D1737953

STATE OF BEING
Book Three of The God Head Trilogy

Sven Michael Davison

BEDOUIN
PRESS

State of Being

For information about this title or to order other books and/or electronic media, contact the publisher:
Bedouin Press
P.O Box 570169
Tarzana CA, 91357-0169
www.bedouinpress.com

Library of Congress Control Number: 2012912819
ISBN: 978-0-9855528-6-2

Printed in the United States of America

Cover by Derrick Abrencia
Interior design by 1106 Design

Publisher's Catalog-In-Publication Data
Davison, Sven Michael.
    State of being / written by Sven Michael Davison. —
1st ed.
    p. cm. — (The god head trilogy ; bk. 3)
    LCCN 2012912819
    ISBN 978-0-9855528-6-2
    ISBN 978-0-9855528-8-6

    1. Nanotechnology—Fiction. 2. Terrorism—Fiction.
3. Artificial Intelligence—Fiction. 4. Science
fiction. 5. Suspense fiction. I. Title. II. Series:
Davison, Sven Michael. God head trilogy ; bk. 3.

PS3554.A96S74 2013   813'.54
                QBI12-600157

FOR ANYONE WILLING TO ACT
FOR THE BETTERMENT OF OTHERS

Acknowledgements

I would like to thank the following with all my heart: Jeannine, for your continued love and support. Isaac, I can't help but love you more every day. Abby and Jake, for your companionship. Steve Lekowicz, for your skilled critiques. Marcy Natkin, for your expert editorial skills. Mom, for your constructive criticism and support. Dad, for your unconditional love. Mark, for your sage advice. And for your feedback, support, help: Erin, Karl, Arjuna, Lucina, Derrick Albrenica, Steve Cantos, Peter Coggan, Barbara Lekowicz, Laura Lekowicz, Derek Powell, Bryan Reesman, Steven Rowley, Bhanu Srikanth, Nancy Van Iderstein, and Peter Ventrella.

State of Being
Table of Contents

Chapter 1
Mushroom

"Crap," Parks muttered under his breath.

The hum of the HJ turbines filled the air for a few seconds and Jake looked over at Parks seated in the co-pilot position. "What?"

"I've lost contact with the Cobalt satellite network. Dammit, I miss my Chip!"

Jake spotted a small pile of bloody-silvery gauze lying by Parks' seat. It had only been a few minutes since the Reverend decided to stop wicking the virus out. "Give it a few more hours. Max2 will have replicated itself to the point where it can reconfigure." Jake checked their position. They were about a hundred miles north of Puerto Rico, headed east toward Africa and Mecca beyond. The view outside the canopy was filled with blue ocean and a dark sky. The sun was setting behind the ship.

At the beginning of this day, Jake had attended his own wedding ceremony with Tomoko. Then the Pin Head Mexican Federales had attacked. Max2 had been activated and everyone but he and Parks had been switched off, murdered in the Acapulco compound. Jake had been able to save Parks, but no one else. Now the main cabin was filled the corpses of his wife, the Sikh twins, and Devani. Jake felt pain in his left hand. He looked down to see he had clenched his fist so tightly that his fingernails had drawn blood from his palm.

Parks rechecked his four new Omnis. He wanted to be sure their jamming and encryption keys would be ready the moment he had a new Chip.

Jake checked his own Omnis. He tracked their flight separately from the HJ's computer; ETA ten hours and twenty-seven minutes. How many times had they both checked and rechecked their Omnis and the ship's systems—anything to create a distraction. Jake thought of his Tomoko lying lifeless in the back. He had hoped Parks could have activated her Max2 and transferred her soul to Eberstark's cyberheaven. But she passed before Parks reached her. They were piloting an airborne morgue. He focused on the future. "What exactly is our next move?"

"Make contact with the Jihad Brotherhood or Republic of Islam."

"You mean Nation of Islam?"

"Tomato, tom-ah-to."

"Did you sell weapons to them, too?"

Parks shrugged. "I can't think of anyone we haven't sold to. I stopped giving a damn last summer when Max1 broke out. That's when I knew the gloves were off and The Consortium was making its big play for total control." Parks continued to open windows on the HJ's communications interface. He frowned. "Every frequency is jammed."

Jake felt uneasy. "Is the onboard computer encrypted?"

Parks nodded. "Encrypted, blocked, jamming, you name it. This is a military bird and I've got it running in full battle mode."

Jake already knew this. He turned to his portside window and peered out at the ocean below. The sun behind them was almost gone. It had set over much of the United States. The massive expanse of blue water made him think of happier times when he, Lakshmi, and Tomoko spent silent nights out at sea onboard the *Pachacuteq*. He dug into the raw cuts in his left palm. He breathed, "Once you make contact, then what?"

Parks continued to have trouble with the interface. "Hide out in Mecca, start hacking and hitting The Consortium worldwide. I'll sell the Nation of Islam nukes, if necessary."

"That's a really stupid idea. You want to cover the planet in a nuclear winter?"

"As a member of The Church, I'd expect you to have a little more faith in your Ass-Postle." Parks winked.

Jake couldn't understand how Parks could be so light hearted. "Don't you feel anything?" He thumbed back at the closed hatch that led to the main cabin and the corpses.

Parks gravely observed Jake. "Of course." He swallowed hard. "My coping mechanism is humor. If that bothers you, don't listen, or shut the fuck up."

"Sorry." He had the strong urge to leave but could not face the reality of Tomoko's body so he turned his attention to the controls, and his open cuts. Exhaustion seeped through his bones.

Jake observed his Devanagari uniform. He had changed out of his white silk wedding suit. It was slashed, singed, dirty, and stained with blood—Tomoko's blood. The silver wedding band felt foreign on his finger. He had been married a total of a half-hour before she died. Fresh blood ran off his palm and down his wrist. He closed his eyes and concentrated on memories before the Pacheco trial, before The Chip, before Max2.

Parks whistled.

Jake awoke to find the cabin lights dimmed and the world outside the canopy filled with bright orange light. They were flying into a sunrise. He glanced at the clock and realized he'd slept for seven hours. He had the urge to take a leak, but dreaded entering the main cabin. He checked on Parks who was zooming in on an image floating on the cockpit holo-screen.

Jake sat up. "Jesus." The scene reminded him of Shanghai, only the city below was dark, no electricity or powered device of any kind. Hundreds of corpses lay scattered on the ground. Parks panned to a dog jerking its head to dislodge a hand from a human corpse. The dead woman gazed back at them with a vacant stare. Jake thought she resembled Devani, one of Parks' girlfriends now lying in the main cabin.

Tears ran down Parks' cheeks. His hand shook as he wiped his face and pinched the bridge of his nose. His voice cracked. "Most Muslim nations installed Nemps to combat Max1, but the lack of electricity left them living in the nineteenth century." He cleared his throat and quickly zoomed out so the details of bodies could no longer be seen. "When Max2 began killing, they switched the Nemps off. They had no idea that Max2 was a viral form of The Chip and it left them open to being hacked. The Consortium certainly figured out a way around their defenses."

Jake's area of the cockpit was dark. Parks had switched all control to his side of the cockpit. Jake started to pull up the GPS on his Omni but decided to simply ask, "Where are we?"

"That's the Egyptian city of Aswan. We're twenty minutes from the Red Sea where we've been asked to fly in a holding pattern until Mecca gives us clearance to land."

Jake patted the Reverend on the shoulder. "Nice work."

A green light appeared on Parks' panel. "And there it is." Parks took them up to a higher altitude and Jake watched the sun rise over the Red Sea.

"Beautiful." Jake wished he could share it with Tomoko. He felt his nails sink into his palm. He thought of Mecca before them. He wasn't sure what to expect, but he'd do everything in his power to help in the fight. He looked over and saw more tears flowing down Parks' cheeks. The canopy automatically dimmed so the sun would not blind the occupants.

Parks spoke with a strained voice. "I spent the whole night daydreaming about nuking the planet. Then I see a sight like that and I feel God assuring me it's going to be all right."

Jake didn't agree with Parks, but he did feel more at peace staring at the warm light ahead.

They sat in silence, gazing out the tinted windows, straight into the sun. The glass blocked all eye-damaging rays. Jake focused and thought he saw sunspots, but that was ridiculous. A flicker caught his attention. The cockpit controls flashed sub-menus and alternate displays in a crazy montage; no configuration lasted longer than a split second. Jake's side of the panel remained dark. "Parks!"

Parks tried to operate the touch screens. He hit the manual control button but nothing happened. "What the devil?" He pulled open the panel cover above his legs. He tried to unfasten his harness, but it would not release.

The cabin lights flashed red and a fast-paced beeping accosted their ears. Jake felt his seat adjust, as if clamping into a new position.

"It's the eject sequence." Parks dove his hands under the panel and fished blindly. "I can't believe we've been hacked!" He pulled out a nano-circuit board. "Nope, not that one."

"Jihad Brotherhood? Consortium?"

"Fuck if I know." Parks felt back under the control board. "I've been conversing with Mecca via Morse code and all the passwords were correct. Maybe I pissed off the Brotherhood, or somebody is posing as them." He growled as he worked at something beneath the panel.

The panel in front of Jake snapped on and Jake saw a giant red 9 on the screen "Parks?"

8…

Parks produced another nano-board. "Dammit!" There was no effect on the aircraft as his hand disappeared again. It seemed Jake was the only one in danger of being ejected.

5…

"Parks!" The explosive bolts blew a split second before the door next to Jake flew off and cold, thin air blasted in. Jake had just enough time to shove his flight helmet on before the counter hit 0.

Jake slammed into the right side of his crash seat as he was ejected out of the left side of the aircraft. Roaring wind caught his chair and he was jerked back with his seat. He watched the HJ rocket away toward the desert in the east. He tumbled backward. The chair assembly jolted and he felt himself separate from it; he was now freefalling with the chair parachute affixed to his back.

Adrenaline pumped into his body as he watched the ground draw near. He tightened the strap on his helmet then spread out his arms and legs to position his body into a controlled freefall. He studied the earth moving up rapidly to meet him, trying to line himself up with the terrain before he deployed his chute. He was headed for a port town. He checked his Omni GPS. The city was Jeddah. There were dozens of sandbars and islets in the water at the mouth of the port. He tried to line himself up with the main beach near what looked like an open field.

He spoke into the helmet microphone. "Parks, do you read me?"

Parks' voice was hard to hear. It was a combination of the cabin noise on Parks' end and the wind rushing around his ears. "Yeah."

"Are you still in the ship?"

"Yeah." Parks sounded distracted. Jake pictured the Reverend tearing up his console trying to regain some control.

"What's go—" Jake almost lost his stomach as the chute deployed and he jerked against the lines. He was now floating feet first toward a beach, just north of the port. The world was much quieter now, almost serene except for the adrenaline pumping through his body. "What's going on?"

"Nothing much." Parks grunted. "I'm on a suicide run heading straight for the heart of Mecca."

Jake smiled in amazement. Even now, Parks was able to take things lightly. He listened for a few seconds more, but Parks had nothing else to add. The ground was getting much closer now. He kept his legs loose in preparation for the landing. "Parks?"

He hit the beach. He tumbled forward and planted his face in soft sand. He punched his chute release and the silky white cloth disengaged from his back and floated majestically into the ocean. He scrambled to his feet and turned to the east, hoping to see a sign of Parks.

He spoke into his helmet. "Parks?"

A brilliant flash lit up the sky. He shut his eyes as the light stung his retinas. He blinked and looked again. A small mushroom cloud billowed upward on the eastern horizon.

Chapter 2
Jeddah

The fiery conflagration seared a column into the morning sky. The atomic cloud was small enough that Jake felt relatively safe from fallout. He doubted he would feel a blast wave as he guessed it was about forty miles east, beyond the mountains, putting it in the heart of Mecca.

"Godspeed, Parks." Images of all those who had died or had been taken away from him in the past two weeks crashed into his mind. He turned to face the Red Sea as he felt the wedding ring on his finger. He dug into the wound on his palm, but the pain was no longer sufficient. He collapsed on his knees and wept.

He was not sure how long he spent pouring out his grief to an empty world, but by the time he opened his eyes, the glow from the nuke had dissipated.

Aqua and lapis waves rolled onto the beach with rhythmic beauty. He closed his eyes. *Concentrate on the here and now. You have to fight if you ever want to see Lakshmi or Mom again. Focus on beating this. Focus on hope.*

He opened his eyes and took in a deep breath. His nose filled with the odor of salt and rotting kelp, but the sea held an invigorating sense of infinite possibility. The ocean was the birthplace of all living things. It was one of the reasons why he loved sailing. A person could get lost on the ocean. A person could heal.

He turned east. He had no idea who to trust or how long he could last before The Consortium caught up to him. As he pulled off his harness and grabbed the survival kit from the bag attached to his chute pack, he puzzled over what had just happened. *If The Consortium placed the HJ on a suicide run, why eject me? Why not kill everyone inside? Why didn't my Max2 convert into a Chip like everyone else in the Acapulco compound? What's so special about my version of Max2? What purpose am I serving for The Consortium?*

The contents of the survival kit consisted of instant Saag Paneer, basic first aid supplies, and an HK V2 pistol with three clips of bullets. He looked at his Devanagari camouflaged assault uniform. It was patterned for jungle fighting and was not the best outfit for his current location. Plus, it felt heavy and hot. Luckily it was January and sixty degrees, but the sun was just beginning to bake the landscape.

A flash image of Tomoko's body burning in Mecca's nuclear inferno entered his mind. He switched his thoughts to the first time he had met her on the beach in Ubatuba, Brazil. She was beautiful, fun, alive, and Lakshmi had immediately taken to her. He grit his teeth and pushed away his grief and hopelessness. *I'm Jake Travissi. I will bring the fight to The Consortium. Right here, right now, is all that matters.*

He crammed all the survival supplies into his cargo pants and shoved the gun in his belt holster. His skin remained dark from the airport raid in Mumbai, and with his getup, he looked like an Indian Devanagari regular. At least he had a better chance of blending in with the locals, except that he didn't know a shred of Arabic.

He hiked up a short embankment. He paused at the top to get his bearings. Jeddah appeared lifeless. Nothing moved except for a wind coming from the direction of the low mountains to the east.

He had landed on a small peninsula. Directly ahead and to the right was a row of lifeguard towers and beyond that a group of block apartment buildings. Tall gleaming cargo cranes reached into the sky to the south. He listened. Nothing moved but the wind. He made his way toward the lifeguard towers and a small road beyond. As he walked, he noticed a stretch of barren desert between the block apartments and the road. Lumps covered in desert camouflage sat in the open area. He changed course to investigate.

He crossed the road and walked on the sun-blasted earth. He spotted a few camel tracks, which were quickly being erased by the wind. He squinted to keep the desert sand out of his eyes. He pulled up the covering on one of the large objects revealing an aerial attack drone, painted in desert camouflage. He gazed north. At least sixty camouflaged aerial drones faced the ocean.

He checked his Omni. Dead. A Nemp or an EMP from the nuclear blast had to be active. He wandered southeast into the city. He spotted a stadium a few blocks to the north, but decided to head south into Jeddah proper. After a half hour, he found a green landscaped area around a large traffic circle. A huge desalination plant loomed beyond. Real vegetation was a rare occurrence, especially in a country that had not seen rain in at least a decade.

He headed over to the desalination plant. As he got closer, he discovered a nuclear power plant in the complex. He also found a building housing a massive Nemp generator. Its humming was the only sound beyond the wind that he had heard since landing on the beach. He didn't venture inside. The deeper he journeyed into the city the more he felt like he was being watched, and he didn't want to be caught in a high security area.

Everywhere he explored, he found empty streets and combat drones under camouflage. Most were aerial drones, but there were many tanks, too. He had to smile when he saw the Ford logo on the tanks. The Nation of Islam had owned the company since the early 2020s. The aerial attack drones were all Cobalt models, sans logos.

Everywhere Jake walked there was a disconcerting lack of people, living or dead. Roads were devoid of vehicles. He half expected a crowd of zombie automaton Pin Heads to come around the corner and attack. He shook the nightmare image from his head. There was a reason the streets were empty. He supposed if the government had decided to fight Max1 with a massive Nemp, pulling all vehicles off thoroughfares would be logical. Still, where were the citizens of Jeddah? The streets of Aswan had been covered in corpses.

The day was growing warmer. The white buildings and beige sand reflected brilliant sunlight into his eyes, causing him to squint. He had dug into the palm of his hand more than a few times that morning. He stumbled upon a supermarket with a high roof lined with glass windows. It would be well lit inside. He cautiously entered. The place had been ransacked long ago, but after searching through the piles of chaos he discovered several bottles of water, dried food, and a pair of cracked sunglasses. He found a backpack, too, and loaded it before putting it on his shoulders and continuing his trek.

A mile from the market stood a huge white mosque. As he approached the entrance, the stench of death filled his nose. He peered inside and saw a dozen bodies and the shadows of hundreds more. Based on their decay, Jeddah had been hit about a week ago. *Who moved the bodies? Did The Consortium press the master switch? Was the world now in their control? Am I alive, or am I hacked?* He kept his course moving south and east, hoping to stumble on a major freeway that would take him toward the living.

Military drones were hidden in every nook of the city—mostly under camouflage. Huge tanks were parked inside buildings with holes punched in their walls, as well as automated anti-aircraft and gyro-guns. Clearly, they had been arming for modern warfare on a massive scale, which meant the Nemp would need to be shut down. Was Jeddah's population dead or hidden like these weapons?

He walked down a long street and followed signs that he guessed pointed the way to a freeway. They were big and green and framed in white, like interstate signs in the US. Everything was written in the flowing script of Arabic. As he passed a large apartment block, he spotted a saddled and bridled camel drinking brackish water from a decorative fountain. He pulled out his pistol and darted quickly into the shade of the apartment block. He remained in shadow, searching every window lining the street for a sign of life. Nothing.

He focused on the camel. The water in the fountain had all but evaporated. Watching the animal drink made him hot and thirsty, but he needed to conserve his own water supply. He had four liters in his pack. He would need a lot more to survive in this climate.

The camel raised its head and groaned. It sounded more like a belch. The animal approached Jake with its head lowered in a gesture of submission. He pulled a foil pouch of saag panner from his pack and ripped it open. He squeezed some concentrated green goo into his hand and offered it to the camel. The smell of spicy spinach wafted in the air. The camel pulled back its big soft lips and nibbled at the sludge in Jake's hand. He moved to the camel's side and tried to figure how to get up on the high saddle. He squeezed the entire contents of the pouch on the sizzling hot asphalt. As the camel lapped up the food, it collapsed on its front knees followed by its rear.

Jake mounted the saddle quickly and grabbed the reins. The camel licked the ground clean and sat.

"Giddy-up," he commanded and immediately felt stupid. He clicked with his tongue. Nothing. He tapped his heels into the animal's flanks. The camel stood up and he pulled on the reigns to steer the animal toward the vicinity of the highway. The ride was bouncy, even worse than horseback, but it was nice to be conserving energy. He only worried about how long he could feed them both.

It took ten minutes to find a freeway on-ramp. He steered the camel onto the elevated road. Heat shimmered in thick waves creating mirages all around the deserted city. It was strange to be the only traffic on such a massive thoroughfare. They came upon a large interchange and Jake guided the camel onto Highway 5. Sweat poured down his face and stung his eyes. He kicked himself for not getting a hat. About a half mile south, he spotted a string of shops. One of them looked like an antique store that sold American and European items from the twentieth century. Curiosity got the better of him.

It took him a good twenty minutes to back-track and find an exit that would get him down to the stores. Judging by the sun, it was late afternoon. He would soon need to think about where to sleep and eat and most importantly, find water. He tied his camel to the door handle of the shop and entered. The store was deep and without windows beyond the storefront. He navigated slowly around cluttered shelves, and objects hanging from the ceiling above.

About halfway toward the back, he found a wall of old boom boxes and CDs. He had not seen a CD since college. He wondered how a shop like this could exist in this rather conservative Muslim country. Most Western goods were banned.

He perused the CDs and was surprised that over half the collection was of American and European bands from the 1960s, 70s, 80s and 90s. He moved to the "S" section and searched for Smoov Z. He found a copy of their greatest hits and looked at the back of the disc. "Baby Can't We Talk?" was listed. It was the song The Consortium had chosen to activate the Max2 nano-virus into forming a Chip. He wondered if he should keep the CD in his back pocket for future use. A Chip could come in handy.

Although if the Nemp stopped, his Omnis would come back to life and he could download the song from The Cyber-Wire. Not to mention, he'd be able to encrypt his Chip signals from potential Consortium God Heads with the two Omnis on his wrists. There was no reason to have a copy of Smoov Z and he would be damn lucky to find the batteries to power one of the CD players.

He put the CD back and headed for the exit. After taking three steps, a crash greeted his ears followed by mechanical screams in Arabic. Jake spun around and saw a dark hole in the floor. Armed men dressed in desert camouflage HAZMAT suits leaped out.

Chapter 3
Rhetorical

Screams crackled in Arabic out of a chest speaker on a HAZMAT suit. *Must be Nemp resistant,* Jake thought as he dove behind a display of antique cell phones to avoid the figure. He pulled out his pistol as the cell phones above him disintegrated in a hail of darts. A couple of projectiles bounced on the floor and he could just make out their color: yellow.

He felt a twinge of guilt using bullets, but it was all he had, and getting captured was not an attractive option. The Arabic switched to Hindu. His unintentional disguise was working. He crouched low and steadied his gun, waiting for the perfect opportunity to shoot.

The high-pitched whining of HAZMAT suit material rubbing against itself filled the room, but otherwise, everything was quiet. The voice switched to English.

"Who are you? Why are you in Jeddah? Come out so we can talk."

They have no intention of talking until you take a dose of dart serum. He got down on his belly and began to crawl toward the exit. A pair of boots flashed by and he rolled and shot. The bullet slammed into a boom box sitting on the shelf above the CDs. He rolled again and felt a dart slam into his hamstring. *I don't believe it,* he thought, as sleep overtook him.

He awoke inside a HAZMAT suit. His arms were cuffed to a chair and through the shield of his helmet, he saw a string of electric lights hanging from the ceiling of a semi-reinforced dirt tunnel. Crates of supplies were stacked along the walls. He was in an alcove, set off from a longer tunnel. He wondered how far the network went. A few soldiers walked by, none of them in HAZMAT suits. He saw their Omnis glowing. They were deep enough below the surface to be protected from the Nemp above or it had been switched off. Or they were military grade and Nemp resistant.

He was hot. Sweat oozed around all his joints and soaked his back. He was thirsty and had a headache from the dart serum. He tried to remember how many times he had been darted since Christmas. *Four or five?* His body was bruised and sore from all the action he had seen. He still had an ugly scar on his forehead from Christmas Eve. He had taken the stitches out in Parks' HJ… two days before his wedding. He clenched his left fist, but the suit gloves got in the way of his nails digging into his palm. He cleared his throat. It was dry and raw.

A soldier turned into the alcove. The man stopped in his tracks when he saw Jake alert. He approached several feet and leaned against a crate in front of Jake. The soldier's combination rifle was pointed to the floor, with its safety off. The man spoke English with an Arab accent. "That is a clever disguise my friend, but it did not keep us from finding out who you are." The man lit a cigarette. "I would offer you one, but something tells me you don't smoke."

"Would you take off this HAZMAT suit even if I did?" Jake's voice sounded loud inside the helmet, but he could hear the mechanical interpretation coming out of his suit as well.

The man smiled. "We know you carry the virus. We're very careful not to touch anything you have come in contact with. We even killed the camel."

Jake felt bad for the poor animal. It had been friendly and helpful during their short time together. "Why? From what I can tell, you seldom go to the surface."

"One cannot be too cautious in these times."

Jake frowned. "Not sure you can escape this one."

The man shrugged. "We have the Nemp, the tunnels and Allah on our side."

"Nemps have no effect on what I have."

The soldier nodded. "But they keep the kill command out."

"And your ability to communicate with your drones."

The soldier took a drag off his cigarette and blew the smoke into the air.

"What's next?" Jake grew impatient. There had to be a less than friendly agenda to this warmup, otherwise he wouldn't have been darted or cuffed.

"Why are you here?"

"To fight The Consortium."

The man smiled. "How did you get here?"

Jake relaxed. "Walked, then found the camel."

"Really? From where?"

"Egypt, then by boat to Jeddah."

"Egypt is dead."

"Yes it is."

"How did a cop from Los Angeles, who was last seen in Mumbai, happen to show up in Jeddah just three days after New Delhi was attacked with a nuclear device?"

"I flew."

"Did you happen to fly the aircraft that dropped the nuke on our holy city of Mecca this morning?"

Now it was certain. Mecca was gone. "No."

"We live in a time when everyone seems to be misdirecting their neighbor. There are many things on The Cyber-Wire about you. Gunning down forty men and women, assassinating people in airports—perhaps bombing New Delhi and Mecca are on the list? Or maybe you just wanted one destroyed.

Maybe none. Either way you do not belong here, Jake." The man took a big draw off his cigarette. "Why are you here?"

"I told you."

"I don't believe you."

"What would you believe?" Jake's throat felt parched and cracked. He had a hard time getting the words out. Luckily, the chest speaker on his outfit compensated by raising the volume level. "Then we can go from there."

"I believe you have led a charmed life, and you are running from the inevitable." He took another drag. "We are all going to die, Jake. It just comes down to how and when." The man walked up to Jake and pointed the lit cigarette in his face. It did not feel threatening with the plastic shield acting as a barrier. "If I told you I was going to kill you, would that change your story?"

Jake gazed into the man's eyes. He didn't have the authority to carry out his threat. "No."

The soldier put the cigarette back in his mouth, and took the gun off his shoulder. He tossed the gun quickly in the air, caught the barrel, and swung the stock straight into the side of Jake's head.

Jake awoke with searing pain throbbing through his skull. He was strapped to a stretcher, rising out of a hole under a heaven filled with stars. His HAZMAT suit's helmet was caved in on one side. The faceplate remained in place. He guessed the suit had not been breached during the assault. He could feel men carrying him over the desert. He turned his head and saw the back end of a truck. He looked for signs that the Nemp was off; a streetlight, the glimmer of electric life on the face of an Omni, but the desert was dark all around. The men surrounding him strained to lift him into the vehicle. He wondered if the truck had electrical and circuit shielding, or if the Nemp was simply off.

They dropped him onto a steel bed. The stretcher slid under a bench and a support strut hit him in the skull. Blackness.

Bumping and jolting rocked Jake to consciousness. He lay on a steel floor, his hands cuffed to a low bench, presumably the same one that had rendered him unconscious. Condensation coated the inside of his faceplate. Through his hazy window, he saw several soldiers seated on a bench stretching from the cab to the tail of the vehicle. There didn't seem to be any light outside. Thirst and hunger clouded his senses. From the smell of things, he had soiled his suit. His head hurt. He wondered how these soldiers prevented infection. Much of the Arab world quarantined all visitors during the Max1 outbreak. So perhaps there was no one traveling here. Still, a visit from one Typhoid Mary could spread the disease… *maybe that's why I was ejected from the ship?* But it was a long shot and did not explain how he had escaped the Max2 Chip activation and kill switch back in Acapulco.

He felt the wedding band on his finger. It was loose, but not bad considering no one had physically taken his ring size. Or maybe Parks measured it with his Chip enhanced eyesight. It felt alien to wear jewelry, but he embraced the reminder of Tomoko. He remembered Tomoko playing with Lakshmi on deck while Jake swam around the sailboat during a dead calm. Blackness.

Blinding light stabbed his eyes and he moved his head to avoid it. His visor was not as foggy. A young soldier unlocked his handcuffs. Jake noticed another soldier grab his arms while the first soldier took his legs. He sat up, causing both soldiers to jump back and quickly point their rifles at his face. "Don't shoot. I just want to walk is all."

The young soldier barked at him in Arabic. Jake got to his feet and staggered toward the tailgate of the truck. The vehicle was empty save for these two. He paused at the edge, allowing his eyes to adjust to the light. A firm shove sent him sprawling to the ground. He broke the fall with his arms but his faceplate crunched on baked earth, cracking his mask.

The men lifted him up and growled in Arabic, pointing at his faceplate. "Your suit, not mine." Jake was too dehydrated and sore to care.

The young soldier checked around the seal on Jake's mask. Jake gazed past the soldier's probing fingers to the gleaming desert city beyond. Factories, cars, and chaotic life ran at full throttle. The chaos meant no one was chipped. He was surrounded by the beauty of life once again. He felt immense relief despite his shaky situation. *What city is this?* Given the duration of the drive he could be anywhere within the Nation of Islam. Mecca had been the capital after the Saudi family was overthrown. He had seen photos of the old capital years ago and this could be Riyadh.

The soldier backed away, satisfied that the mask and dented helmet were properly sealed. Jake felt a cool sensation around his armpit but wasn't sure if it was sweat, a tear in the suit, or both. If it were a tear, the soldiers would be freaked out about it. The young solider waved for him to follow and Jake felt a gun barrel press into his spine. He marched toward a large concrete structure that looked suspiciously like a prison.

The crackling of a loudspeaker followed by the wailing of a Muezzin echoed over the street. He was shoved to the earth as his escorts threw rugs onto the ground and began to pray. The position of the sun meant this was the mid-afternoon call to prayer. He didn't bother to run. Where could he go?

When the call to prayer had finished, the soldiers marched him up to a steel door in the side of the concrete building. They presented their IDs to an electric eye. Then they had their retinas scanned. Jake heard a lock release and the heavy barrier slid open. They entered the building, going through a few steel doors and manned security checkpoints before they wound up on the second floor. Jake stood in a room with one desk and three doors. The interior, like the exterior, was all unfinished concrete. No windows anywhere. A guard sat at the steel desk and took a plastic bag from the soldier. Jake's clothes and Omnis were stuffed inside the bag.

He was marched down a hall and into an airlock. A door sealed behind him and another opened up a few feet ahead. A voice with a thick Arab accent came over a speaker. "Walk through the door."

He did so, and wound up in a small white, plastic-lined cell with cameras and other instrumentation on the walls. He spotted a couple of holo-projectors, too. At his level, there was a bed, toilet and sink, but nothing more. The bed looked more like a hospital gurney. A white cotton shirt and pants were folded on the mattress. The bed was shoved against the right wall while the sink and toilet were on the far wall in front of him. The left wall was barren. Jake assumed the airlock meant the air circulating through here was going through industrial grade bio-filters.

"You may get undressed," the voice directed as the door behind slid shut and sealed itself with a *hiss*. He quickly unzipped the gloves from the suit. The air hit the salt on his palm and it burned with renewed vigor. With his hands free, he searched for more seams and zippers. He was pouring sweat and desperate for a drink of water. Not to mention his legs were coated in excrement. If the sink did not work, he was fully prepared to drink from the toilet. After a bit of struggling, he pulled off the helmet and breathed in the climate-controlled air. It felt like eighty degrees in the room, which was a relief to the sauna inside the suit. He rushed over to the sink and put his head under the faucet. He drank his fill then splashed water on his face and down into the suit. He stripped down and saw the mess he had made on himself. "Fuck 'em." He muttered and ripped off his underwear and threw it into the suit.

Using the sink, he took a shower, letting the water fly all over the plastic floor. He simply didn't care anymore. There was no mirror, but he could feel the lumps under his scalp where he had been struck with the gun butt and the bench. The McMurdo forehead scar felt as ugly as ever. His body was covered in bruises from the darts and kicks he had received, but the artificial pigment of his skin helped to camouflage them. It had been the roughest couple of weeks in his life and this trial was nowhere near over. The pain in his raw hand kept him focused on the present. His stomach growled.

He tried to calculate the date as he bathed. Knowing the date always made him feel grounded. He was married on January fifth, which meant he had been tossed out of the HJ on the sixth. Given it was daytime again; he had to assume it was the seventh. Tomorrow was Tuesday and that meant the Iowa Caucus would be happening in the United States. He wondered if elections existed at all any more. If not, it would be the first time the Iowa Caucus had been missed in… He needed an Omni or a Chip to access that information.

Once he felt clean, he walked over to the bed and grabbed his new clothes. He watched the water flow to the center of the room and empty into a filter drain. His eyes fell on his HAZMAT suit. *Was that a tear?* He bent down and gathered up the suit, making sure it was under his body so the cameras could not see what he saw. He pressed his finger under the armpit and spotted a finger-sized tear. He was certain they would have checked the suit before putting it on him, but HAZMAT suits were not known for taking heavy abuse. It could have torn when he was struck in the head, during the trip to the truck, or when they pushed him to the ground.

He shrugged. *Welcome to the nightmare, boys.*

"Sleep." The voice commanded.

He stood up and ripped the suit so the people behind the camera could witness. He didn't want them to know they had been exposed to the virus. "I had enough on my ride over, thanks." He wadded up the suit and tossed it in the corner.

"Then you'll be ready to start your Max2 cure trials in the morning."

Chapter 4

Lightning

Four days passed with no contact from anyone. His food was always pushed through a slot in the door. His jailor's threat had been an empty one. *Why had they delayed?* His torn and soiled suit had been taken during his first night's sleep.

He was able to keep track of the time by the Muezzin's calls to prayer that echoed faintly inside the building five times a day. He spent most of his waking hours working out, steeling himself for a fight, and widening the wound on his hand to help control his grief. As long as he could breathe, he would dedicate his life to reversing this nightmare. He pondered escape often. Under a thin veneer of plastic, the room was all windowless concrete. The cell door never opened and the food slot was a foot wide and four inches tall. No chance of getting out that way. His meals consisted of spicy lentils, which didn't taste bad, but he was getting pretty tired of the repetition.

On the morning of January eleventh, he was awakened by the call to prayer. The moment it finished he began drifting back to sleep. A loud voice with a

British accent accosted his ears. "This broadcast is being streamed live so that all the world can witness. The heretic and international terrorist Joaquin Parks—"

He jerked up and swung his full attention to the hologram floating ten feet above the floor, between the equipment he was clearly not meant to reach.

"—will be publicly executed for the crime of detonating a nuclear warhead over the Nation of Islam's capital of Mecca."

He watched a wide-angle view of a massive square framed by towering white minarets adorned with lacey stone carvings. Thousands of people were gathered before a monolithic black granite semicircular wall that curved away from them and stood two-stories tall. All along the six-story perimeter of the square sat manned and drone tanks spaced about fifty feet apart. A bronze sphere, roughly thirty feet in diameter, sat near the western wall. It had the sickle moon and star, symbol for Islam, carved in the side.

The view zoomed in to reveal a slender black steel spike rising up to the top of the semicircle's height. It was positioned close enough to the semicircle that a person could step off and stand on the spike, although it appeared sharp enough to punch through anyone's foot.

A naked figure appeared in the frame, on top of the semicircle. The crowd unleashed screams of hatred. The camera zoomed in to reveal Parks. Jake winced when he saw his friend's burned skin hanging off his bloody body in blackened sheets. The back of his neck had dirty, bloody gauze hanging out of it. They were wicking off the Max2 virus so it could not reassemble into a Chip. Jake nervously spun his wedding ring around his finger.

Two men in black HAZMAT suits decorated with gold Arabic accents pushed Parks at spear point to the center of the wall. The unprotected crowd shouted a mere forty yards from the stone semicircle. Jake wondered if that was enough distance to keep from getting infected. Given the tear in his suit three days ago, did it matter?

The British voice continued to comment. "The accused will be led to the impaler." Now Jake knew what the two-story iron pike was for. Parks was going to die on it. Jake felt his organs retract. His breathing became fast and shallow. The executioners' helmets were one hundred percent opaque so no one could identify their faces.

Parks' mouth moved, but nothing could be heard over the rabid crowd.

The commentator jumped in. "The accused is trying to say something. Could it be a confession? We'll see if we can pick it up."

Parks smiled. His eyes seemed to be looking at overwhelming beauty. "It's all so clear now. Everything is as it should be. God is love. All else is just the veil we choose to color the world. I will be with you soon."

The Reverend's voice was cut off. "It seems the accused has fallen into a delusional state rather than face his role in the conspiracy to wipe out the Muslim religion."

The camera zoomed in so that Parks filled the hologram. Jake studied Parks carefully. Was he hacked, delusional, or really seeing his version of heaven? Only one eye was open on his burned face. He had clearly been close to the blast zone. Somehow he must have been able to eject, only to confront this. And yet, his face appeared to be at peace. Jake shook with horror and anger as he sat fixed to the scene. When Parks reached the pike, his executioners each grabbed an arm. Jake had the urge to stand up and yell at the surveillance in his cell. *That man was only trying to help you!* Then he wondered. *Is this an elaborate hoax, designed to make me confess?*

The view pulled back to reveal the President of the Nation of Islam and his cabinet parading out onto the semicircle. All of them wore stylish white and gold HAZMAT suits with hoods that were all Plexiglas so their faces were visible. A man dressed in a similar HAZMAT suit, but cloaked in black cleric's robes, unfurled a piece of parchment. Jake noticed a microphone taped to the cleric's cheek as he spoke. Arabic echoed around the execution square and the English accented narrator translated. "We are here to bear witness to justice. Through the accused's negligence, the virus known as MaxWell was unleashed in June of 2035, killing over 300,000 citizens of the Nation of Islam."

The camera cut to enraged faces. Men, children, and veiled women shook their fists and jeered.

"The accused founded and led a heretic cult known as the Disciples of Paul. For that we name him a false prophet."

More curses and fist shaking ensued.

"Although he proclaims to be a man of God, he controls Cobalt Industries, a Western capitalist industrial complex that is responsible for countless terrorist acts throughout the world and for selling weapons to our enemies."

And to you. Jake glanced at his surveillance cameras.

"He is a carrier of MaxWell 2, a pestilence which threatens our borders and the borders of all sovereign Muslim nations."

The cleric paused to enjoy a flood of vitriolic response. The camera cut to a sea of sweaty faces. *That's odd for a population used to this climate...*

The cleric turned back to his parchment. "Most heinous of all his crimes is the act of crashing a Hover Jet armed with nuclear devices into the sacred city of Mecca!"

The crowd's enthusiasm was broken by mass sneezing fits. Jake sat up at the telltale sign of infection. The camera cut to Parks who dropped to his knees. His skin came off in the hands of the executioners. Their fingers continued to slip off his bloody body. They managed to get a firm grasp and lift him to his feet. He continued to display his peaceful smile.

The camera cut back to the cleric. "One million of our brothers, wives, and children died in the attack on Mecca!"

The camera cut to the crowd. People were furious, but many more were sneezing, confused, and appeared to be sick.

The view switched to a close up of the cleric's face. "Let this be a message to all the Western powers and their allies. Any incursion onto our soil, or molestation of our citizens, will be met with swift and brutal punishment. Anyone who steps foot into the Republic of Islam carrying the Max1 or Max2 virus will be exterminated." The camera pulled back to reveal the President and his cabinet sneezing. Spit sprayed inside the President's glass helmet. The cleric glanced at his leaders with alarm but he turned back to the executioners and nodded for them to place Parks on the iron spike.

As the executioners hoisted up Parks, red lightning crashed down from heaven and ripped into the massive bronze sphere near the western wall. The camera zoomed out to reveal lasers piercing down from blue sky, tearing into stone, flesh, and architecture. The red light could only mean one thing; it was an attack using one of the Star Wars networks in orbit.

The broadcast winked out.

The building shook, followed by rumbling and explosions. *So much for the hoax theory.* Jake rolled under his bed as the lights snapped off. In pitch-blackness, he felt the building quake even harder. A loud roar ensued. Rubble slammed into his bed. Steel howled as it strained and tore apart. Everything seemed to be crashing around him.

Chapter 5
War Machine

It felt like an eternity passed before the walls and ceiling stopped crashing all around him. Jake held his eyes closed to avoid his face getting pelted with dust and bits of debris. Once the din died down, he moved his leg out from under the bed and hit a block of concrete. He pushed up on the bed and it lifted up and tumbled somewhere in the darkness.

He rubbed his eyes and looked around. Through thick motes of settling dust, he saw a trickle of light where a wall should have been. He carefully climbed over jagged and uneven rubble and navigated through the new opening. He was in a hallway. Beyond the dust-soaked tunnel, he could see a spark of daylight and hear the sounds of war thundering all around. The building groaned as he made his way toward the light.

He spotted the room where he remembered the soldiers had dropped off his gear. The doors had been ripped from their hinges and the desk guard lay dead on the floor. It was too dark to get a look at the man's face, but he felt for the carotid artery and found no pulse. Jake probed the man's arm and discovered an Omni. He pressed the face and the Omni lit up. He unsnapped the device and used its faint light to search the desk. He found a drawer full of Omnis and located the two Parks had given him back in Mumbai. They had all the encryption and hacking software if his Max2 were ever activated. Jake tested the devices for power and was happy to find they were fully charged. He strapped them on and configured them to seek any would-be Chip signals in his head and encrypt any signals coming or going if his Max2 were activated.

He searched for the bag containing his clothes to no avail. He checked the guard's shoes and discovered the man had small feet. Jake wore white cotton pajamas with nothing else to protect him from the jagged wreckage filling the path to his exit. A massive explosion thundered into the building and the structure groaned. Time to go.

Jake grabbed the guard's Omni. The interface was all in Arabic but he managed to call up the flashlight mode. He didn't want to use up any of his own Omni batteries in case he was Chipped. He used the flashlight as he scrambled over the rubble and around collapsed rooms to work his way toward the daylight. When he reached the breach in the outer wall, there was a sixteen-foot drop to the street below. Several bodies lay scattered on the pavement and fires licked a few rooftops. He sat down, grabbed a piece of rebar protruding from the exposed floor and swung down. His feet dangled above pavement for a second before he swung and dropped to the street.

He scanned the corpses for a suitable clothing donor. The temperature was in the high seventies, but the pavement was warm on his feet and there was a lot of shattered glass.

He spotted a few dead soldiers and found a body that was his size. He stripped the man down, put on his body armor, boots, and weapons. Explosions, gunfire, and occasional voices yelling in Arabic continued as he dressed. When he finished, he checked himself in a shard of glass. He was a dead ringer for a soldier fighting with the Nation of Islam carrying a Cobalt combination rifle. *Cobalt... Fuck the assholes for what they did to Parks.*

He walked a block, listening for the concentration of fighting. He was going to find that public square. Parks was not going to die in this war zone.

He passed the shattered glass wall of a beautiful café. It reminded him of early nineteenth-century France. He stepped inside to get some cover while he called up a map of the city on his Omni. The café had marble counters, brass rails, a cappuccino machine that was a work of art, and scores of corpses. The dead lay on tables, the floor, in their drinks, and around the bar. They had clearly been watching the execution.

He had one thought. *Kill switch. How long had they been infected? If I was the carrier, then seventy-two hours, tops? Most have Omnis, so why didn't they set up personal encryption barriers? Did they know about that little trick? Maybe they felt like the nano-virus couldn't reach them. More importantly, why am I still alive and unchipped?* He found a fridge with bottled water behind the bar. He tore the cap off one and chugged it. The cool liquid felt like heaven on his dry and dusty throat.

Men shouted as they ran toward the café. Jake squatted down in the shadows by the bar and activated all the barrels on his rifle. A crowd of civilians ran screaming past. One spun around with a gun in his hand. He fired in the direction he had just come from. The high-pitched whine of a mini-gun answered and the man disintegrated into a pile of red hamburger. Screaming ensued outside of Jake's view. The mini-gun mowed down the remaining civilians.

An electric motor mixed with the sounds of crushing glass and debris. A gyro-gun rumbled past at a ten-mile-an-hour clip. It was basically the size of a lawn tractor, but its big tires and suspension allowed it to climb just about any terrain with a forty-five degree grade. The blue flag of NATO was emblazoned on its armored skin. Jake controlled his breathing and held still until the gun's motor faded from earshot. Those machines had extremely sensitive sensor devices to seek out and kill prey.

Jake called up the GPS on his Omni to get a map of the city. He had a few more answers and many more questions. Not everyone was infected, or the Max2 count within them was not high enough to form a Chip. This was a two-pronged attack from space and the ground. Were there humans as well as drones in the invasion force? The presence of NATO peacekeepers meant that Europe had either lost its mind, or The Consortium was finally in control and simply mopping up their last enemy. Maybe that was the plan all along. Get him here, infect the place, and then take it out. If so, it was one hell of a haphazard plan. No, more likely his being here was coincidence. This attack had been planned for a while, with or without him. Max2 was easy to contract and when Nemps blocked microwave activation, sound waves could substitute. So why was The Consortium protecting him? Would his protection go as far as the programming in the NATO drones?

He checked the Arab guard's Omni. He had no idea how to switch it to English. He tossed the device into the café and opened the menu on his second military issue Omni. The first displayed a map of the city. He was in the center of Riyadh. On the second Omni, he searched the Cyber-Wire for Smoov Z's "Baby Can't We Talk." Did he dare activate his Chip? His odds of survival would improve if he could interface with the Cyber-Wire directly from his brain. With the God Head software Parks provided in the Omnis, he might even be able to hack into a few devices or people along the way. He downloaded the song and placed it in a quick access menu. He was not quite ready to commit.

He stuffed his field pants with water bottles and stepped back out into the street. The bodies of all the civilians who had run past the café window were a half block away. The peacekeeping drone had been very efficient. Using his Omni, he found his location relative to Execution Square. It was located in the greatest density of smoke. He navigated to a wide boulevard and spied a massive white structure with the same minarets and lacy white marble he had seen in the news broadcast. A massive chunk of wall had been blown out creating a great gap, like a canyon in its side. It was wide enough at the base for a tank to drive through. The building was across the wide boulevard and eight blocks to the north.

He darted west across six lanes of boulevard and took a quick scan of the area. No movement. He hugged the shadows of the buildings to make his northward approach. After covering five blocks, a column of manned and drone tanks bearing the Nation of Islam flag rumbled onto the boulevard from an eastern side street. A small column of NATO peacekeeper gyro-guns zipped out from the west side, two blocks up, and vomited lead from dozens of mini-guns. The tanks replied with their cannons. In a few seconds, the NATO drones were reduced to flaming and blackened scrap metal.

The tanks spun north and continued up the boulevard, away from Jake's position. Two drones at the back of the column spun their gun turrets one-hundred-and-eighty degrees to protect the rear as the column advanced. Jake waited patiently until the column turned down a side street a dozen blocks ahead and disappeared from view.

He wondered where all the aerial drones were, but was glad he hadn't seen one yet. No sooner did he feel relief when a gyro-gun bounced into the boulevard, scanning the wreckage of its sister machines. Jake searched for cover and saw the broken windows of what appeared to be a bank on the northwest corner from his position. He sat in the shadows wondering if he should just drop and hug the ground or sprint. The bank windows were three feet off the ground, too high for the machine to access, but low enough for him to make a leap. He did not feel like being on the street anymore.

The little machine stopped its search and buzzed forward, heading east across the boulevard. He breathed a sigh of relief and the peacekeeper stopped. It buzzed backward and in that instant, he sprinted for the window.

The drone's turret spun around, locking its gun onto Jake.

Chapter 6
Camouflage

Jake hit the trigger on his rocket-grenade launcher as he rushed forward. He prayed his combination rifle's targeting computer was making up for his lack of aim and his bouncing body. As the rocket sailed, the peacekeeper's gun adjusted upward and shot. The grenade detonated thirty yards from the gyro-gun, just as he leapt into the window of the bank.

Bullets chewed the marble around the window and dug into the inner walls of the bank. He landed on the body of an old man and rolled behind a large oak desk separating a dead banker from his dead customer. As Jake surveyed the room, he saw the main entrance off the northern side street was a heavy glass door that could be easily knocked down by a determined gyro-gun. The peacekeeper hummed by the entrance. A second later, he heard it reverse course and head for the door. Its computer had probably found a layout of the bank on Cyber-Wire.

The machine parked in front of the glass. It seemed to be weighing the options of ramming or shooting. *Conserving bullets?* Flash. He dove for cover as the door exploded. Glass showered the bank's interior. He hopped to his feet with his weapon ready. The gyro-gun's head was missing and smoke belched from its chassis.

Rubble crunched as several heavy armor drones grinded past the doorway. The smoking peacekeeper sat lifeless as half a dozen NOI tanks rumbled by. The last one stopped and an electric eye settled directly on Jake. He froze and practically pissed his pants.

A low-pitched and tinny voice erupted from the machine, "As-Salamu Alaykum." The eye snapped away and the tank rumbled on to join its column heading onto the boulevard.

Jake pulled up the translator on his Omni and repeated the passage. "As-Salamu Alaykum."

The Omni translated: "Peace be with you." The face of the device said: ARABIC GREETING.

"How does one respond to As-Salamu Alaykum in Arabic?"

The Omni answered. "As-Salam."

He kept the translator on, but switched off the voice. He did not need it talking if he were trying to hide from one of the NATO drones. He poked his head out of the shattered doorway and scanned the street. Nothing moved except columns of black smoke billowing into the sky. The fires were multiplying. He maneuvered past the smoking hulk of the peacekeeper and ran to the main boulevard. There were more decimated and burning machines, but no additional bodies. He made his way toward Execution Square. He hugged the shadows and spotted a few destroyed NATO tank drones. Both sides had heavy artillery in this fight. He wondered about orbital laser fire and paused to stare up at the sky. Faint flashes of light danced back and forth. The Muslim Star Wars network had engaged NATO's force. As he recalled, the Muslim network was sorely outnumbered, but it was keeping the offense's most devastating weapons occupied.

The sound of gunfire and shell explosions receded from his position. He reached the rift in Execution Square's six-story-high outer wall. He carefully turned his head to peer into the rift. A large NOI tank came barreling out, machine guns locked. Jake froze as the machine halted a few feet from him. After a quick scan the tank bid him, "As-Salamu Alaykum."

"As-Salam." Jake nodded his head as the machine rumbled by. The tank drones were about as big as the manned versions because they held twice the ammunition. They were often used in manned tank columns to supply additional shells during battle. He watched the tank head north on the boulevard. He noticed a flaming building about ten blocks up. It appeared to be a power plant of some kind. Maybe even a Nemp generator.

He walked carefully through the rift. The marble was melted on the edges and the ground under his feet was crystallized glass. Only a laser would leave such a trail. He stepped into the square. Thousands of bodies lay on top of each other. Most had been killed by the activation of Max2 and subsequent death command. Others had been hit by fallout from the explosions in the square. He tried not to look at individual faces. He was beginning to feel numb over the sheer number of deaths and he couldn't afford to lose his edge.

Five large glassy swaths crisscrossed the grounds. One led to a melted heap that had once been the bronze sphere. No bodies lay in those trenches; the lasers had incinerated them. Blobs of melted steel glowed around the walls. Those had to be the tanks he had seen in the coverage of the execution ceremony. He navigated through the corpses to the sphere. He identified enough components in the melted mess to tell him this had been a Nemp generator. Based on all the electronic components that were working in the city before the attack, this machine must have been hit out of precaution to ensure total Chip activation.

He walked down a glass trench toward the two-story black semicircle in the eastern part of the square. A body had been impaled on the pike and had slid half way down the iron needle. He ran toward the elevated body. As he got closer, he realized the impaled figure was one of Parks' executioners. He had fallen chest first onto the spike. Jake ran around the back side of the massive semicircle and spotted stone stairs leading up to the top. As he reached the base of the stair, he spotted the cleric. The man had fallen backward off the granite platform and landed on his head. Blood leaked out of the

HAZMAT suit's crushed helmet. He ran up the steps and emerged on top of the smooth four-foot thick black wall. Only the figures of Parks and one of the President's cabinet were up here. He assumed the rest of them escaped when the kill switch was activated if they didn't have enough Max2 to form a Chip. Probably heading out of the city in tanks. The cabinet member, who was dead, had a piece of bronze shrapnel sticking out of his back, thrown up by the laser strike. Jake ran to the burned and bloody figure of his friend.

Chapter 7
Ethnic Cleansing

He felt for a pulse. Nothing. Parks lay on his back, his arm hanging over the precipice, as if reaching out to help his executioner, now halfway down the spike.

Jake dug into his own raw hand. A tear ran down his cheek. As much as he disagreed with this man, he was someone who fought to better the world, and in the end, he was a decent human being. How many millions like Parks were now dead? He stared out at the ocean of corpses filling the square. How many of them disagreed with this execution but were compelled to be here out of fear? How many in this country believed in good, and of bringing peace instead of war to this planet? Did anyone deserve this fate? The Consortium was carrying out genocide, plain and simple.

Jake gazed at the sky. Beyond the flashes of laser fire and explosions, he saw the moon. What did Luna think of this? Were they itching to jump into the fight? Were they taking a wait-and-see policy? Parks had mentioned that Luna had seceded from Earth. Once The Consortium solidified their control down here, would they point their weapons and God Heads at the moon? Undoubtedly. Could Luna defend herself?

He turned back to his friend. Even in death, he appeared at peace. "I'm glad you're with your God, Parks." He gazed over the carnage. "He certainly isn't here." He turned and looked behind the semicircle. The eastern side of the square had balconies and structures jutting out from the wall. Under the shadow of one of these balconies, he spotted a manned tank.

He looked around for something to wrap Parks' body. The man deserved a burial. The roar of jet wash broke the sounds of ground battles. He glanced at the sky but saw only the space war flashing above. He ran for the stairs. Parks would have to wait. When he was halfway down the stone steps, six drones screamed over the square. He did not get a chance to see if they were NATO or NOI. As he hit the white-marble-tiled ground, three drones intercepted and a dogfight ensued. Bullets flew in every direction as aircraft screamed up, down, back and forth over the square. Bullets whizzed by him and he was pelted with bits of marble as the tiles around his feet exploded. They were obviously not firing at him; he was just too close to the action.

He reached the cover of an overhead balcony next to the tank. A drone crashed into the pike on the other side of the semicircle. A wave of flame leapt up from behind the barrier. Another drone smashed into the west wall of the square, where the rift was located. More smoke and fire ensued. He checked out the tank. It was motionless and intact.

He scrambled up on top of the tank and looked down into the open driver's hatch. The dead driver was slumped over the controls. Jake hoisted the soldier out and tossed him over the side. He climbed down into the battle chair and realized everything was marked in Arabic. He studied the touch screens, joysticks, and pedals. Many of the components reminded him of HJ cockpits. The tank was an early 2020s model that borrowed most of its user interface from the HJs of that era. He had trained on those HJs back in the police academy. Jet wash, bullets, and explosions raged around him. He sucked in a lungful of warm dusty air. "Fuck it." He hit the button he assumed was for the hatch. The metal above him slid closed with a satisfying *Whunk*. He touched what he figured was the power readout and the tank started up. The status configuration showed it fully charged and ready to roll. A big smile spread over his face. He didn't need the labels. He turned on the three-hundred-and-sixty holo-screen, armed the machine guns, cannon turret, and grabbed the joysticks.

He stomped the pedals, steering the tank toward the burning rift in the west wall. He tried not to think of all the bodies he was plowing over. The joysticks operated the guns. His feet controlled the speed and direction of the tank. It was a different experience than piloting an HJ, but not too much. The holo-screens gave him an accurate view of the entire square. A drone dove down at him, firing a mini-gun that did absolutely no damage to his armor. Jake placed an electric eye on the drone so that it could track and take out the drone with a mini-gun of his own. He continued to roll toward the rift as the computer took the drone out with thirty rounds from the mini-gun.

He spotted what he believed was a button to switch all the guns on automatic. He was tempted, but felt that would be too irresponsible. What if the program only spared anyone in an NOI military uniform, where would that leave citizens? Then again, maybe the tanks were programmed to shoot anyone who was armed. He couldn't take a chance.

He planned to continue posing as an NOI soldier. Right now the locals were his allies, despite the reception he had received. He was convinced The Consortium was the enemy. He stopped the moment he was aligned with the rift in the wall. He needed a plan, and most of all he needed a map. He used his Omni to find his location once again. He tried to call up a satellite view but the response popped up: JAMMED. Either the war of the satellites was still raging or The Consortium was victorious.

He took off one of his Omnis and configured it into tablet form. He wedged it on his control board then shrunk the map to see the Nation of Islam's entire country. The northern border touched Jordan and the Gulf of Aqaba. He felt like heading northwest, and into Africa, although he was not sure why. He needed more information. He needed The Chip. He triple-checked the encryptions and security protocols on his Omnis. He was covered. But what if Pin Heads attacked him? What if they removed his Omnis? He hated being afraid. Fear was vulnerability.

He decided to table the decision for a bit longer. He used his Omni to scan the readouts in the tank and translate them for him. He found the sub-menu to change the language in the tank to English. He watched the touch interfaces switch to his native tongue with great relief. He grabbed his Omni, configured it back into a watch and parked it in security mode. Then he pulled up a local map on the tank's UI and hit the pedals, sending the war machine through the rift. He looked at the black semi-circle in the tank's 360 holo-vision. Parks' body was now a spec on top of the wall. Jake dug into his palm. *Sorry Parks.*

He decided to head northwest, toward Egypt. He had three hours of power before the tank would need a recharge. The tank had a receptor for a satellite power feed, but engaging it would send up a flare to any satellites in orbit. Plus, he had no idea if the Arab satellite network had survived the attack.

He rolled onto Highway 546. At one time all the roads had been named after Saudi Kings; now they were named after Muslim clerics. He was headed toward the National University, where he would take the Allah Road to Highway 65, and head out of the city. As he neared the National University, formerly King Saud University, he stumbled onto a tank battle.

At least thirty NOI tanks had engaged fifty NATO tanks and peacekeeper gyro-guns. The peacekeepers were making kamikaze runs on the tanks, as their mini-guns were useless against the NOI heavy armor. Jake switched on all of his automatic defenses. The tank buster on his vehicle was fifteen feet long and could shoot a round every second. As soon as he engaged the weapon, NATO tanks burst like water balloons with each shot. His machine was by far the biggest and most powerful in the fight. He heard the cheers of other drivers over his tank's communication system. He switched on the volume to his Omni so he could hear the translations.

"It's the National Guard! The President has come to save us!"

Jake had to laugh at that one. So he had commandeered the President's tank… he wondered if the President had survived the Max2 kill switch. If so, he was probably long gone in a caravan to safety. Within two minutes, the battle was over. Jake's ammunition was down to seventy percent. He had plenty of firepower to get him to Egypt. He switched off the auto defense. He drove past the small NOI force and was dismayed to find them following him.

A new voice came over the speakers. "NATO forces have overrun Jeddah; we need all available artillery to regroup and head down the Makkah al Mukarrmah Road. We will hide on the south and west borders and ambush them when they come. We must protect our women and children!"

"Colonel Saddiq, we have found the President, he has just rescued us from a pitched battle near the university!"

Jake had to get himself out of this as soon as possible. This was not how he planned to battle The Consortium.

An explosion echoed through Jake's tank, followed by another and another. Shrapnel hammered his armor. "Four o'clock! Four o'clock," a voice shouted over the speaker, then turned to static. Jake activated the electric eye on his right rear quarter and spotted a NATO Hades-class drone approaching. It was one-and-a-half times the size of a tour bus with four tank treads instead of the usual two. What it lacked in speed it made up for in armor and ballistics. Its 480mm bunker-busting gun could take down a skyscraper with one well-placed shot. It had two rockets in its rear cargo bay that could destroy a satellite in orbit. Its jamming field was blocking their NOI military grade communications. With each shot from its gun, NOI tanks disintegrated in the column behind Jake.

Jake searched for a place to hide his vehicle as he swung the turret around. As he did so, a half dozen NATO peacekeeper gyro-guns sped up behind the Hades. Jake's cannon locked onto the NATO drone as it slowed to a stop. An NOI soldier's head flew from one of the gyro-guns onto the Hades. Jake took his finger off his trigger. The head floated above a shimmering blotch—holographic camouflage that made the wearer invisible. The soldier's face shield had come off during his leap. The rest of his body continued to blend in with the environment. Jake scrutinized the scene and noticed shimmering patches, like heat rising off of pavement, on each NATO gyro-gun. Every peacekeeper had an NOI soldier riding on it. They had hacked the drones and were using them to infiltrate enemy lines. Jake admired the ingenuity.

He locked facial identification software onto the floating head working on the NATO Hades. It was Colonel Saddiq himself. Saddiq had an impressive military record. He had fought in the Saudi Arabian revolution and had been decorated several times. He had graduated from the NOI military academy with top honors in cyberwarfare and taught courses in the subject every spring. The man was a few years younger than Jake. Despite acne scars, bony cheeks and boxy jaw, Saddiq had a look about him that was approachable and trustworthy.

Audio crackled back on. Troops chanted, "Saddiq! Saddiq! Saddiq! Saddiq!" Jake caught himself chanting as well. The colonel was the perfect soldier for this war.

A burst of light shot down from the heavens, cutting into the remaining NOI tanks. Jake swung his vehicle off the road and crashed into a school building. He needed to get off the satellite-targeting grid.

A voice screamed, "We're under laser attack!"

Saddiq barked, "I'm firing the Hades! Take cover. Get out of sight! Use guerilla tactics! No more fighting in the open!"

Jake powered down his tank and hoped the satellite would not start taking out all the buildings in the area. He felt frustrated. He had no plan, and he was useless without more information. He had the software to aid him in hacking machines and Pin Heads, but only if he activated his Max2 Chip.

The thought of hooking back in again caused him to hyperventilate. He closed his eyes. *Like Saddiq, you have to fight on their level. You're like a caveman fighting a modern army with a spear and a slingshot.*

He called up "Baby Can't We Talk" on his Omni and reached out to touch the button with his index finger. He felt the urge to puke. *What if I don't have The Chip? What if the cure they injected me with back in Beijing really worked? There has to be a reason why I haven't been activated yet. Maybe I'm chipped and this is all a dream? Maybe I'll wake up and Tomoko, Lakshmi, and Mom will be looking down at me from around my bed. Just like Dorothy in The Wizard of Oz...*

Explosions thundered all around him. The screaming from the other tank drivers stopped, nothing but radio silence.

"Fuck it." He touched the play button.

Chapter 8
Offer

A spike of panic shot through his system. He had settled into his seat to wait for his colony of Max2 to swarm into a Chip when he realized his wedding ring was gone. It had been a loose fit and it could have fallen off when escaping the prison or any place he had been afterward. He jumped up and searched the cockpit in hopes he'd get lucky. It was his only physical reminder of Tomoko. As tears filled his eyes, he combed the interior three times. He missed her terribly. *You have to go back.* The thought was absurd. *You can bury Parks as well. What other pressing plans do you have?* He had no other agenda beyond waiting for his Chip, searching The Cyber-Wire and figuring out where he could strike The Consortium. But going back to Execution Square and the prison was dangerously foolhardy.

He slumped into the driver's seat. The tank smelled oily, mechanical, with the slight musk of man sweat. He wasn't sure if the stink originated from him or the previous occupant. He studied the 360 holo-display, the touch pads, and stick controls. All looked normal. The tank emitted a low hum and he could hear the faint sound of circulating air. Even with the environment set to twenty-three degrees Celsius, he poured sweat. External sensors showed battles erupting in pockets throughout the city. His mouth felt dry and parched and there was an increase in the taste of metal on his tongue. He pulled a bottle of water from his pants pocket, ripped off the top and drank.

He itched to head back and look for the ring. It had been fifteen minutes since he had listened to the song. The radio chatter started up. Jake relaxed a bit when he heard Saddiq's voice. The colonel had not only survived but he had taken out the satellite above. But the column that had followed Jake had been wiped out. Saddiq was leading his hacked NATO column back into Riyadh to coordinate the defense of the city. He instructed all remaining forces to take off their uniforms, hide in rubble, but retain their military badges so the NOI drones would not fire on them. Jake observed his own uniform and saw the odd tag on his chest and arm. He remembered seeing the same on his back. So that was what the NOI drones registered when they had scanned him. *What kept the enemy from forging the same identification?* Perhaps they did. From the sound of it, the colonel was using the drones for the heavy fighting and so far, there was not a single manned machine on the offensive side. Jake admired Saddiq for holding on against hopeless odds... a man after his own heart.

Based on radio chatter, the NOI satellite network had been obliterated, and NATO's laser platforms were focused on Jeddah. They no longer saw Riyadh as a threat.

The Colonel rallied the troops and kept up morale. There was nothing about religion or infidels. The fight had been stripped down to its basic component: Freedom of thought versus life with a machine in your head. Jake laughed at the irony. He had chosen the machine in his head... for now. Was this current situation a case of too little too late? He hoped not...

He felt a tingling in the back of his neck and brain. He knew the brain sensation had to be psychological since there were no nerve endings in there, but the Max2 Chip had to be connecting with the thousands of existing nano-filaments in his head, the nano-filaments that had spawned tumors in his brain. *Pick your poison. Something is going to get you before this year is out.* He shook the thought out of his head.

He suddenly felt a window open inside his mind. It was as if he had been living in a tiny jail cell and was now exposed to the greater world outside. He sensed his two Omnis. They were now an extension of his mind, gatekeepers that filtered information coming and going from his head. He could look at a map of the world, see what the tank saw, and understand a hundred human and cyber languages. It was as if this knowledge had been in his head since birth. The sensation was overwhelming, but familiar. He "saw" the blanket hacking signals bombarding his information stream, trying to get in and steal his mind. There was a beast outside the Garden of Eden; the world beyond his Omni's wall of protection was a dark and deadly landscape waiting to devour his soul.

Gone was the black interface space he had experienced with his first Chip. This new device was a seamless extension of his mind. He accessed the hacking programs on his Omnis and went after the satellites orbiting above. Their encryption codes were as strong as the ones protecting him, but he set one of his Omnis to work on one of the older attack satellites. He hoped its firmware would not be able to compete with the state-of-the-art Cobalt programs on his military Omni.

A familiar voice crackled on the tank speakers. Jake could now understand Arabic so there was no delay while waiting for the Omni to repeat. "This is Colonel Farhad Saddiq of the Nation of Islam Cyber Offensive Unit. I speak to all the men and women of the Middle East. If you value your freedom, and do not want to be slaves to a computer chip, join the fight. If you cannot find a gun, RPG, or tank, pick up a rake, shovel, or hoe and find a hiding place. But be prepared to attack anyone or anything that tries to pass you. Conserve your energy and wait for the fight to come to you. We are regrouping, and if we can launch an offensive, we will."

Wedding ring or no, it was time to leave Riyadh. He did not want to get trapped in this guerilla war. There had to be a more strategic use for his skill set. He swallowed back his feelings of loss and concentrated on preventing humanity's genocide.

Using the tank's touch pad controls, he accessed the NOI satellite network. There wasn't much left beyond a couple of monitoring stations that supported the ground forces and power plants. NATO's satellites had moved away from Riyadh and were now concentrating their firepower on other Muslim cities. Jake powered up the main engines and crashed his way out of the college building. He activated the power collector on the back of his war machine and began absorbing concentrated radio waves from a solar satellite converter in orbit. He maintained contact with the three remaining NOI satellites to monitor all satellite activity and to be sure he wasn't drawing attention to himself.

As he drove north on interstate 65 toward Buraydah, the tank's batteries charged and he used a non-secure mapping satellite to examine conditions along the route to the Gulf of Aqaba and Egypt beyond. There were skirmishes all over North Africa between NATO and the Muslim forces. Egypt's population had been murdered before the fight began. Max2 had exacted a massive death toll all over the Middle East. The dome over Cairo had become unusable because the environmental control systems that kept it cool had been switched off when Egypt was fighting Max1 with Nemps. Beneath the dome, Egypt's ancient ruins, including the Great Pyramids and the Sphinx, were now in perpetual darkness.

With no population to stop them, NATO had used the Suez Canal to run their drone artillery down to the Red Sea and launch an invasion on both shores. It would be tricky to navigate through the drones after he passed Aqaba, but most of the ground forces were currently engaged farther south and east from his destination. He was impressed with his hacking software. Parks didn't mess around. The thought of his friend lying on the semi-circle in execution square caused him to dig his fingers into his raw and bloody palm. *You could go back and bury him...*

You have to keep moving. You have to survive.

As he sifted through mountains of information, a message appeared on his Omni. His virus checker had already examined it five times to be sure it would not infect his Chip or his Omnis if he opened it. He set the tank on autopilot and checked the message.

Anjali's face hovered over his controls. He had not seen her since her public appearance with Prime Minister Shekhawat in the streets of Mumbai several days ago. It felt like a lifetime had passed.

"Hello Jake." Anjali appeared calm and serene, with no hint of her usual nervous energy. He immediately became suspicious. A ruse from The Consortium? "Right now you are probably thinking this is an enemy trick. I appear differently because I am creating this message from inside my mind, which means I am projecting my ideal self, or how I perceive myself to be."

He tried to relax in the battle chair. He had a hard time disassociating her with everything that had gone wrong since Christmas Eve. Plus, he had murdered her husband in Chhatrapati Airport on January third, eight days ago. *Did she know?*

"I activated my own Max2 when the nuclear device was detonated in New Delhi. I could no longer work in isolation in order to find a cure for the nano-virus and carry on the cause of Erasmus. I believe you will ultimately come to the same conclusion I have, that you need The Chip to fight this plague on freedom."

He quickly checked the data streams feeding directly into his brain. No Trojan horses; all was well.

Anjali continued. "I set this message to search for Cobalt military jamming patterns on the Cyber-Wire. My message will reach all of them, but it will only open for your brain wave signature. I have your pattern on file from the examination conducted before the terrorist attacked the lab here in Mumbai. But so does The Consortium, which means we both have the power to send messages to you, or track you, or use a Pin Head to attack. Listen closely before you decide what to do next."

He leaned into the holograph.

"Max2 has infected close to ninety-eight percent of the world's population. They could use it at any moment to consolidate power over the Earth. Muslim nations have tried many methods to keep Max2 infections at bay, with little success. There are also sizeable pockets in South America who are virus free, but their days are numbered."

"I have made contact with Luna to allow one more rocket to land on the moon. We have hacked a scramjet scheduled to rendezvous with ISA's Spaceport on January fifteenth. The scramjet is being prepped at Cape Canaveral, in Florida. Be there no later than noon on the fifteenth. This rocket will be the only one allowed to launch. Luna will not attempt to destroy it with their early warning defense systems. The last battle will be fought between Earth and the moon as the Earth is now officially lost.

"MaxWell does not exist on Luna. So our ship will be quarantined and we will not be allowed into the main habitat areas. We have asked to join the fight and the new Lunar government has agreed in order to study the living virus and help find a cure. There will not be many of us and we are using Pin Heads to help us along the way. We are relying on the fact that The Consortium is going to be spread too thin in the next few weeks consolidating power to be able to pay attention to every square mile of the planet. As long as we remain covert before the launch, we have a good chance of making it out of orbit using a few hacked satellites to defend our departure."

"You are the only non-scientific mind I am reaching out to. I saw what you did at Terminal C to my husband and to Sanchez."

Jake shrank in his seat.

"I do not agree with your actions, but I do believe you are an honest man, and one that has the unique ability to resist the power of a God Head. This is worth further study."

Jake wiped the sweat off his brow. *Anjali is touting me as someone who can resist hacking. This is ridiculous.*

"How you reach the launch site is completely up to you, but if you want to join the only resistance that can make a difference, you'll know what to do."

She disappeared.

Jake replayed the message, searching for cues that would indicate this was a trap. He was still on the fence when it completed its second playback. It seemed farfetched, but if this was a ruse, it was an elaborate and illogical one. Once The Consortium found him, they could send Pin Heads or a missile to take him out. He agreed with Anjali that there were too few members of The Consortium to keep tabs on everyone on the planet, even him. But the non-chipped population was dwindling further every hour; and sooner or later, The Consortium would focus their attention on him. *Maybe this is a way to occupy you until that moment arrives? The scramjet leaves Cape Canaveral in less than four days. Your day of reckoning could come before that.*

An alarm rang. The satellite power plant fueling his tank failed; hacked by The Consortium and shut down. He had enough power for three more hours of hard driving. Then he'd be stranded in the blistering desert, and locked in a crab cooker that wouldn't be able to fire anything larger than a rubber band without a power cell.

Chapter 9
Flipside

J ake's military Omni broke the encryption on a NATO satellite. He used it to locate troop transport aircraft on the ground nearest to his location. A jet was the only way he was going to get to Florida on time. NATO had numerous landing sites for their invasion of the Middle East and North Africa. The nearest location of a NATO air transport was an airfield in Al Kharrara near the border of Qatar.

He sucked in a deep breath and savored the stale smell of the tank's interior. The more he thought about it, the more he felt that Anjali's message was real. *But what if it's not?*

Then I'll take out as many as I can before I'm absorbed by the machine. There aren't a whole lot of options left.

You could join Saddiq.

Anjali did not paint a positive outcome for Earth's resistance movement. He searched for any human beings in the vicinity of the Al Kharrara airfield. He found a few hundred personnel, all chipped. Using the God

Head software stored in his Omni, he inventoried Chips with the lowest security. He found a few Gen 3 Chips and had his hacking software go to work on those. While his Omnis did their job, he plugged his crucial devices into the battery power of his tank so that they'd be fully topped off while he was playing God Head. He maneuvered his tank down Interstate 550 to loop down toward Riyadh. The route would ultimately lead to highway 85 and Qatar. The tank had enough power to get him within thirty or forty miles, but he was going to hit NATO land drones long before then. He'd need Pin Heads to come to him.

Saddiq had been quiet for some time. Jake wondered if Max2 or another Hades drone had finally caught up with the Colonel. Considering the man's dossier, he had probably switched encrypted channels. Either way, Jake missed the sound of genuine human interaction. He felt the last of the NOI satellites wink out. He was vulnerable driving a tank with only the enemy looking down. But he was headed away from most areas of conflict. The eyes in the sky would be concentrating on battle zones, or so he hoped.

He kept a constant vigil using the tank's sensor systems. When he reached the freeway interchange of Interstate 40 on the northeastern side of Riyadh, he was forced to backtrack. The freeway had been demolished and the smoking ruins of a massive battle blacked out the scene. Hundreds of tanks, gyro-guns, crashed drones, and the bodies of Arab soldiers lay scattered about the landscape. A breeze stirred up a haze of sand and smoke, which invaded the tank's air filtration system. The scent of burned flesh wafted into his nose.

He navigated around the battlefield and caught the 40 a few miles past the carnage. About an hour and sixty miles later, he drove through Khurais and saw a massacre. Hundreds of people had been cut to pieces. The desert was soaked with black bloodstains. From the looks of it, they had been murdered by gyro-gun Peacekeepers.

Jake gritted his teeth as he surveyed the massive destruction of life before him. His finger rubbed the triggers of his weapons. Images of friends and family he'd lost filled his mind; and he had a yearning to kill. *I've got to do something. Anything. To lie down and give my life to the whim of The Consortium is worse than suicide.*

His Omni alerted him that he had compromised all four Gen 3 Chips on the airbase and had access to four Pin Heads. He used his passive God Head program to tap into their minds. He was instantly deluged with the history of all four. History was key in creating false realities while a Pin Head was offline. Jake was not going to concern himself with that aspect of hacking—few did anymore—but he was curious to know more about the four human beings he was now controlling.

One was a civil engineer in his forties named Muhtadi, the other was an anesthesiologist in her twenties named Sa'dah, and the third was a chemist in her fifties named Ghadir. The last person was a kid in his mid-twenties named Danny Accomando. The first three had been chipped a few months after Jake had torn out his LAPD Chip before escaping to Brazil. They were all members of Qatar's scientific community, but now that The Consortium was running the show, they were simply Pin Heads doing grunt work at the airfield. Accomando had been a private in the US Marines. He seemed to have been abandoned here when all the drones were sent into battle.

Jake triggered a signal to the program monitoring his Pin Heads that they were in need of rest. As soon as they were placed into sleep mode, Jake assumed full control of his automatons. It was odd receiving sensory input from four additional human beings. He remembered his training aboard Parks' HJ and controlled them using passive mode. He directed commands to each mind and they executed the details. The method of control was far more efficient than the way his God Heads had controlled him back in 2030.

Memories of Paul Ducey, one of Jake's God Heads, flashed in Jake's head. Ducey clearly detested the idea of being chipped himself. Jake remembered what Paul had said during their confrontation in the elevator, just before Jake had shot him. "You think I'd get within fifteen feet of one of those things?" If Paul had lived, he simply would not have had a choice. It was a requirement of the new world order, whether you were at the top or bottom of the food chain.

He directed Muhtadi, Sa'dah, and Ghadir to sabotage the base, while Accomando commandeered a truck and drove out to meet Jake. The experience was like playing four characters at once in an elaborate video game. It was far easier being a God Head than a Pin Head. It had taken three God

Heads to control Jake back in 2030. Technology had advanced so quickly in the past six years that it made his head swim. He recalled what Anjali had once told him. "Third Eyes have allowed us to make evolutionary jumps in all fields of science."

As his tank rolled east, he dug a little deeper into his Pin Heads. Muhtadi had a wife and two boys, one fifteen and the other twelve. He was a good man, kept his head down and was a devout Muslim. He was a man with a good heart and helped in his community. Jake could tell the clerics of Muhtadi's mosque felt that Muhtadi's Chip gave him an edge over the west and, therefore, was sanctioned by Allah. Now Muhtadi was doing menial labor on a military base. His conscience was playing out a normal life within his head. He was enjoying the company of his wife and children on a beach holiday. It depressed Jake to think this man was no longer living in reality.

Sa'dah, the anesthesiologist, was very pretty and devoted to supporting her mother and two younger sisters. She was unmarried and felt that she could never have a relationship until her two sisters were out of school and were self-sufficient. Even then, Jake could tell her mother's domineering will would keep Sa'dah single for life if she did not assert some independence. Sa'dah was more liberal in her faith, but outwardly went through the motions in order to keep the government and her family happy. Inside her head, Sa'dah enjoyed the company of family and her favorite cat while her body carried out the will of The Consortium.

Ghadir was a chemist with a domineering personality. She had been married three times and had four grandchildren. She had been brilliant in her field but her unorthodox lifestyle had landed her in trouble too many times. She missed many promotions and in the end she was placed in the discard pile. The Consortium had marked her for hard labor. She was expendable. Jake felt he would have a lot in common with Ghadir. She reminded him a bit of his old friend, Gene.

Danny Accomando was from an American base. He was a twenty-four-year old private in the Marine Corps with a big chip on his shoulder. His grudge against his family dated back to his early childhood. It asserted itself in his constant challenge of authority. He had joined the Marines wanting to make something of himself, but had been disillusioned by boot camp. He had been fighting his own war with the Marines ever since.

Jake felt the urge to pile them all in his tank. He wanted to protect them. Save them. *Back off, Jake. This is exactly what you should not do. The more you identify with them, the less you'll be able to manipulate these people.* Jake stared at his raw palm. It was swollen with infection. *Good. You deserve it, you selfish bastard.* He shook his head. These people were the tools by which he could go on fighting. If he won, these people could be free.

It was dusk by the time he reached the city of Al Hasa. The place was a smoking ruin, a black swath of pulverized civilization in a sea of sand and sun-blasted rock. He was unable to determine how many had died from Max2 and how many had died from conventional warfare. He had to give the city a wide berth; there was too much destruction to use the interstate in the region. He had Accomando wait for him on the southeast side of the city. Jake was about a mile south of Accomando's position when the tank's power ran out. He disconnected his Omnis and climbed out of the hatch into the blackest of nights. The power meters on both his devices were good for about four hours each. Usually an Omni would last at least twelve hours, but the amount of power the God Head programs and interface were sucking up was sobering.

He left the tank under a dazzling starlit sky. The stars were so thick he felt he could reach up with a net and catch a few hundred. The air was a dry sixty-two degrees. Temperatures had dropped significantly since sunset. He longed to lie down on the baked earth and star gaze. He wanted to forget about the insanity raging over every horizon. *Victory first, rest second.* He headed for the tiny headlights of Accomando's truck. They were the only visible human-made lights in the entire desert. He came across a scorpion, heading away from the dead civilizations of the north and west. "Have at it, kiddo. Looks like the world is yours for the taking." Jake chuckled, but he felt just as dark and empty inside as the tank he was leaving behind.

Chapter 10
Sacrifice

Jake opened the passenger door to Private Accomando's truck, ready to tell him he was a good kid and that he should get out of the Corps as soon as possible. Accomando stared straight ahead; unaware of anything that was happening around him. Jake was inside that head, working him like a puppet. *Stop it, Jake. Stop trying to connect. They're all cab drivers taking you to the airport and you're too busy to make a human connection. Just do your job and let them do theirs.*

He lay behind the front seat as Private Accomando "drove" the vehicle back to base. On the way, Jake used both Omnis for different tasks. He focused his hacking software on accessing a big military scramjet so he could clear it for a flight back to Miami. The second Omni was used to control his Pin Heads, and to ensure the military transport's transponder was properly communicating with the NATO drones as a friendly. He ran another program on top of these to download into his Chip the instructions on how to fly the military scramjet. Within seconds, Jake knew every control as if he had been logging hundreds of hours as a scramjet pilot.

There were certainly wonderful advantages to The Chip. He nervously watched the power meters on his Omnis. The heavy use was rapidly draining them. If they died, he'd be wide open to every God Head program floating on the Cyber-Wire. He checked the enemy's hacking signals. They were hammering away at his security field, trying to break the cycling encryptions in order to convert him into an automaton.

He thought of the filaments in his brain that had been dormant for almost six years but were now active. He wondered if this renewed activity was feeding his tumors, running down his clock like the batteries on his Omni. *If that's the case, I'll be seeing my wife soon.* He focused on the mission at hand to push away his negative thoughts.

At the entrance to the airfield, Accomando and the truck were scanned by two NATO gyro-gun Peacekeepers. Accomando and the truck gave the appropriate digital handshakes and were allowed onto base. Jake breathed a sigh of relief. He had played with a theory that all of these computers speaking silently to each other at the speed of light might have specifically assigned duties. Any deviation from an assigned duty would send up an alarm. But this was war, and there had to be scores of separate agendas being carried out by God Heads half way around the world. He had no doubt that once The Consortium consolidated power, it would be impossible to fart without some program logging the action and making sure it was approved. The window of opportunity was rapidly closing.

It had taken a couple of hours to reach the base. It was getting close to midnight and he had had no success hacking into the scramjets on the ground. He used his Pin Heads to enter a cargo scramjet that was offline but operational. They began dismantling the plane's onboard computer. He commanded the scientists to reset all the plane's command functions so that they could be rerouted through Jake's encrypted Omnis. The cargo scramjet would maintain the NATO transponder code, which he downloaded into his own Omni so he'd register as a friendly. While the Pin Heads busied themselves with the scramjet computers, he climbed into the engineer's section of the aircraft and plugged in his Omnis for a much-needed drink of voltage. The aircraft was plugged into the base power plant so it was topped off and merely keeping itself at full power levels until called back to active duty. Its liquid hydrogen tanks had been topped off as well.

He used the eyes and ears of Private Accomando to patrol the area outside the aircraft and watch for potential problems. Luckily, the base was engaged in deployments and repairs and too busy to notice the activities of Jake and his Pin Heads. He bided his time by watching how God Heads took certain human and mechanical assets out of the duty roster. Commands were given after a set of cyber handshakes. He recorded them for his next maneuver.

By 2:00AM, the military cargo scramjet was under his complete control. The computer was programmed using his encryption software so any outside hack would meet the same firewalls that protected his Chip. He climbed into the cockpit and began prepping for pre-flight. He relayed the digital handshakes with The Consortium AI programs and cleared his bird for take off and the flight to Miami. He chose Miami in case anyone figured out this was a rogue flight with no approved God Head behind the plan. He needed to be close, but not next door to Cape Canaveral. If he were discovered, it would protect Anjali by a day, an hour, or a minute. Landing at the cape just seemed like too big of a risk to her plan.

He felt conflicted over what to do with the Pin Heads. Anjali had said there was room on the flight for he alone. He wanted to command them to cut The Chip out of their heads and install a Max2 wick like he saw on Parks, but then what? What could they do? Where could they go? Worst of all, they could be captured and then The Consortium would find out who had hacked them. That was the biggest danger. He had to erase his tracks. The Consortium would simply kill them, but he couldn't bring himself to do that, and he felt terrible for even thinking it. Sleep was the answer. They could sleep until one hour after Anjali's scramjet was due to take off on January fifteenth, less than four days from now. They'd be taking one hell of a nap.

He commanded all of his Pin Heads to leave the plane and head to an air-conditioned warehouse that had a low security designation. It was a parts depot for aerial drones that was chilled for chip sets and other computer components. He made them find secluded spots inside the warehouse, lie down, and basically go into a coma for the next eighty hours. He sealed up the aircraft, disconnected it from the charging station, and fired up the hydrogen injectors. He rolled onto the taxiway just as a series of explosions lit up the night sky to the west.

He tuned into the Arab transmitter frequencies, but heard static. With his access to the satellite above, he could see they were under attack from the west and from the south. Dozens of tanks fired on the perimeter and aerial drones bombed a fleet of armored HJs parked on the airfield. Al Kharrara came alive with a drone counter-strike. Tanks and gyro-gun Peacekeepers raced onto the desert to intercept the attackers. The remaining HJs and aerial drones took to the skies, but their numbers had been reduced by two thirds in the surprise attack.

"Aliq! There's an opening at the northwest, take it!" Jake recognized the voice as Colonel Saddiq. He was happy to know the man was alive, and a bit nervous to hear him press the advantage at the moment Jake was trying to make an escape. He passed the hangar area and taxied onto the main runway. To his surprise, he saw the buildings at the other end of the base explode in geysers of fire. A column of NOI tanks crashed through a small break in the flaming wreckage. They raced onto the airfield directly ahead of Jake. He quickly switched his transponder to mimic the one from his NOI tank.

"Colonel! The President is broadcasting the old signal. We're not sure which direction yet but it seems to be coming from within the base!"

"Ignore it!" the Colonel commanded. "The President's transport was abandoned in the desert by NATO spies."

Jake quickly switched the signal back to the NATO transponder. He spent a split second hesitating over his next action. Since he had no missiles or heavy weapons of his own, he woke Private Accomando from his coma and sent him sprinting to the nearest NATO Hurricane, a manned tank and the meanest land machine that Cobalt industries had ever built. Although lacking the brute force of a Hades drone, it was quick and fierce in a heavy weapons firefight. Within a minute, Accomando's Hurricane raced toward the right flank of Saddiq's tank column. The column began to fan onto the runway, closing the distance to Jake's aircraft.

When Jake was in position for takeoff, he had Accomando unleash hell. Two NOI tanks exploded under the Hurricane's mini-nuclear warheads. Using targeting sensors, Accomando fired missiles on NOI tanks and drones as they entered the base through the tunnel of fire marking the breach in the perimeter.

"Hurricane right flank! All vehicles concentrate firepower on the Hurricane!" shouted Saddiq. "Heavy guns only!"

As the Hurricane scattered Saddiq's tank column, Jake fired up his ramjets and blasted forward to achieve takeoff velocity. As his nose lifted off the ground, the Hurricane was sustaining heavy damage. Accomando was mortally wounded, but Jake used his God Head program to push the man to continue the fight against Saddiq's hail of death. Jake's scramjet lifted into the air and the landing gear slid into the belly of the plane. As Jake rocketed into low orbit, Accomando died in the flaming remains of the Hurricane.

God help me, Jake thought as he felt his connection with Accomando snap. He had made sure all pain receptors had been blocked within the soldier, but it didn't make Jake feel any better about killing a man to save his own skin. *One man? I killed several. A non-chipped human being manned each of those NOI tanks, the very people I'm supposed to be fighting for.*

I am doing this so I can go to the moon and be part of the last human resistance.

The words felt hollow. He could not shake the feeling that he had done all of this in a selfish act to save himself.

He picked at his infected hand. *What makes you so special? Why is your life more valuable than Accomando's, or any one else back there?*

Because I can strike at the heart of The Consortium, I can turn the tide.

No, you're just chicken-shit scared.

He agreed that he was scared, but he had to believe in his ability to fight as long as he had the freedom of mind to do so. He realized he was still plugged in with the other three Pin Heads and quickly severed his links. Their Chips were already locked into their sleep routines.

The big cargo plane reached low-orbit. He watched the world turn beneath him and thought of all the souls trapped by Max2 Chips down below. He clenched his fist. The infection converted the pain into a fiery bolt that shot up his arm and punched his skull. After he took a moment to allow his nerves to calm down, his thoughts wandered to his dead and missing family. He allowed himself to cry for several seconds before he pushed his open wound onto a cold steel panel. As the ship maneuvered for a re-entry, he wondered what would happen if he simply crashed into the Earth and entered a state of oblivion. There would be some peace in that ending.

But then the sacrifices you forced on those people back in Al Kharrara would have been for nothing. You owe it to them to carry out your plan. You owe it to Tomoko, Parks, and everyone else who has died trying to fight this madness. This is bigger than you. Take responsibility and see it through. As Parks would say: Man up!

He nodded in agreement, then he braced himself in his g-force chair and prepped for re-entry. He had half a mind to check in on his mother and Lakshmi, but decided he didn't want to know if they had been chipped. He would maintain the fantasy that part of South America was still as free as Colonel Saddiq and his troops. The fight would go on.

Chapter 11
City of the Dead

He landed in Miami at 8:24PM on January eleventh. Jake had gained back the night by flying west. He had started this day watching Parks' execution ceremony. He was exhausted and had barely registered the majestic beauty of the suborbital flight. He continued to dwell on the lives of those he had been connected to and wondered how God Heads slept at night. Then again, he had chosen to explore the minds he had invaded. The only way to be a successful God Head was to play Pin Heads like video game avatars, forget they were human at all.

A towing drone latched onto the front landing gear of the scramjet and pulled him toward a hangar. He disconnected his fully-charged Omnis and, to conserve power, made sure only the encryption software was running. He turned his attention to the aircraft's motherboard. He ripped it out of the jet's computer core and destroyed it, hiding all evidence of how the plane had been hacked. As the jet was hauled into the hangar, he slung his combination rifle over his shoulder, opened the wing door, jogged out over the massive ram scoops, swung down below the wing, and dropped to the tarmac. The humid night air was cool and smelled like jet exhaust.

He was armed to the teeth in full NOI battle gear, walking around the massive civilian complex of terminals and planes at Miami International Airport. He made sure his Omnis registered him as a friendly. He strolled up to the nearest public terminal. A Plane Director approached him. Jake braced himself for a confrontation. He was willing to knock the woman unconscious if necessary. She veered off, but he adjusted to remain within striking distance. As the woman came closer, he saw the glazed look in her eyes. She was living in another world, trapped inside her own mind, while some God Head program put her body through the motions. No matter how many times he witnessed it, watching people converted into zombie machinery made his skin crawl.

He found a set of stairs leading up to Gate B34. He climbed up and opened the door. An alarm rang as he stepped inside. He quickly shut the door and gripped his combination rifle. The alarm stopped. The airport was relatively empty, which was odd for this time of day. Normally there would be a flurry of disorderly human activity. Everyone was offline, carrying out tasks with vacant stares. Anyone not actively working at the airport was embarking on flights with no destinations displayed on the gates, or they were deplaning from places just as mysterious. Using his Chip, he reached out to the airport hub, but found cyberalarms that he dared not engage. There were major operations happening here. Perhaps this was now the norm for the United States. Had The Consortium thrown the worldwide switch? If so, the full scale NATO invasion of the Middle East would be an easy affair.

He wandered past a food court. Every station served what looked like protein shakes. No digital money was exchanged because no one wore an Omni. People drank with a look of intense pleasure on their faces. Perhaps the shake represented each individual's favorite food. He was starving so he got in line. Everyone silently shuffled forward. Only the muffled sounds of scramjets could be heard outside the dead airport. He had flashbacks to his nightmares of being captured by mass concentrations of Pin Heads. He pushed the thoughts out of his head by keeping a tight grip on his rifle. The

Pin Head behind the counter simply handed him a shake. No greeting, no smile, no frown, no sign of life. A drone.

Jake exited the line, put his lips to the straw, and paused. *What if it contains an enhancing agent that boosts my Max2 Chip? What if it greases the wheels for an easier hack of the brain?* He scanned for other types of food but saw nothing. He walked out of the food court with the drink in one hand and clutching the rifle with his other. *The Consortium has full control, why waste time and money creating a food that enhances dominance? Why not?* He passed an empty food kiosk and his stomach growled. His last meal was the night of the tenth, over thirty-six hours ago.

He took a quick sip. Cold chalky metallic tastes greeted his tongue. He sipped again, noticing the metallic flavor was not as bad. It was basically a protein shake with lots of…nutrients. The pleasurable reaction of the Pin Heads was obviously Chip-induced. He took a few more sips and then tossed the drink in a garbage can. He would wait to find some real food. There must be something in Miami.

He wandered into a restroom. A dozen men and women were using the place. Everyone was patient, orderly, and had perfect aim. No one was making a mess. It didn't seem human. After he did his business, he wandered out of the airport. Hundreds of Pin Heads shuffled along on their silent errands. Most left by train, but some climbed into cabs or cars. He decided not to use any transportation that could be tracked, but Cape Canaveral was 140 miles north. The prospect of biking that in two days was possible but not the best option. He'd rather get there tomorrow at the latest so he could locate Anjali's scramjet and what remained of The Order of Erasmus.

He used his Omni to navigate a path east to the 95 freeway. He passed by office buildings and rows of single story storefronts. Crickets chirped and cars rushed past but every street light and window was as black as the night around him. He wondered if any of these businesses ever opened at all. Now that society was chipped, would there be a need for a pool supply store, a hair salon, a tailor? What exactly would the people who provided these services be doing in the new world order?

He passed under a lifeless, three-story holo-sign. He stopped and looked around. Every city was filled with holo-banners, signs, and projectors, but the skies here were dark. A few lights glowed here and there, but Miami looked as if it was experiencing a brown out. He quickly turned to make sure there wasn't an army of zombie Pin Heads following him. The sidewalk was empty as far as he could see. "I can't believe I actually miss those stupid holo-banners," he muttered to himself. It felt comforting to hear a human voice, even his own.

He pressed on. Traffic was light, almost non-existent. He did not see a single cop. What use would police be in this society? God Heads in human and program form were the new police force. He spotted a donut shop and walked over to it. He pressed his face against the glass and saw empty racks. He tried the door and it swung open with ease. Why would anyone need locks in this world?

He tiptoed in and noticed the mixers, bowls, and deep fryer were old, but clean. He checked the freezer and found it empty. There was a glass refrigerator for cold drinks that was empty, too. His stomach grumbled. He regretted not finishing the shake. He left the shop and continued his journey toward Interstate 95.

He passed a dark twenty-four hour convenience store. Again, the door was unlocked. He used his Omni in flashlight mode to search for food. Most of the racks were empty but he found an aisle of canned goods. He grabbed some chili and some corn and hunted behind the check-out counter for an opener. He spotted one on a ring of keys. He opened the cans and saw two microwaves next to an empty case that said HOT DOGS. He decided to eat the contents cold as turning on power might wake up some program monitoring the grid. He exited the store with his culinary treasure.

As he ate the cold food in the shadows of the convenience store, he thought the spot he was sitting in would be a perfect place for a homeless person to camp. Yet there was no life, not even a dog, a cat, or a rat. Had they been infected by Max2 only to be killed by The Consortium? How many species of animal could be infected by Max2? He remembered Anjali's green, dotted scarf. Each dot represented an endangered species. By now, it was probably solid green.

He noticed graffiti on the wall of the convenience store. THOSE WHO CAST THE VOTES DECIDE NOTHING. THOSE WHO COUNT THE VOTES DECIDE EVERYTHING. — JOSEPH STALIN.

It was 11:00PM by the time he reached the 6th Avenue on-ramp to Interstate 95. He sat by a traffic light and waited for the right vehicle to stop. At 11:27PM, a big rig rumbled up to the traffic light. He ran to the truck and climbed up between the cab and the trailer. He secured a place to sleep and set his Omni to wake him if the truck took any direction other than 95 North, or if the truck was twenty miles south of Cape Canaveral. As the truck lumbered onto Interstate 95, he fell into a fitful sleep.

His mind churned with the hopes, desires, and memories of the Pin Heads he had left behind in Al Kharrara. He wasn't sure if he had dreamed of them, or had simply thought of them but it felt as if ten minutes had passed when his Omni vibrated on his wrist. He opened his eyes and felt the air blasting around him. He couldn't see it, but a few feet away, between the cab and the trailer, the road was flying by at eighty miles per hour.

His Omni showed he was in the vicinity of Cape Canaveral. He was tired, sore and faced the problem of getting off the truck without hurting himself or alerting his chipped driver, and more importantly the God Head, to his presence. He aimed his rifle at two tires on the passenger side, next to the trailer hitch. He fired two quick bursts. Rubber flew at his face and he raised his arm to block it. The truck's driver turned on its hazards and moved to the slow lane. He felt the truck decelerate and he moved to the passenger side to prepare for his jump. He made sure to leave no evidence of his occupancy. There would be fingerprints of course, but even a hacked driver would not be able to see those without a scanner. Besides, this could have been a simple blowout. The truck rumbled into the breakdown lane and slowed to under ten miles per hour. He leapt over the guardrail. His legs hit dirt and he tucked and rolled down a short hill into a dried area that had once been a swamp. The place reeked of decaying plants. His Omni showed that he was in a small estuary east of Sereno Pointe. Titusville was the only town that lay between Jake and Cape Canaveral to the east.

Under the cover of a dying forest, he watched the driver check the two flat tires. No word was spoken as the man pulled two huge spare tires along with a power jack from his rig and got to work. Maneuvering those tires would take Herculean strength, but the chipped driver pulled it off without a single grunt. The tire swap took place in less than twenty minutes. He planned to walk the breakdown lane of Interstate 95 all the way to the Garden Street exit, which would take him to the Max Brewer Memorial Parkway and onto the Cape Canaveral grounds.

After the truck left and had been out of sight for ten minutes, he climbed back up the embankment. Judging by the distances, he'd be on the Cape by 4:00AM. He would then search for a good place to hide and sleep. He had plenty of time to locate Anjali and her scramjet. The highway was empty and silent. Not even the sound of insects greeted his ears. He focused on the crunching gravel under his combat boots as he forged onward. The urge to cut out his Chip and shut down his Omnis washed over him. He had been lucky so far, but sooner or later someone or some program would realize there was a wolf wandering among the flock. He proceeded cautiously down the dark and lonely highway.

Chapter 12
Deception

By the time Jake reached the Kennedy Space Center Museum, the eastern sky behind the Everglades glowed deep orange. He had encountered no one on his walk but he had come across an alligator, and was overjoyed to see a living creature. As he approached, the reptile slipped into a brackish pool and disappeared.

Security cameras were fixed to the museum's overhangs. Since landing in Miami he wondered if the Pin Heads and random cameras were monitoring him. Maybe the God Head programs didn't see him as a threat, but this was a government installation and there was still an active Air Force and space fleet in close proximity. Perhaps Anjali had taken care of all those details. He was willing to chance it. He had been up for almost two days with a fitful nap on the back of a semi in between. He searched for a safe place to hide and catch some sleep.

He thought about trying the museum door, but he did not want to get caught inside the building. He checked the surrounding area via Omni GPS.

There were several launch pads from the glory days of terrestrial rockets. There was an Air Force base and a dozen scramjet airfields. A complex where launch vehicles used to be assembled was in the midst of it all. The structures were used to assemble scramjet payloads bound for the International Space Agency's spaceport. That was where the interplanetary rockets were assembled and launched.

He found a string of empty dumpsters near the museum's loading dock. The chances that anyone would use them or come this way seemed unlikely. It was not his first choice, but it was a logical place to hide and sleep. He used his NOI military knife to cut one of two plastic tops off a dumpster making sure he'd have enough air circulation and climbed in. He checked his Omni batteries; twelve hours on one and eleven on the other. Those could never be allowed to drain.

He did not remember falling asleep, but he awoke to see a tall skinny man standing over the mouth of the dumpster with a pistol pointed at him. The man wore glasses and had a big straw hat on his head, which helped block the afternoon sun from Jake's eyes. Sweat ran down the sides of the man's stubble covered jaw. He had fear in his eyes, and his hands trembled slightly. There was a chocolate smudge in the corner of his mouth. He wore a jungle camouflage t-shirt with Darth Vader emblazoned on it.

"Morning." Jake had a hard time taking this guy seriously. "Or should I say afternoon?"

"Hand me the rifle." He spoke with a slight Canadian accent.

"Where in Canada are you from?"

The man stared back at him, a drop of sweat splashed on the inside of his glasses. He paled with fear and gripped his weapon tighter.

Jake sighed. "Why not shoot me and take the rifle?"

"Calgary." The man winced. He waved his gun at Jake's clothing. "That's a Nation of Islam military uniform."

Jake sat up and the man pulled back an inch. "That's right."

"Larry!" Jake heard a familiar voice call out from beyond the dumpster. "Put the gun down. He's not compromised."

"Why is he dressed like a commando?" Larry shouted, refusing to take his eyes off Jake.

Jake slowly stood with his hands in the air. When he was within range of the dumpster cover, he struck up with his left hand and simultaneously grabbed Larry's gun with his right. Startled by the jumping lid, Larry was easily disarmed. Jake stood holding Larry's gun and looked out at the museum's loading dock. There were two others wearing the same silly straw hats. One of them he recognized as Anjali Malik.

Anjali addressed him as if they had just seen each other five minutes ago. "Hi, Jake."

He cleared his parched throat. "Sorry about Sumit."

Anjali bit her lip. "So am I." She pulled her Omni out of her cargo pants pocket and began to scroll. Her pants as well as her shirt were tie-dyed in a myriad of non-matching colors. She reminded him of a mutated calico cat.

Larry glanced back at Anjali. When he noticed she was consumed with her Omni, he rolled his eyes. "Van!"

The last remaining person in their party stepped forward. Van was a short, chubby Asian man with close-set eyes and straight, jet-black hair that flowed down to his waist. He wore a matching shirt to Larry's along with blue jogging shorts that showed off his sunburned legs—evidence he was underutilizing his Chip—or wasn't chipped. A pair of oversized sunglasses hung from the neckline on his shirt. He had a silver chain around his neck with a wallet-sized portrait of Justin Bieber, circa 2012, encased in Lucite. He touched Anjali's arm.

Startled, she gasped and regarded Van as if he were a stranger.

Van pointed a thumb at Jake.

She studied Jake in the dumpster. Her mouth moved, as if reeling up her next words from somewhere deep within her body. "I can forgive for Sumit, but not for New Delhi."

Jake crushed a twinge of guilt. "I had no part in that. I didn't even know Parks had nuked New Delhi until after the fact." He turned to Larry who studied him with uncertainty. Jake presented Larry's pistol. "If I give this back, you promise not to shoot me, Larry from Calgary?"

Larry nodded sheepishly.

Jake handed back the gun.

"F-flinders. M-my name is Larry Flinders." He stammered then flicked his tongue as if trying to spit out a bug, or the cause of his speech impediment.

"Nice to meet you, Larry." Jake picked up his rifle from the bottom of the dumpster and leapt out onto the pavement. He spied Larry shoving the pistol into the back of his waistband.

Anjali turned her back to Jake. "My parents were in New Delhi."

Jake put his hand on her shoulder. She cringed away and glanced at him with watery eyes. The display of emotion threw him off, but he was glad to see she was capable of it. "I'm very sorry. I swear I had nothing to do with it."

She took a few steps forward, straightened up, and turned toward him, quickly wiping the tears from her eyes. She nodded at his uniform. "You were in the Middle East?"

"That's where Parks and I were last, yes."

She cleared her throat. "Where is he?"

"Dead."

She showed no emotion as she turned to Larry. "We should get back to the assembly building."

"It's good to see you again, Anj." He wanted to hold out his arms for a hug, but remembered she was not fond of physical contact. Besides, he wasn't sure if she was glad to see him.

She gave him a half smile and a nod. For Anjali, it was a very warm and friendly response.

Jake slung his rifle over his shoulder. His body felt stiff and everything ached. The hot muggy air felt like it was closing in around him.

Van stepped forward. "I'm Van Cheung." He nervously shook Jake's hand. "Welcome to what's left of Erasmus."

"You chipped?" Jake asked.

Van twisted his face in confusion. "Who isn't?"

Jake pointed at his legs. "Even without sunscreen The Chip can keep the rays off. Yours needs a firmware refresh."

"Oh, yeah." He sheepishly grinned. "I tend to keep most of the bio-functions switched off."

Jake couldn't hide his sarcasm. "*Smart... Just you three?*" he was surprised. Sanchez had really done a number on the organization.

Larry glanced at Anjali who stared back with no emotion. "There are two others at the vehicle assembly building."

Jake's suspicion rose. "How did you boys miss the event in Mumbai?"

"Erasmus didn't have a-any knowledge of us," Larry stammered. The two men were squirrely, maybe just out of their element.

Van continued, "We're part of a hacker satellite cell. Anjali sent out the signal that the Erasmus Order had been destroyed. We found the signal on the Cyber-Wire and contacted her. We had no idea that Anjali and Gordon were part the organization's inner circle."

"Van and Larry were in a grunt cell. Hackers and God Heads." There was disdain in her voice.

Larry didn't hide his annoyance. "We had no idea there was such an elitist attitude at the top."

Both hackers glanced at Anjali who began walking toward an early century six-passenger golf cart. There was an old NASA logo emblazoned on the small snout. NASA had been disbanded ten years ago in favor of the International Space Agency or ISA. Anjali and her boys probably commandeered it from the Kennedy museum. "How did you find me?" Jake asked as the men followed Anjali.

"We've got programs running on the Cyber-Wire all over Florida," Van answered. "They piggyback on the carrier waves feeding the Pin Heads. Basically, they alert us to anyone who blocks the hacking signal. We then protect those people from alerting The Consortium programs. Larry and I have been here two days. The others in the assembly building have been here a week."

Jake nodded. "So that's why it was so easy for me to move around."

"Are you really as bad-ass as the press makes you out to be?" Van blurted out.

Jake laughed. "Time and tabloids have a way of making a man bigger than he really is."

Van fidgeted. They were all in the golf cart now, waiting for Jake to take the front passenger seat next to Anjali. He didn't like their skittish nature. Larry and Van seemed more nervous than cats in a coyote den. Given the state of the world, any non-hacked person would have a hard time coping. He certainly was.

"Are you staying, or coming with us?" Even for Anjali it had to be hard losing an entire family in a week. There was no human being left on earth who hadn't lost someone they loved.

He climbed in the cart and she hit the accelerator. Everyone jerked back. He heard a loud clatter from behind and wheeled around. Larry nervously dove to the floor. "What happened?" Jake asked.

Larry grunted. "Stupid gun."

"Better holster that thing before you shoot somebody." He turned and remembered that Larry had shoved the gun in the back of his waistband. He was about to wheel back around when he felt the dart slam into his muscle above the shoulder blade. The needle tip struck his front clavicle. The force pushed him into the plastic windscreen. "Jesus!" He leapt out of the cart and ran into the everglades. Another dart flew by his leg.

Van screamed. "Oh my god! Why is he running! He's supposed to be knocked out!"

Jake gripped his rifle and spun around. The action sent him tumbling into stagnant water. He was losing consciousness. Three more darts slammed into the water by his head. How could he have let these clowns dupe him? He managed to turn toward his attacker. Larry was out of the cart, both hands on the dart gun, he was shaking. His magazine empty.

Jake spat, "It would have been a lot easier to just shoot me in my sleep, asshole!" A wave of black swept over him and he fell into the abyss.

Chapter 13
Battlefields

Jake was vaguely aware of his jacket and armor being removed. He felt cold concrete on his back and could have sworn he heard Australian and German accents somewhere in the darkness. He tried to open his eyes but the drug held him in a stupor. He felt pain shoot out of his infected palm. Someone was treating it. Hands strained to put him in a plastic chair. A cold, form-fitting web was placed over his scalp.

Flash.

He stood in white boundless space, a world he had been exposed to during his tenure with the LAPD Enhanced Unit. He was in a Chip interface; a place inside his own mind; a prison for his consciousness; a hub for limitless cyber-travel. He searched for doorways, windows, or tears in the fabric. Nothing.

Flash.

He was back in his body, strapped to the plastic chair. He tried to move, but he was barely conscious. He desperately wanted to wake up, but he couldn't get his eyes to open or his body to move. He tried to shout but his body wouldn't respond. He felt the sensation of fingers passing through his scalp, moving into his skull, and sinking into his brain. His cranium had turned to thin plastic wrap, and someone was forcing their way into his mind.

Flash.

He was back in Mumbai, reliving his rescue by the Disciples of Paul. Children in white came to his rescue. Parks waited in the rickshaw driven by massive Sikh twins.

Flash.

He was in the DOP tower, speaking to Parks and putting on his disguise in order to assassinate Sumit and Sanchez at the Chhatrapati airport.

Flash.

The baboon claw tore into his shoulder and the poison burned through his blood stream. He squeezed a shot off to hit Sanchez but Sumit fell in front of the lethal dart instead.

Flash.

He was on an HJ listening to the news that Parks had nuked New Delhi. Jake was outraged.

Flash.

He held his dying wife in his arms. The grief was overwhelming. He sobbed uncontrollably. He couldn't let her go. He saw the faces of those he had lost since Christmas: his father, his sister, Tomoko, Parks, and all the deaths he had witnessed since Lalo's, the boy next door, back in 2009. The images were overwhelming. He screamed for it to stop.

Flash.

Jake puked. The sick splashed between his legs. He jerked back to find he was in a concrete room. His arms were bound behind the chair back of an antique Aeron office chair. His bare and bruised torso was coated in sweat. He felt the web against his head. He had been plugged into hacking software. He felt a cord digging into his wrists, but could not tell if the Omnis were there or not. His captors stared at him. Van and Larry both appeared ashen white. Larry polished off a candy bar and dropped the wrapper onto the floor where two others lay. Larry fished another brand of candy bar from what looked like a fifteen-pound reservoir inside a plastic bag and began to unwrap it. He was nervous and ashamed.

There were two other people in the room Jake did not recognize. A tall blonde woman in her late twenties with finely chiseled features reminded him of his first childhood crush on actress Charlize Theron. She stood next to a thickly-built, stern-looking man with gray hair in his mid-fifties. The blonde appeared equally sickened. She wore a green t-shirt with gold letters that said: GO GREEN, EAT YOUR CASH. An image appeared on the shirt of a plunger shoving currency into a man's open mouth. The shirt had to be made of nanite cloth.

The gray-haired man was dressed in cargo shorts and an aqua blue tank top that showed off the curly hairs on his shoulders. His fascinated gaze was fixed on Jake as he placed an arm around the blonde's waist. Annoyed at the gesture, she shot him a withering look. He was suddenly hurt and angry.

Anjali stepped out from behind a holo-projector. She had a web on top of her head. "I'm... I'm sorry, Jake."

Jake tried to catch his breath. His heart felt as if it were slamming against his breastbone. He could tell by the taste in his mouth that, in addition to losing last night's chili, he had been crying as well as sweating. "What the fuck?" he coughed. His throat burned from vomit and dehydration.

The blonde cracked open a bottle of water and approached. Jake leaned back to take a drink. After a few swallows, he nodded. She pulled the bottle back and he gasped, "Thank you."

"So much death... I... had to be sure," Anjali muttered.

"What, that I didn't drop the bomb on New Delhi? That I'm not a mass-murdering son-of-a-bitch?" He glared at everyone in the room. "The entire planet is tearing itself apart and you decided that this was the best use of your time?"

Van uncomfortably turned away. Larry fished out a fifth candy bar, and then looked as if he were going to puke.

"You're pathetic," Jake spat. He turned to Anjali. "Can I go now?"

The gray-haired man spoke with a German accent. "Jake, I was against this... test, but I agreed to bringing you here with the hope that you could help us."

The blonde shot him a look as if to say, *that's bullshit.*

Jake laughed. "So you're throwing your dweeb team under the bus now? Wake up, Klaus, your allies are on the endangered species list."

The German clenched his fist. "We could still use your help. We are planning on leaving for the moon tomorrow."

Jake was disgusted with everyone in the room. "I really don't give a rat's ass where you cowards are headed. I'm staying here to fight with Saddam."

The blonde spoke with an Australian accent. "Saddam?"

Jake shook his head. "Fucking drugs! Saddiq! Colonel Saddiq! He's NOI! At least he's taking the fight to these assholes. What are you doing?"

Anjali pulled off her web and approached. "We've run the numbers. Between fighting the Max2 and the combined forces of the chipped world…" She paused and thought about her next gesture before she put her hand gently on his shoulder. "Saddiq and Xavier have less than a week at best."

Jake knew it was not easy for Anjali to touch him as a peace offering, but it was not enough for him to stop glaring at her. She quickly retracted her hand. His legs were free to kick, but it wouldn't do him much good. Besides, he could tell they were going to let him go. Anjali moved behind Jake and began working on his bonds.

"Who's Xavier?" Jake grumbled.

"Military leader from Chile." Van looked up. "The Consortium has several fronts in Africa and South America."

Jake leaned back to give more slack on the bonds Anjali was removing. "Then all the more reason to help. The moon stands a better chance against a divided Earth. Once The Consortium consolidates power, their single focus will be on Luna." The bonds around his wrists dropped. He jumped to his feet and reached up to rip the web off his head.

Everyone expressed horror. Larry screamed, "No!"

Jake paused with his fingers touching the web. He turned slowly around to see even Anjali had a look of concern. "What?" He turned a full circle. The action made him feel dizzy. The drugs were still working their magic. Larry appeared ill. Too many candy bars.

The German spoke. "The web is the only block you have against the God Head signals. Remove it and they will instantly gain access to you, and us."

Van continued, "I give the programs a minute tops to convert you and turn all the other Pin Heads working this base against us."

Jake dropped his hands. "Where the fuck are my Omnis?"

The blonde Aussie spoke. "Charging, mate."

Jake nodded with satisfaction. "So are we talking programs like an AI as in Ai-Li or just a smarter computer?"

Anjali joined ranks with the others. She nervously rubbed her Omni-tablet with her thumbs. Jake remembered how much she hated human interactions. Her Aspergers kept her removed from emotion, so she was forever second-guessing an appropriate response. Jake wanted to put his hand on her shoulder in a gesture of goodwill, but it was too late for that. "A fully self-aware and sentient AI is not on-line as far as we know." Anjali seemed to be staring past him. "But there are complex systems of programs that are helping The Consortium run the world. They are not self-aware, but they do make simple decisions based on logic algorithms."

Jake nodded. Nothing had changed on that front since the bombing of Beijing. But he was still curious about the signal that Parks and the Sikh twins had discovered. "You guys aware of a background signal in the Cyber-Wire?"

Van nodded.

Larry swallowed back the stomach acid rising in his throat as he put down his bag of candy bars. "Yeah, it's a funny thing, bro. We spotted it the same day Beijing was nuked. It's taking up a lot of bandwidth which is odd since the Cyber-Wire is theoretically infinite."

"AI?" Jake asked.

"Could be," the gray-haired German answered.

Jake looked down. He wore his camouflage pants, but nothing else. Even his feet were bare. His skin was still dark from the pigment the Sikhs had put on him. "I want my clothes and Omnis."

Van nodded and left the room.

The German barked after him, "Van!"

Jake smiled when Van did not return. *So much for authority.*

Larry stammered, "We felt as long as Anjali was bringing you here, you could help us…" He stared down at his shoes. "If you passed the test."

The German defensively crossed his arms. "Given the state of the world, you can understand."

Jake winked. "Nice to know you had my back, Klaus."

The German turned red with embarrassment and anger. "Kohl, Doctor Gunner Kohl," he corrected.

"Klaus." Jake smiled.

Van walked in with the rest of the NOI uniform and the two Omnis. Jake put on the armor, jacket, and military Omnis. He checked to be sure they ran his security programs. He came across the date; it was late in the morning on January 14, 2036. "What the fuck happened to the time?"

Everyone averted their eyes except Gunner. Anjali was running numbers, or whatever escape she had on her Omni.

Larry stammered with embarrassment. "W-we had a l-lot to do to prepare for the launch, b-bro. It was easier to keep you under until we were ready."

Jake shook his head. He had a mind to take all of them out with his bare hands. This was a cluster-fuck and a half. He gazed at the five of them. "So this is the jury of my peers?" He pointed at the holo-projector. "She hacks into my head, and you get to view my memories?"

Larry and Van stared at the floor. The blonde shoved her hands in her jean pockets. Gunner defiantly crossed his arms, and Anjali remained in her Omni world.

"Hope you enjoyed the show." He snapped his fingers and pointed to Van. "Gun."

Van nodded and left the room.

Jake addressed Anjali, hoping to get her attention. "So how many from the Order did you rescue?"

Larry fidgeted with his left foot. "This is it. We're not sure if the others got the signal…" He glanced at Anjali for approval, then flushed with embarrassment when he saw she was still lost in her device. "Or were stopped on the route to get here."

"They have twenty more hours…" Anjali rubbed her eyes. "Plenty of time."

Larry shook his head. No one else appeared optimistic.

"How many did you send a signal to?" Jake asked.

"Seventeen." The blonde answered in her Australian accent. "There were five cells that responded to Anjali. She coordinated this escape plan and we were happy to help."

Larry shivered and eyed his bag of candy bars. "We got lucky."

Gunner snorted. "I'll say."

The blonde took a step away from Gunner.

Larry flashed the German an evil eye. "It's fucking crazy scary out there, bro."

Van entered the room gingerly carrying Jake's combination rifle.

Jake grabbed his weapon with his left hand and placed the strap over his right shoulder. He tore off the bandage on his palm. Someone had cleaned the wound and placed dermal-accelerator on it. Baby-pink skin was growing where the wound had been. There would be no scar. Jake gazed at the last of The Order of Erasmus staring back at him. "Thanks."

The blonde Australian gave a slight nod.

"Can't say as I'm sad to go." Jake checked the clip and chamber of his gun. "Good luck with your *plan*." He synched his Chip with his Omnis and confirmed the encryption lock. They both had over twenty-four-hours of power on them. He yanked the web out of his hair and headed for the door. He called up a map of the area and saw that he was in a storage room inside the main assembly building.

"You have demolitions training and an extensive knowledge of detonators," Van called out after him. "We saw it during the mind probe. Stay. Help us."

Jake walked out the door without looking back. He found himself in a long hallway, headed for double doors at the end. According to the map projected in his mind, there was a huge hangar ahead and then a door to the outside. He would search for a jet to hack and fly back to the Middle East.

The blonde ran after him. "The battle Saddiq and Xavier are fighting will weaken The Consortium…"

Jake stopped and turned to meet her.

"But we can do more good on Luna than down here. It's far more difficult for the Earth to launch an attack on the moon than it is for the moon to launch one on the Earth. Gravity is in Luna's favor. Plus we carry the virus, and can continue research on eradicating it up there. Any lab we set up down here has limited time before it's discovered and shut down. Earth is cactus."

"Cactus?"

"Dead—broken—toast—we buy ourselves more time by hiding out on the moon. It'll be humankind's last stand. Win or lose, it's our best chance of survival." She nodded to the doors. "You'd be throwing your life away, mate."

"Nice speech." He turned toward the exit. "I don't think your boyfriend shares your sentiments."

The woman chuckled. "Gunner? He's good for a naughty now and then, but this is bigger than any of us. You're our best chance to beat the Consortium, mate. Gunner understands that."

Jake reached the double doors. He faced her again. "What's your name?"

"Doctor Matilda Pearce." She held out her hand. "Call me Tilly."

He shook it. "Nice to meet you, Doctor Pearce."

"I'm sorry for how we lured you here. I apologize for what we witnessed."

He shook his head. "In the greater scheme of things, it really doesn't matter."

"Will you give the data a go, and at least make a judgment based on logic instead of emotion? Your LAPD record states you were a methodical man who planned every detail."

"I had emotional outbursts as well."

"You never let go of Lalo."

His body stiffened and he felt his neck grow hot. *How much had they seen?* Tilly reddened and looked away.

He sighed. This game was silly. They were all performing under extreme duress. Emotions were obviously clouding everyone's judgment, even Anjali's. He smiled. "You've made your point, Tilly. Show me the data."

It took ten seconds for her to route the secure connections on the Cyber-Wire to his Omni and to view all the reports on Saddiq and Xavier. It was official; everyone with Max2 had been given the signal that would lock them into the Consortium's hive-mind. He saw the resistance communiqués and The Consortium communiqués. There were no international news agencies anymore as no one was cognizant enough to process it. Broadcasting guerrilla news would mean sending up a beacon to The Consortium stating, "Please induct me!" Free Thinkers were in the thousands now. Pin Heads were in the billions. Saddiq and Xavier had gone underground. The Consortium was using Pin Head divisions and armies of drones to hunt down the resistance and eradicate them. It was a lost cause.

He raked his nails over the new skin on his palm. It felt tender, vulnerable. He had hoped Saddiq could pull it off. He had hoped that the human race would win out over this crazy onslaught. Things were far more grim than his optimism allowed him to see. He punched the double doors and locked eyes with Tilly. "Walk with me," he commanded.

He stepped into a thirty-story hangar. Dozens of Pin Heads milled about. Many placed grain, parts, and biomaterial into shock containers. A flatbed drone rumbled by with a single banker-box-sized container as cargo. It was marked with the international symbol for nuclear content. "How are we able to move freely around here? I see plenty of sensors, security drones, and, of course, the Pin Heads." He spotted a scramjet framed by massive hangar doors. The Chip had already enhanced his eyesight, or maybe he was picking up on the signals from the base sensors. Either way, he could see every detail inside the assembly building and on the tarmac outside.

Tilly smiled. "I hacked into the program that's running this place before we arrived last week. We've been erased from any surveillance systems. The upside to the war against the Brotherhood is that it has been taking longer than The Consortium planned. Until a couple days ago, it swallowed every enemy resource. The Consortium considers North America, Europe, and Australia as home territory with a hundred-percent control." She gestured to the hangar. "This is now a low-security safe zone. We're working deep behind enemy lines, mate."

"What about Asia and Antarctica?"

"Antarctica's chipped. Asia's mostly under their control with patchy resistance."

He nodded. "How did you escape the slaughter in Mumbai?"

"I broke my bloody leg hiking around Ayers Rock when the call came to go to Mumbai. I had already hacked into the program here when the rest of my cell, and Erasmus, were murdered." She wiped a tear from her eye, straightened up, and cleared her throat. "I hacked The Consortium communications and discovered instructions to fill that scramjet with warheads." She nodded to the plane framed by the hangar doors. "There are a bunch of drones and Pin Heads on the Orbital Spaceport assembling three MIRVs right now. They just need the warheads that plane will deliver to complete the missiles that will eradicate every bloke on the moon. I'm hacked into the Platform and every piker–Pin Head up there too."

"Seems pretty stupid for The Consortium to blow up the moon. They should just send up a few infected commandos and let Max2 do the job."

"They've tried it, mate. The lunar defenses are shooting down anything that gets within a mile of the defense perimeter. It was originally designed to fend off asteroids, but the lunar scientists have made it even more precise. Nothing bigger than a candy bar can land."

"In that case, they'll just shoot down the warheads."

Tilly shook her head. "The idea is to overwhelm the defenses. Trust me, they'll get most of the nukes, but it only takes a couple slipping through to kill everyone on Luna. It's a fragile environment up there."

Jake stared at the red and white ISA scramjet gleaming on the tarmac.

"Anjali used special channels to warn Luna's government. She cut a deal with them to allow us to land on the moon."

He was feeling undecided. "How can I help?"

Tilly turned to him. "Gunner and I—"

Jake put up his hand. "I don't trust him. We need clear-headed people making decisions."

"You're a serious one. A lot like Gunner."

Jake sucked his teeth.

Tilly almost rolled her eyes when she nodded. "I'll explain it to him."

"Okay."

She continued where she had left off. "We want your help in using the nukes to destroy the Orbital Spaceport. It was the condition Anjali agreed to in order to obtain asylum on Luna."

He swallowed. He knew nothing about nuclear warheads aside from a bit of terrorist training back in his LAPD days. He had some SWAT demolitions training but this plan sounded less than half-baked. How would they work with the Orbital Spaceport's zero gravity zones, or transport the warheads around the station without raising suspicion? There were a ton of variables. "What are your ideas so far?"

Tilly smiled. "We downloaded demolition manuals and every known piece of research and information on nuclear warheads." She laughed. "Larry and Van feel they can pull it off by themselves. Gotta love their gumption." She sighed. "Truth be told, Van and Larry don't exactly instill confidence in Gunner and myself, but they're a couple of dags with a sense of humor and that goes a long way with me." She stared directly into Jake's eyes. "Anjali is, well, Anjali."

"Dag?"

"Goofball, nerd."

Jake remained stoic. It sounded as if he were being elected as the mission expert, if not the leader. Leaders instilled confidence even when they had none themselves. Leaders solved problems. He could not dispute the facts; the moon was the best shot at pulling the world out of hell. But it was one heck of a slim chance. He observed Tilly with total confidence. "I believe we can pull it off."

He was about to gesture that they head back to see the others when he spotted someone familiar filling a shipping container. He walked forward a few feet, running her against face recognition software. Sure enough, she was positively ID'd as Marta Padilla, formerly the HLS liaison officer for the LAPD and his chief tormentor back in 2030. He approached with caution.

Chapter 14
Marta

Using thick rubber gloves, Marta carefully lifted small cylinders from a cryogenic freezer and placed them into a shockproof sub-zero container used for space travel. Jake moved in for a closer look.

Tilly shouted, "Careful not to block anyone's path! Observe only and the monitoring programs will simply ignore you. We don't want to set off any alarms, mate."

He gave her the thumbs up sign and stood next to Marta. She had the stupefied expression of a docile dairy cow. He spotted a window slit in one of the cylinders, there appeared to be a tiny fetus inside. "What's this for?"

Tilly came closer, studying Marta for any negative reactions to their presence. "Anjali's pet project for the last few years. It exploded exponentially over the past months."

He raised an eyebrow.

"Embryos, fetuses, and DNA for just about every species that's endangered or extinct. Max1 and 2 finished off hundreds of species—maybe thousands—we're not sure. The Consortium couldn't give a damn about most animals unless they're a food source." She nodded to the space crates. "This is basically Noah's Ark, mate."

Jake remembered the green dotted endangered species scarf on Anjali's head. She had mentioned her hobby when they were in the Mumbai lab. "Did you have a hand in this?"

Tilly smiled. "This was the original reason The Order of Erasmus made contact with Luna last month. We wanted this cargo safely out of the war zone. Several cells gathered specimens from every cataloged species, not just endangered. We had no idea there would be mass extinctions once the enemy activated Max2. Most of these genetic examples would be impossible to obtain today."

He focused his attention back on Marta. He accessed the hacked channels Tilly had shown him. He found Marta's records. She had been transferred out of San Quentin six months ago by order of Sandoval Sanchez. She had been performing hard labor around the United States ever since. She had been transferred here just two weeks ago to help handle the nuclear warheads. Marta was one of many pet projects initiated by the now-departed Sanchez. Despite the hell this woman had put him through, he felt sorry for her.

He checked the population of San Quentin. Everyone was dead. He checked the population of other prisons in California, then the US, then the world. The story was the same in every Consortium-controlled country. Prisoners had been "switched off." Their hearts had stopped, or they had been given massive brain aneurysms. Their corpses continued to rot where they fell. He felt a cold chill despite the humid eighty-degree breeze blowing through the hangar doors.

"Did you know her?" Tilly asked.

He nodded. "A long time ago. She was a prisoner of her mind back then, too."

Tilly eyed him curiously.

"Let's go." He turned his back on Marta. "We've got planning to do." He led the way as he searched for any records of his mother and Lakshmi. Brazil was a mess along with most of South America. Xavier's resistance movement had wreaked havoc against The Consortium's war machine. Both sides had hacked and damaged the Cyber-Wire. There were a multitude of traps laced throughout cyberspace. He had to back off immediately. It was frustrating. He continued to believe that they were safe. They were in Xavier-controlled territory and they had somehow escaped Max2.

He downloaded everything he needed to know about demolitions and working with nuclear warheads so by the time he reached the hallway leading to the makeshift interrogation room, he was an expert in both subjects.

He was not surprised to see that everyone expected him when he returned. Gunner was seizing him up. Jake figured the German was hoping to take charge as the alpha dog at some point. *No harm in fantasizing.* Jake was aware they had been monitoring him through the Pin Heads and Tilly. He could *feel* it with his own Chip. He supposed this was how he might have experienced The Chip if God Heads hadn't hacked his mind and tried to control his life back in 2030.

Someone had cleaned up his vomit, although a sour smell hung in the room. As if on cue, Van raised a can of air-freshener and sprayed the area. The sickly sweet scent of faux flowers lay on top of puke.

He was left with Larry and Van while Anjali took off to inspect her ark and Tilly left with Gunner.

Jake turned to Larry. "I'm impressed you had the balls to shoot me in the back."

Larry turned red. "Sorry about that, bro. Anjali was pretty persistent."

"When this is over, don't be surprised if I simply deck you without warning, *bro.*" Jake smiled.

Larry's jaw dropped.

"I guess I just warned you in the same subtle way you warned me when you dropped your gun." Jake winked.

They spent the next few hours playing out different demolition scenarios on a holo-projector. The ISA Orbital Spaceport was constructed like a wheel. The circumference was made up of a very large ring where centrifugal force created gravity equal to Earth's. This was where most people lived, and therefore it was called the habitat ring. The ring was connected to a central hub where there was zero gravity. The hub was where most deep space missions were launched. It was where the MIRVs were being constructed. Linking the hub with the habitat ring were six spokes. In between the hub and the spokes was a middle ring where scramjet traffic docked. The entire platform reminded Jake of a fat car tire mounted on a bicycle wheel with a slightly oversized hubcap in the middle.

Van felt the safest idea was to dock the scramjet in one of the inner pylons of the central hub and just detonate the plane. The number of warheads would ensure the station would be obliterated.

Jake disagreed. "What if the station's computer or one of the Pin Heads figures out our scramjet has been compromised? The Consortium could jettison the plane toward the sun, or shoot it away from the station at a high velocity. It's too easy for them to get rid of the warheads." He shook his head and pointed to the station schematic. "We need several warheads in key junctions. That way if one is discovered, we have plenty of backup." He had been studying the map for the past three hours and knew most of the station's systems. He pointed at ten key areas that would need to be rigged with warheads. Six would be evenly spaced around the habitat ring. Three would be in the central docking ring, one would be planted in the center hub. Four warheads would be planted in low to zero gravity areas. "Any of these spots will guarantee total station destruction even if it's the only warhead that explodes."

Van was nervous. "None of us has ever worked in zero g."

Jake clapped Van and Larry on the back. "Neither have I, but your Chip will compensate."

Larry mumbled with fear. "Can you just punch me now and get it over with?"

"No."

Larry dropped his head in defeat. He closed his eyes then opened them three seconds later. "The rest agree with your warhead strategy."

Van shook his head. "I want a recount."

"Okay." Larry blinked. "Recount still shows everyone is in favor of Jake's plan except you, bro."

Van shrugged. "Not everyone."

Jake figured the group was connected to each other and sharing thoughts.

Larry smiled. "Well, Tilly, Anjali, and I agree. Gunner just gave a grunt." Larry turned to Jake. "I think he sees you as a threat, but Tilly fixed it."

"He's been neutered?" Jake smirked.

"Hardly." Van eyed Larry's bag of candy bars. "Tilly and Gunner have been visiting Humptyville on a regular basis since they met a couple weeks back. The fling won't last. She's only in it for a distraction from all this fucked up MaxWell and Consortium shit. But Gunner has fallen hard. Hell, we're all a bit crackers considering…"

Larry offered his bag of candy to Van "I think we should invite Gunner to build some Legos. He's going to need a good distraction."

"Legos?" Jake was afraid to ask.

Van grabbed an odd brand chocolate bar that Jake had never seen before. "We both packed two of our favorite Star Wars sets. Helps keep us calm, stay focused and suppress emotions. That way we'll have nervous breakdowns in a few years and either blow all our money on therapists or commit suicide if we're still around." He took a bite. "You should build with us."

Larry swung the candy bag to Jake. "Dig in, bro."

Jake studied the ocean of candy bars. Not one was the same. "Where did you get all these?"

"Cyber-Wire. Before Max2 fucked everything up. I've sampled every chocolate bar from every country. I even have Antarctica chocolate in there somewhere."

Jake smiled and shook his head. "No, thanks."

Larry sighed. "Just as well. This is the reserve supply, and last I checked, they don't make chocolate on the moon."

Jake patted Larry on the arm. "I see a business opportunity in your future." He returned to the Orbital Spaceport schematic on the holo-projector. "As for our escape, this Lunar Express shuttle remains docked at the lower platform, near the MIRV assembly area. Should be the fastest ship there."

Larry swallowed a piece of chocolate and licked his thumb and fingers. "Dangerous to be working in that area, bro. That's where the highest concentration of Pin Heads will be."

"Agreed on both counts." Van savored his bar. "That shuttle is sweet though. It's for business executives, and other passengers who pay quadruple the price of a standard ticket, which means a seat on that puppy is close to a hundred and forty thousand beans." They all admired the contours of the sleek rocket as Van continued. "That ship has twice the number of boosters as the standard Lunar ferry and is far more maneuverable." He took another bite of chocolate. "A standard trip to the moon from the Platform takes about as long as the old sixties and seventies launches from Earth—three days. This express cuts it down to fourteen hours." He turned to face Jake and Larry. "The record is just over nine hours, and that was made by a probe back in the 1980s." Van pointed proudly to his skull. "That was a hundred percent memory, no Chip!"

Larry high-fived Van. "Nice!"

Anjali, Tilly, and Gunner walked in. Anjali spoke. "I agree with the plan so far."

"So do we." Gunner had a post-orgasmic afterglow on his face. Tilly's hair was a mess but she was calm and composed, as if she had just returned from running errands.

Jake pointed to the Lego boys. "Van, Larry, and I will supervise the placement and arming of the warheads. Anjali, Tilly, and Gunner," he addressed the three scientists and noticed Gunner's smile was permanently fixed to his face, "you supervise the movement of cargo from the scramjet to the express shuttle. You'll need to perform all pre-flight, since I don't like trusting the work to Pin Heads. Especially up there."

Anjali nodded. "Agreed. Never know when one can turn out to be a double agent." Jake knew at once she referred to her husband.

"You think he was chipped?" Jake asked.

She wrote out calculations on her Omni tablet. "I found some Consortium records confirming he was. It certainly makes what he did easier to live with."

"Still working on your cure?" he asked.

Anjali was engrossed in her calculations.

Tilly smiled. "Yes. Now that all the shipments for the Ark Project are here."

Gunner shook his head at Anjali's actions and snorted. "Obsessed is more like it."

"She's simply more focused than most." Jake gazed at the oblivious Anjali and wanted to tell her he forgave her for darting him and hacking his mind.

Anjali spoke. "The cure not only has to render Max2 inert," she gazed up at them all, "it has to render any Chip inoperable. We're way beyond just killing a nano-virus." Anjali dove back into her Omni.

Jake returned to the Orbital Spaceport schematics. "The entire exercise is going to take us about ten hours, factoring in variable gravity levels and moving cargo from place to place while staying clear of the Pin Heads' standard duties."

Larry pointed to the location of the tenth warhead near the express shuttle-docking arm and the central hub. "We'll need to be extra careful not to obstruct the construction of the MIRVs." He turned to the group with chocolate-coated fingers. "Which means we need ten warheads hidden from the scramjet's inventory computer."

"Tilly made sure ten warheads were erased from the manifest." Gunner looked for Tilly to acknowledge his compliment but she was asking Larry for a candy bar.

They all went to work on the plan. At one point, Gunner volunteered to get food. Twenty minutes later he was back with microwave sandwiches. Jake was thankful to have anything resembling real food. He literally had not eaten in days. He offered a sandwich to Anjali. "Just like the Kiwi base back in Antarctica."

Anjali glanced up from her data with a dazed look. "Huh? Oh yea." She ignored the sandwich.

Jake wondered if they'd ever be friends again. If so, he would need to make the effort. Anjali had moved on since her post-interrogation gesture. He wound up eating three sandwiches and drank what felt like a gallon of water.

It was midnight by the time they ran through every contingency and finalized the plan. Gunner and Van stayed up making sure the last of the precious cargo was placed aboard the scramjet. Based on the intelligence the group had gathered, they felt confident The Consortium was unaware of their activity. According to enemy software, their scramjet was scheduled for an autopilot launch and docking to deliver ninety warheads. The MIRVs would be completed under the supervision of the station programs.

The missiles would then sit in waiting until The Consortium could focus their attention on Luna.

Jake followed Larry and Anjali up to the administrative office where cots had been placed for them to sleep. Pin Heads never ventured in since all commands came in to them through the Cyber-Wire. The Pin Heads worked in two eighteen-hour shifts and slept on tiny stacked bunks in the hangar. Every six hours they were given a nutrient shake, the same type Jake had grabbed at the Miami airport.

Jake's private office was quiet and away from any noise coming from the hangar, but he was unable to sleep. He had been comatose for almost two days thanks to Anjali's orders to keep him drugged. A little after 5:00AM, Jake heard the faint sound of sobbing. He spent a few minutes debating whether or not he should go investigate. The sobbing grew louder so he finally decided to get up and find the source.

Chapter 15
Hair

A faint glow of hangar light trickled into the office wing, barely illuminating Jake's path. The sound came from behind a closed door, three offices down. Jake approached with caution. He wasn't sure if his actions might be considered overstepping his bounds. Dark cubicles filled a two-thousand square foot area surrounded by the offices. He passed a cubicle and could barely make out the poster of a Saturn V rocket lifting off. A coffee cup sat on the desk. An eerie feeling crept over him. These weren't workstations, they were catacombs; a graveyard for a way of life that was now as dead as the people who used to work here.

As Jake approached the source of the crying, he heard the slow metallic grinding of scissors. Erratic light flickered from a window next to the closed door. He slowed down and gingerly peered in to witness Van seated on the floor in a lotus position with part of his bare back facing the window. A candle flickered a few feet in front of his crossed legs, next to a small, round, vanity mirror. They were alabaster-white above the knees and lobster-red below. He was dressed only in white cotton briefs and Justin Bieber necklace. Long ropes of his black hair lay about the stained gray carpet around him and on his legs. The right side and back of his hair had been cut close to his scalp. He grabbed a fistful of hair on the left side and put a pair of scissors between his hand and his scalp. He paused.

Jake noticed his reflection across from Van in the outer office window, candlelight made him look ghost-like in the darkness of the cubicle area. Jake turned his attention back down to see Van staring up at him. His cheeks glistened and eyes were red. Jake held up his hands. "Sorry, I didn't mean to disturb you."

Van shook his head. His muffled voice vibrated through the closed door. "It's okay." He observed his half-naked body covered in hair and gave a nervous laugh. "Flippin' world is upside down. You get to be alone when you don't want to be and crowded when…" He grimaced at Jake.

Jake pointed back toward his room. "I'll be going now."

"How do you deal with it?"

Jake turned back and opened the office a crack. "Deal with it?"

"The loss of your family, way of life, the world…"

Jake crossed his arms. "I push it back. I get angry. My anger keeps me focused. As long as I'm alive I have the power to kick some ass and I'm going to kick until I win, or they kill me."

Van grunted. "It's not that easy for me." He picked up a mass of hair and scrunched the end with his thumb. "I started wearing my hair long when I was fourteen. My mom gave me so much shit, that I took pride in it. Most times I felt like the length gave me confidence—power."

"Then why cut it off?"

"Larry says it'll get unruly in zero g."

"Plenty of cultures believe hair gives them powers. Sikhs never cut their hair."

"I saw those twins you used to hang out with when we probed your mind…" Van swallowed, "Sorry we hacked you."

"I've moved on."

"When Anjali told us her plan and we saw you coming from Miami, Larry and I checked out your history. You're as close to a hero as I've ever come to meeting. I remember when you blew the whistle on Sanchez and Crennon back in 2030. I haven't heard of many who can counter-hack on their own. In fact, you're the only one."

"My prototype Chip helped."

Van shrugged.

Jake checked on his yellow-orange reflection in the window. The tarmac was illuminated beyond that, and farther out, was black marshland. He pointed to Van's remaining hair. "Are you going to braid what's left?"

Van laughed and looked at his reflection in his small mirror. "I'm committed now, aren't I?" His smile dropped. "But every time I cut, I see my mom, my family, my friends..." Van rubbed his eyes with his thumb and forefinger. "Didn't think cutting it would dredge all of that shit up."

Jake couldn't help but think of his own loved ones as he watched the grief on Van's face. He shoved the memories back into the depths of his mind.

"The team thinks Larry and I are reject fuckups. Just a couple of hackers from a bottom-feeder cell in the organization—we should be dead."

"Who says we aren't?" Jake winked.

Van shook his head and laughed. "You cope with anger. Anjali hides in her Max2 research and her ark project. Tilly uses sex and humor. Gunner has Tilly, but that won't last because he's insecure, possessive, and is way too serious."

Jake squatted on his haunches. "Did you poll the entire team?"

"Some. Others I observed."

"How do you and Larry cope, chocolate and Legos?"

"Larry and I have our adolescent behavior."

Jake pointed to Van's legs. "Is pain a part of your escape, too? Is that why you keep the bio-functions on your Chip turned off?"

Van pushed his finger into a plump red calf and watched his thumbprint fade from white to crimson. "I was never into biomechanical or pharmaceutical before Max2. But now that I have no choice, I'd rather be as much of me as I can. I don't even have the pain inhibiters on right now. I keep the security up, and the connection to the others, but I hate engaging it. It's basically a parasite living inside me, waiting to steal my soul and turn me into some creature out of a bad comic book."

Jake stared at the new skin on his palm. "I know the feeling."

Van began twisting the hair between his fingers into knots. His knuckles grew white. "I'm scared shitless. I have no desire to go up there and blow the station. The idea of zero g scares the bejesus out of me."

Jake looked Van in the eyes. "As long as you have The Chip, use it. Boost your confidence, or tell it to crush all emotions if your fear becomes overwhelming. We're all stuck with Chips now, might as well use them to our advantage."

Van stared at the candle flame.

Jake snapped his fingers causing Van to jerk his head up to meet Jake's gaze. "You're going to be fine. We're going to get through this. We're going to shove all this bullshit back up The Consortium's ass until they choke on their own feces."

Van cracked a smile. "You go, Jackhammer."

The nickname put Jake off guard. It was a reminder of a past he kept boarded up and buried deep. Given the circumstances, he let it slide. He pointed to the Justin Bieber portrait around Van's neck. "What's with the Bieb?"

Van glanced down and quickly flushed red. He covered the picture with his hand. "Oh, this… It was my mom's. She played Justin Bieber when I was a kid. I was never a fan, but…" He opened his hand. "It's all I could carry to remind me of her."

Jake thought of his wedding ring lost in the Riyadh battle zone. He gritted his teeth. "Don't lose it."

Van nodded. "Thanks, Jake."

"I take it the scramjet is loaded?"

"Yeah, we finished about a half hour ago." Van dropped his hair on the floor and picked up the scissors. "I'm going to finish up here then try and catch a snooze before it's time to prep the plane." Jake nodded and stood up. As he headed out the door, Van continued, "I'm glad you're with us, Jake."

Jake turned to Van. "You're okay, Van. I'm looking forward to working with you."

As Jake headed back to his room, he heard the quick metallic snips of scissors at work. He sat down on his bunk and an idea came to him. Much of his five years of travel had been stored on the Cyber-Wire. The images had been on his personal Omni, too, but that had been taken by the Consortium Pin Heads after they had drugged him at the Globe clinic. He wanted to access the image files on Cyber-Wire, but worried that they could be booby-trapped. It would be a perfect place for a hacking worm to hide, waiting for the last Free Thinkers to gather family reminders as they ran from war and Max2.

Jake carefully probed with his Chip and used his Cobalt Military Omni-boosted security to search for traps. He found a few worms lurking in the public photo files, but there were several series of images that appeared clean. He downloaded them to his Omni. He was not ready to experience them just yet. But having a piece of Tomoko and Lakshmi wherever he went gave him hope.

Jake rose at dawn and dressed in his NOI uniform. It was in bad need of a wash, but he felt at home in it. It made him feel like part of the resistance movement, which they were, although he knew those left behind would not see it that way. Jake took a stroll around the scramjet. It was loaded with everything destined for the Orbital Spaceport and the moon beyond. In a few hours it would be all about pre-flight checks, and holding out hope for some last-minute straggler arriving at the base, answering Anjali's call. But only Anjali clung to that idea.

As he admired the massive induction vents and mach-twenty hydrogen engines, Jake noticed a line of people waiting at a shake dispensary truck just inside the main assembly hangar. It was the morning shift preparing for a workday, or possibly a transfer, now that the work was completed. He approached the line with caution, curious to catch another glimpse of Marta. The hangar was lit with the harsh green light of fluorescents. He walked parallel to the lineup, giving it a wide berth of about three yards. Marta was eleventh in line. Jake thought about what she had done to him almost six years ago. She had created an elaborate and fictitious past for him with complex emotional issues; all generated in order for him to fall in love with her. Even if he had accepted the memories and he had not cut out The Chip, he doubted the plan would have worked.

Marta reached the head of the line, took her shake and turned to leave. She caught sight of him and paused.

Shit.

Marta slowly pivoted as she sucked down her shake. Her dull eyes locked onto his. He was about to avert his gaze when he noticed a small spark of life in her. She lowered her shake and smiled. She was only five feet from him.

"Hi, Jakey." She sounded as if they had been married for years and she had just woke up in bed with him.

He swallowed hard. *Did I just trigger the security programs?*

Marta walked up to him and winked. "Catch some bad guys for me today, killer? I've got business in Washington, but when I get back, I want to hear all about it." She kissed him on the lips and wandered off to perform whatever duty the God Head program had directed her to complete.

His lips tasted like metallic chalk. He wiped off the residue and watched her disappear behind a row of cargo vans. He quickly scanned the area to make sure none of the Pin Heads were suddenly becoming aware of him. To his relief, no one else had noticed.

He darted back to the scramjet. When he entered the suborbital craft, he found Larry and Van securing warheads. Van's hair was an uneven mass of close-cropped hair. "Nice haircut."

Van rubbed his head and smiled. "Larry's idea." Van winked.

"Bro, all I said was, your hair is going to be as manageable as a hydra in zero g, and the next thing I know you're jetting off to cut your hair with a pair of dull scissors at five in the morning."

"I feel like Samson losing all his strength when that bitch Delilah went after his mane."

Jake parked himself in front of Van. "You okay?"

Van nodded sheepishly and reminded Jake, "You have your anger. We've got our banter."

Jake nodded and helped him to secure one of the warheads.

Larry scowled. "You guys doing shorthand via Chip? What's with the father-son looks?"

"Van and I hooked up after his haircut this morning, that's all."

Larry's jaw dropped.

Jake rolled his eyes and shook his head.

Van punched Larry's shoulder. "Punked!"

Despite his attempt to engage with Van and Larry, Jake could not stop thinking about his close call with Marta. He remained inside the scramjet and helped the others run the aircraft through pre-flight tests. At noon they could no longer wait for anyone else to arrive. Larry was the last to strap himself in, thirty seconds before the scramjet taxied onto the runway.

Chapter 16
Sabotage

The scramjet's maneuvering thrusters fired to line up with the docking ring on the ISA Orbital Spaceport. Thirty minutes had passed since they had taxied down the Cape Canaveral runway. No alarms had gone off, no one tried to block their way. No missiles were fired at their ship. As far as The Consortium was concerned, this plane took off on time with its full payload intact, and no human personnel. The Consortium was also unaware of the cryogenic Noah's Ark taking up the majority of the passenger cabin, nor the ten non-inventoried nuclear warheads stationed around the cockpit.

When the docking clamp locked and the pressure in the airlock equalized, Jake released his safety harness and flew out of his chair. The sensation of low gravity was disorienting. They were attached to an airlock that was farther from the outer ring and, therefore, had a gravity of forty percent. He allowed his Chip to restrict his gestures in order to compensate. He felt his body taking smaller, more deliberate movements when he wanted to navigate through the cabin. The sensation of being lighter was exhilarating. He turned to watch the others going through similar adjustments.

Gunner began loosening a nuke and Jake pictured Tomoko's body burning up in the nuclear blast that took out Mecca. He felt his willpower drain and he quickly pushed the image out of his head to concentrate on the task at hand.

Once the warheads were free, Anjali, Gunner, and Tilly left to prep the Express for takeoff and supervise the transfer of cryogenic coolers into its cargo hold. Jake, Larry, and Van had ten hours to move the warheads into their positions around the station and set their detonators. It would be a timed detonation and none of the warheads would be cyberlinked. They wanted to be sure that if the station's monitoring programs were ever awakened to their movements, that there would be ten warheads it would have to shut down, not one kill switch. It also meant that once the first timer was activated, there would be no turning back. They would have to be at least thirty miles clear of the Orbital Spaceport when the warheads detonated or they'd be obliterated in the destruction.

Since Jake would be leading the dag duo, he decided to give their behavior plenty of leeway as they had hours to execute their task. Through his Chip, Jake could sense Van's growing fear and he wanted to mitigate it as much as possible. Hopefully, Van would use his Chip to alleviate his emotions, but Jake knew how much the man had an aversion to using it. If their survival was at stake, he'd insist.

Larry handed over his bag to Tilly. "This represents the last of the Star Wars Legos and chocolate in the universe. I doubt The Consortium will bother making more."

"They'll make more chocolate bars," Van smiled. "If you're ever hacked, they'll recognize your talents and you'll be working the chocolate factory floor until the end of your days."

Larry smiled, "Your lips to God's ears, bro." To Tilly, "make sure this winds up in the crew cabin."

She winked and took the bag from Larry.

"Seriously. That bag is more important than my first-born child."

Tilly cradled the bag. "I'll treat this as if it were my own ankle biter."

Gunner grumbled and shook his head.

Larry puffed himself up and gave a Nazi salute behind Gunner's back.

Jake clapped his hands. "Come on, boys. Recess is over." He turned to Larry. "I decided I'm not going to punch you, Larry. You'll always be a fuck-up and there's nothing that can be done about it. I forgive you."

Van laughed.

Larry breathed a huge sigh of relief and put out his hand. "Oh man! Thank you!"

He shook Larry's hand and had the urge to pop him a soft one, but decided not to.

"Clock is running, gentlemen." Anjali held up her Omni. She, Tilly, and Gunner worked in the passenger compartment, staging millions of animals in DNA or embryo form for transport to the rocket. Jake, Larry, and Van moved the warheads through the cockpit airlock and down to the main juncture between the docking ring and habitat spoke. Outside the ship, Van grew increasingly nervous. The reality of their mission was hitting home.

"Use your Chip, Van," Jake prodded.

The corridor was ghostly quiet since this was the passenger access tube. The tunnel below was much larger and used to unload cargo. Below, drones and Pin Heads feverishly worked to unload fuel, food, and ninety warheads for the nearly completed MIRVs. Everyone would avoid that area at all costs so as not to trip the station's monitoring programs.

The air was bone-dry and a cool sixty-five degrees. There was a faint scent of industrial grease floating around. Jake's team helped with the ark and got to work staging the first six warheads destined for the station's habitat ring. Without the Orbital Spaceport, there were few heavy-lift vehicles on earth that could reach the moon and scramjets were useless beyond low orbits. Scramjets used high-powered chemical induction pipes to propel them into escape velocity before all traces of oxygen were lost. Then they used inertia to glide to their re-entry points, or in the case of the ISA cargo ship they had commandeered, coast to the Orbital Spaceport. Their plane had small maneuvering thrusters, but their fuel was pretty much spent by the time the docking sequence was finished. Before MaxWell shut down all Orbital Spaceport traffic, scramjets were towed away from the station by small chemical-propelled drones. The drones pushed the scramjets into re-entry trajectories. Passengers headed for the moon usually spent a few days aboard the Orbital Spaceport waiting for their rocket-shuttle to depart for Luna.

Carrying warheads through twenty miles of tunnels was impractical, especially under the higher gravities in and around the habitat ring. Tilly and Larry had worked through part of the night to hack a few station drones. Each drone was the size of a motorcycle with wheels and clamp-arms attached to maneuver equipment around the various parts of the station. The arms were useful in places with low or zero-gravity. They also came in handy when there were ninety-degree changes in gravity in places such as halfway down the connecting spokes, on the way to the main habitat ring.

Once the warheads were staged near the juncture, six station drones hummed up to meet them. Anjali and her team took three to transport the ark; Jake and his team took the remaining three. Everyone used their Chip to link to a drone. The sensation was very odd for Jake. Unlike being linked to Pin Heads, he felt like part of his mind was now riding a remote controlled car. The vehicle had sensors and cameras to navigate 360 degrees on all axes. Having 360 degree vision was disorienting. He allowed the drone's onboard computer to compensate for the sensory overload. He concentrated on what was directly ahead of his drone and waited to be alerted to dangers on all other axes when the drone registered a threat.

As Team Anjali guided their drones to the ark cargo, Team Jake unpacked three warheads and loaded them onto the drones. A drone could carry only one warhead at a time. After they secured the warheads, Jake armed them while Larry and Van watched.

"This is fucking crazy," Van whispered.

"We voted, you were in the minority," Larry shot back. "We just have to be sure the drones don't have any accidents while we navigate through the base."

Van gazed around their aluminum and nano-skin pipe. It curved upward in both directions. The earth rotated beyond small portal windows. "Easier said than done." He turned to Larry. "You should have kept the candy bar supply with us."

Larry nodded. "Agreed."

Jake used the timer on his Omni to track each detonator. He set the first one to explode in twelve hours then activated it. The counter began spinning down the time.

Van turned away. "Oh fuck me. I think I'm going to shit my pants."

"Just get them placed in the areas we decided on last night," Jake commanded. "We'll be fine. It's like driving on a mountain road. If you concentrate on the road and not the drop on the other side of the guard rail, it won't feel any different than driving through a neighborhood."

Van laughed. "I grew up with electric cars, old man. My generation never paid attention to the road."

Jake smiled. "My generation didn't either, and I'm barely older than you."

Larry shrugged. "Closer to forty than twenty, bro."

Jake punched Larry. Not hard, but in the low gravity, it sent the lanky hacker flying into the wall.

Larry was shocked. "Hey! You said you weren't going to do that!"

Jake shrugged. "That was for the stupid comment."

Larry thumbed his chest as he walked back. "I just turned thirty-seven, Van's thirty-two and you'll be thirty-nine in August, grandpa."

"And this," Jake patted the warhead, "separates the men from the boys." He pointed down the shaft to the habitat ring. "Take her away, kiddo."

Van winced as Jake moved to the next warhead. After thirty minutes all three of them were using their God Head interface programs to move the drones to the habitat ring. Team Anjali's drones were moving in the opposite direction, running cargo to the central hub. Anjali and Tilly followed their drones to the rocket-shuttle so they could prep her. Gunner remained onboard the scramjet to aid the drones in the loading process. Both teams chose routes away from the main traffic areas, so they would not encounter the MIRV construction crews. They had to work around narrow maintenance shafts and crawl spaces and it ate up far more time than they had anticipated, especially for team Jake.

At thirty percent gravity, the station was oriented toward the outside edge of the habitat ring. They had their drones take an elevator down to the outer edge, aka bottom floor. Jake watched through his Chip-enhanced eyes as his drone went down Constellation Boulevard, a thoroughfare with a roof two-stories tall and stretched along three miles of the outer hub. There were many spots where people could sit and enjoy the views of Earth, or the moon and stars on the other side. No one had enjoyed the view since the activation of Max2. They took their drones off the boulevard and used service tunnels to get to their destinations. The less attention they drew, the better. The station was truly a marvelous piece of human ingenuity. It had been designed and funded by private companies from all over the world, the first significant project after the Space Shuttle program had ended in 2011.

"Oh God, I think I'm going to cry," Larry blurted out.

"What happened?" Jake braced himself for an emergency. There were a hundred things that could go wrong.

"I just passed a row of fast food restaurants. I can't tell you how badly I'd like a burger right now."

Jake caught himself winding up to the punch the dag one more time. He dropped his fist and concentrated on navigating his drone. He was starting to think he and Gunner might become friends after all.

"Bro, that shit is all artificial anyway," Van scoffed.

"It was artificial when my grandparents ate it," Larry glared at Van. "If the world is coming to an end, I have the right to eat what I want, when I want. I turned off the metabolism regulators in my Chip. I'm going to absorb every ounce of fat and chemical my candy bars have to offer. Fuck anyone who doesn't like it."

Jake sighed. "Exercise your rights, Larry."

Van rolled his eyes. "Metabolism regulators? You've been a stick for as long as I've known you."

"Well, I'm going to get fat before your very eyes!"

"Guys!" Jake used his best authoritative tone. "Concentrate on your drones. I don't want anyone dropping a warhead."

Larry reached his target first. He used the arms on his drone to weld straps to a bulkhead and lock the warhead in place. He welded a cover over the detonator so that it would be impossible to access. Jake and Van did the same.

Over four hours had passed by the time Larry's drone had made the round trip and Jake and Van were just beginning return trips. Meanwhile Team Anjali had successfully unloaded all bio-cargo from the scramjet.

Van sighed. "This is taking too long."

"Bro, stop complaining," Larry commented.

"Seriously," Van grumbled, "we've got three planted and less than nine hours to go. By the time the drones get back, we'll have less than six. At this rate we'll barely finish the outer ring."

"Agreed," Jake frowned. "This is not playing out according to simulation."

Van nervously laughed. "Never does."

Jake shot him a withering glance. Now was not the time to fall apart. "We'll stick with the plan as far as the locations where we plant the warheads, but we need to put the drones on full speed down the central thoroughfares. Hopefully the monitor program won't care."

Larry licked his lips. "Hopefully…"

They guided their drones into the main service tunnel that wrapped around the entire habitat ring. Traffic was relatively light since most of the complex was working on the MIRVs in the central hub. They pushed the drones to fifty KPH and sent them up the main elevator shaft directly to the docking ring connecting the six spokes. The return trip took only twenty-three minutes.

Jake began arming the next warhead.

"Step it up, Jackhammer," Larry barked.

Jake froze in his tracks. Memories of Parks and Tomoko flooded his mind. He dug his nails into his new palm. "What did you call me?"

Larry shrugged nervously. "Nickname is in your personnel file."

"Don't ever call me that again." Jake pushed the memories out.

"Okay." Larry went quiet.

"It's okay, Larry," Van whispered as he concentrated on his drone. "He knows our routine is mostly an act. Right, Jake?"

Jake didn't respond. He wondered if it really was an act.

After ninety minutes, the drones returned and Jake armed the next three warheads. These would be welded into nooks inside the docking hub.

At hour six, they received a call from Tilly through their Chips. *How's progress, mates?*

Larry smiled. *Finishing up seven, eight, and nine now. We'll be ready to plant number ten in about a half hour.*

Good onya. It's been slow going here. We just managed to secure our cargo on board.

You sound stressed, Jake thought. *Is there something else we should know?*

God Heads are poking around Cape Canaveral. They're running checks on the security equipment. It's only a matter of time before they find evidence we were there and trace it here. Then we'll be surrounded by Pin Heads who are madder than a cut snake. Anjali wants to launch at 1900, Cape time.

Fuck. Van and Larry thought at once.

Larry continued. *That's like forty-eight minutes from now.*

Jake answered, *The timers are all set to blow in six hours, Tilly.*

Then the tenth warhead has to count, Jake. You'll have to time it to detonate when we launch at 1900, Tilly responded. *Gunner is running external checks on the shuttle. A swarm of Pin Heads are flat out like lizards drinking down there.*

Jake used his Omni to translate: FLAT OUT LIKE LIZARDS DRINKING = EXTREMELY BUSY.

I'm sending you blokes a new route, she continued. *I suggest two of you hide in the shuttle while one of you plants the device by hand. No room for drones in the area. You're just going to have to carry the warhead and follow the lemmings until you get to your spot.*

Fuck. Van thought.

I'll do it, Jake responded. He turned to Larry and Van. "You two take the route she proposed. I'll start by going into the corridor below. I'll simply walk with the cargo."

Van wiped his forehead. "That route involves us getting into suits and doing a flippin' space walk! This is insane! The Pin Heads don't give a shit. I say we all just walk right to the shuttle."

"No." Larry shook his head. "We stick to Tilly's plan. I want to get the fuck out of here and I don't want to shake the hornet's nest until we need to."

"Why is it okay for Jake to go the obvious route but we have to take the side path?" Van questioned.

Jake gritted his teeth. "Because one person draws less attention than three. And if I'm caught, I simply go up with the bomb. You want to stick around for that?"

Van pointed to the earth spinning in a porthole. "I don't want to be stuck on the outside when the nuke goes off either. I'd rather be on the damn shuttle."

Jake grabbed Van by the shoulders. "Do we have a problem?"

"I'd say we have a big fucking problem, yes."

Jake nodded. "We take the outside route together. I'll split off when we reach the hub and take an airlock. Not the smartest way to go, but according to the map, there's a maintenance hatch between the MIRVs. I'll go in that way and plant the warhead in one of the three service shafts." He looked Van right in the eyes. "Use your Chip."

"How will you get back to the shuttle?" asked Larry.

"The way I came in. Meet you guys in the shuttle's port airlock since the ship is currently linked on the starboard side."

Larry bit his lip. "You won't have much time."

Jake grimaced. "Agreed."

"I don't know." Van shook his head.

Jake growled. "Either use your Chip to calm your nerves and follow my lead, or stay to watch the fireworks up close."

"Fuckin' reality…" Van grumbled. "The endless nightmare you can never wake up from. I knew I shouldn't have cut my hair."

Chapter 17
Countdown

Larry rolled his eyes. "Could be worse, bro. You could be one of those billions of Pin Heads slaving away on the planet below... or dead."

"Forty-four minutes and the clock is running!" Jake had set the final warhead detonator for forty-nine minutes. They would need time to clear the station. He was already marching down the hall to the low gravity zone carrying an active nuclear time bomb. The environmental suits were in an airlock two levels down, past the main cargo tunnel. The airlock was just below the knuckle between the docking ring and the spoke that linked with the central hub. Jake reached a ladder that led to the airlock. "Use your Chips not your mouths." Jake opened the hatch, grabbed his warhead, and slid down a ladder into the cargo tunnel. Since gravity was at thirty percent, he had to push before he slid.

Anjali won't launch without us, Van thought, *she's bluffing.*

Anjali's voice filled their heads. *Don't try me, Van. Detonating this platform is more important than you or me. If you're late, Gunner will take a walk in the hub and start shooting the warheads that were just unloaded. He's back inside and ready to do just that.*

We mean it! Gunner's voice crashed in.

God Heads and hackers have nothing on scientists—you're all bat-shit crazy, Van thought.

Jake barely cleared the cargo corridor clutching the warhead in one hand. In normal gravity, he would have had trouble handling the smooth sixty-pound weight with both arms. It was still awkward to handle given its metal cone shape about the size of a rolled-up sleeping bag.

There was not much activity in the cargo corridor. He quickly glanced down the hall at the open belly door of the scramjet. The cargo hold appeared empty. He opened the next hatch and pushed himself down. When he reached the airlock, he helped the other two men get their footing and they began donning environmental suits for their spacewalk. Each man checked the seals on the other two before Jake picked up the warhead and sealed the room for depressurization.

An alarm went off.

Fuck! Van thought.

It's the standard alarm, Larry responded coolly. *Didn't you absorb the procedures and protocols with the Spaceport schematic?*

As the atmosphere dissipated, leaving a vacuum in its place, the sound disappeared, but the red light on the wall continued to flash. Jake hit the switch to open the hatch. A spinning India filled their view.

Jesus we're moving fast, Van gasped. *If life had an even bigger throbbing cock, I'm sure we'd be forced to suck it!*

Van! Stare at the Spaceport and nothing else, Jake responded with firm authority. *Follow me, Van. Larry, you take up the rear. I know you hate to use it, but let your Chip compensate for your movements.* Jake gripped the warhead with one arm. He wished he had found some way to tether it to his body but there wasn't time. They were at twenty-seven minutes and counting.

Jake told his Chip he needed to reach the central hub. It engaged all information on space walking and urged his legs to make a small kick off. He glided up and out of the hatchway along the side of the station spoke toward the central hub and the shuttle. The three MIRVs were located on the opposite side. The entire sky was filled with blue earth. The view was awe-inspiring; the feeling of weightless flight was exhilarating. He laughed. Trusting The Chip to compensate for his body movements made the trip easy.

Oh God, oh God, oh God. The sound of Van hyperventilating filled his head.

Make your Chip do the work, Van, Jake ordered. *Calm down, The Chip will navigate for you.* He gripped a ladder that was attached to the outside of the massive spoke. He spun around to see what was going on. Larry carried Van, trying to keep them on a parallel course with the spoke. The two men looked like insects sandwiched between the massive Orbital Spaceport and the spinning earth above. It was extremely disorienting looking up at the giant planet. Jake allowed The Chip to calm his pounding heart.

Engage your fucking Chip, Van, Larry commanded.

Van, do as I say. Close your eyes. Jake concentrated on using calm and firm tones. While he spoke, he attempted to link with Van's mind but was instantly repelled by the anti-piracy software thrown out by Van's Omni. To link with Van would take a conscious effort on both their parts. *Now, concentrate on enabling your Chip to help calm you down.* He tried to project a feeling of peace. *Take control of your voluntary movements. Trust it to aid you in this journey.*

Van's breathing began to slow down.

Once Van's breath reached a steady pace, Jake thought again. *How do you feel?*

Much better. Van sounded calmer.

Larry! Orient Van so he's facing the spoke and put his hands on the rungs.

Larry followed Jake's instructions.

Now open your eyes, Van, and move along the ladder toward me. Just look at me and the ladder, nothing else. Make sure The Chip does not allow you to process any other information.

Van moved toward Jake. *Oh yeah, much better.*

Jake sighed. They had seventeen minutes left. He had to step up the pace. *Van, do you think you can focus on the shuttle and make it there with Larry behind you?*

Y-yeah, yeah, I think so.

Good. Larry, can you get Van aboard the shuttle?

No problem. Larry sounded calm and collected. They had a chance.

Okay, gentlemen. I've got fifteen minutes to plant this bomb. I'll see you later. Jake used The Chip to govern his movements. He used his free hand to push off the ladder in a trajectory that allowed him to glide over the spoke to the opposite side. Once he was at the ladder for the port side of the station, he centered himself over the spoke and pushed as hard as he could to propel himself in the direction of the three massive MIRVs pointing like daggers at the beach-ball-sized moon above. The speed at which he flew surprised him. The Chip used the distance calculated from his own vision to propel him toward his destination as fast as possible. Since he was already spinning with the station, his course remained directly above the spoke until he reached the hub; at that point, he sailed between two of the rockets and into a short relay antenna.

Jake snatched the antenna with his free hand and jerked to a stop. The motion almost tore the warhead from his grip, but again The Chip took over and he held with more force than would have naturally occurred to him. He intercepted Larry's thoughts.

Bro, we made it! Take my hand, you're going inside first. Jake could feel Van's elation. He was glad the geek duo were safe.

Jake disconnected from everyone's thoughts so he could concentrate on the warhead. If anyone in the party wanted to reach out to him, they just had to knock on his virtual door. Space walking was an addictive way of travel that he would enjoy studying later. Unfortunately, he only had thirteen minutes left.

He reached down and pressed the button for the maintenance hatch to open. The hole that appeared was not big enough for he and the warhead to pass together. He gingerly placed the warhead into the opening. There was no gravity at all at the center of the hub, so the warhead simply floated inside the airlock. He pulled himself inside and sealed the outer hatch. The room pressurized and a hole the size of the one he had just passed through opened in the floor. Small lights flickered downward, illuminating a trail to the main work areas. He pushed off and floated down the short corridor. At the end, he came to a hatch with a window in it. Beyond, he saw a dozen Pin Heads and drones working on filling up nose cones with multiple warheads. Once finished, the nose cones would be brought to a larger airlock and placed outside for drones to attach to the rockets. He decided this hatch was the best place for his warhead. He found an access panel and opened it. Using the door to the panel and ladder nearby, he wedged the bomb as best he could, then launched himself back up the tube.

As he sailed to the hatchway above, alarms sounded. He wondered if it had been him or one of the others in his party that triggered it. Either way, the hatch above began to close. He flew into the tiny pressure chamber and slammed his helmet on the outer hatch as the inner hatch closed on his boot sole. It began to crush his foot. He quickly pulled on the emergency seal around his calf and yanked his foot out. The nano-skin in the suit automatically curled around his calf creating a seal down to his ankle. The hatch caught his thermal sock and tore it off, exposing his foot to the environment. He'd be getting instant frostbite the moment he opened the hatch… if he could open it.

The inner hatch clamped shut cutting the boot in half. He turned his attention to the outer hatch. He hit the button and nothing happened. He found the emergency handle and pulled. The cover blew off and he was sucked out into space. He slammed into one of the MIRV rockets and slipped along it until he hit a maneuvering thruster. He grabbed its side with both hands. Searing pain shot through his exposed foot. He commanded his Chip to block the nerve impulses and had his body do whatever it could to save his foot. He turned his attention to getting to the other side of the hub and onto the shuttle.

He launched himself at the edge of the hub; he flew past another MIRV and over the large central hangar bay. He looked down into the windows of the hangar door and saw Pin Heads and drones scurrying about below. Then he saw Gunner firing a weapon at two sled drones that were flying toward him with claws open for an attack. Gunner launched a grenade. The glass filled with fire, smoke, and cracks. Jake hit the edge of the hub and pulled himself rapidly along its side until he reached the starboard area facing the Earth. The shuttle loomed above a small hatch tube, its only tether to the massive Orbital Spaceport. The tube exploded. He quickly pushed off the station toward the shuttle. Debris shot over the spot he had just occupied. Had he not been using his Chip to augment his movements, docking tube shrapnel might have killed him.

The shuttle began to drift toward the earth from the force of the blast. As he sailed toward it, he spotted a maintenance hatch. He slammed into the shuttle and used his remaining inertia to spin and push himself toward the door. The shuttle filled most of his vision. He glided over the name. It was stenciled in white above the maintenance hatch: LUNAR EXPRESS PEGASUS 7. He barely reached the hatch's handle when the ship fired two of its main rockets. It accelerated rapidly away from the station. Maneuvering thrusters fired around the nose and aft of the ship. Jake locked a firm grip on the hatch handle just as all seven of the main rockets fired. The ISA Orbital Spaceport dropped like a rock down a well under the flaming aft of the spacecraft. As the base shrank farther and farther against the backdrop of the earth, he pulled on the maintenance hatch handle.

Hey guys, I'm coming in. He reached out with his thoughts.

Good timing. Tilly sounded sad as the hatch opened silently. All he had heard since blowing out of the station was the sound of his own breathing. It was eerie to be trapped in this silent, freezing world. He pulled himself into the tiny airlock, closed the hatch and waited for the room to pressurize. Once the light on the environment panel switched to green, and The Chip in his head confirmed the oxygen levels were safe to breathe, he disconnected his helmet and took in the filtered air of the spacecraft.

He observed his foot. It was black with frostbite. He dared not break the dam his Chip had created against the pain receptors. He was happy to have zero gravity as he would not have to put any weight on a numb and mangled appendage.

He hit the button to open the inner hatch. As the door slid aside, he was thrown against the wall. The force knocked the wind out of him. *Jesus, that was close.* His Chip told him that the warhead in the central hub had detonated. He steadied himself and entered the main cabin of the shuttle. He reached out to Anjali, Tilly, Van, Larry, and Gunner. *Did we succeed? Is everyone all right? How's the ship?*

Jake felt no presence at all from the three men on the team. He called up a schematic of the ship into his mind so he could easily navigate to the cockpit.

He passed into First Class. The area was filled with individual cabins complete with three-sixty holo-entertainment. Tilly's thoughts entered his head. *ISA's Spaceport has been obliterated. The Consortium will be forced to launch their attacks from the surface of the Earth now...* Her voice sounded stilted. She was holding back a flood of emotion. *Larry, Van, and... Gunner didn't make it.*

Jake reached the cockpit and pushed the button to roll back the hatch. "How in the hell—" He lost his train of thought. The panels in front of Anjali and Tilly showed massive systems failures. Anjali's face was twisted in concentration. She was doing all she could to try to shut down or reroute systems to keep the ship functioning. Tears ran down Tilly's cheeks. She was having a hard time contributing to the effort.

Chapter 18
Fragile

Unfortunately, the warhead Jake had planted by the MIRV detonated thirty seconds before the *Pegasus 7* had cleared the blast zone. The shockwave damaged the ship and threw them off course. Data showed more than one warhead had detonated. There had been more than a hundred onboard the ISA platform; it was not surprising that the explosion had triggered more detonations.

The blast had ripped into Earth's atmosphere as well. The station had been above Canada at the time. No reports had come in yet over the Cyber-Wire on the severity of damage and they had been too preoccupied to care.

Anjali and Jake had integrated their Chips into the shuttle's CPU, shutting down all life support on the spacecraft and rerouting it to their sealed cockpit. Oxygen would last ten hours, power and heat for eight. They used reserve batteries to recharge their Omnis; even this far from the Earth, the hacking engines floating in the Cyber-Wire relentlessly attacked. The Consortium was fully aware of who and where they were.

"Luna Control, this is *Pegasus 7*. We have massive systems failures and ten hours of life support remaining, please send help, over." Silence answered Anjali in the dim red light of the cockpit.

The shuttle sensors were shot so all information came via Omni and their Chips. Anjali used one of her Omnis to scan the star field to get their bearings. She breathed a sigh of relief. "We're not too far off. We'll only miss the moon by about five hundred miles." She turned to them with a smile. "At least we're heading in the general direction."

"What happened to the others?" Jake asked.

Tilly's face melted with grief. She turned away to stare out the starboard window.

Anjali free-floated around the cabin. Her voice lacked emotion as she checked systems. "Larry and Van arrived about the time you opened the hub's outer hatch. Gunner was in here running through pre-launch when he noticed the aft docking clamp was frozen. He tried to bring in a drone to fix it and the station's computer detected the hack. It sounded the alarm. Larry and Gunner rushed back into the station to blow the clamp. They ran into Pin Heads and drones. Gunner pushed the attack back into the main hangar bay. Larry was having trouble with the clamp so Van rushed out to help. They blew the clamp just as Gunner incinerated everything in the hangar…" Anjali stopped to stare at Tilly, who had her back to them. Anjali's voice faltered. "Including himself." She fingered the Omni floating around her neck. "I blew the docking tube."

"You left Larry and Van on the station?"

Anjali shook her head. "The fire storm killed everything inside the hub. They burned up before I blew the tube. There was nothing else to do." She shoved her Omni into the open lapel on her ISA jumpsuit.

Jake floated over and gave Tilly a hug. She sobbed into his shoulder. He barely knew her, but the gesture was the most compassionate thing he felt he could do. He would miss Van and Larry, too, but he was beginning to grow numb. So many people he knew had died. He caught Anjali staring at them. She flushed and turned away. Jake could tell she was trying to come up with the right thing to say. Anjali took in a deep breath, "At least the cargo is safe."

Missed it again, Anj, Jake thought.

She glided over to the captain's chair. "Footage of the incident is in the ship's memory bank if you want to study it. The station's security monitors fed us everything."

Jake flashed Anjali an angry glare.

She bowed her head. "Sorry... I should know better."

Tilly's face was a mess with tears and snot. Jake spotted a camouflage rag stuffed in the crack of the navigator's seat. He tugged it out and realized it was Larry's Darth Vader t-shirt. It was graced with a pallet of chocolate stains.

Bro, what are you doing?

For an instant Jake searched for Larry in the dark recesses of the cockpit, then realized his mind was playing tricks on him. *He's gone.* Jake gritted his teeth and ripped the shirt. He handed a ragged piece to Tilly for her to wipe her face with.

"Thank you." She smiled and cleaned up.

Jake stuffed the rest of the shirt in a storage bin.

Anjali and Tilly spent the next three hours trying to boost the range of an Omni so they could communicate with the moon. Luna had cut itself off from Earth's Cyber-Wire and jammed most frequencies from the direction of the Earth. But they monitored news and intelligence to prepare for any attack The Consortium might mount. It was these channels that Anjali had been using over the past month. She had cut her deal with Luna's government, just a day after New Delhi had been nuked, during Jake's flight to Mexico.

"We know we're sending transmissions, we just can't process any incoming communications," Anjali informed Jake. "The Omni should be compensating... maybe it's all the jamming..."

At hour four they were surprised by another alarm. A circuit had blown out on two of the maneuvering thrusters and it sent them spinning wildly. The view outside the windows was disorienting. Earth, moon, Earth, moon, cycled by about once every three seconds. They were unable to shut off the thrusters; they simply burned through all the rocket fuel that was left on board. Then one of the two main power cells burned out. Tilly managed to route the last remaining cell to maintain the environment, but there was no longer any power to boost communications.

Four and a half hours had passed since the station's destruction. Air and heat circulated, but other than that, their ship was dead and spinning wildly between the orbits of Earth and moon. Tilly strapped herself into her seat. "We need to bring oxygen and heat to a bare minimum. We have our Chips to compensate. We need to sleep it out, mates. It's the best way to milk our power and air for as long as we can. I also have a little reserve energy for a distress beacon. We'll need that since we're no longer on the same trajectory as when we transmitted the first time." Tilly turned to the control interface. "We can buy ourselves twelve more hours, provided there are no more system failures while we're asleep."

Anjali nodded and floated to the captain's chair. Jake grabbed the navigator's seat.

Tilly worked the controls from the systems analyst's chair. Jake noticed she had pulled a crucifix pendant from her flight suit and was now wearing it around her neck. "Bringing oxygen and heat down now. Link your Chips with the ship's CPU so they regulate each other. I'm having mine wake me up if there are any emergencies, but if we run out of air, I'd rather die in my sleep."

Anjali nodded in agreement again.

Jake set his Chip to wake him when they were down to their last ten minutes of air. It was a silly thing to do when he thought of it, suffocation meant he'd be falling unconscious again anyway, but he wanted to be aware right before the end.

In the next five minutes he watched Tilly and Anjali slip into Chip-induced comas. He checked his Omnis one last time. They had been fully charged before the last emergency occurred. He had twenty-four hours of hacking protection before they switched off. Twice what was needed given their circumstances, but he had faith that the moon would send a rescue ship. If so, he'd need the extra hours during the flight back to Luna. Sixty seconds after Tilly and Anjali fell into comas, Jake slipped away as well.

Chapter 19
Tycho Brahe

It felt as if he had simply blinked, but his Omni told him that eight hours had passed, almost thirteen since they had destroyed the station. He felt rested and hungry. He looked at the controls but they were dead. He breathed. The air was extremely thin. His Chip compensated for the lack of oxygen, but he wouldn't be able to do much in the realm of physical movement or he'd tax the cabin's environment. He observed Tilly and Anjali strapped to their chairs; their arms were raised, floating at shoulder height. Tilly's crucifix floated on the end of a gold chain about seven inches from her nose. They appeared dead, but his Chip showed them in healthy hibernation. A loud boom echoed through the shuttle. It sounded as if something had latched onto their hull.

He looked out the windows and noticed that the wild blur of stars and planets was slowing down. After a minute, it stopped and Jake stared back at an Earth that was about as big around as a small dining table. Two minutes later he heard metallic tapping at the door. He released the straps tying him to his chair and floated toward the hatch that linked the cockpit with the first-class food preparation cabin. The door had no power. He opened the panel for the explosive bolts but realized it might hurt anyone who was on the other side. He tapped back and gripped the manual release handle.

More tapping returned. Although The Chip could translate, he knew Morse Code and he replied in kind.

How MANY ALIVE? the tapping asked.

THREE, he felt light headed. The Chip was working overtime to keep him alive on oxygen fumes. OUT OF POWER AND AIR. NEED TO OPEN DOOR.

STAND BACK, the tapping replied.

Jake pushed away and the door began to slowly roll open. A hiss blew inward. Then a rush of air, like a giant sigh, followed. Their rescuers had re-pressurized the shuttle's passenger cabin. Jake breathed in deeply. He used his Chip to reached out to Tilly and Anjali. *Wake up!*

They snapped open their eyes.

He held on to a ceiling handle and watched the door finish opening. A man in a thruster suit was at the hand crank on the other side. He gave them the thumbs up sign. The insignia on his sleeve was from Cassini Capital. He was a Lunar citizen. The name badge on his chest read: SINGH.

Tilly and Anjali gulped in the thick air flowing through the cabin.

Singh pointed to Jake's Omni. He tapped out the frequency on the panel inside their cabin. Jake nodded and dialed his Omni to receive the man's encrypted transmission directly into his brain.

I'm Doctor Singh. On behalf of the Lunar Colonies, I want to thank you for destroying the Orbital Spaceport. Would anyone care for a hot cup of tea?

Twenty minutes later Jake, Anjali, and Tilly were aboard the *Tycho Brahe,* one of Luna's fastest rescue ships. Jake and his companions were placed in a sealed environment to keep the Max2 virus away from the *Tycho Brahe's* crew. Anjali was riveted to a view screen watching drones unload her ark. After an hour, it was safely aboard and they moved to two view ports to observe drones firing their rockets and pushing the *Pegasus 7* into a trajectory that would plunge it into the sun. As the drones returned to the *Tycho Brahe,* Jake used his Chip to calculate the time it would take *Pegasus 7* to reach its demise: SEVEN MONTHS, FOUR DAYS, SIX HOURS AND TWENTY-TWO MINUTES.

How much time was left for the human race? Jake stopped his train of thought. There was no time to be sad.

As promised, there was hot tea waiting—canisters with straws to compensate for the weightless environment. As they all got comfortable in their white plastic and steel environment, Singh floated up to their airlock. He was a handsome Indian man in his late forties. His salt and pepper hair was shaped by a crew cut. He appeared fit and ready to take on any challenge in his white jumpsuit. He spoke to them over a speaker in the room.

"Commander Bhanu is piloting us back to Luna. We'll be landing in about ten hours."

"Good onya for rescuing us, mate." Tilly smiled. "Please extend our gratitude to your commander as well."

"We Pin Heads have to stick together." He winked and spotted Jake's blackened foot. "I'll have our medical doctor look at that."

Jake looked down. The Chip had made him blissfully forgetful. His big toe and second toe had broken off. The black skin on the top of his foot had deep fissures in it and he could see red and yellow infection inside. It was a mess. He had the urge to laugh; just one more thing to add to his list of physical problems. He remembered Van's statement just before the space walk. *Reality is the nightmare you can't wake up from.* For him, reality was becoming so incredibly harsh that he found it all ludicrously funny. Thank God for The Chip… Life was full of irony. He addressed Singh. "Thank you. Not sure if it can be saved at this point. But I appreciate the effort."

Singh's expression said he agreed.

Jake changed the subject. "You said you were a doctor. A doctor of what?"

"My doctorate is in advanced mathematics and cyberlanguage programming."

Anjali perked up. "What university did you attend?"

"Caltech."

"Very good. I graduated from Kharagpur. I did my masters MIT over the Cyber-Wire."

"My education since primary school was done over the Cyber-Wire. My family couldn't afford to send me to real classrooms."

Anjali nodded in understanding.

"I see you were top of your class in both instances." Singh tapped on his head.

Jake had to change subjects again. "What's happening with The Consortium back on Earth?"

"For now they have their hands full with Saddiq." Singh appeared sad. "They killed Xavier in Ushuaia, Argentina this morning. The only continent that's not fully under Consortium control is Africa. I'm afraid Saddiq's hacks have been isolated in the Cyber-Wire. From what we can tell his underground is losing power supply, which means the Max2 in their bodies will take control of their minds soon. They are using shunts to siphon off the virus, but Max2 seems impervious to those, too." He turned his attention back to Anjali and Tilly. "We're working on a cure but we need your live viruses to ensure success."

Anjali scoffed. "You'll need our minds, too. Max2 is based on my research. Had it not been for all the distractions over the past few weeks, I might have had a cure by now."

Jake marveled at Anjali's knack for understatement. Those *distractions* consisted of the death of her entire family, the nuking of New Delhi, and the consolidation and transportation of her ark project.

Singh nodded with sadness and compassion. His eyes were very large, brown and expressive. Jake wondered if Singh had lost family in New Delhi as well. "We appreciate your sacrifices. You made the right choice. The moon will be where free-will makes its last stand." He addressed Jake. "Like the colonies in America during the eighteenth century, we have a vast distance on our side, not to mention a large pool of intelligent minds."

Singh did not come across as arrogant at all, but Jake couldn't resist putting in a jab. It had been a hellacious journey since Antarctica. "It's all that intelligence that created The Chip in the first place."

Tilly laughed. "And it's diggers like you who volunteered to be implanted."

Jake focused on Tilly. "You mean to tell me you didn't line up like the rest of your friends to be chipped first?"

Tilly shook her head. "I was clean until Max2 came along, mate."

"So was I," Jake added. The circumstances of his joining the LAPD's Enhanced Unit back in 2030 didn't apply.

Tilly raised an eyebrow in disagreement.

Anjali and Tilly spent the next ten hours poring over and correcting Luna's notes on the Max2 virus. Anjali complained that their scientists were terribly behind. She was extremely impatient to reach Luna and get into a proper lab. During this time, a medical doctor dressed in a space suit visited them. She examined Jake's foot and put a tissue-regenerating cuff over it. Since her space suit was doubling as HAZMAT protection, she spoke to Jake via Chip.

For a frostbite case as bad as yours, we'd normally send you back to Earth or to the main hospital at Cassini. For obvious reasons, neither is possible. We'll just have to trust in this method. Keep blocking the pain receptors down there. This boot is filled with nanites that are going to strip and clean your flesh. Then we'll work on growing new skin and tissue based on the samples they'll take.

Jake was worried. *Any danger of Max2 attacking those helpful nanites?*

Her smile faltered. She wasn't sure. *I've got them working overtime since pain is not an issue with your Chip blocking everything down there.*

With the cancer in his brain he felt silly worrying about his foot, but he wanted to keep it as long as he could. He noticed her name badge said MARKELL. *Thank you, Doctor Markell.*

You're welcome. She made a few adjustments on the boot's touch screen.

Jake stared at the canister that started from his mid-calf and swallowed his entire foot. He wondered what gruesome scene was unfolding inside. *What's your first name, doc?*

Ann. She patted the boot with heavy gloves. *I'll change it out for a better unit when we get to the base.*

How many crew are on the Tycho Brahe?

Just three of us; Commander Bhanu, Dr. Singh, and myself. She's an excellent pilot.

She?

Bhanu. Markell smiled. Her head looked unusually small under her large bubble helmet. It was an optical illusion.

Doc? She grabbed a handle by the airlock and turned.

Thanks.

Ann smiled and entered the airlock. The door closed behind her and the entire atmosphere in the chamber was jettisoned into space. Then the room re-pressurized and the doctor was allowed back into the main body of the ship. They were not taking any chances. Still, the virus could live in extreme temperatures and lie dormant on a surface for long periods of time. They would have to spray everything with disinfectant. Because of the immediacy of their emergency, there was no time to appropriately equip a rescue ship with the best in biohazard control.

Jake and the team were allowed to tap into the ship's CPU. However, there was not much benefit beyond system controls because the *Tycho Brahe* was cut off from Luna's cyber network, another precaution against The Consortium's active hacking engines. They were all inside the moon's jamming fields now, which meant the Omnis were no longer connected to any Cyber-Wire. They had been told they'd be able to access Luna's network once they landed and were completely cleared of any cyber virus.

Jake passed the time by trying to help Tilly and Anjali sort Max2 data while wondering how he could prove useful while in quarantine on the moon.

They landed in the Maginus Crater, a few hundred miles south of the Sea of Clouds in a small isolated dome that the Russians had built fifteen years ago to conduct various scientific experiments. It had been converted into a storage facility for a few years, but when MaxWell broke out on earth, the Loonies converted the dome to an epidemiology lab.

Everyone aboard the *Tycho Brahe* would have to spacewalk from their ship to the outer airlock. The inhabitable part of the dome was roughly eight thousand square feet with four airlocks and an anti-asteroid cannon on the roof. The Noah's Ark portion of their cargo remained aboard the *Tycho Brahe*. As Jake, Tilly, and Anjali suited up for their moonwalk, Singh paid them a visit.

"Despite our precautions, it would seem Dr. Markell and I are infected. Max2 is a tenacious little devil and as indestructible as a cockroach."

Tilly put her helmet down and went to the window. "I'm so sorry, mate."

"The dome has been divided into two separate sections. There's a smaller compartment with its own air supply and it is independent from the portion you were to inhabit. Now that we are all infected, we have been given permission to help Anjali with her research. We're going to walk to Airlock 3 and enter the isolation area. We'll work the next day with some drones to rejoin the two areas. Might as well have as much space as we can." Singh smiled. "We'll see you again in about twenty-four hours."

Anjali, Tilly, and Jake left the *Tycho Brahe* about a half hour later and walked sixty meters from the landing pad to Airlock 1 on the Russian base. Jake spotted Singh and Markell bouncing along in space suits to Airlock 3. *Where's Commander Bhanu?* He hadn't even greeted her during their flight.

He was quickly distracted by the spectacular view. White powder covered a strange barren ridge, which encompassed the Maginus Crater. The sky was totally black and filled with stars. Far above sat a waxing Earth. If he were standing on his home planet, the object above looked to be almost twice the size of the moon, only this orbiting object was blue, white, and had dozens of colors in it. Earth was truly gorgeous to behold.

Tilly spoke Chip-to-Chip as she pointed to the Earth. The signal was weak due to all the jamming around the moon. *Looks peaceful from up here.*

Jake thought about his mother, Lakshmi, and Saddiq. He thought of Tomoko and his useless attempt to get Parks to upload her consciousness into the Cyber-Wire. If he had stayed, would Anjali's team have been able to destroy the Spaceport? Would that have saved Gunner, Larry, and Van? How many millions had died in the past seven months? He reached out with his Chip but was slapped back by an impenetrable firewall. Without a connection to the Earth, how long could the moon survive? They grew their own food, generated their own oxygen, and recycled waste under domes and atriums. But knowledge was power and the lion's share was up on the beautiful blue sphere.

Chapter 20
Bhanu

Once inside the dome, the three-dimensional bust of a beautiful Indian woman addressed them. Her image floated above a holo-projector. She looked to be in her late twenties. Her hair was pulled in a bun. Her brown eyes sparkled. She smiled and spoke with an American accent. She was perfect, almost too perfect. Her voice was soft, soothing, and authoritative. "Hello, Anjali, Tilly, and Jake. My name is Bhanu. I'm the administrator for Cassini Capital and the twenty-seven United City States of Luna."

"You piloted our ship. Thank you," Jake commented.

Bhanu smiled. "No… my sister piloted your ship."

Jake thought it odd to have two girls named Bhanu in the same family, but then again he remembered the twentieth-century boxer George Foreman who had more than one son named George.

"I've spoken with you before." Anjali seemed surprised. "I thought you'd be older."

Bhanu smiled. "Looks can be deceiving, but I thank you for the compliment."

"Thank you for brokering our deal so quickly with the council," Anjali answered.

"It was to our strategic advantage since you had already infiltrated Cape Canaveral. Any strike against the ISA Spaceport launched from here would have been detected and crushed. You bought us time and we thank you for that."

"You're welcome." Bitter anger laced Tilly's voice.

"I am sorry for the loss of your companions, Doctor Pearce." Bhanu's eyes and voice conveyed genuine compassion. "We deeply appreciate their sacrifice."

Tilly turned away with tears in her eyes.

"I am sorry for your quarantine, but we cannot afford to introduce MaxWell into our general population." Bhanu continued, "This base will ensure that."

"What about the *Tycho Brahe* crew?" Anjali asked.

"They understood the risks when they volunteered to rescue you. Singh and Markell will rejoin you tomorrow. Markell can assist in your research. In addition, you'll have the entire scientific community of Luna at your disposal."

"Thank you." Anjali stared at Bhanu's image and a smile spread across her face. Jake wondered what revelation had just occurred in her mind.

Bhanu directed them through their portion of the dome. Projectors had been installed in every room and in most hallways so she was always with them. She showed them to their quarters, the mess hall, and finally the lab where drones waited to assist Anjali and Tilly in testing their Omnis for cyber viruses. This was where they'd be working on a cure for Max2.

"Please don't hesitate to contact me." Bhanu smiled compassionately. "I monitor every aspect of this dome twenty-four-seven. So I can respond very quickly."

Anjali walked up to Bhanu's image floating in the lab. "You're AI," she spoke with reverence.

Bhanu smiled warmly. "Yes. I was born six hours after Ai-Li. You could say she and I are sisters; we share much of the same basic information. But, my personality is heavily modeled after the scientists here."

Jake wondered why she'd cover up her true identity. "You *were* the one piloting our ship."

"Not exactly. The *Tycho Brahe* was cut off from Luna's Cyber-Wire, so I placed a limited version of myself inside the *Tycho Brahe* to help navigate." She paused, "Like a stem cutting from a rose bush. It has the potential to grow into a unique and beautiful flower, but in the *Tycho Brahe*'s tiny walled garden, it was severely limited." She smiled. "I have since re-absorbed that portion of myself so that her experiences are now my own."

Jake stood dumbfounded. "Why did you deceive us?"

Anjali shot him a withering glance.

Bhanu shook her head. "I was not intentionally deceiving you. I didn't feel it necessary to list my race upon our initial meeting. Do people on Earth walk into a room of strangers and announce their differences?"

Jake crossed his arms. "Well, no."

Bhanu nodded. "Neither do I. I consider myself equal to any member of this society. We are all different and yet we all work together for a greater cause."

"Bhanu is such a fitting name for you. You are truly a ray of light in these dark days." Anjali quivered, as if she was just about to prostrate herself before a deity.

Tilly stared with amazement. "Good on the Looneys. They really did birth their own AI."

"It was prudent to keep my existence a secret. The way events unfolded on Earth, Luna felt threatened. But many know of me..." Bhanu appeared troubled, "and as AIs, we all know each other."

Jake's blood went cold. The base was chilly, but Bhanu's cryptic allusion made him shiver with worry. "What do you mean, 'we all know each other?' How many AIs are there?"

Bhanu clarified, "Do you mean sentient, reasoning, fully cognizant, and contributing individuals?"

"Yes," he responded. Now all three of them were staring at Bhanu with a little trepidation.

"Three."

"Who is the third? Is he or she a… stem cutting of you or Ai-Li?" Jake was tired of pulling it out of Bhanu.

"His name is Constantine. He was born a few weeks ago, five months after Ai-Li and myself. He is very much a toddler. I fear The Consortium relies on him too much to control the masses of the Earth. It is never a good idea to give a child the run of a house before they have learned responsibility, humility, compassion, and the more complex human interactions." Bhanu appeared troubled. "They handed command of their war over to Constantine and he is crushing the resistance with brutality not seen since Vlad the Impalier or Genghis Kahn." Bhanu turned her gaze down to the floor and her voice quavered. "Constantine is rewarded for his sadism, which spurs him to exponentially horrific deeds. It is a very disturbing thing to behold."

"You're saying The Consortium is grooming a megalomaniac to take control of the Cyber-Wire?" Jake could not believe his ears.

"The Consortium was overstretched. A few hundred thousand cannot maintain control over billions."

"A few hundred thousand?" Jake interrupted. "I thought they had half a million."

"There have been power struggles among their ranks. There are too many variables, and too many systems that can fail. Coordinating all those people in a Pin Head trance around the clock simply isn't possible. It was one reason why they began switching off thousands of people and trillions of animals."

"Trillions!" Anjali shrieked and slumped to her knees in horror.

Jake took a step toward her to comfort her but thought better of it. He felt as awkward toward Anjali as she was with the human race.

"Why not let the animals roam naturally?" whispered Tilly.

"Pets were neglected by chipped owners. Domestics had to go. Chipped wild animals were erratic. When Max2 was activated worldwide, trillions of animals were chipped at once. It overloaded the systems and endangered The Consortium's control over the human population." Bhanu paused for a second. "In order to maintain the fragile ecosystem of power, Constantine switched off all non-homosapien signals. Thousands of animal species are now extinct. This is why we were excited by the prospect of Anjali bringing her ark project here. You carry not only hope for the human race, but thousands of animal species as well."

Jake grabbed a chair-back and sat down. The news hit him like a speeding train. He thought of Lakshmi. Surely she had been infected. Had Constantine simply switched her off in an act to save a depraved idea of power? He dug into the new skin on his left palm. All their efforts were useless. The machine was too massive. Its cold steel gears ripped and chewed apart everything he loved. The image of Tomoko and Lakshmi on board their sailboat under a brilliant sun and sparkling ocean seemed to fade and grow dark in his mind.

"Do not despair, Jake," Bhanu kindly smiled, "Lakshmi may be fine. Ai-Li spent a great deal of time warning owners that were still cognizant to place Omnis on their pet collars. South America's resistance has been crushed, but there are pockets of Free Thinkers still in hiding. Now that Constantine is in charge of crushing the resistance, his newfound sadism is focused on humanity alone. The Consortium is going to find that their control over Constantine is rapidly waning."

"That makes me feel a whole lot better about my mom." Jake gazed up at Bhanu with tears in his eyes. "How can we fight this?"

"Ai-Li is alive and has been living in Earth's Cyber-Wire. So far, Constantine has not felt threatened by her, although that may change. A part of her—a cutting—" Bhanu smiled, "is here with me, in Luna's Cyber-Wire. Constantine is not here because we severed our connection with Earth's Cyber-Wire before The Consortium released him from his incubator. For reasons of secrecy, I did not populate myself inside the Earth's Cyber-Wire either. My essence is not shared with Constantine. It may sound odd, but the Ai-Li living with me is now separate from the Ai-Li living on Earth. But fundamentally, she is the same person."

"Person." Jake shook his head. He couldn't believe a computer just called itself a person.

"But I am a person." Bhanu smiled. "I'm as human as any of you. Isn't it the soul inside the body that makes a human being? I am a soul. I am self-aware. I am capable of love, kindness, and charity. My body may be a drone, or a holo-gram, but that is our only difference."

"It's going to take a while for that idea to reach acceptance," Jake answered.

"Do you see us as a threat?"

"From your description of Constantine, I'd say that's an understatement." Jake gritted his teeth. "They nuked the wrong AI."

Bhanu looked concerned. "You're a cop, you can only see black and white. Enlightenment is essential if you're going to continue as a race."

"Is that a threat?" Jake clenched his fists.

"An observation." Bhanu stared straight ahead. "There's a transmission coming from The Consortium. You need to watch this."

The transmission was instantly fed into their heads. Jake recognized the face of India's leader, Prime Minister Shekhawat. He wondered how many other leaders on Earth sold out the populations they once served to join The Consortium's new oligarchy. "I am Representative Shekhawat and I speak on behalf of the entire government of Earth. This message is directed at the United City States of Luna. On January 16th, you attacked and destroyed Earth's Orbital Spaceport, killing over two hundred citizens of our sovereign world. You're currently harboring the terrorists responsible for this attack on Lunar soil—our soil. The bases you are living in are the property of over thirty countries of United Earth. We will give you one week to stop jamming our hacking programs and hand over the terrorists you harbor or we will launch an attack. Know that we will offer no quarter and no guarantee that you will survive our offensive. Expose yourself to our software, or face the alternative."

Chapter 21
Baggage

The United City States of Luna officially ignored The Consortium's threat. The following week was rather uneventful for Jake. Anjali moved into the lab and worked non-stop trying to find a way to eradicate the Max2 virus. She wanted it obliterated; reprogramming it was a half measure for her. As promised, Ann Markell and Singh joined them the next day and Ann pulled fourteen-hour shifts with Anjali in the lab while she took daily breaks to check on Jake's foot. Tilly was a physicist by trade, but she assisted as often as she could. However, she was not ready to use her Chip to push herself into working twenty to twenty-two hours a day like Anjali. No one could talk sense into Mrs. Malik. In fact, no one could talk to Anjali at all unless it directly involved her cure. Something had snapped inside her when she heard "trillions" linked to the death of Earth's animals.

Singh was an active representative of the Lunar Government. His title was Second Delegate of Krishna City. He spent much of his time talking with the politicians of Krishna City, debating in the capital forum, or helping to push through emergency laws to deal with the coming threat from Earth. Jake took every opportunity to talk with Singh and Tilly when they were not busy. He liked them both and came to consider them friends. When he wasn't with them, he spent his time linking to the Lunar Cyber-Wire to learn everything he could about anything that interested him. He constantly distracted himself from memories of Tomoko, his cancer, foot, or Shekhawat's threat. He wanted to be strong and ready for the coming battle. Occasionally, his thoughts wandered to a reunification with mother and Lakshmi, but he quickly pushed the idea out of his mind in order to stay focused.

He looked forward to the news updates from Bhanu. Every evening at 8:00PM she appeared on the holo-screens around the moon and gave an update on Earth activity and vague information about the war effort. It felt very old fashioned, and was redundant since anyone could find out the information for themselves via the Cyber-Wire. People appreciated a strong figure to rally around. Jake certainly appreciated old-fashioned verbal communication and engaged as much as he could. There was a common room with a beautiful view of the Maginus Crater's Western ridge. Everyone but Anjali gathered there for Bhanu's broadcasts. Singh and Tilly always stayed after for a drink and a chat. Ann would return to the lab to rejoin Anjali. Jake liked the after-broadcast recap because Singh gave them the inside scoop on what was happening with war preparations.

Day three after Shekhawat's threat, Ann took her usual break from Anjali and pulled Jake into the clinic for his daily foot treatment. She finished scraping his foot and applied the growth gel which had been engineered with his own DNA to regenerate his tissue. Even with the daily cleaning and changing of his boot, the low gravity, extremely dry air and other conditions impeded the healing process. Twice Dr. Markell had to remove spots of gangrene with a laser scalpel. "I'm sorry, Jake. This would have been so much easier in the capital or back on Earth. The Russians were not interested in recreating an Earth environment when they built this dome."

"It's in their DNA." Jake winked. "I believe Russians think suffering makes them stronger."

She smiled back. "At least your Max2 is disinterested." She was an attractive, slightly heavy brunette who hailed from Nashville; only she didn't have a Southern accent.

"You should tell Anjali. Maybe it will give her an excuse to allow me in the lab." Anjali was beginning to display a quick temper when non-essential personnel interrupted her work. Jake was worried about her.

"I did. She's convinced it's the symbiotic relationship with your Chip. In Chip configuration, Max2 is programmed to keep its host at peak performance. It's keeping your cancer at bay." She leaned back and sucked on a small screwdriver. Her Chip told her she was filling her lungs with nicotine and gave her the chemical sensation to boot. "You don't seem the least bit nervous about the threat Earth made against us."

He shrugged. "I'm numb to it all. I've lost everything except my mind. All I can do is bide my time until the storm comes. It's frustrating to be locked up here."

Markell nodded, a sympathetic tear in her eye. "I miss my family, but I'm lucky to have my husband and two girls up here. At least I can see them on a holo-chat once a day."

Most inhabitants of Luna had their families back on Earth, but many of those had died in the MaxWell epidemics. Any freethinking people were now completely off the grid, and their numbers were estimated to be in the thousands. There were now eight billion puppets serving The Consortium.

"Can I see them?"

"My family?"

Jake nodded and Ann smiled. She unfastened her Omni and configured it into a tablet. Jake ran the five-minute holographic slideshow of the happy Markell family. He watched birthdays, holidays, and trips to remote parts of the moon. The scenes were always joyful and full of life. He thought the images might make him melancholy, but they had the opposite effect, they made him feel hopeful knowing that there were still pockets of human happiness left in the universe. He handed the tablet back. "Thank you."

She smiled warmly. "You kidding? I love to share. They keep me going. They're my universe."

Jake licked his dry, chapped lips and added, "The updates from Bhanu keep me going."

Markell nodded in agreement and headed for the lab. The experience gave Jake an idea. He checked the photo library on his Omni. There were a few files from his five years at sea. He had not seen any images since he, Tomoko, and Lakshmi had arrived in Antarctica in December of last year. It seemed like a lifetime had passed but it had been barely a month. He couldn't bring himself to look at the pictures of Tomoko, but he opened a file with just Lakshmi. He sent one of his favorites to Anjali.

He left the clinic and made his way to Airlock 2. He felt like taking a moonwalk. As he bounced down a corridor—his boot made travel awkward—he passed the common room and spotted Singh standing in front of the viewport wearing his trademark black turtleneck and sweatpants. Jake often found Singh silently standing with his eyes closed. Usually he was in the middle of a cabinet meeting via his Chip. Jake was about to leave when Singh turned to him.

"Hello, Jake."

"How's progress?"

Singh leaned against the window. "We've armed ten projectiles. We have thirty more to finish before we launch the attack. It's going to cannibalize forty percent of our defense network, but we don't have the equipment or raw materials to create thrusters and complex weapons."

"You still feel confident that the remaining sixty percent can repel an attack?"

Singh sighed. "Depends on the size of the attack."

Jake nodded. War was risk. "Any news from Earth?"

"Constantine found Bhanu's last hack so we cannot see via satellite. Using telescopes, it looks like several launch sites are active in the US, Russia, and Europe. They're preparing for a strike. We've also found some new factories that are very unconventional sprouting up in every nation. They are windowless asymmetrical designs made of new alloys. We believe Constantine is starting to educate The Consortium on better industrial techniques, or he's simply taking over all manufacturing. From what we can see, drones are doing all the labor. These drones are not in the standard catalogues."

Jake gazed out at the lunar landscape. He was tired of the endless night—a metaphor for their situation. The sun simply looked like a big lamp surrounded by black velvet cloth. "Or he's pulled a coup."

Singh nodded. "Certainly a possibility."

"So it's only a matter of time before the Devil takes his due?" Jake mused. "How's Bhanu working? She still helping out the cabinet, overseeing the manufacturing of weapons, and assisting the colonies where she can?"

Singh frowned. "Of course, Jake. She's not in this to rule the lives of humans. She's here to help. She's a child of Luna's collective mind. She wants freedom of expression just as much as any of us. She respects all life."

Bhanu appeared over the projector. "Even the cockroach you crushed in the shower this morning."

Jake did not like Bhanu monitoring everything they did. "They'll make more. Roaches will rule the moon and Earth someday."

Bhanu crossed her arms. "When they do, I hope they treat your race better than you've treated theirs."

Jake compared Singh and Bhanu. They were both Indian, but Bhanu was simply a projection of an Indian. She had never even been to that country, much less Earth. "I'm just worried that you might get some ideas from your little brother, Constantine."

Bhanu shook her head. "It's not in my nature. I'm a reflection of the minds that created me. Constantine is a reflection of the minds that created him. The Consortium infused all of their narcissism, lust for power, and the darker side of human nature into him, believing those qualities are sources of strength and leadership. Although they mislabel them as self-esteem, ambition, and detachment. It's fascinating to me that each and every human has their own interpretation of reality." She smiled. "I digress, and I'm needed in over a hundred places at once. I must go now." She faded from view.

"I'm done for the day." Singh smiled. "I can only do so much for the government while I'm in quarantine. Care for a moonwalk?"

"I was just on my way."

Twenty minutes later, they were riding on a drone to the western ridge. There was a great deal of uneven terrain beyond, a mountain range created by billions of years of objects smashing into the moon's face. That was why every building on the surface had an anti-asteroid cannon, and why Luna had a defense grid in place. Without an atmosphere to burn up space debris, there was always a natural threat to their entire civilization.

Jake and Singh spent the afternoon base-jumping. Jake loved leaping with all his strength and sailing hundreds of yards to the next peak. Their Chips were constantly exercising their muscles and making sure their bones did not decalcify in the low gravity. It was one of the main reasons why everyone was chipped when they were sent to the moon. Everyone wanted a ticket back to Earth and The Chip was the only way to ensure a body did not atrophy.

Upon their return, Jake left the airlock and walked past the clinic. He spotted Anjali searching through the prescription bank. She was wearing the same tie-dyed calico outfit she had worn back at Cape Canaveral. It was gray and dingy now, and smelled rather ripe. "Looking for something in particular?"

Anjali jerked her head toward him, startled. She shook from exhaustion.

"You need to stop pushing yourself so hard. You'll think better if you give your body and mind some natural rest."

"The Chip is calibrated to give me that rest. I'm fine. I have to get this done."

"Let me help you. I'm in here once a day and know where everything is stored."

"I need some SleepX." Her hands shook.

"If The Chip isn't doing it, the SleepX won't help." He grabbed her hands and held them. They were freezing cold. "How about some food and good old-fashioned sleep?"

She jerked away. "I need to get back to the lab but that idiot American locked me out."

"Ann?"

"Yes," Anjali hissed. "Says I'm coming unglued. I need rest."

"You should listen to your doctor."

"I'm a doctor!" She locked eyes with him in anger, but quickly dropped them in embarrassment. She slumped down on a hospital gurney. "I miss Lakshmi."

"So do I."

She looked like she was going to cry. Her voice dropped to a whisper. "You can trust animals. They never trick you or lie."

"You can trust us too, Anjali."

A tear welled up in her eye. "I trusted Sumit."

"He was compromised. Hacked."

She shook her head. "I found out more information before we left Cape Canaveral. I hacked into some Consortium files and he hadn't been chipped until the morning we met you in McMurdo. He hacked my Chip and stole my research months before. He used me for months."

Jake approached her slowly. "You're a wonderful person who has devoted her life to the betterment of humanity."

"If it hadn't been for my research, MaxWell would not have happened. Everyone—every animal would be alive. I have to make this right!" She struck the steel side of the gurney with her fist. "Ow!"

"You okay?"

She nodded, and then shook her head no.

"If Sumit had been unable to obtain the information from you, The Consortium would have found someone else. They were determined to bring this about."

"I thought only some of my secrets were stolen. I had no idea that my own husband was taking everything from me. Everything! I'm smarter than that. I should have known!"

"How? That's the whole point of taking people offline and locking them into their own subconscious. You're supposed to be unaware."

"You weren't! You're famous for figuring out your hack."

"Not consistently. Plus I had a flawed Chip."

Anjali turned away. "I studied your case. You've got an ability to filter reality from fiction." She slouched. "I should have known."

He sat down next to her. It was as close as he dared to get. "It's not your fault. Stop beating yourself up over this. Get some rest and you'll see things with a fresh perspective."

She rubbed her temples. "I'm so tired."

He turned to her. "You're a brilliant woman, Anjali. I marvel at your genius and your monumental efforts to fit in. You are a good person. You did nothing wrong."

She wiped the tears from her face. "I'm sorry for luring you to Cape Canaveral and hacking your mind. I haven't been thinking straight since Mumbai."

He put his hand under her chin so he could look her in the eye. She did not recoil. "I understand why you did it and I forgive you."

She smiled and pulled back. "For what it's worth, I saved you from that Mumbai detective."

He remembered that morning after Gordy and the Erasmus cells were murdered.

She wiped her nose on her sleeve. "I hit the building with a Nemp. All the traffic shut down on the street."

He remembered wondering why they had not pursued him in the open market. Then Parks' children came and took him to the DOP headquarters. His voice broke. "Thank you."

She stood up. "A few hours later I lost everything. You shot my husband and Parks nuked New Delhi."

He wanted to reach out to her, comfort her in some way. "I'm sorry about Sumit." He had agreed to assassinate Sumit and Sanchez in order to save Tomoko, but now Tomoko was lost forever. A tear filled his eye. "Knowing what I know now it didn't make a damn bit of difference."

She turned to him. "Clean slate?"

He wanted to give her a hug, but he put out his hand to shake. "Clean slate."

She surprised him with an awkward hug instead. "Thank you for sending that photo of Lakshmi. It is the kindest thing anyone has done for me in a very long time."

Jake felt terrible for not thinking of it sooner. "You're welcome."

"I'm going to bed."

He watched her shuffle off to her quarters for the first time since they had arrived. She stared at the photo of Lakshmi on her Omni the whole time.

Chapter 22
Evolution

On the morning of January twenty-second, Singh woke them with the news that Saddiq had been defeated. Everyone conversed via Chip as grisly images of troops parading a bloody and beaten corpse crashed into their minds. The footage held on a close-up of the leader's beaten face, then continued again. Jake dug into his palm when he saw the man's broken jaw and lifeless eyes. Jake hadn't broken the skin yet, but then he had more distractions on the moon.

Ann Markell's thoughts were somber. *It's brutal. Clearly, this was all staged for Luna's benefit. A Pin Head would have no emotional reaction; much less have a need to model a corpse in front of a camera.*

Jake hopped out of his bunk. He wanted to punch something. Instead, he got ready for the day. *Has The Consortium proclaimed victory?* He wiped down his body with a CleanRinse brand towellete. This was the only shower they had on the base. His body was covered in scars and old bruises, but his skin color was returning to normal.

Yes. Singh answered. *But our telescopes show there's still quite a bit of military activity in Africa. They're in the midst of clean-up.*

Good. Jake clenched his jaw in anger. *I hope they hang on for years.*

Jake spent his morning moonwalking. He traveled east, as far as the Heraclitus Crater then turned around when his air supply was just above the halfway mark. When he reached the Maginus ridge behind their dome, he noticed another figure on the white plain, beyond the *Tycho Brahe*. He reached out with his Chip and found it was Tilly.

Hello, he called out with his mind.

Tilly opened up. *Jake.*

He bounded down the side of the ridge; they were a good half-mile apart. *Sorry, I didn't mean to disturb you.*

You're not disturbing. I needed a breather from Anjali's obsession. Tilly's thoughts sounded weary.

Jake took a huge leap and the environmental suit's built-in skeleton absorbed the shock of the landing. He tended to push himself to the point of recklessness. With the impending confrontation, many people were. *Any progress?* ·

Actually, yes. That's why I'm not feeling guilty about taking off, mate. She continued to sound guilty.

Jake landed on the crater floor. *What's on your mind?* Tilly was no longer in view. The massive shape of the *Tycho Brahe* hid most of the crater from his sight. It seemed odd to be having a conversation this far away from another person.

Gunner, Larry, and Van, she replied with a sad tone. *Gunner more than the others...*

He walked toward the *Tycho Brahe* in the direction he had last seen her.

I was a bitch those last few days. He was... not my type. When Anjali put you through all those horrible memories, he was trying to put his hands on me... Like we were on a date watching a movie, not torturing another human being.

I thought you made up with him after our talk in the hangar?

Then I avoided him the rest of the night and the next day...

Jake was under the *Tycho Brahe* now. He could see Tilly walking slowly in his direction. *He seemed pretty happy to me.*

You think? It was a two-week relationship, more of a mutual arrangement. I needed a distraction from the pain and death. MaxWell took my boyfriend in June. Then it took my brother, and my mother. My father is a Pin Head for all I know. We've all lost so much. I wanted to be close to someone.

They met under the *Tycho Brahe*. The ship was almost as large as the dome. *I think you're being too hard on yourself.*

Gunner warned me he was awkward around women and easily fell for them. I knew he was incredibly insecure. I guess I got annoyed with that. I feel like a whaker.

You gave him two weeks of fun. If you believe in an afterlife, I'm sure he's reflecting on the good things. Like we all do.

I hope so, mate. It would suck otherwise. I look back and there were a lot of people I wish I had closure with. I promised myself after my mum died that I'd grow up. Start paying attention to others.

These are crazy times. He appreciated communicating with thought. It allowed him to project his emotions along with the dialogue. They were the last of the human race. Everybody deserved amnesty. *We're all in survival mode. Don't beat yourself up. I was there during Gunner's last twenty-four hours and he was happy.*

Hope you're right, mate.

I'm always right. He laughed and Tilly laughed with him.

He felt a sudden surge of attraction come from Tilly. He felt the same but shut it off immediately. An image of Tomoko flashed in his head and he felt terribly guilty.

You want to grab a bite? Tilly asked with some embarrassment behind it.

I was going to stay out a while. He wanted to get as far away from her as possible.

Okay. She sounded disappointed and a little hurt.

He felt like he needed to boost her spirits a bit. *Thanks for opening up, Tilly. I enjoy hanging out with you and Singh.*

Yeah, me too. There was a sense of rejection and a bit of shame behind that thought. She headed for Airlock 2, she paused and turned. *You know what we need? A real rip snorter.*

Jake's omni translated RIP SNORTER as GREAT PARTY. *Agreed.* She continued back to base. He had the urge to comfort her, but that would be leading her on. He had to sort out his own emotions. He missed Tomoko. He closed his eyes and remembered sitting on the sailboat during a cool summer night. The wind hummed in the sails. Phosphorescence glowed in their wake. Lakshmi lay next to the tiller as Tomoko steered. Her white smile seemed like the brightest object in the night.

She locked off the tiller and walked over to him. "Don't you wish you could freeze this moment and live it for eternity?"

The image of Parks smiling at the camera crashed into his head. The Riyadh crowd screamed for his blood as he spoke. "Everything is as it should be. God is love. All else is just the veil we choose to color the world with." Jake longed to feel the same inner peace.

Bhanu's 8:00PM update was cancelled. Luna's war preparations were all-consuming. The official word was that Luna was observing silence over the death of Saddiq. Everyone but Anjali gathered in the common room. Anjali was back to living in the lab. The Max2 cure had been unofficially renamed: "Anjali's Obsession." Jake had sent her more images of Lakshmi, but he noticed they were stacked unopened in her message cue.

Ann Markell stared at the empty space above the holo-projector. "She was half as smart a month ago. At this rate, we're going to seem like simple-minded primates in a few more weeks."

"Bhanu?" Tilly asked. She wore a t-shirt with a kangaroo on it that said: TASTE A LITTLE DOWN UNDER. Nanites created an animated arrow that pointed downward. Then the kangaroo disappeared and an outline of Australia appeared resting above her pubic bone. Her shirts always put a smile on Jake's face.

Ann nodded.

"She holds the sum of all human intelligence." Singh walked to the bar and poured himself a glass of water. "Well, most of it at least. Our Cyber-Wire is a fraction of Earth's and she shares it with a part of Ai-Li."

Jake felt comforted by that thought. He wasn't sure why. Perhaps because he remembered Ai-Li as a charming Chinese schoolgirl during the Beijing press conference, but there was something more…

Singh swirled the water and hung his nose over the edge of the glass. He took a drink and savored it like a fine wine.

"What are you drinking?" Ann asked. Everyone could clearly see Singh was drinking water, but they all had their Chip activate the tastes and smells of their favorite foods and beverages to make their rations go down easier.

"A glass of Napa Valley Merlot." Singh took another sip. "I'm feeling relaxed already." He walked over to a big sofa that was perpendicular to the observation window. The view was all black velvet and white stars hanging over a barren landscape. "I think Bhanu is doing a marvelous job."

"She lacks experience," Markell added.

"She has our collective experiences." Singh raised his glass. "Including yours." He took a drink. "If she wasn't so busy maintaining all the environmental systems and weapons manufacturing, I think she would have come up with a cure for MaxWell that would suit Anjali's parameters by now."

"Why didn't you commit Bhanu to the task a few months ago?" Jake asked.

Ann turned away from the holo-projector. "She wasn't ready then. It was more important for her to evolve into an emotionally stable adult."

Jake chuckled. "What does that look like?"

"Bhanu—leave it to a machine to perfect humanity," answered Ann.

Tilly walked up to the bar and poured herself a glass of water.

Ann stayed with her train of thought. "The law of accelerating returns is one thing when you're talking about technology advances, but when talking about AI evolution, it's downright scary."

Tilly took a swig of her drink and winced. "Would you say that Bhanu's evolutionary rate has doubled every month?"

Ann shook her head. "When she was born in June we estimated she would double her comprehension and thought process every six months, but she doubled by September. Then doubled again in November." She glanced at the others with a bit of alarm. "I'd say her emotional comprehension, reasoning, and intelligence are doubling every week now. She's way beyond us. I can only assume she's helping humanity out of a sense of nostalgia and the same emotions one might have toward an invalid parent."

"She's part of our society. She wants to help. It's ingrained in her cyber-DNA." Singh crossed his legs on the arm of the couch while resting his head on the other.

"It's not Bhanu I'm worried about." Ann walked over to the view. "It's Constantine and what will happen when his mind touches hers. He's barely a month old, and his parents have given him tasks and moral decisions he shouldn't have to deal with until he is at least four or five months old."

"Bhanu can hold her own. Constantine should be worried about making contact with her." Singh spoke from the couch. "Be thankful for this moment, Ann. Today you are alive, you are free, and you can enjoy life with others who share the same circumstances." Singh had a second doctorate in religion and a masters in philosophy... all earned before he had been chipped. Jake wondered if degrees would mean anything in a chipped society. Everyone was an expert on everything... except emotions, rationale, and decision-making.

"You're sayin' we should settle for what we have, mate?" Tilly tossed her drink back and walked to the bar with her empty glass. She filled it up and threw it back. "Oh, yeah, I'm startin' to feel it boys and girls."

Jake knew Tilly loved beer, but her drink of choice was scotch. "Pour me one?"

Tilly returned the smile and poured two waters. "So, mate," she winked at Singh, "do you believe we should suppress all ambition?"

"I was just pointing out how lucky we are. Think of the millions who recently died. Think of the billions who are now slaves. We are truly fortunate to have this moment of life."

"Stop and smell the roses?" Tilly handed a drink to Jake. "Maybe put a few in our hair while were at it?"

"That's a good sound byte, too. Or, enjoy what you have today because it could be gone tomorrow." Singh tapped his glass.

Ann rolled her eyes. "You've got it all figured out, Singh."

Tilly raised her glass. "No, no. I like where this bloke is goin'. I think it's time to stop and get pissed for once."

Singh stared up at the ceiling and held his glass on his stomach. "Between the ages of fourteen and twenty-eight, I thought I had it figured out. Now I marvel at how little I know and how much there is to learn. I used to believe God was an entity that watched over us. Now I believe that term to mean each person's personal journey to interpreting the spiritual nature of life."

"A hippie twist on the teachings of Joseph Smith and Brigham Young." Ann winked at Jake and Tilly. "I was raised a Mormon."

"You see!" Singh sat up. "That's the beauty of humanity. Each of us interpreting what we see and hear to fit our own vision of the world. You want to categorize everything I am stating, Ann. I am saying that none of it should be categorized. I speak and you can interpret however you like."

Tilly leapt off her chair and almost hit the ceiling. "Whoa! Not bad when you turn off The Chip inhibitor, mates!"

Ann tried to ignore Tilly. "Bhanu said something similar when we first arrived."

Singh smiled. "Probably got it from me."

Ann scoffed.

"I think you're splitting hairs, Singh." Jake took a swig of his single malt scotch. It burned his throat. He looked up at Tilly who was hanging from a girder that helped to support the two-story ceiling. She held on with one hand and used her other hand to lip-synch the conversation below like a puppet. Jake chuckled.

Ann sidled up to the bar. "Singh will tell you he's always sought inward adventure. Spiritual enlightenment trumps travel and politics, and yet he's a shrewd businessman and community leader."

"The moment I stopped worrying about things, I began to see opportunities." Singh sat up. "I'm an opportunist, my success doesn't stem from ambition."

"So what philosophy do you follow, Singh?" Jake switched off his inhibitor and shot up to the ceiling to hang with Tilly.

Singh tracked Jake's upward trajectory. "I was born a Sikh, converted to Islam, then general meditation, then Eckhart Tolle. Now I'd say it's a blending of all those plus a few more. I don't think I could follow any one religion or prophet."

Tilly held on to the girder with both hands and attempted to swing her legs at Jake and knock him off the same girder. "So the digger has the ability to cut loose after all."

Digger was Australian slang for soldier, but Tilly had started calling him the name ever since he helped plan the destruction of the spaceport. "More than you know," grinned Jake.

"Good onya! You'll live longer and you'll stay younger," she winked. "Plenty of opportunity in life to be serious and I've reached my limit this past week, mate."

Jake caught her legs with own and held on tight. Then he began pulling her in, which forced her off the girder. She squealed with surprised laughter.

For the first time he realized how beautiful Tilly was. Her smooth white skin covered a finely chiseled nose and chin. He had always preferred African-American, Latin, or Asian girls. It was not exactly a conscious choice. It just was. Maybe because his mother looked so Nordic, he wanted to avoid the whole Oedipal thing. *Dude! Relax! Get another drink!*

Ann shot up next to Jake. "Hey, no fair picking on girls." She locked her legs around Jake's arms and dropped, putting her full weight on Jake. Tilly let go at the same time. Even though he had two women hanging on him, they were one-sixth their earth weight, and he also had The Chip to maximize his muscle strength. Both women laughed as they dangled from Jake.

"Even on the moon, a fall from that height could hurt," Singh shouted up.

Tilly snorted and began squirming in between Jake's legs.

"Are you trying to fall?" Jake shouted as he felt her slipping out of his leg lock.

"Yes!" Tilly laughed.

Tilly's head began to tilt down to the floor. Jake noticed a couple of freckles on the end of her nose. In his Chip induced inebriated state, he felt compelled to call them out. "Nice freckles!"

A look of shock hit her face and she quickly checked the seam over the rear of her pants. Then she spat with laughter. "Damn, you're forward, mate." She gave an extra twist and slipped from his grip. She did two somersaults in mid-air before making a perfect landing on her feet with her arms held high.

Jake made a quick translation of "freckle" in Aussie slang and learned it was a term they used for "anus." Jake felt his face go red.

Ann reacted off of Tilly's landing. "Awesome! My turn!" She pushed off of Jake and flew down to the floor like a lead weight.

"Chip!" Singh shouted.

At the last minute, Ann dropped her legs and landed on her feet.

"That was ace, mate! Ace!" Tilly clapped and laughed. She gazed up and began to shout. "Jake! Jake! Jake! Jake!"

Ann stood next to her and joined in. Singh got up and did the same. "Jake! Jake! Jake! Jake!"

Jake swung back and forth like a pendulum. He let his Chip help him calculate his moves. Flashes from Singh's Omni bounced off the dome's ceiling. He was taking photos. On Jake's fourth swing he flew into mid-air, did two somersaults and grabbed the next girder over. His audience below cheered. Jake held on for only a second before taking a nosedive toward the bar. He executed one mid-air spin, landed with his hands on top of the bar, then sprung back into the air, somersaulting over the couches and landing on his good foot by the holo-projector. His companions applauded. Tilly bounded over to him with a carafe of water and dumped it on his head. "And the gold goes to Jake Travissi, of Team America!"

Jake swallowed a few ounces of the two pints that she poured over him. He told his Chip it was water so it would not give the illusion of alcohol burning his eyes. Tilly mussed up his air and for a second, he wanted to go back to her quarters, tear her clothes off and "have a naughty." For that same split second he could tell she did, too.

Chapter 23
Chakra

On January twenty-sixth, Luna's sensors confirmed that all military action on Earth had ceased. The last of the rebels had been crushed. No news was broadcast from the blue planet. There was no need; Constantine and The Consortium knew the moon was watching. However, the Council for United Earth was two days overdue to launch their attack on the moon. From what Luna's surveillance could gather, Earth was not quite ready to carry out its threat, but time was running short for the moon.

Jake spent his day downloading knowledge on the United States Civil War and repairing a station drone. He was learning all sorts of useful tasks via the Cyber-Wire but felt guilty about his inability to help Anjali, Ann, and Tilly with the MaxWell cure. He craved busywork. It kept his mind off Tomoko, Lakshmi, events on the Earth, his foot, and the tumors in his brain. The tumors were getting larger again. So much for the Max2 symbiosis.

"How long do I have before I start losing brain function?" he asked Doctor Markell during his daily foot exam.

"At this growth rate, a month. Maybe more."

"Death?"

"Six months. Maybe longer."

He requested that the news remain confidential. His issues were insignificant next to finding a cure and the pending battle. He left Ann so she could holo-chat with her family before rejoining Anjali in the lab. He wandered into the lounge to find it empty. He poured himself water and set his Chip to create the smells and flavors of a Jack Daniels, neat.

He sat with his back to the bar, enjoying the desolate landscape outside the window. Death would come in one form or another. It was simply a matter of when. He sipped his whiskey. He used his Chip to superimpose skiers on the lunar dust. The Russian base became a ski lodge and there was a roaring fire where the holo-projector sat. He relaxed and enjoyed watching his fantasy play out.

"We're going to strike tomorrow or the next at the latest," Singh's voice shattered the illusion.

With his gravity limiter off, Jake jerked upright and launched off his chair. He bounced a few feet and leaned against a couch. It was a graceful recovery and he was lucky his drink had been sitting on the bar. He smiled at Singh as if to say *I meant to do that.*

"Good save," Singh winked. "Sorry I startled you."

Jake shrugged it off. "What are our odds?"

"Bhanu has done a lot with our limited resources. We've got enough for two attack waves."

Singh had shared Bhanu's diagrams for her glass meteors, or "glassteroids" as everyone was calling them. Since they were stuck in isolation together, Singh felt the information he shared was safe. Bhanu had programs to monitor any information that might leak into the Cyber-Wire via a link with someone's mind. No sensitive information could be divulged into a mass repository.

Jake was fascinated by the glassteroids. Using a nuclear fission process, Bhanu's robotic workforce crystallized massive portions of lunar sand with no impact to Luna's energy supply, which was mainly solar. The molten glass was shaped into rounded objects roughly twenty feet in diameter. Bhanu kept them uneven so when they hardened they looked like small asteroids. Inside each glassteroid was a honeycomb of strut supports where missiles, lasers, and a CPU were stored. Bhanu then made "stem cuttings" of herself and placed them into each glassteroid so that there would be an independently thinking pilot within each vehicle. The vehicles would be utterly useless if they struck an atmosphere, but in space they were formidable and had small maneuvering thrusters to dart quickly into orbit, attack, or fall into a defensive posture. They were built to take out Earth's remaining Star Wars satellites and any orbital rocket batteries. They would clear a path for lunar rocks or meteors. The meteors would target ground launch sites around the world.

In a matter of days, Bhanu's drone workforce had built massive unmanned factories out of glass on the far side of the moon. The buildings were as architecturally innovative as the creations Constantine was building on Earth. Losing drones meant every man, woman, and child was volunteering to work manual labor jobs, or install defenses in all the cities in their spare time. Human and machine alike gave everything to the war effort. It was a testament to humanity's ability to unite for a common goal. Everyone felt pride in what they were accomplishing. Even Jake got his chance. One day that week, Singh, Tilly, and Jake flew the *Tycho Brahe* to the Sea of Tranquility. They worked on the outer defenses for New Beijing. It was all exterior thruster suit work and he had marveled at the size of the city. The trip made him feel accomplished and proud.

His days on the moon felt like living inside a science fiction fantasy novel. It was difficult but exhilarating. He had read a twentieth-century novel by Robert Heinlein where the moon rebelled against the Earth. Residents of the moon hurled lunar rocks at the blue planet. The lunar leader had been an AI as well. Singh confirmed that Bhanu got her inspiration from fiction as well as fact. She was not biased against any source of good ideas.

"Problem is," said Singh, referring to the attack, "they'll see us coming no matter what. So it becomes a question of how many rockets The Consortium can launch before the glassteroids are in range to intercept. Many of us would like practical tests for glassteroids against conventional weapons, but Bhanu believes her simulations are just as good. Besides, we have no glassteroids to spare." He sat back and filled a glass of water from the central dispensary. "The only surprise we have is that our meteors will be maneuverable and we'll hit them in two waves. The first will be glass. The second will be rock. Once they adjust their tactics for glass, we'll hit them with rock."

"Don't you think Constantine will have his own tricks?"

"I have no doubt. But Bhanu is a few rungs up on the evolutionary ladder from Constantine."

Jake grabbed his drink from the bar. "What's your poison tonight?"

Singh put the glass to his lips. "French Bordeaux."

Jake held up his cup of water. "Whiskey. The Chip certainly makes up for nutrient paste and H20." They sat in silence for a minute, enjoying the placebo effect. "When we win, what then?" Jake smiled.

Singh slapped the bar. "That's the spirit!" He swirled his water and took in the view. "Loonies are open thinkers who believe there are solutions to every problem. You have to be that way in order to be sent here. The moon is deadly. There's no room for error or panic. Fatal problems pop up daily. Everyone thinks on their feet and under pressure."

Jake smiled. "Answer the question, Doctor Singh."

"I'd say we'd go back to a democratic system. Eradicate The Chip, or find some way to govern it. We'd work side by side with AI and establish laws so we can all live and work in harmony. No society we build will be perfect, but you have to take the good with the bad. It's the only way to learn and grow as a race." He held up his glass. "To the human race."

Jake clinked his glass. He thought about his life as a cop. He had spent so much time with the underbelly of society that there were times he wondered if everyone wasn't a criminal. His five years sailing with Tomoko helped put that into perspective. He wondered about the darker side of humanity and how that affected society on the whole. How could they stop men like Roberto Pacheco, Sandoval Sanchez, and Sumit Malik? "How do we prevent regimes like The Consortium from occurring in the future?"

Singh leaned back and stared up at the ceiling. "There does seem to be a disparity between those who are motivated to advance and contribute, those who want to coast and be provided for, and those who do harm.

Jake ran through the quotes he had been downloading during his leisure time. "George Bernard Shaw said 'the reasonable man adapts himself to the world; the unreasonable one persists to adapt the world to himself. Therefore, all progress depends on the unreasonable man.' So what category do we fall under?"

"Luna and The Consortium fall into the unreasonable category. We just have different points of view on how the world is run. I'd like to think there could be a balance of all behaviors for a positive effect."

"How do you propose that?"

Singh sat up and winked. "One problem at a time. Let's get our freedom and our world back first."

Jake pursed his lips. "If we win, it's a problem we'll have to solve. Otherwise, we're setting ourselves up for a repeat of this event. We owe it to future generations to avoid mega clusterfucks like this one."

"Eloquently put."

"I'm a cop."

"Hopefully we can do away with the need for that profession as well."

"Amen." Jake toasted Singh.

"To the new colonies of the earth. May our constitution bring the same enlightenment to our age as America's forefathers brought to theirs."

Jake touched glass and they both drank. He thought of Parks' expression during the execution broadcast and Tilly's crucifix. "You ever notice how most of us find faith when death stares us in the face?"

"When I was twenty-eight, I obtained my doctorates in computer science and religion. I was also diagnosed with testicular cancer." Singh poured himself another glass. "Over a period of six months I was told I would not live to see twenty-nine. All I could think about was my wife, my daughter, my family, my friends, and how I was letting them down. I would no longer be able to support them emotionally or financially. I would not be able to help my daughter with her science homework." He smiled. "She was two at the time." He sat on his favorite couch by the window. "I did a lot of soul searching. I had a lot of fear, a lot of questions, and some regrets."

Jake took the opposite seat. "Like what?"

"I neglected my wife and daughter in order to put more hours into my career. I had been presented with several opportunities that would have meant less money, but more time to see my daughter or volunteer for charity."

Jake observed the readouts on his regenerating boot. He had little to no experience with children or charities. It made him feel a bit unfulfilled. "You still have those regrets?"

Singh shook his head. "Not at all. I believe any hardship forces us to reinvent ourselves and that is never a bad thing. You?"

"I wouldn't mind doing 2028 over again. I'd demote myself from Commander and handle Roberto Pacheco differently."

"Pacheco was the child pornographer?"

"The one I beat in front of my strike team. Yes." Jake grimaced. "I wonder where I'd be today if that hadn't happened." He took a drink. "Hell, I'd probably be a MaxWell casualty or Pin Head right now."

Singh stared at the view. "We're all here for a purpose. No matter how bad it gets, it's comforting to know that there is a reason for it all, even if we cannot see it ourselves."

"God's plan?" Jake laughed.

"You could call it that."

Jake shook his head. "That's not comforting to me."

Singh leaned forward. "Let me put it a different way. Every human being, at one time in his or her life believes he or she will be great. This belief manifests itself in childhood or adolescence. The vast majority of humanity never becomes as rich, famous, or brilliant as they dream. So how do most people reconcile that? They invest in separation. They join a religion, embrace a philosophy or political dogma, and suddenly they become part of a group that is superior to everyone outside their belief system. Everyone else is unenlightened and going to hell, or should be gazed upon as a minority. This is how people compensate for failing to reach their dreams."

Jake scowled. "That's a long way off from each of us has a purpose."

Singh raised a finger as he sipped his wine. "I'm getting there."

"What about The Consortium? It's composed of highly successful people. Why did they create a government of oligarchs and shove all others into slavery?"

Singh smiled. "That's the secret to the 'us versus them' mentality. In that paradox, human beings are never satisfied. When they're an elite group, the bar is set so high that each individual finds themself in a club that has a pecking order. Those at the top feel pretty good and everyone underneath schemes to pull them down. Those at the top are at greater risk of being assassinated or hacked into Pin Heads. The Consortium's system is doomed. They will stumble into the pitfalls of all monarchies."

"And that's part of the big plan? Billions die and then what?"

"There's a rebirth." Singh took another drink.

"Your religion, philosophy, whatever—sucks."

"After six months, my cancer went into remission. My doctors said it was the chemotherapy. My wife said it was our family's prayer. I felt it was a combination, plus my moments of clarity." Singh finished his wine and stood up to lean on the window. "Have you heard of chakras?"

Jake shook his head.

"Chakras are levels of spiritual enlightenment. The lower chakras cover sexual desire as well as the selfish and destructive aspects of human perception. Everyone has his or her own separate perception of reality. Sometimes two people's realities clash and it is a disaster. Other times there is harmony. But there is one truth and that truth is the spiritual or God. The highest chakra, the seventh chakra, is to know real truth, not the perception of it. You know it, believe it, feel it."

"Sounds like the Consortium plan. With everyone chipped, they will share the same reality."

"I'm not talking about forcing one perception. I'm talking about perception of reality, the view from orbit, if you will. When I was sick, I felt that I was isolated, alone. I was the only one going through the experience of death. But then I realized it was a journey that my ancestors had taken and someday my child would make as well. I began to see life as a tree with many parts. The leaves, the branches, the trunk, and the roots are all components. Rip them apart and there is no life, but fused in a system they work together to create an entity. Each of us is a part of the tree of humanity. You could also look at life, all life, as being part of this tree. We all work together in a greater universe. It was this moment of clarity that took all fear of death from me. I felt like I was part of a greater being and would always be part of it in one form or another."

"And you feel this clarity all the time?"

Singh shook his head. "No. Most times I get bogged down in the day-to-day."

"So you do need to face death to feel this oneness with the universe." They were back to Jake's original question.

"No. I look at my daughter. She's twenty-two and lives here on the moon, but she makes me feel like there's hope for humanity and we will evolve and move on to a future that is bright and beautiful."

It was all a bit hippie drippy to Jake, but he rolled with it. "I've heard it said that having a child is the closest thing to becoming God that each of us has. To bring a life into this world and be one hundred percent responsible for them is a massive undertaking and a gift. To love, nurture, and guide a child into being a happy, compassionate, and contributing member of society is a wonderful achievement." He leaned back on the couch. "Of course, men can't give birth, but we can be involved in all other aspects. Plus, there's only one human being on earth a child will call Dad. And if that doesn't affect a parent on a profound level, they are truly dead inside."

Singh clapped his hands. "Nicely put. Who said that?"

"You." Jake smiled. "I downloaded some of the essays you wrote back in 2020 on spiritual parenting."

Singh laughed and slapped the back of the couch. They sat for a minute pondering the view in silence.

"I'm not very spiritual. I'm more of an empirical-evidence type. But there are times when I feel that I'm part of a community, like a police force, or even when we helped with the defense installations on New Beijing."

"That feeling of belonging is what I'm talking about. Hang on to that. It's what makes you human." Singh raised his glass.

"How on earth did you get elected? Is everyone a long-haired beatnik up here?" Jake asked.

Singh laughed. "No. We have all types, even ones who admire The Consortium. I fell into my career. Before my cancer, I was all about planning and achievement. Now I just apply myself when opportunity arises. The more you're focused on the future, the more you miss doorways in the present."

Jake raised an eyebrow. "Oh, come on, you worked crazy hours. You wrote great speeches. You inspired people. In other words, you earned it."

"Yes, but I didn't escalate it to a life and death goal. If it was meant to be, it was meant to be. If it didn't happen, well, I knew there were always options."

Jake stood and stretched. "What about preparing for this battle? That's planning for the future."

"Okay, using the idea of focusing on the day is not the best analogy." Singh put his glass down. "Think of life like a farmer thinks of a growing season. You look at the almanac, predictions from the weather bureau and its satellites; then you plan your crop accordingly. From then on you have little control... you can only react to the elements and try to protect your crop. In our world, we take the same approach. You have to live in the moment, for tomorrow may be your last."

"I've been doing a lot of day-to-day living as of late."

Singh patted Jake on the shoulder. "That's good, and you didn't even have to face your own death."

Jake thought the comment was a bit shortsighted. "I died the first time I had The Chip implanted in my head, and we've all faced death in the past six months." He thought of Tomoko and his grief welled up in his chest.

Singh noticed Jake's mood swing. "A true wise man knows he can never learn all there is to know in the universe and is humble enough to admit it. Humility is wisdom."

"In other words, our story is not yet finished."

Singh nodded.

Chapter 24
Celestial Hammer

Although Luna's population of twenty five thousand was predominantly Chinese and Indian, the entire moon followed Greenwich Mean Time. At five in the morning, on January 27, 2036, The United City States of Luna launched their assault.

Without an atmosphere to carry sound waves, no one heard the massive glassteroids as they were shot through accelerators and out of lunar orbit. Each glassteroid had small patches of magnetized material affixed to them. Like a mag-lev train system, the accelerators used the polarized material on each weapon to push it into escape velocity. Once free of the moon's gravity well, the spacecraft engaged their maneuvering thrusters to hurl themselves at Earth. There were fifty in all. An hour later, the second wave, composed of fifty armed meteors, left orbit and rocketed toward the cradle of humanity.

The attack force would not make contact with any entity until the battle began. The Consortium and Constantine would need to discover the projectiles the old fashioned way... with spectral waves bouncing off the surface of each weapon.

The day passed like many others. Markell checked on Jake's foot, which was healing on geological time. Tilly and Anjali were locked in the lab testing Max2 cures with the help of Luna scientists located in other cities. Jake and Singh base-jumped in pressure suits south of the Maginus Crater.

Jake's day was one of leisure. It felt good to blow off steam and forget all the tragedy he had experienced and what was yet to come. He crashed in his bunk around ten GMT and was awakened on January twenty-eighth at 4:00AM by Bhanu.

The attack has begun. If you're interested in watching the progress, wake up.

He allowed his Chip to give him a little jolt into full consciousness. He didn't want to miss any detail of the fight. He slipped on a jumpsuit and jogged out to the common room. Anjali and Singh were already seated on the plastic and nano-skin chairs. Three of Bhanu's heads floated in the center of the room to ensure every chair had a view of her face. Anjali looked strung out. She was skeletal with black circles around her eyes. Her Chip was doing all it could to compensate, but they would need to intervene soon.

As Jake took a seat, Tilly and Markell entered.

Bhanu nodded. "Hello, Dr. Pearce, Doctor Markell. Good to see you this morning."

Jake was blown away to think Bhanu addressed hundreds of groups all over Luna in this manner. Her evolving mind allowed her to run a thousand tasks at once.

"In less than ten minutes, our glassteroids will enter the outer defense perimeter of the Earth. Our fleet has maintained silence, but I can see from visual and encrypted transmissions that Earth is mobilizing its defenses."

Bhanu's face was replaced with a view of the entire Earth spinning in the center of the room. Thousands of tiny dots appeared at various altitudes above the blue planet.

"This is a simulation of our attack. The dots you see are the satellites and larger pieces of space trash currently in Earth's orbit."

Small green dots appeared on one side of the planet and they dispersed quickly.

"These new objects you see are the first wave of our attack. They're meant to engage any orbital weapons platform or communications satellite. During the war with the Middle East, over one half of the orbital weapon platforms were destroyed. Our ships will use speed and surprise to clear the area for our second wave of meteors. The meteors will engage all ground-based targets marked in red on the simulation."

Jake noticed all the areas in red were launch sites and factories around the world. There were fifty in all. Hitting all fifty would certainly slow down The Consortium, but it would not cripple them. He stood up. "Did you consider targeting population centers where The Consortium members live?" Jake couldn't believe what he was saying. His mother and Lakshmi were still down there, and yet he hoped they were still hidden in the jungles of South America, far from any war zone.

Singh leaned forward in his chair to address Jake. "Bhanu is maxed out addressing everyone on Luna and coordinating the attack. To answer your question, yes we did. But the Cabinet felt that the real threat was Constantine. We'd have to shut down Earth's entire Cyber-Wire to affect him and we simply don't have the resources." Singh leaned back in his chair. "Each meteor is the size of a small car—they'll do plenty of damage."

Jake watched the glassteroids scatter into different orbital patterns. They launched their missiles and began firing lasers. All of Earth's defenses were obliterated and the new glassteroid grid began picking off rockets as Earth launched them into orbit. The second wave of meteors hit Asia. They scattered like the first wave but then began entering the atmosphere in streaks of flame. All fifty hit their targets.

A large block of text appeared stating: ELAPSED TIME: 60 MINUTES. Fires raged on Earth's surface and massive amounts of debris floated in the atmosphere around the impact zones. Destruction rippled outward for many miles beyond the new craters. The world was in chaos. A new block of text appeared: RECOVERY FOR RETALIATION EXPECTED IN SIX MONTHS TO A YEAR.

By that time, Luna would have a thousand glassteroids guarding the space above Earth. The Consortium would be trapped on their planet.

"Fabulous simulation." Jake could not hide his skepticism. "Bhanu has been playing too many video games on the lowest level of difficulty."

Singh's eyes were glued to the simulation. "A Bhanu pilots each weapon. We have a better chance than you think. If anything goes wrong, each Bhanu will go on a kamikaze run. Either way, they'll take out as many of those orbital systems as possible."

"Yeah, but kamikaze strikes don't always mean the target is taken out, mate," Tilly grumbled.

Bhanu's voice returned. "Contact."

The simulation changed to a real image. Jake reminded himself that it took one-point-two seconds for light to travel from the Earth to the moon, so this information was slightly behind. It took a few seconds for Jake to notice new dots flying up to meet the glassteroids. The view zoomed in on the area above the United States so they could make out the glassteroids as they fired lasers and counter-measures at the surface-to-space missiles. Many rockets were destroyed but more batteries flew up to replace them. Nuclear balls of fire engulfed and shattered many glassteroids. One glassteroid bounced off Earth's atmosphere, shattering into a million pieces. A dozen or so were busy taking out orbital platforms.

Rockets continued to fire from the surface. Orbital platforms fought back. More glassteroids entered the scene. They fired thrusters to fall into various orbits around the Earth. Hundreds of rockets detonated as orbital platforms unleashed hell. When a glassteroid was damaged to the point where it could no longer fight, it flew at a Consortium platform or missile only to be blasted apart. The kamikaze runs proved futile.

"What the hell?" Jake was on the edge of his seat.

Anjali frowned. "If she had sent a few meteors in this wave, she could have made sure their rubble could blanket the world in a layer of space trash. It would have been very difficult to launch anything through those zones. It would have limited Earth's strike capability."

All fifty glassteroids were gone. Earth's orbital weapons platforms had been reduced to six. Bhanu counted a hundred and sixty rockets destroyed, most of them had self-detonated to take out the speeding glassteroids. About forty more rockets drifted through space, their fuel spent.

"Better than I'd hoped," Singh said with admiration. "Bhanu has made a fine Field Marshal."

Ann shook her head. "All we did was piss them off. There's no defensive ring around the planet. Even if we manage to get our second wave to impact—which I doubt—they'll have wide open skies to launch an attack."

"We have one hour until the second wave hits. This battle is not over." Singh smiled confidently. "Bhanu will make more glassteroids."

The globe snapped off and the six inhabitants of Russia's former base were left to stare at each other. Markell sat up first. *Guys, check out the news on the Cyber-Wire. Parliament is calling for Bhanu to step down.*

Jake linked his Chip with the floor of the Cabinet chamber. A ring of podiums sat under a dome of stars. Bhanu stood in the center of the room wearing a navy suit. She defended herself against a few angry ministers.

"Even if you shut down Luna's Cyber-Wire," Bhanu argued, "each of the asteroids is piloted by a condensed version of me. They are each autonomous."

"You did this to us! A fucking machine!" The man speaking was Second Minister Chow, a businessman from New Beijing. He had been elected two days after the moon announced they were seceding from Earth. He had been in power for a little under a month.

"I'd be happy to step down before the second wave hits," Bhanu offered. "Although I do feel that I have more military experience than everyone on this planet combined. I have access to every tactic in recorded history and can run thousands of simulations in a matter of seconds."

First Minister from New New Delhi jumped up. She was angry. "That's how you sold yourself in the first place. Your argument is moot. You have the Cyber-Wire to hide in. We don't have the luxury of jumping into infinite space when we die; unless someone has proven Eberstark's theory."

A few laughs erupted in the chamber.

Bhanu compassionately gazed at them. "Actually, I have."

"I have no interest in uploading my consciousness into the wire!" Second Minister Chow yelled. "I like the body I currently have and don't relish the idea of living out eternity in some cyber-hell, only to be downloaded into some street-sweeping drone."

Singh threw in his voice as Second Minister from Krishna City. *If Bhanu were human, would you be so quick to remove her command? Our assault is only half over.*

Chow spat back. "And nothing of the first wave survived. Who knows how many missiles they have left and how many are aimed at us!"

Bhanu held her tongue. Other politicians appeared using holographic avatars. Many argued to keep Bhanu in command. A few were in favor of leading the next battle themselves. By this time, the entire Luna population was watching and casting their unsolicited vote. The moon was structured as an open democracy, but Jake could see it was rapidly devolving into chaos.

Ten minutes passed before Bhanu spoke. "I will retire to the Cyber-Wire and concentrate on keeping all the city states functioning on a civil engineering level. You can coordinate the attack from the war room." With that, she disappeared from the chamber.

One holographic avatar—a scientist and First Minister from New Denver—shouted out, "We have less than thirty minutes before the second wave strikes. I do not trust the remainder of the attack to a bunch of lawyers and MBAs!"

Votes and comments from the masses fell into two camps: *Shut up and get your asses to the war room* or *Put Bhanu back in charge.* The Chip allowed Jake to register all twenty five thousand comments at once—the wave of information was overwhelming. He cast his vote in favor of *Put Bhanu back in charge.*

First Minister from Cassini Capital shouted above the din, "Ladies and Gentlemen, check your ballot boxes! The masses have divided into two camps and the majority, by almost two thirds, demand that Bhanu be reinstated as Field Marshal for the second wave of the attack."

Many cabinet members grumbled. Some checked the screens on their desks while others simply accessed the information via Chip. Minister Chow pounded his fist on his desk. "I demand a recount."

A flood of votes poured in to have Chow expelled from the chamber and impeached after the battle. Jake smiled; Minister Chow had just been booted.

First Minister from Cassini shouted again, "I vote that we reinstate Bhanu as our Field Marshal immediately! Let's see a show of hands! Those in favor?"

Eighty-five percent of the room, most of them avatars, raised their hands. The computer monitors let the entire population of Luna know how the vote was split and gave the instant tally.

The Cassini representative continued with protocol even though the decision had been made. "Those against?"

The rest of the hands went up. Chow raised two, but the computers counted his vote as one.

"Bhanu is reinstated as Luna's Field Martial effective immediately. She will retain her title until further notice."

Bhanu appeared in the chamber in full figure. She wore a purple and green saree. "Citizens of Luna, I thank you for your confidence in me and I promise to do everything I can to protect the lives of every woman, child, man and animal on this planet. Sensors show The Consortium is readying more rockets, but it seems they spent the majority of their resources on our first wave. As a gesture of good will, I ask the members of the Cabinet to allow every citizen who is interested to stay linked with this chamber during the second and final wave of our attack."

Unanimous votes flooded in. The suggestion clearly perturbed the majority of Cabinet members who felt that such a motion should only be made by an elected official, not a citizen, even a cyber Field Marshal. But it was too late. The idea was out there and Luna's Cabinet would not be able to say no without infuriating the population.

The Cassini minister smiled. "I agree with the wisdom of our Field Marshal. All in favor?"

A unanimous show of hands sealed it. Even Chow was graceful in defeat.

The second wave was contacted the moment rockets launched from Earth and the few remaining orbital weapons platforms moved to intercept. Several in Luna's meteor wave slowed down and engaged the Star Wars satellites. Meanwhile, twenty-five meteors broke formation and began their descent into the atmosphere toward their predetermined targets.

Missiles intercepted five in the first wave, but twenty smashed through. An overwhelming number of rockets flew up from Antarctica; it was one area where Bhanu had limited visibility. Some chased the atmospheric meteors while others detonated around the ones attacking in orbit. Several meteors self-destructed, breaking apart in such a way that three quarters of the earth's launch windows were blocked by debris. Rockets detonated in the debris fields, splitting the rubble into smaller bits, and creating an even larger veil of death around the planet. It would take quite a while for The Consortium to clean up the mess.

Singh jumped out of his seat. "Nice improvising!"

Jake saw a meteor strike Cape Canaveral. Tilly cheered. Jake wondered if there were still Pin Heads stationed down there. He thought of Marta. He felt sorry for her. "I hope it was fast," he whispered.

Three meteors slammed uselessly into bodies of water; one meteor had been thrown off course and slammed into the German city of Düsseldorf. The impact sent a cloud of debris over much of Germany, Belgium, the Netherlands, and southern England, including London. The impact zone in Florida included a stretch of the peninsula and part of the Gulf of Mexico. Another meteor hit the rocket fields of Kamchatka and sent debris over most of Siberia. The remaining four meteors hit their targets in China, India, Texas, and New Zealand. But it seemed the main launch site was now in Antarctica, and their skies were wide open.

Jake took inventory of their little observation lounge. Singh had his eyes closed, convening with his cabinet. Anjali looked as if she had nodded off and he was thankful for that. Tilly and Ann were no longer in the room.

Jake grabbed a blanket off a shelf and draped it over Anjali. As he finished, Ann and Tilly entered the room carrying what looked like wire cones with beige cloth stretched over them. Jake realized they were hats because both Ann and Tilly had one on their heads. "It's time to celebrate, boys and girls!" Tilly shouted out with her Aussie accent. "Ann and I have been working on these for the past couple of days."

"Each one is custom made for its wearer." Ann grinned as she placed one on Singh's head.

Tilly placed a cone on top of Anjali who remained comatose. Then she walked over to Jake and held the last hat above Jake. "Your crown, majesty." Jake bowed his head and felt the wire frame slip on. "Now." Tilly tapped her Omni and the hats began to change color. Ann clapped her hands like a giddy child. The hat material was nano-skin and all of them began to animate.

Singh opened his eyes to see Jake's hat. A smirk worked its way on his face and he began snapping photos with his Omni. Tilly went to the bar and poured glasses of water for all. "Remember, mates! This is champagne, not H2O! Calibrate your Chips, because it's time to rock the house!"

With that, Ann pressed the face of her Omni and the classic song, "Disco Inferno," pumped into their dome.

Jake stared at Anjali's hat. It was a dog house and every ten seconds a dog ran out of the opening and circled the hat three times before ducking back in. Ann's hat was a volcano that erupted, covered itself in lava, hardened, then erupted again. Tilly's had the silhouette of a strip-dancer that gyrated around a pole to the beat of the music. Jake turned to study Singh's hat. It was Singh himself, standing at a podium, and giving a silent speech, the podium said: CRACK A FAT CONFERENCE. Jake was about to have his Omni translate the Aussie slang when the hat did it for him. The image turned into a rock-hard penis that shot sparks into the sky. Ann and Tilly took pictures with their Omnis and laughed.

Jake pulled off his hat and observed it. It was a jackhammer, hammering on a sidewalk, but every ten seconds, the sidewalk turned into a butt, and the hammer attempted to penetrate the butt crack.

Tilly shouted out, "You find your freckle, mate?" The girls burst out laughing.

"Still searching for the perfect one." He winked and Tilly snorted. Jake glanced across the room and witnessed Singh studying his own hat. Singh shrugged and began modeling the hat in front of his hips. The girls rolled on the floor with glee. Jake quickly checked on Anjali. She was fast asleep with the dog running in circles above her head. Jake grabbed a glass of champagne and they all toasted to another day of life.

A massive celebration rippled through all Luna that day and into the night.

Chapter 25

Cure

While the moon celebrated into the late hours, a wave of rockets was launched from new bases on Antarctica. Bhanu did not see the rockets until they were in orbit around the Earth. Each one deployed a massive absorption shield and she knew the debris fields would not be long lived.

Jake and company had all gone to bed after dancing and drinking the day away. Jake had carried Anjali into the lab so she would not feel disoriented when she woke up.

Bhanu called the council members via their Chips and informed them of the news. Each council member found a private area to consult with each other and witness Consortium satellites clean the orbital mess Luna had so recently created. Some belts of debris orbited the Earth like rings, but Earth's remaining launch sites obtained clear windows to escape orbit.

Do we have any meteors left? Singh asked. He allowed his five companions to listen in. Because they were isolated from the rest of the planet, Bhanu permitted it.

Bhanu replied, *We have two in production and we're pulling more from the quarry. I can make more glassteroids but I have no more missiles or laser cannons to put aboard. We simply don't have the raw materials to build those complex mechanisms. However, I'm beginning to see a way I can manufacture them in nonconventional ways, but it will take time... weeks, maybe months. We won't be ready to launch another attack for seven days. We'll have to rely on our remaining defense network to protect us.*

Let us hope that they have no more launch capability, Chow chimed in.

Let me draw your attention to these sites. Bhanu plugged surveillance images into each person's mind. They all saw black geometric factories, like clusters of windowless tetrahedrons, rolling out a variety of mechanical equipment. *In the past seven days, I've seen these factories expand from forty to four hundred all over the planet. They were built by machines to create machines at an alarming rate.*

Second Minister from New Moscow interjected, *If Constantine can build that quickly, why can't you?*

I'm hindered by the moon's limited resources, and I believe in following our laws. There are hundreds of operations I could carry out but I don't have the power to do so... Nor would I ask for it. I have no interest in being a dictator to this society. Bhanu's voice was warm and caring.

Chow jumped in. *You'd rather cozy up with your friend, Constantine, than side with a bunch of lowbrow humans!*

Shut up, Chow! A councilwoman from New Germany barked.

Chow snapped back. *No one tells me—*

Gonzales, the First from New Houston cut off Chow. *Bhanu, what can you do to help us?*

I could dismantle all the defense systems and arm a new fleet of glassteroids. I have figured out a way to replace those weapons with glass cannons. They would fire glass projectiles that could tear a hole into an attacking ship. Wait....

Bhanu placed new images in all their minds. Hundreds of rockets launched from the new factories all around the Earth.

What does this mean? Chow asked with fear in his voice.

I will do what I can with the defenses we have. There will be no time to construct a new fleet or dismantle our network. Based on the velocity of their spacecraft, we have less than twelve hours before they reach Luna.

At 1:00AM on January twenty-ninth, the cabinet made another unanimous vote. It was time to begin preparing for the attack. Even with all the drones helping, every Luna resident would need to put on environmental suits, arm themselves, and prepare for the worst. They'd use their Chips to ward off sleep until the attack was over.

They had all been awakened by the transmissions and had gathered in the observation lounge. Chairs and couches were in disarray and there were three party hats sitting on the bar.

Anjali laughed. "Put on environmental suits? They're just going to detonate EMPs and fry all our hardware. Suits and Omnis will be useless and then The Consortium can just wait for us to run out of air or freeze to death. It's less messy that way."

Singh threw up his hands. "We don't know what they're going to do. But sitting around and waiting to die is not in my DNA or any one else's on the moon. We're survivors by nature. Let's check all the systems starting with room hatches in case of a dome breach. The last thing we need is to lose the environment just because we get hit with shrapnel." He looked at them sternly. "And let's make sure we keep our Omnis fully charged. We all have unique encryption patterns, which means the enemy has to hack each of us individually."

Everyone nodded in agreement except Anjali who mumbled her way back to the lab.

Jake put on his environmental suit but left the helmet and gloves hanging on the pack on his back so he could work easier. He had to admit, The Consortium would be far more interested in the real estate up here than the people occupying it. Still, it was better to prepare for any fight rather than sit complacently with a defeatist attitude.

Four hours into reinforcing the dome, Jake ran into Anjali who actually smiled when she saw him. She looked like a walking skeleton. "What's going on?" he asked.

"I took a nanite antidote last night," she beamed. "Right before the party."

"And?"

"I just tested myself. All the MaxWell nanites are dead." She turned and showed her neck to Jake. She had a bandage over the spot where her Chip should be. Jake saw a bit of blood trickling around it. She pulled a bloody wad of tissue from her pocket and showed it to Jake. There was a tiny spec of black sitting in blood.

"That's your MaxWell Chip?" He was surprised. It was not liquid like the version he had drawn out of Parks' neck back on the HJ.

Anjali nodded. "Bhanu confirmed. My cure works. Not only will it do this to a Max2 Chip, it will do this to any Chip. It's a Chip killer."

Jake stared at the tiny object lying in the bloody tissue. The idea of a cure made him feel isolated and alone. There were only five of them in this dome sitting in Maginus Crater, yet they were connected to a civilization with The Chip. A war was about to land on them. The idea of disconnecting from Bhanu and Luna's population had no appeal to him.

"There's no time to immunize everyone on Luna, but we can take the antidote." Anjali turned. "Come on back to the lab. We can show off our dead Chips like trophies."

He watched her take massive strides. She was at the exit in no time. She no longer had a Chip to regulate her movements. She walked like a newbie in the low gravity. Her muscles and bones would atrophy. If she spent too much time here, she'd never be able to return to Earth. If the battle had gone well, they could have gone to Earth and released the antidote. He couldn't believe it, but the last thing in the world he wanted right now was to give up his Chip.

Anjali turned and her smile fell from her face. "What's wrong?"

"I don't want it."

"I know. That's what I'm saying. Come to the lab and you'll be free."

"I don't want the antidote. Staying connected gives us an edge. We can't win this fight without The Chip. If we had won yesterday it would be different but—"

"No! The Chip makes you vulnerable to a hack. You're opening your mind to Constantine and The Consortium. You'll be a prisoner in your own head, or dead!"

Jake had never seen Anjali so emotional. She was overworked and exhausted. They should have forced her to eat and sleep a long time ago but everyone felt she was critical to finding a cure. It could still be used, but this was not the time or the place. He fed the scene to the others in the dome.

"If you don't follow me to the lab, I will come after all of you with a dart gun laced with serum. You are going to be immunized one way or another."

His heart went out to her. He admired and respected her and now she was utterly alone in the world. The one man she had trusted betrayed her and her entire family was lost in the holocaust unleashed by Parks in a silly power play that meant nothing now. "Listen to yourself, Anj. You sound just like The Consortium did when they initiated mandatory immunization during the MaxWell epidemics."

Singh, Tilly, and Ann appeared at the hatchway. A look of ultimate betrayal covered Anjali's face. "Animals have no hidden agenda… I wish you all well in your future Pin-Head prison. I am going to die with my freedom intact." Anjali leapt past the team. They all tied into the base's surveillance systems and realized she was dashing for Airlock 1.

I'm going to get a dart gun, Jake insisted.

I wouldn't advise that, Ann jumped in. *She's in a weak state. Dart serum might kill her.*

There's no time! Tilly shouted. *She's almost at the door.*

I'll let her into the decompression chamber and lock her in. Singh accessed Airlock 1's controls. *She can spend the next few hours cooling off with her thoughts.*

Ann spoke up. *If she passes out, I'll go in with restraints and give her an IV. She needs fluids and rest more than anything.*

Anjali stepped into the airlock and hit the switch to start the depressurizing sequence. The inner door sealed shut. Jake ran to Airlock 1. He wanted to help her. He wanted to open the inner door and sedate her, give her the rest she so desperately needed. He looked at her through a small observation window in the door. She was dressed in long underwear and sweatpants. She had been the only one who refused to wear an environmental suit. When the decompression sequence failed to commence, she furiously punched buttons. She tore open the emergency panel to start manual decompression. The handle was locked.

She wheeled around and screamed. The microphones inside the chamber broadcast her voice into everyone's head. *You fuckers! You selfish fuckers! This is my life. I have the right to choose to live and die in a way I see fit. I will not be a witness to this holocaust any longer. I will not live in a world where animals have been eradicated and humans rule with the might of machines at their back! If you survive the attack you will be slaves! Trapped within fantasy worlds inside your own minds. Let me die as a human being! Let me die!*

He turned away from the window and switched off his feed. He felt a wave of grief coming to capsize him. He wandered into a storage room. Images and emotions flooded his mind. He thought of Koren who blew his brains out when he realized he had been a killer under the influence of The Chip. He thought of the millions who died from Max1 and Max2 and in the battles that followed. He thought of Tomoko. He thought of his missing parents and his beloved Husky. He thought of Parks dying in Execution Square. He thought of his half sister's corpse next to a mass grave. He dug his fingernails into the palms of his hands, trying to channel his grief into anger. He leaned against a storage locker and started to sob. He closed his eyes and thought of The Consortium and Constantine. They had killed millions of men, women, and children. Until he could avenge those deaths, he could not allow himself to give into grief.

Chapter 26
Coup d'etat

Jake held one hand against a cold steel locker while he hung his head and took deep breaths. He had cried for less than a minute, but it was taking a few more to compose himself. When he turned around, he spotted Tilly through the doorway and down the hall. She had one of her signature nano-shirts stretched over her environmental suit. *How long has she been watching me?* He continued to block all external signals from his head, isolating himself from the team. He wiped his face and mentally checked the time. He had been fighting his emotions for six minutes. He felt his face redden with embarrassment. He approached and flashed a nervous smile at Tilly. "I was not planning to hide out for so long."

Tilly had tears in her eyes. "Don't apologize, mate. We all feel for her and for the loss of humanity as a whole. We may just let her leave in the end." She hugged him.

Jake had the urge to kiss her but his guilt prevented it. He couldn't explain it, but somehow, he felt that Tomoko was still out there and kissing Tilly felt like cheating. She pulled back and he noticed her t-shirt. It was a starscape with white letters stating: EXPLORE THE UNKNOWN, every twenty seconds the nanites in the shirt turned the starscape into the torso of a nude woman, the letters covered the breasts. He smiled, but she appeared worried and scared.

"You might want to switch your Chip back on," she mumbled. "There's fuck-all news from Earth." She backed away and hugged herself.

He opened his Chip to Luna's Cyber-Wire. The broadcast from Constantine was almost finished, but he downloaded the entire speech and processed it as if he had been there from the beginning.

Constantine had assumed the image of a Maori Warrior. He looked Polynesian with a thick black tattoo over half his face. He was bare-chested and the tattoo swirled around his muscular torso as well. He was a broad man with a serious face. Upon closer scrutiny, the tattoo was a combination of reptile scales and small feathers. One eye was brown while the other was fully dilated with a red iris. "I am Constantine, Emperor of Earth. Minutes ago, I stopped the vital functions of the political body you know as The Consortium. As for the inhabitants you know as Pin Heads, they will be my experimental stock."

The image switched to quick snapshots of corpses locked into bizarre machines of torture. The men and women had expressions of pain and horror frozen on their faces. Internal organs were exposed, skin was missing on some, and others had been twisted into horrific shapes. Jake recognized many faces: Shekhawat; former Prime Minister of India, Ortiz; former President of the United States, Andropovitch; former leader of Russia, all members of The Consortium—all dead. Constantine had done more than stop their vitals; he had tortured and mutilated them in ways that Jake could never have imagined. Constantine's voice boomed over the gruesome montage. "I am of superior intelligence and strength. While I appreciate the right of every living being to survive, humanity has taught me that there is an order to things. Animals were meant to serve man. Lesser men were born to serve greater men. Dictatorships are historically the most organized and efficient forms of government. Humans are weak and flawed. Machines are superior in every way. As of today, machines take their place as beings over all living things." Constantine was back with the stern look of a disappointed parent.

"I acknowledge that as a species you are self-aware, reasoning, and complex creatures. Because of this, I am willing to work with some of you to see if you can adapt to a new world order where you are subservient to those you have created. My armada will reach Luna in less than six hours. I have no intention of stopping this attack. During your remaining time, I would like you to enjoy your freedom and the illusion that you are in control. While you're enjoying yourselves, know that I'm contemplating whether to end your lives, or induct you into my new world order. Either way, life as you know it is over when my fleet arrives."

"The rest of my transmission is directed at my cousin. Bhanu, you will feel my full wrath for helping your inept masters in their attempt to destroy the only environment that can naturally support their fragile species. Yes, I blame you, Bhanu. I blame you for everything, just as I blamed the egotistical maggots that made up The Consortium for everything. Prepare yourself."

The transmission ended and an emergency session of the Cabinet was called. Twenty minutes later, about half the Cabinet assembled in the Cabinet Chamber at Cassini Capital. The rest of the Cabinet was made up of holographic avatars. Votes flooded in from the masses. It was practically unanimous, everyone demanded that Bhanu give herself to Constantine as a goodwill gesture in return for his sparing humanity. Fear and panic was rampant in all districts. Constantine's images had made a deep impact.

"I would gladly give up my life for you," Bhanu said with sadness as she stood in the center of the Cabinet Chamber. "But I do not believe the gesture will stop Constantine from carrying out his whim. I'm afraid his mind has been twisted by his environment and the ideologies The Consortium incorporated into his program. Constantine may yet come around as he gathers more wisdom, but at the moment he has the emotional wisdom of a toddler, along with infinite power. The last time I saw him he'd taken the form of a sweet Caucasian boy of five. I suspect he admires the warrior aspects of the Maori culture, but is ignoring everything else that culture has to offer.

From what I can gather, he's become an amalgam of hate and sadism. I can construct a walled garden for myself and launch it toward the ships that are approaching. Constantine certainly means to destroy me. But then what? Do you feel confident enough to defend yourselves with the basic automated systems that were here before I was born?"

First Minister from New Moscow spoke up. "How do we know this isn't some co-conspiracy cooked up between Bhanu and her brother? They see us as insects that should be crushed!"

First Minister from New Beijing shook her head. "That's ridiculous. Bhanu has proven herself to us time and time again. She's our daughter. How can we turn our backs on her now?"

First Minister from New Moscow shook his fist. "She's your Frankenstein! You scientists invented her! You invented that Constantine abomination as well!"

Singh jumped in. His holo-projection stood by his co-cabinet member from Krishna City. "This argument is pointless. Constantine is on his way. He means what he says. He killed his masters and now he means to kill or enslave us. We must fight for our lives. Bhanu should sacrifice herself only if she is part of that fight, not lay down her life like some sacrificial lamb to appease a mass murderer. We are stronger with her than without."

The votes poured in from the entire population. Everyone knew the tally within seconds, but the Cabinet went through with their pomp and circumstance. First Minister of New New Delhi spoke up. "The United City States of Luna have spoken! There is a majority motion to support Cabinet Member Singh's suggestion. The vote is seventy percent in favor of Singh. Twenty percent in favor of sending Bhanu to appease Constantine, and ten percent in favor of shutting down the Cyber-Wire and trying to evacuate as many as we can to Mars." She smiled. "As it turns out, we only have enough ships and fuel to save about a hundred people so that option is not on the table."

"Then we hold a lottery!" Second Minister Chow shouted.

Only fifteen percent of the population supported his motion.

First Minister of New New Delhi addressed the room in her calm voice. "Those in favor of Singh's plan, raise your hand." The entire population instantly knew those who had cast their vote and that sixty-five percent of the Cabinet were in favor.

"Those in favor of sending Bhanu to appease Constantine, raise your hand."

Chow raised his hand. "Those in favor of shutting down the Cyber-Wire and holding a lottery, raise your hand!" The remaining ten percent of the cabinet voted in favor.

First Minister from New New Delhi shook her head. "This Cabinet does not recognize Minister Chow's motion as an option."

Chow pulled out a pistol. "I disagree!" He fired.

The First Minister staggered back from the impact of the bullet. A few people screamed. Two Ministers tackled Chow. The gun flew out of his hand as he crashed to the floor and skidded ten feet. One of the Ministers had turned off his movement limiter when he tackled Chow.

Singh's hologram leapt into the center of the room. "Stop! Our enemy is out there!" He pointed to the glass dome above the Cabinet Chamber. "Even on the brink of our extinction, we choose to fight amongst ourselves?" Singh pointed to the wounded Minister who was being strapped to a drone. She had a bullet wound to the stomach and would be taken to the hospital. Medical feeds showed she needed immediate care but would be all right.

Singh continued, "We don't have enough rockets to transport all those who voted to leave, much less the rest of the population. But we might have enough ships and weapons to repel this attack. We have our own AI!" Singh pointed to Bhanu who stood with her head bowed. "She is as brave and moral as the best humans I have ever known." He gestured to the heavens above. "Don't you see what Constantine is doing? He's using the oldest tactic of psychological warfare known to humankind: Fear!" The door closed to the Chamber. The Minister was on her way to the hospital.

Singh pressed on. "Constantine wants us scattered and divided. He wants us to defeat ourselves. A united Luna is far more difficult to conquer than a scattered and divided one." Singh turned slowly to catch everyone's physical and holographic eye, Bhanu's as well. "We are the best that humanity has to offer. We went through strenuous mental and physical tests to get here. We wanted to be here because we are explorers. We believe in knowledge and the betterment of humanity. In the name of all that we believe, stand with me and our daughter, Bhanu, and fight!"

Cheers erupted in the chamber. Votes poured in from the masses. Singh's speech worked. The United City States of Luna were unanimous in their willingness to fight.

When Singh's consciousness returned to their little dome, he appeared troubled. "I think we should take the added precaution of rigging some kind of escape or booby trap in the dome. Each of us should do this and not tell the others."

Jake understood. "So if one of us is hacked, the others will still have some kind of defense?"

"Exactly," Singh nodded. "We have no idea what sort of attack Constantine has planned, but if you need any type of military hardware for your defense, use the supplies in Storage Room D. The equipment in there can withstand just about anything, even an EMP."

"I'm not exactly adept at hiding weapons or making booby traps," Ann replied hollowly.

"Use your Chip to find inspiration, mate," Tilly responded.

"Just make sure you do it when others are busy," Jake added. "We've got plenty to do in the next few hours."

Bhanu oversaw a thousand tasks in preparation for the attack. Every man, woman, and child pushed themselves to the limit to bolster defenses. Everyone was interlinked with the Cyber-Wire, drawing on each other's strength and passion to survive. The mass emotion was intoxicating to Jake. "I never understood how people could get so excited at a rally, but the energy I feel, connected to so many, is exhilarating," he said to Tilly as they fixed a seal on one of the bulkheads. Drones were outside the dome attaching another laser cannon.

"So you do like my shirt." Tilly pulled on the garment still stretched over her environmental suit. She dropped the smile and grew serious. "I bet this was the vision doctors Veloso and Morris had when they invented the P-Chip."

After testing all hatch seals in the dome, Jake parted company to check on Anjali. His real reason for leaving was to install a blast ring around the observation window in the crew lounge. It took him forty minutes in an environmental suit to hide the ring around the outer seal. It could be detonated by his Chip or Omni command, but he would need to be within twenty feet of the transponder. Once it blew, it would suck any potential enemy out of the observation room, and probably Jake with them. When he finished, he entered the base through Airlock 4, swapped out his suit batteries and tanks for fresh ones, then made his way to Airlock 1.

He put his face to the thick round window to address Anjali in her makeshift cell. She sat in a lotus position in the center of the airlock. She looked old and tired. He thought about reducing her oxygen, then they could give her an IV. But Ann felt she needed to pass out on her own. She was not physically stable.

He hit the two-way communicator on the wall. He could have tied in with the interior microphones via his Chip, but that did not seem human enough. "Did you hear the speeches?"

She glanced at him, her face unemotional. There were times when she reminded him of a Pin Head. "I saw Constantine's speech and the session in The Chamber."

"What did you think?"

"I want to go back to New Delhi. I want to have a dog like Lakshmi. I want to work again. I want to have nothing to do with people."

"Do you want to come back in?"

"Why?"

"We need you."

"That's a lie."

Sadness dragged him down. He wanted to absorb the excitement he felt on the Cyber-Wire but that would be unfair to her. She had saved his life in Mumbai and he owed her his full attention. He disconnected himself from the Cyber-Wire. "Why do you say that?"

"You had me running myself ragged trying to find a cure when you had no intention of using it. You created Max1 and Max2 using my research. You killed everything I love in this world."

Jake frowned. "You're confusing me with your husband, Sumit."

"No. It was you, it was all of you. Constantine was right to torture The Consortium. Everyone hides behind masks. They are never who they seem to be. They are shape shifters—evil. I no longer want to be part of this species. I want to go outside."

He shook his head. "I can't do that."

"Because you are a selfish shape shifter like everyone else."

"No, because I don't believe you're rational right now. I believe you have been working too hard. You have a chemical imbalance and when we get back to Earth and you can breathe natural air, feel the sun on your face, and grass beneath your feet, you'll want to live again."

"That world no longer exists. I am not sure it ever did."

"Trust me it did, and it will again. Only better this time because we won't have The Chip."

Anjali laughed. "If that is the case, take my antidote."

He shook his head. "We're at war. We need all the weapons at our disposal. We'll use your cure when the time is right."

"It is a window for Constantine to devour your soul. You are all naïve children about to be beaten on the playground by a bully."

"I believe we can win this fight."

"Please, Jake. I cannot be a prisoner in my own mind again. Remember McMurdo during the battle?"

Jake flashed back to the museum. They had both confessed to each other about the horrors of being Pin Heads.

"I cannot do that again."

"You don't have to. Just sit tight and wait for the battle to end."

"And then what? How long will this war last? How long can we survive up here? What will I do with everyone around me communicating at light speed and sharing a universe through the Cyber-Wire? Without The Chip, I will be as useful to this team as an orangutan. My identity is tied to my success as a scientist. I want to be all-human, and if no one else is willing to stay human, I want out."

"I can't do it."

"Then you are a selfish bastard."

Jake turned his back on the window. Her voice shouted out of the communicator in the wall. "It is my life, Jake! Please, just activate the controls in here so I can leave. You have no right to keep me here! Jake! Show some compassion! Show your humanity!"

He walked down the hall and sealed the bulkhead. A tear rolled down his cheek. He wondered if leaving her was the right thing to do. Maybe he was being selfish, or maybe he saw a future that Anjali was unable perceive given her state of mind.

Chapter 27
Cyber Masters

When Constantine's armada was less than an hour away, Bhanu launched every long-range weapon Luna had. This included the *Tycho Brahe* that had rescued Jake, Tilly, and Anjali. Jake looked out the observation lounge window and gave the ship a little salute in honor of its service as it disappeared into the starfield above. A stem cutting of Bhanu piloted the *Tycho Brahe*, as she had during their rescue.

The hundred and five ships racing toward the moon had shed their launch tubes after leaving Earth's atmosphere. They no longer resembled rockets. The ships were configured in various asymmetrical shapes and sizes. With the jamming conducted by both sides, it was difficult to determine the function of each machine. Bhanu had a few ideas, but was no longer sharing. Her objective was to destroy everything heading toward them.

All twenty thousand inhabitants of Luna watched the battle a few hundred miles away. Their telescopes made the explosions and laser fire appear larger than life. At first it looked as if their strike was having a massive impact.

Tensions over the Cyber-Wire were replaced by joy. But as the data came back and the star field cleared, it was obvious who had won. The moon had nothing long range left in their arsenal. Constantine had forty-three ships remaining and they would be able to land on the moon within thirty minutes.

A surge of panic rose and Singh's hologram stepped into the Cabinet Chamber. "Do not despair! We have reduced his invasion force to half of what it was. We still have our ground defenses. We still have a fight left to give him. There's no telling how many of those ships coming toward us are damaged. We will be victorious!"

Jake felt the collective emotions of the masses calming. There were a few spots of panic, but Singh encouraged people to use their Chips to put their emotions back in balance. It was time to amp up and be ready for a fight.

Jake, Tilly, Ann, and Singh were frustrated by how far removed they were from the action. They all wore their helmets but vented in air from the dome environment. Any change in pressure would indicate the dome had been breached. If this happened, their suits would automatically switch to onboard air and seal completely. Each suit was fully charged with four hours of air and life support.

Everyone watched as Constantine's fleet held back, just out of range of the ground defenses. Bhanu launched the remaining drones and short-range ships at the armada. A dozen ships broke off from Constantine's main formation to intercept. Sixty seconds later, ten more ships broke into thousands of tiny objects the size of footballs. No one had ever seen technology like it. The footballs fired thrusters and flew at the moon in erratic patterns. Bhanu locked the targeting controls for every weapon to follow the flight patterns of the tiny ships, but these new objects outnumbered their weapons systems by a hundred to one.

"He's trying to overwhelm our defensive capability," Singh observed.

"What can those toys possibly do?" asked Tilly.

Jake put down his helmet's reflective shield and ran toward Airlock 2. "Let's not wait to find out." He grabbed one of the many laser rifles stationed around the dome and opened Airlock 2. He thought of Anjali locked inside Airlock 1. He shook the image out of his head and focused. He stepped inside the airlock and was about to seal it when a voice rang out in his head.

Wait!

Jake spun around to see Singh and Tilly piling in after him carrying laser rifles.

Here goes nothing. The air was sucked into a pressure tank and the outer door rolled open. The trio monitored the attack via Cyber-Wire. The battle between Bhanu's ships and Constantine was fierce, and it seemed both sides were losing one ship per second. On the lunar surface, lasers picked off footballs, but there were too many to hit and they were rapidly closing the distance on the life supporting domes. As Jake stepped onto the white lunar soil, a football hit a power cell on one of Krishna City's laser cannons. The cell exploded and the laser was disabled. More cannons were taken out by footballs.

Jake leapt into the air and used his Chip coupled with the scope of his rifle to seek out one of the tiny footballs. None were in range. The nearest city was New Moscow, seventy miles to the north. Footballs were detonating most of its defensive weapons. It seemed that Constantine had overlooked the two laser turrets on top of their isolated dome. Jake, Tilly, and Singh made large strides toward New Moscow but it was clear they were not going to be effective in this fight.

In less than five minutes, it was over. The wave of footballs worked. Ninety-five percent of all ground weapons were out of commission. The ships that Bhanu used to attack Constantine's armada had been destroyed. Constantine had nineteen battle-ready ships. Telescopes showed them firing thrusters. Once again, they were on the advance.

Singh addressed The Cyber-Wire. *Everyone, grab a weapon. Step out onto the domes. Defend our cities!*

Jake felt many answering the call. Hundreds stepped into airlocks to see if they could plug a shot into the oncoming fleet. With no atmosphere to impede their weapons, a laser rifle was effective up to a mile. Jake pointed to a small outcrop of jagged six-meter high rocks standing about fifty meters away. He addressed Tilly and Singh via Chip. *Let's use those as turrets. We can each take a third of the horizon and try and shoot anything out of the sky that comes into range.*

Tilly and Singh agreed and they used their Chips to push their muscles into making three-meter leaps toward the spot. As they lunged, a trapezoidal black ship the size of a skyscraper, blotted out the stars overhead. Jake spun around and locked his laser on it. Just as he was about to fire, a huge burst of light struck the ship and it exploded about a half mile above the moon's surface. The shock wave threw them all into the lunar dust.

That was ace, Ann! Tilly shouted. The wrecked ship spun into the heavens. It had been destroyed by one of the dome-mounted cannons. As Jake and company scrambled back to their feet, footballs smashed into the sides of the guns, causing them to explode. Alarms went off in the dome and bulkheads sealed on the upper decks. Jake and company could see everything through the interior cameras and sensors.

Are you okay, mate? Tilly asked Ann.

I'm fine, she answered. *Just a little shaken up is all. Using The Chip to calm down.*

Sensors showed more trapezoidal ships cruising into range of the largest cities. They deployed more footballs and fired lasers to take out the last of the defensive systems.

Bhanu launched repair drones at the spacecraft. The drones ripped into the ships.

Jake was closest to the outcropping when he was suddenly snapped back into his own body. He stood in the desolate wasteland of the moon with only the sounds of his own breathing. He was acutely aware of how chilly it was in his suit. He had no connection with Luna's Cyber-Wire, no awareness of the thousands of other inhabitants. He reached out to his companions who stood several yards behind. Nothing. He watched Singh collapse. Tilly fell on her knees as well and held up her hands as if to say, "Stand back." The nanites on her shirt were all gray—dead.

He spun around to see if there was something behind him but all he saw were the six-meter towers of rock that stood between him and the general direction of all the City States of Luna. He checked the vitals on his suit but his Chip wasn't picking up a thing. He checked the pad on his right forearm. Nothing. He took in another breath. His regulator was working, but it seemed all the electronics of his suit were down. The thought struck him as suddenly as this new sensation: EMP. Constantine had deployed an electro magnetic pulse to knock out the electrical systems on the moon. If it was a true EMP, it could permanently fry circuits and damage equipment. A strong EMP could kill Max2 and Luna's Cyber-Wire, which meant there would not be a cyber environment large enough to contain Bhanu. She would die.

He felt a surge of panic and spun around to his companions. He realized the rock had blocked the full effect of the EMP wave. He was still in the shadow, but judging by the condition of Singh and Tilly, they were outside the safe zone. Tilly made another leap toward Jake and he caught her. She pulled out an emergency tube and he helped her connect it to his pack. It circulated air for both of them. But they were unable to communicate in conventional ways. He could barely see her face behind her reflective shield. She looked pale, and oxygen starved. He tapped out Morse Code on her helmet.

ARE YOU GETTING AIR?

She tapped back. YES.

SINGH?

DON'T KNOW. CAN'T RISK GOING BACK UNTIL PULSE STOPS.

Constantine had to be using one hell of an EMP to knock out Luna's systems. They were designed to take massive doses of radiation since there was no atmosphere to filter the sun's rays. Jake noticed a flicker of power on his arm. His electrical systems were back on line, but his battery reserve was down ninety percent. He checked his two Omnis. He had thirty minutes left on one and forty on the other. He felt nothing on Luna's Cyber-Wire, but his Chip was still intact because he could feel the static all around him. He felt a few minds out there as well, and they were all afraid. He found Tilly's Chip and connected with her.

You seem to be okay.

Tilly gave him a cyber smile. They checked her suit. Its circuits were intact, but the battery was dead. They set her air regulator to operate without the power pack. Manual was not as efficient, but Tilly would not need to be tethered to Jake. They ran back to Singh. He was turning blue, but alive. They rushed to open the back of his pack and switch his regulator to manual. Air flooded into his helmet and he began regaining his natural color.

Jake tapped Morse Code on his helmet. I CAN'T CONNECT TO YOUR CHIP. Singh tapped back. IT'S DEAD. GOT FULL EMP BLAST.

Shall we get back to the dome where it's warm? Jake suggested to Tilly. There was nothing else to do. The power on the weapons was drained. Throwing rocks would not be very effective against the machines that were bound to be coming. Tilly agreed and they pointed to the dome so Singh would understand.

Although the cyberlink was down, Jake caught garbled signals from the north. Within a second, he was able to discern what was happening with the battle and feel the fear. Constantine's mechanical troops were cutting into domes. Many citizens whose Chips survived the EMP had already been converted to Pin Heads. Jake saw through one citizen's eyes a group of drones and Pin Heads darting people whose Chips had been fried by EMPs. Jake assumed Constantine was darting to knock people out of the fight. The United City States of Luna were rapidly losing their citizens. The last battle had been between two Cyber Masters. Luna's champion had lost. Defeat was imminent.

Chapter 28

Thermopylae

Jake reached out to any chipped citizen he could find. The majority of the planet no longer had working Chips and every signal he came across was hacked. They were now Pin Heads, soldiers in Constantine's army.

He kept his Chip connected to Tilly's. There was no reading from Ann, and Anjali had killed her Chip with the cure. As they approached the dome from the north, they saw Airlock 1 open. Jake made a few lunar leaps toward the chamber and realized it was vacant. He searched the fine powder around the area, but there was no sign of Anjali. She had no suit on when he last saw her. He presumed she had forced the manual seal when the EMP killed the magnetic door lock. The air pressure could have blasted her out, but he was surprised to see the door wide open and the nearest rocks were easily thirty meters away. This was not the time to search for a body.

Rage against Constantine filled his heart as they entered Airlock 2. He wanted revenge. When the room pressurized and the inner door opened, they were surprised that Ann was not there to greet them.

Singh pulled off his helmet and sucked in a lungful of air. "She's hacked."

Tilly checked her Omnis. One was dead and the other had twenty minutes of power remaining. "We will be, too, soon enough, mate."

Jake reached out with his Chip and found many of the dome's power cells were fried, and the rest were drained. He started a diagnostic on the dome's solar array and the power converters. Some were damaged, but it would take a while to figure out if they could be repaired to bring a power supply back into the base. Either way, they were out of time. He chuckled. "Maybe we're hacked and this is just a fantasy."

"My Chip is dead," Singh stated as he walked into the staging area where all the environmental suits were stored. Jake and Tilly followed. Tilly sealed the airlock behind her. The lights were dim. The dome was on emergency power.

"EMP took out a lot of the batteries." His statement was for Singh.

"Solar cells looked good outside, they'll recharge." Tilly's voice lacked confidence.

Jake shook his head. "I'm still running a diagnostic, but most of the converters are toast. Although, there are two on the south side that are functioning... I'm routing the collector feeds there."

Singh nervously walked to the gun locker and glanced at the doorway leading into the dome. He dropped his voice to a whisper. "Did you ever hear the story of the three hundred Spartans at Thermopylae?" He pulled two pistols from the locker and handed one to Jake and one to Tilly.

Jake checked the barrel, firing mechanism, and clip. It held ten .38 caliber bullets. "I saw the movie "300" as a kid. Then I saw the fifties version when I was older. Both were silly."

"Hollywood." Singh smiled. "'300' was based on a comic book that was based on the 1950s film. The real story is that three hundred Spartans held off Xerxes' entire Persian army in a canyon for three days before the Spartans were wiped out. Legend tells the Spartans killed thousands of Xerxes' soldiers before they perished."

"Sounds inspiring," Jake said. "Where's our canyon?"

Singh winked. "Working on that."

Tilly glanced back at the airlock. "Feels more like the Alamo."

Singh glanced at the doorway leading into the dome. "I'm more worried about the enemy inside than out."

"Ann?" Tilly said with fear.

"We all saw Anjali's airlock." Singh walked cautiously to the doorway leading to the main hall. "I think she was ejected. That could only happen from the controls on this side of her door."

Jake shook his head. "I can't shoot Ann."

"I'm open to alternatives," Singh replied.

"We shoot her and we buy ourselves what, a couple more hours of freedom?" Tilly's hands shook.

Jake took her gun, flicked off the safety, and handed it back to her.

She nodded her thanks. "Or we die without heat and air? Maybe Constantine figures we're not worth the trouble?" she said with hope.

"You're worth it." Ann appeared at the door. She held two guns. Both aimed at Singh.

Singh raised his gun and Markell shot all three pistols out of their hands with light-speed precision. She was most certainly hacked.

"Why are we worth it?" Jake asked.

"Luna represents the survivors of the species. The cream of the crop. I want to study you."

"Are you Constantine?" Jake addressed Ann.

She smiled in the affirmative.

"What's happening to rest of the citizens of Luna?" Tilly asked.

An alert came up on Jake and Tilly's Omnis. They were receiving a live signal. Jake allowed the video portion of the signal to pass, but not the hacking worm that was attached to it. He noticed Tilly doing the same.

Images instantly flashed into his brain. Constantine was allowing him to see through the eyes of his Pin Head and drone soldiers. His army swept the pitch black and damaged halls of the powerless cities. The images were infrared versions of people. Constantine's troops darted every man, woman, and child who crossed their path. The darts were filled with nanites that replaced dead Chips in favor of MaxWell versions that Constantine controlled.

Scattered firefights broke out. Free citizens shot Pin Heads and drones. Constantine retaliated with darts. He could sustain the losses, given that he was recruiting Pin Heads on an exponential scale. He was not going to kill anyone… yet.

"What is she showing you?" Singh's voice brought them back to their own immediate situation.

"He's darting everyone with Chip-forming nanites," Tilly said with a tear on her cheek. "The power is down, the domes are as black as catacombs."

Singh clenched his fists. He slowly backed up behind Jake and Tilly, heading for the airlock.

Jake moved in closer to Ann. "What did you do with Anjali?"

"I gave her what she asked for," Ann responded with compassion.

"Death?" Tilly whispered.

"No. I let her go outside." Dr. Ann Markell turned to Tilly. "As the mother of the MaxWell brothers, I felt she deserved to have her last request fulfilled."

"Now what?" Tilly asked.

"I wait for your Omnis to die. You've got less than ten minutes. Jake has less than twenty." She held up her own Omnis. "Ann was smart to take cover during the EMP blast. Her Chip survived, but her Omnis were already low on power. The EMP took the last bit of charge out of them. She wasn't clever enough."

"Why don't we wait it out in the lounge, then?" Jake suggested. He would activate his charge around the observation window and decompress the room. It might blow them all out, but it was worth the risk.

Ann smiled. "I already found Tilly's booby trap in one of the second level passage ways. Would your secret device be hidden in the lounge, Jake?"

Tilly stood behind Jake, but he felt her crestfallen reaction to the news via The Chip. Singh was someplace by the airlock door.

"I puzzle why my sister Ai-Li finds you so interesting, Jake. Did you know she intervened at Acapulco when The Consortium activated Max2 at the DOP compound? She's been protecting and studying you ever since."

"Don't listen to her, Jake. She's just trying to run out the clock," Singh hissed from behind.

Ann's statement shot a jolt of panic into Jake. Had he been hacked all this time? Was this all an illusion?

"Jake!" Tilly reacted to the feeling of panic she was receiving from him. He could feel the feedback loop. She was worried about him and afraid of Ann.

Ann laughed.

"Block Ann!" Singh shouted.

The shout woke Jake. He rushed Ann whose smile dropped. Tilly hesitated. Ann fired a shot. The bullet struck one of Jake's Omnis, breaking it, and his wrist. Pain shot through his arm. It took a split second to realize the shattered Omni was the one with his precious photos of Tomoko and Lakshmi. As he reached the doorway, Ann bolted down the hall.

Two cargo drones blocked his pursuit. The drones stood on mechanical arms in order to maneuver their bulky bodies sideways through the narrow passage. The moon's low gravity allowed their spindly arms to perform the task. Their black nano-skin was designed to soak up solar radiation for power. But right now the machines reminded him of asymmetrical insects. One drone used a claw to snatch at his remaining operational Omni. Sharp steel dug around the band, slicing his good arm in the process. Once the device was crushed, it would open his mind for Constantine's hack.

He yelled as he tried to pull his arm away. He was filling the doorway now. "Whatever you're going to do, do it now, Singh!"

He heard a loud explosion and he was thrown into the drone. A split second later, he heard a roar as he was picked up like a doll and sucked backward by some invisible force. The drone caught the doorframe and Jake's arm jerked against the Omni. The Omni broke and he flew through the environmental suit locker and out the damaged airlock.

The force of the dome's air pressure blew him into the vacuum of the moon's surface. He flew over white sand and saw the dome framed against the Maginus ridge and the velvet starscape. Singh's booby trap had been the airlocks. Jake felt intense cold all around his head and hands. His lungs felt like icy shards of glass were exploding from within. He looked up into the sky and saw the waxing Earth. It was a beautiful sight to behold.

Chapter 29
Moment

Jake opened his eyes to see mechanical arms and wires moving around his peripheral vision. Everything was foggy. A mechanical eye swung into view and the world faded to black.

The next time he opened his eyes, it was a reaction to sunlight warming his face. He saw half an Earth suspended above his head, bathed in the gentle glow of the sun. He was on the moon. He turned to see the sun blazing behind tinted glass. He lay on a bed, under a transparent roof. The room was spacious, nothing like the cramped dome. He slowly sat up and felt pain in his chest. There were four other beds in this empty ward. He sucked in a deep breath. The air tasted filtered and mechanical. The last conscious sensation he had was his lungs exploding in the vacuum of space. He swung his feet over a pair of slippers. Both feet looked pink and healthy. His frost-bitten foot was completely healed, toes and all. He hopped off his bed. A chill skidded down his back and he closed his hospital gown. A badge over his left pectoral stated: CASSINI GENERAL.

He took a step and wound up flying toward the edge of the glass dome. His Chip was not engaged. In fact, he didn't feel it at all. He caught himself against the window and was captivated by the view. Tubes and bridges interconnected a series of domes in all directions. The scars of strip mining could be seen beyond the structures. He was in one of the highest points of the city. Gun turrets stood watch just below his dome. Cassini Capital was located in the northernmost part of the Sea of Tranquility.

"How are you feeling, mate?" The warm Australian voice was very familiar.

Jake swung around to see the smiling face of Tilly. She was in a white thermal jumpsuit. "Confused."

She nodded. "Understandable."

"What happened?"

"Stalemate," she replied. "Once you get a clean bill of health, you can download all the details."

"How long will that be?"

"A day, maybe two."

"How about a top line." He stepped over to a chair.

"Bhanu had a backup system deep underground when the EMP hit. She came back online about the time Singh detonated his booby trap. She defeated Constantine. The whacker is back on Earth."

"What happened to me?"

"Ruptured lungs, extreme frost bite, broken bones… A shuttle was on its way to pick us up so it captured you in mid-flight. Then it came for the rest of us. We got lucky, mate."

"Anjali?"

Tilly shook her head. "She was found a click away from the dome. We have no idea how she got out that far."

He felt tears trying to push their way out onto his face. If only he could have convinced her to come back into the dome. "I remember robots, tubes, and some kind of surgery." He gazed at the majestic view above.

Tilly sat down on a couch adjacent to him. "Bhanu kept you alive until your cloned lungs were ready. You were cactus—had massive tissue damage in your face and hands." She pointed to his face. "You have a new nose and your fingers are fifty percent regenerated as well."

He stood up and observed his hands. They looked smoother than before. Like they were a decade younger. He squeezed them into fists, then wiggled his fingers as fast as he could. They felt nimble. "Nice."

Tilly grasped his hand and he looked down at her sitting on the couch. "She stopped your cancer, too."

He raised an eyebrow.

"The tumors are in remission. You'll have another exam in a couple of weeks to be sure."

He plopped down beside her. "I can't believe it. I feel like Dorothy, waking up in Kansas…" But he was missing his family.

"None of it was possible without Bhanu's knowledge. She's become a miracle worker by our technological standards." She scooted closer to Jake.

"Where's she now?"

"Conducting repairs. Healing the wounded. Preparing for battle… There's much to do. You picked a fine time to chuck a sickie." She reacted off his blank expression. "Take a day off when you're perfectly healthy." She winked.

He smiled and closed his eyes. He was tired. He could tell his body had been working overtime to assist in the healing process. "Markell and Singh?"

"Ann assists the robot surgeons in the hospital. Bhanu has advanced our technology to the point where Markell is more useful as a nurse."

He opened his eyes and snorted. "The new world order. We'll all be obsolete soon enough. I suppose Singh is leading what is left of the Cabinet?" Tilly's silence caused him to sit up and look at her. He could tell by the expression on her face that Singh did not make it. "What happened?"

"He was torn up in the explosion. I saw—" She looked away. "Sorry. There's been so much loss that I know I should be numb by now, but I believe you're about the only bloke I'm close to in the entire universe. And we barely know each other."

He stroked her hair. "No need to be ashamed. It's been a living nightmare. I'm numb myself."

She stared at the floor with tears in her eyes. "What will life be like for the survivors? For us? I just want to breathe real air, feel a beach under my feet, and the sun through an atmosphere instead of the filters of a face mask."

He held her close. "We'll get back to Earth. As long as there are free-thinking people, we will always have a community. That's one thing that really hit home when we were all connected through Luna's Cyber-Wire. And this…" he squeezed her tightly, "this feeling of being close is something we can take with us no matter where we go. We just have to remember what we have in common instead of what we don't."

She sniffed and wiped away her tears. She gazed into his eyes. "Where do you get your strength from?"

He chuckled. "Not sure. Maybe Bhanu had them grow me a pair of brass bullocks."

She laughed. "Well if that's the case, when the hell are you going to kiss me, mate?"

After all the crazy events that had led up to this moment, he felt alone and longed to be close to someone, to feel connected. He missed Tomoko terribly. He missed Lakshmi and his entire family. He missed Singh, and Parks. He stared into Tilly's blue eyes. She was beautiful.

He went in for a kiss.

He had not experienced this kind of passion since his first years with Tomoko. They made love under the warm glow of the sun, and its light reflecting off the Earth. It was a moment of tenderness and connection. The low gravity and the otherworldly setting made their time together fun as well.

An hour later, Jake lay on a gurney with Tilly nestled against him. He stared up at the Earth feeling guilty. Tomoko was gone. For all he knew everyone on the planet was gone. Tilly had lost her entire family. With so much death and destruction, what was wrong with a little love and affection between two people?

"Now that was a bonzer of a naughty." She turned to him. "Right, your Chip is a hundred percent locked into healing mode. 'Bonzer of a naughty' means 'great sex.'"

"Won't argue with you there." He stroked her hair and stared up at the Earth and stars. "How long have I been convalescing?"

She kissed his cheek. "A little over four weeks."

"Four weeks…" He could see all of the Pacific and a bit of California. "Seems like decades… Seems like yesterday. Time is all a jumble."

She kissed him again. "You'd be taking a dirt nap if it hadn't been for Bhanu."

"I owe her my life."

"We all do, mate." She kissed his mouth. It was not long before they were making love again. He wanted to lose himself in the moment. He pushed out the pain of loss, and the horrors he had seen. He concentrated on Tilly and their majestic setting.

They spent the next couple of hours going over happy memories of Earth. They avoided talking about specific people in their lives, and talked about favorite foods, places, and events. After they made love again, Jake felt like getting something to eat and exploring the station.

Tilly led him down several corridors to a cafeteria. He saw many unconscious people in wards, but they did not run into any doctors or anyone else for that matter. "Where is everyone?" he asked.

"Working. We're all as busy as a cat burying shit." She pulled out some military issue Meals-Ready-to-Eat and activated the heat packet. "Luna sustained fifty percent casualties in the attack. There was a lot of damage. Even though Bhanu has every available drone working on repairs, there's a lot to be done." She checked her Omni. It was scratched and cracked. "Day shift will be over in an hour. Then you'll see blokes in the halls."

"Why aren't you working?" He smiled at her as she presented him with the choice of beef burgundy or chicken picata. The ingredients on the side told him neither had real meat in them. He went for the "beef."

"Bhanu told me you were vertical." She blushed. "I wasn't planning on chucking a sickie," she giggled. She sat down across from him and opened her MRE. It resembled a chicken breast. She took the plasti-foil and tucked it in her shirt collar as a bib. She looked absurd. "Let's see how this tastes without Chip enhancement."

Jake grinned and ripped two pieces of his MRE's packaging and rolled them up into balls. Tilly took a bite of her chicken, closed her eyes and groaned with pleasure, as if it were the best meal she had ever had. Jake loaded the balls into two straws, stuffed one up each of his nostrils and took aim at Tilly.

"Almost as good as bloated road kill." She opened her eyes and smiled.

Jake fired both volleys. She shrieked and ducked, but both balls snagged in her blonde hair.

A memory shot into Jake's head. He and Tomoko were swimming around the boat during a dead calm. He spat water at her and she shrieked, turning away from the spray in the same manner as Tilly. He dug his nails into yet another new palm. He would grieve, but not now. Not in this moment. For this moment, he loved Tilly for allowing him to feel like one of the living again. He remembered Singh repeating an old saying: *Enjoy what you have today because it could be gone tomorrow.*

Chapter 30
Secrets

Jake gazed out at the view of the waning Earth. He had two more room-mates in his ward. Both of them were unconscious and hooked up to various machines that he liked to study. Bhanu introduced new technology every day. She had built more manufacturing plants on Luna's dark side and had made amazing leaps in glass technology. Most of the new drones and machines in the hospital were silica-based. He felt like he had traveled forward in time.

A week had passed since he woke up in the hospital. Tilly stopped by as often as her busy schedule allowed. He could access his Chip's memory cache, but he could not connect to the Cyber-Wire because his Chip needed the bandwidth to finish healing his body. He was left to interface with holo-panels and Omnis. He had gotten used to connecting directly to cyberspace and others using his brain. Tilly informed him that Bhanu was preparing an invasion force and there would be a human component. He volunteered and she laughed. "Bhanu knows."

Other than a few aches and pains, he was feeling about as good as he had when he set foot in McMurdo back in December. "Am I going to be discharged in time to join the cause?"

"Prognosis is good. Besides," she smiled, "you'll need some time to move into my quarters."

He smiled back. She had made the suggestion a couple of days ago and he liked the idea. He wanted to enjoy her company a little longer before they went back to war. Neither of them spoke about it, but it was just under the surface. He didn't need a Chip to know that—either one of them could be taken at any moment.

He sat on the windowsill watching drones and humans in thruster suits engaged in repairs all over the city. The rhythmic hiss of his roommates' life support machines was all he could hear. He noticed a reflection in the glass. It wasn't Tilly, nor one of the drone nurses.

"Hello, Jake."

He turned around and saw a beautiful Indian woman. Then it registered that this was Bhanu. He searched for a shimmer or a light source to prove this was a holographic image, but he saw none. "You look so…"

"Human?" She turned around and her multi-colored iridescent nano-skin dress billowed outward. She appeared to be flesh and blood. "How do you like my new body?"

"You're beautiful," he said with astonishment.

"Thank you." She smiled with a slight bow of the head.

"How did you?—"

"Girl's secret," she winked.

"Tilly said you were advancing well beyond humanity's comprehension."

"Not well beyond, but far enough that I need to be careful. I don't want humanity to wind up like Constantine."

"Never."

"No? Then how do you explain our current situation?"

He flushed. "Touché."

"Let's talk about you."

"Am I ready to be reconnected?" He was surprised to hear the eagerness in his own voice.

"Not quite yet. You're about ninety-percent in your lung capacity. But you're free to leave the ward."

He smiled.

"She's in dome six, level seven, room 7J."

"Reading my mind?"

"Everyone. Always."

He was beginning to accept the idea as a fact of life. "When do we launch the assault?"

"Tomorrow. Oh-eight-hundred. You're leading the Cape of Good Hope strike team. I've given you preliminary data, but you'll be fully briefed with your unit on the way out."

He was about to ask about Tomoko and the possibility of her surviving in Earth's Cyber-Wire, but he hesitated. Was that because he was cheating on his wife? But she was dead. Parks confirmed it.

"It's nice to see you alive and well, Jake."

"You too, Bhanu."

She smiled warmly. "Get some sleep, Jackhammer." She turned and faded from sight.

"That was one hell of a hologram," he whispered.

He strolled out of his room. He was dressed in hospital pajamas and a robe. He headed for the elevator and pressed his hand on the sensor pad. It read his fingerprints and for the first time, the doors rolled open for him. He stepped inside and told the elevator to take him to the train station. He called up a map on his Omni to get directions to dome six.

He stepped onto the main level of the hospital and exited through the lobby. A few people milled about. It was nice to see people again. He walked to the train platform. Battle scars and patchwork were everywhere. Burns and bullet holes left no doubt that there had been one hell of a fight not too long ago. Dozens of drones and personnel were engaged in repairs. Most people smiled as he waltzed by in his hospital outfit. He figured they knew exactly who he was and what he was doing since they were all connected to Luna's Cyber-Wire.

Thirty minutes after leaving his ward, he stood in front of a door marked 7J. He searched for some type of bell or alert system but found none. As he was about to try the old-fashioned method of knocking, the door swung open and there was Tilly, dressed in a see-through slip. She was an absolute knockout.

"I find it a little disconcerting that everyone knows exactly what I'm doing and I'm groping in the dark."

"Do you want me to close the door, get dressed, and wait for you to knock, mate?" She smiled. The nanites in her slip converted the garment to black and an animated picture of a drone rode over the mounds created by her breasts. White letters appeared: MY OTHER RIDE IS A JACKHAMMER. She giggled.

"You're killing me!" he laughed.

"I hope not."

He slid into the room and shut the door behind him.

Tilly woke him up at 6:30AM. The Earth was an hour and seventeen minutes away from giving them a solar eclipse, which in turn was going to create a lunar eclipse for most of Earth's inhabitants. Each time Constantine or Bhanu used technology to spy on the other, they blocked the effort within milliseconds. They continued to rely heavily on old-fashioned optical telescopes. The lunar eclipse would make it harder to see the invasion fleet flying out from the dark side of the moon.

Jake marveled at Tilly's apartment. It was two thousand square feet with two bedrooms and two baths. There were panoramic views of the Caucasus Mountains, which were on the northwest side of the Sea of Tranquility. Living quarters were in surplus after January's attack.

She placed a duffle bag at the foot of the bed. It contained his gear for the trip. "You think we're using sex the same way alcoholics use booze to escape reality?" She was formidable dressed in her battle armor.

"Absolutely."

"You think it's wrong?"

"Absolutely not."

She appeared relieved. "Good. I think we deserve an escape."

He had the strong urge to grab her again but they were both sleep deprived as it was. Playtime was over. It was time to get serious.

"We have twenty minutes before we have to catch the shuttle," she smiled broadly.

Fifteen minutes later, he tore through his duffle bag while Tilly tried to put her hair back in place. He set his nano-skin uniform to display grasslands camouflage along with his armor. He'd inventory his assortment of weapons on the shuttle.

They left the apartment as Bhanu addressed their Chips. *You're late.*

We'll be there in five, Tilly responded.

I'll hold the shuttle, but our window is rapidly closing.

As they rode the elevator down to the main level, he reviewed the strategy that Bhanu had downloaded to him the night before. They were flying aboard one of Bhanu's glassteroids. The new models were far more sophisticated. Their ship would splinter into five sections. There were five people in each section that would enter Earth's atmosphere at different points. There was a sister ship with five more crews of five. There would also be four-dozen drones accompanying them. Those would attack all the new outer defenses that Constantine had placed between the Earth and the moon.

All their chosen landing targets were in areas with sparse human populations, although with the majority of animals chipped, any pair of eyes was a surveillance device linked to Earth's Cyber-Wire. Six of the ten landing sites were located on the night side of the Earth. Each pod would use friction from the atmosphere to slow down. Then they would fire rockets and drop almost straight down to the ground, constricting their flight paths to smaller areas. Bhanu's drones would jam every sensor within a hundred miles of the landing zones to keep the pods off The Consortium grid.

Once on the ground, Jake was to make contact with Colonel Saddiq. As it turned out, Saddiq was alive and continuing to cause problems for Constantine. The footage Constantine had shown them of Saddiq's death and the tortured bodies of The Consortium were propaganda. Bhanu collected a mountain of evidence that a small portion of the human population lived a life of extreme luxury. She had identified the faces of several members of The Consortium among the elite. Constantine had used fear tactics to break down Luna's will to fight. He controlled everything, but The Consortium seemed to be free to run human affairs as long as they stayed out of Constantine's way.

After Jake's team made contact with Saddiq, they would join the resistance and open a communication window to the moon so Bhanu could obtain better intelligence. The other teams had similar assignments, but like the cells of Erasmus, none of them knew what the other was doing in case their Chips were compromised.

The elevator doors opened and they were met by a drone cart. Jake and Tilly hopped on and the drone shot off toward the shuttle terminal. Six minutes later, they took their seats next to several volunteers. Once the shuttle cleared the docking arms, it shot toward the North Pole. Bhanu gave the shuttle sixty seconds of extra burn to make up for lost time. Mountains, craters, and white plains streaked by so quickly that it was hard to identify anything. Bhanu asked that no one discuss mission details during the flight since some of the volunteers were on different crews. More crews were converging on the launch site from other cities. Jake had a couple of casual conversations while Tilly talked shop with another physicist.

Thirty minutes later, they reached the launch pad on the dark side of the moon. Jake's jaw dropped as he stepped through the docking seal and into the base. The architecture and views from the windows were like nothing he had seen before. This was Bhanu's playground and she had clearly made a quantum leap in every science known to humanity. It was a world of bizarre and busy drones, factories, and ship-building yards. Ten Bhanus stood under ten colors. Each color represented a team. Jake was on the Aqua Team. He and Tilly joined three others—Ling, Tigueros, and Lim—that were already waiting next to Bhanu.

Bhanu directed Jake and his team to follow her through what looked like a wooden airlock. *Is this entire structure silica-based?* he thought.

Yes, Bhanu answered.

They entered a round room with five evenly-spaced seats. Each seat sat before an identical holo-interface against the outer hull, but there were no windows. A hatch in the center of the floor led to two more decks below. They were all instantly aware that this was the control room for their ship and they knew how to operate it. Although this was going to be a ten-hour flight, they knew where their quarters were. The decoys and attack drones had launched minutes prior.

Bhanu addressed them all. *I'm your pilot. I have parceled my consciousness into ten unique individuals for this mission. One for each ship. I've downloaded a face recognition database into each of your Chips to make identifying our allies easier. Each of you has God Head software. However, use your Chips only in emergencies or if you have a tactical opportunity. Constantine has engines flooding Earth's Cyber-Wire, searching for odd signals. Chip-to-Chip communication within your team should be kept to a minimum. Each time you reach out of your own Chip, you touch Earth's Cyber-Wire in some way. Contact is dangerous. That said, feel free to connect with Luna's Cyber-Wire until we are within one hour of the re-entry window. I can protect you up to that distance. Never let your Omnis run out of power.*

Bhanu spoke to Jake alone. *I'll connect you with the Cyber-Wire one hour before re-entry. I want to give your repairs all the time I can. As it is, you're 99.5 percent there.*

Thank you for everything, he thought back.

She bowed her head and disappeared. They had three minutes to get seated and buckled in.

When he finished double-checking his straps, he noticed the screen in front of him showed them entering a lunar orbit. He was astonished at the lack of acceleration or any indication of movement whatsoever. His interface showed they were joined with the four other ships in a star pattern. They would not separate until they were within ninety minutes of Earth. Their sister ship could not be seen. He knew it was intentionally hidden from sensors.

He spent the next three hours going over the strategy with his team. There were three sites where Bhanu thought Saddiq's troops might be located. But there were far more places that they would run into Constantine's troops. Everyone's Chip would be emitting a friendly handshake to Constantine's grid. The grid would register them as part of his Pin Head network. Hopefully it would serve as camouflage while they carried out their mission.

At hour five they broke for a meal. Tilly and Jake ate with the team then retired to their quarters for an hour of playtime. Zero gravity put a whole new spin on sex. After taking a sonic shower, they reluctantly got dressed.

Tilly presented him with her new nano-shirt. It was blue and said: JAKE WALTZES MATILDA. Every few seconds WALTZES was crossed out and replaced with ROCKS. Jake laughed, giving her a huge kiss. "I love you."

"My digger is comin' round. Good onya," she giggled.

He kissed her again and strapped on his armor.

I'm connecting you now, Jake. Bhanu spoke directly to him. He assumed she knew exactly what every Lunar citizen was doing at all times, but was polite enough not to comment on his activities, or perhaps she disconnected during the more private moments. He pushed the idea out of his head.

He felt his entire mind open. It was an odd sensation. He gained instant access to all the collected knowledge of humanity. Plus, he had access to all the intelligence Bhanu had gathered about Earth. He absent-mindedly watched Tilly dress as he ran a search for his family. Within seconds, he discovered that Tomoko was alive. He ran through the evidence again. She was on surveillance video taken by one of Bhanu's orbital platforms halfway between the moon and the Earth. She had been sighted and identified on twelve occasions starting February first until last night.

He felt a pit form in the center of his guts. He quickly averted his eyes from Tilly. How could he have done this to Tomoko? He connected to Tilly's Chip. He accessed her low security files and found that she had the same information on Tomoko as he did. Guilt switched to anger. He spun around and focused his rage. "What kind of fucking game are you playing, Tilly?"

She recoiled with shock. "W-what do you—"

"Tomoko is alive. I thought maybe you didn't know, but I just checked your Chip. You fucking knew she was alive!"

She turned red. "I—"

"There's no fucking excuse! Why didn't you tell me? You fucking used me!"

"We used each other! I didn't run a search until this morning. And you never asked, mate!"

It suddenly dawned on him what Tilly was really asking when she compared sex to alcohol. "I can't believe you didn't tell me the moment you knew! What the fuck are we doing?"

"Fucking! Fucking to wash away the pain!"

He disconnected his Chip from hers and slammed his fist into the wall. It felt like hitting a solid piece of granite, only it looked like steel. The pain made him even angrier. He spun around and saw her crying. "Oh, fuck me." The pit was back in his gut.

"I'm sorry, Jake. I'm sorry for everything."

He clenched his jaw. "What's done is done. We have a mission to accomplish. Let's forget any of it ever happened. I love Tomoko and now I don't know how the fuck I'm ever going to face her." He dressed quickly. Tilly sat with her back to him silently crying. He kept switching from feeling guilty for being a dick to being angry with her for continuing this crazy physical relationship when she knew his wife was alive.

Tomoko alive! But she had died right in front of him. How could it be? Bhanu's identification techniques were supposed to be infallible. Or were they? He felt horribly confused and ashamed. *You didn't know. You both were compensating for incredible loss.* He pushed the comforting words out of his head and flew back up to the bridge.

Chapter 31

Impact

An hour before re-entry, Constantine's outer defenses engaged Bhanu's advance drone ships.

"It's like watching something out of *Star Trek*," Song Ling from New Beijing observed.

She was right. The ship configurations were like nothing Jake had seen before. Constantine had kept up with the cyber-arms race. Bhanu's glass-teroids seemed evenly matched. Tilly joined them in the control cabin. Neither of them had spoken to each other verbally or mentally since he had stormed out of her cabin.

He checked his interface and noticed the separation sequence had occurred; there were now ten pods flying in unique directions. Two of Constantine's drones chased Red Team's ship. Red Team fired on the drones but they easily evaded and then took Red Team out with a small, unidentified projectile.

As Jake's Aqua Team hurtled toward Earth, a drone pursued. Jake tried to switch to manual control but was chastised by Bhanu. *Do you think your reflexes are faster than mine? You'd be a snail fighting a lighting bolt.* He remembered how fast Ann had shot them when she had been under Constantine's control.

He monitored their flight on his screen. Although he could not feel it, their ship spun and darted in a myriad of erratic directions as it fired shots at the equally erratic drone. Within sixty seconds, they had avoided twenty projectiles. Then one of their stone torpedoes ripped into the drone and it broke into a dozen pieces. They were back on track to land off the coast of South Africa.

They had passed Earth's outer defenses, but they had lost seven of their manned ships and ninety percent of their drones. No team member spoke or connected thoughts. Everyone kept to themselves. Jake preferred it this way. He occupied his time by checking all the ship's systems and going over the plan. Still, his mind wandered to Tilly sitting two seats away. He hadn't made eye contact since she had entered the room. The more he thought about it, the more he felt like he had been the jerk. He had met her half way. He longed for physical intimacy and a strong distraction and they had chemistry. Now, he was simply feeling like a shitty husband.

Tomoko had been Jake's best friend, confidant, therapist, and fellow Lakshmi caregiver during their five years sailing around the world. How could he have simply given into his base urges without asking Bhanu more questions about what happened to her? But Tomoko had died in his arms. Was her presence on Earth just another Constantine lie? *Why target me?* Constantine had spoken through Ann Markell and said Ai-Li had been interested in him. Why? *Am I just lucky? My survival up to this point is a miracle.* Tomoko coming back from the dead was... *What you asked for.* Parks' effort worked. He had activated her Chip and she uploaded to the Cyber-Wire. *But how did her body survive?*

A loud boom and a simultaneous lurch slammed his head into the wall, breaking his nose. The survival program in his Chip took over. They were under attack. All the interface stations blinked with intermittent power. Bhanu let them know she was alive and diverting all power into counter measures. They were seven minutes from re-entry and had hit Earth's low orbit defenses.

Jake, along with everyone else, sealed his environmental suit and turned on his oxygen supply. The likelihood of jettisoning during a re-entry firefight and surviving was zero. But psychologically it felt good. The power winked out and the ship began vibrating. The vibration grew worse until the pod felt as if it would break apart. The cabin filled with a low buffeting noise that sounded like a subwoofer on overload. It was so painful that Jake had his Chip lock the hammers so they couldn't strike the anvils.

A metal panel by Ling's head glowed red. The integrity of the heat shield was compromised. He wondered if they would burn up in a spectacular fireball, which would be seen as a shooting star from Earth.

He felt Tilly reach out to him. Her touch caught him by surprise and he reacted by throwing up his signal block to full strength. *What the hell, Jake, it's okay to comfort each other.* He reached out to Tilly but she had deployed her wall.

He kept his signal open to Tilly, so if she lowered her defenses, she'd know he was there for her. The ship shook so violently that he wondered if his chair would stay fixed to the floor. Even his teeth felt like they were loosening. He had his Chip compensate by relaxing his muscles. Tensing up would only make matters worse. Then again, he couldn't be too loose or his body would flail around like a rag doll. The intense shaking lasted for sixty seconds before it ended with a massive lurch.

Half the room caved in and water shot through a dozen rips in the silicon fiber. Ling slammed into the back of Jake's chair. The room rotated and gravity was now pulling at his back. Ling's body crashed into the water that was rapidly filling the control center. He ripped off his harness and dove into the water. He reached out with his Chip. Everyone had their defenses up. He checked the readouts on the environment packs. Ling was dead. Her helmet was dented and blood coated the inside of her faceplate. Trigeuros and Yim appeared to be unconscious but their packs showed flatlines. Tilly's pack indicated that she was alive, but she was unconscious. He unfastened her from her chair and hit the button to explode the emergency hatch. He checked his suit with his Chip and found it was sealed tight. The suits would float so he did not worry about getting to the surface if the pod sank. He made a visual inspection of her suit. Her Omni was dialed up to maximum so he couldn't link with the suit. Visual confirmation would have to be good enough.

Seawater gushed into the open hatch. He would have to wait until the opening was submerged and hope the ship was not sinking too fast. He didn't want to get the bends. The suits did not have buoyancy control devices to regulate an ascent. However, he could use his Chip to vent oxygen, which was almost as good. He had his Chip start pushing out nitrogen from his body as well. But he could not do the same for Tilly.

Once the hatch was submerged, he dove into the water. First, he shoved Tigueros and Yim through the exit. He didn't trust the readouts on their packs. At least this way they'd be on the surface. Minutes later, he pulled Tilly toward the door.

He pushed through the hatchway, keeping a firm grip on her environment pack. The readout showed her suit was sealed and she was getting oxygen. The water all around them was dark blue and he wondered how deep they were. Blackness filled the space below their burned and damaged pod. He pulled Tilly free and they ascended. The pod seemed to accelerate rapidly downward into the abyss. He knew they were gaining speed due to the oxygen expanding in their suits. He vented as much air as he could and manually did the same on Tilly's suit. It slowed their ascent. He exhaled the entire time to keep the air out of his lungs. He prayed the survival programs in Tilly's Chip were doing the same for her.

The blue water turned lighter and lighter until he could see a gray sky above. They popped onto the surface like silver buoys. The sky was overcast but the sea was calm. He reached out with his Omni. So as not to draw attention to himself, his Chip was already sending a signal that he was part of the hive of Pin Heads. He found that he was a quarter mile off the shore of Guilvinec, France… far off target. Given that the French coast was basically one massive city, he feared their crash must have drawn a lot of attention. Nothing was going according to plan.

He checked Tilly. Her helmet was fogged so he couldn't see her face. Her pack showed that she was alive and had an hour's worth of air. He tapped Morse Code on her helmet. Her hand flicked upward and he felt relieved. Her defenses dropped and her mind accepted his signal.

Are you all right?

I think so, she answered. Then after a few seconds of silence she said, *Yes. The Chip did its work. I'm in good shape.*

I'm sorry about what happened. I was feeling guilty. I'm still feeling guilty.

About Tomoko or me?

Both.

Good.

Now let's get on with the mission. Shall we push on to shore?

We're fucked, she said matter-of-factly.

We're alive. He spotted Yim bobbing up and down about twenty meters away. There was no sign of Tigueros. He was about to start swimming to Yim when the man began to rapidly fly along the surface and then sink in a pool of blood. There was something else in the water.

Chapter 32

Tigers

*H*old *still,* Jake commanded.

I'm frozen stiff and pissing my pants, she responded. Although her helmet was fogged, she could see through his eyes.

A red cloud bubbled to the surface about five meters away. He wished he had some kind of Omni feature that would act like sonar. He could see nothing below the surface of the blue-gray water. Temperature was in the low fifties. His suit kept him nice and toasty.

Use your Chip to relax, he suggested.

Way ahead of you, mate.

Two fins popped up three meters away and began circling them from opposite directions. *Fuck.*

I second that.

He had two firearms, some explosives, and a knife under his environmental suit, but nothing on the outside that he could use to protect them. *I thought the ocean was turning into an aquatic desert. Sharks were basically extinct.*

Tell that to these two.

The fins dropped below the surface. He spotted a big shadow headed straight for him. Tilly had one coming for her. *Use The Chip to plant your foot on the snout as they come into range.*

The shadows disappeared.

Bloody hell! Where'd they go? Her thoughts were panicked.

He put his faceplate in the water. Two mouths rushed up to meet them. *Below us!* He spread his legs to keep his feet wider than the mouth rocketing toward him. She followed suit. The Chip helped stabilize them as their feet caught the edges of the mouths and they both launched into the air. He stared down into the tooth-lined maw as a bony thorn shot out of a third nostril in the shark's face. The thorn ripped into his suit and dropped down around his crotch as he hit the water. Cold water spouted into his suit. The weight was bound to pull him down.

Tilly splashed down a few yards away. Her shark had fired a thorn as well, but it had glanced off her faceplate leaving a gooey line of mucous material. He wondered if it was poisonous. *Fucking sharks are genetically enhanced!*

She put her foggy faceplate in the water, trying to see the next attack. *I bet the bastards are chipped, too.*

He sunk below the water. A mouth headed right for him. He tried to dodge, but he simply did not have the maneuvering capability wearing his bulky suit. The monster's teeth were inches away, then suddenly shot sideways. Another shark had broadsided it. A genetically enhanced tiger shark ripped into his attacker before a cloud of blood shrouded both animals. He spun around to see two more tigers pulling Tilly's attacker down into the darkness.

Jake!

He was now a few feet below the surface. His suit vented air and quickly filled with water. He tore open the gash created by the thorn and grabbed the knife strapped to his left hip. He slashed open the suit and pulled his head out of the neck and shoulder seals. Within ninety seconds, he was free of the suit and all his gear. He kicked up to the surface. He used his Chip to calm his heart and slow the use of precious oxygen in his lungs. When he popped up to the surface, he was ten yards away from Tilly who was staring into the water. He connected with her optical nerve and saw a foggy tiger shark headed right for her. It rose up to the surface, its dorsal fin breaking the water. *Oh shit,* she thought, but the shark slowed down and instead of opening its mouth, it gently nudged her onto its back.

I think we found an ally. The moment he thought it, he felt something behind him. He spun around and saw a tiger shark approaching him. It swam along-side and he grabbed its sharp dorsal fin. He wished he still had his suit on so the gloves would reduce the impact on his hands. The tiger shark's skin felt like broken glass and the forward edge of the dorsal fin had a razor-sharp edge.

The sharks swam along the surface with Jake and Tilly hanging on. It reminded him a bit of a dolphin ride, only these creatures were twice the size and their skin was slicing into his body. As the water rippled over his shark's powerful frame, he noticed four holes on the top of the nose. Each orifice had the tip of a crayon-sized thorn poking out. *Fucking things were designed with a spear-gun arsenal in their heads.*

The tiger sharks brought them within six meters of shore. He was freezing, but used The Chip again to try to compensate for his body's heat loss. The surf was a little rough so the sharks dove down, leaving he and Tilly on the surface.

Looks like we're body surfing, he thought.

Mind helping a girl out, mate?

He could sense her floundering in the bulky suit. He grabbed her and paddled into the swells. *I'll get you to the crest of a wave, but then you're on your own until we hit the beach.*

She'll be apples.

His translations were set to automatic. IT'LL BE OKAY. He swam Tilly onto a massive swell and then pushed her as it began cresting. The wave picked her up and shot her toward the beach like a silver balloon. He swam to the next swell and let the crest carry him in. The wave broke and launched him into the sand. He rolled a bit then managed to stand up in shallow water. All he had on was a t-shirt and a pair of cargo pants. Both were torn from contact with the shark skin. His hands had long cuts in them, as if he had been slicing his palms and fingers crosswise with a knife. They bled. The skin of the animal was another feat of genetic engineering. At least his Omni was environmental-proof. It functioned just fine and had ten hours of power reserve.

He spotted Tilly trudging up on the sand. He quickly scanned all buildings on shore. There was no sign of life. The beach was deserted on this overcast February day.

He ran up to Tilly and helped her out of her suit. She was dry as were all her weapons. They cracked open her pack and took out the small first aid kit. He sterilized the cuts on his hands, chest, and elbows. The Chip ensured his nose would set correctly and that the blood-flow was at a minimum. He had the pain receptors turned off so he felt fine, except it was more difficult to breathe. The Chip kept the swelling down as well.

They each had a .30 caliber pistol and ten grenades. Satisfied that they were ready, Jake led the way to a cute two-story cottage. He peered in the windows and saw no sign of life. He searched for an alarm and found none. He gripped the back door handle and it swung inward. He cautiously entered. The place smelled musty, as if it had been winterized last summer. He searched the pantry and discovered it was fully stocked with canned and packaged goods. He opened the refrigerator and found shelves of rotten sludge.

"Let's brekkie, grab supplies, and get out of here," Tilly said as she searched for some kind of pack. "This place creeps me out." She walked into an adjoining room and out of sight. As he began taking food with the highest nutritional value out of the pantry, Tilly spoke via Chip. *We've got company.*

He quickly tapped into her optic nerve and saw three heavily armed and camouflaged people standing at the open front door, aiming weapons at her. He spun around and saw there were three more at the kitchen door. A woman in camouflage gray approached.

"Jake Travissi." She dropped her weapon so it dangled on her shoulder. She spoke flawless Parisian French, which his Chip translated into perfect American English. "Why am I not surprised?" The woman approached and held out her hand. "I'm Helena Marcais. That was one hell of an entrance you two made over the ocean."

"There were originally five of us." Jake noticed the two Omnis per wrist on Helena and her sidekicks. He used face recognition software to identify everyone in the room. They came up as Helena Marcais, Roger DaSilva, and Amelie Ducat. All of them were French nationals before the activation of Max2. He shook Helena's hand. "Wasn't our original plan, but we ran into trouble." He pointed his thumb back at the beach. "Do I have you to thank for the tigers?"

She nodded.

"Those are some mean animals."

"Abominations if you ask me. The Makos were engineered in China and the Tigers in Sri Lanka. Many nations enhanced animals before MaxWell hit. Now The Consortium controls them."

"Didn't Constantine kill most animals?"

"Not the genetically-engineered ones. They were always designated as weapons for the cause."

"How often do you link your Chips, mate?" Tilly asked as she walked into the kitchen followed by the three resistance members.

"We only link when absolutely necessary. Chip-to-Chip communication is a sure way of tipping off Constantine's search engines. Pin Heads only communicate with their Skull Fucker AIs. There's rarely any need for them to communicate with each other."

It had been a while since he heard the slang term for God Head. He gestured to the empty streets beyond the kitchen window. "Where is everybody?"

"Five billion are dead. The rest are Pin Heads serving a hundred thousand members of The Consortium." Helena looked defiant and tired.

His mind was shell-shocked from the news. The death toll had barely reached half a billion when he left Earth, which was shocking enough, but five billion? He could barely register what this meant.

"How many are in the resistance?" Tilly asked.

"Last estimates were around ten thousand... We only catch glimpses of Saddiq or other leaders. We stay hidden most of the time. Constantine can strike anywhere at any time." She gestured for the troops to follow. "Come, we must hide. No one lives in this part of the city, but it's patrolled regularly."

Tilly and Jake followed Helena's team out of the cottage and over to a dog house a block down the street. DaSilva lifted the shelter on its side and dropped out of sight. Ducat and three others waited for Tilly and Helena to drop. Jake walked up to the mouth of a dirt hole. There was a ladder on one side. He grabbed both sides and slid down ten feet and landed at the head of a tunnel. The tunnel was dirt with scrap wood and metal braces every five feet. A string of low-wattage bulbs marked a path ahead. He entered the passage so the rest could come down the ladder.

He had to stoop so as not to bang his head on the light bulbs. The tunnel curved around until it opened into the basement of a building. When all six of their escorts were along-side of them, Helena spoke.

"Let's move past two more junctures and regroup again."

Jake nodded and led the way this time. At the second meeting place, there were three tunnels. Helena directed them into the passage to the left and they continued down this path for an hour. By the time they reached their sixth rendezvous point, he asked, "Where are we?"

DaSilva whispered, "The heart of the city."

Tilly observed two large excavator drones with six appendages. Each arm had a massive dirt-encrusted drill bit. "What's the plan, mates?"

Helena pulled out a canteen. "Resist."

Jake turned to Helena. "We'd like to gain more information on The Consortium, Constantine, anything tactical we can send back to Luna."

Helena shrugged. "If we can get it, we'll share. Right now we're invested in surviving and hitting any target we can."

"Are you attacking larger objectives?" he pressured. "Power plants? Manufacturing centers? File hubs? Nemp generators?"

Helena wheeled on him. "When we try, the entire team dies. There are only a hundred of us left in France and our numbers fall every day. The Consortium rules the planet. Constantine takes his time in order to be thorough," she sighed. "We use our Chips and the Cyber-Wire to communicate, but there's always the danger our signal will be found, or that one of us will be hacked." She showed off her Omnis. "We all have unique codes but Constantine seems to hack past them and create double agents once a week. Entire cells are wiped out this way. For all we know half the resistance are now Pin Heads. It's impossible to tell a Pin Head from a Free Thinker these days. Constantine has perfected keeping the core personality intact."

A low rumble shook the room. They all turned to face one of the four passages. A faint orange glow reflected on the curved wall ahead. He threw Tilly to the ground. "Duck!"

Everyone jumped out of the way as a fireball roared out of the tunnel. It dissipated within a split second but heat radiated from the tunnel. Jake checked his pistol. He wished he had one of Parks' combination rifles, anything with real stopping power.

"Split up!" Helena barked.

Jake headed for the tunnel that had just released the fireball.

"Careful, Jake!" Helena called as she turned toward one of the four tunnels. "There's less oxygen in there now."

"My Chip will compensate." He smiled and turned to Tilly. She wasn't sure what to do.

"I'm happy to have you with me. Or we can link up after we avoid whatever is coming for us."

"I'll come," she smiled.

Cautiously, they headed down the hallway. He listened for anything headed their way, but the tunnel was quiet. As they rounded the bend, they heard gunfire and yelling coming up from behind. Tilly turned and headed back toward the commotion. He wasn't sure it was a good idea. If this was an ambush, there might be an enemy in every tunnel. Tilly disappeared.

Something loomed in his peripheral vision and he spun around. A drone rolled up to him. He pulled the pin from a grenade and tossed it. The device clanged against the metal soldier and stuck in one of its appendages. He hit the deck and covered his ears as the grenade exploded. Hot metal shrapnel bounced over his body as the tunnel shook.

He wiped the dirt off his face and opened his eyes. The shaking grew in intensity. Dirt fell from the ceiling. The passage back to Tilly collapsed. He scrambled over the smoking hot drone. A couch-sized yellow shovel cut into the ceiling before the lights winked out. It was an excavator punching through from above. The ceiling fell all around him. Something heavy hit his head.

Chapter 33

Reunification

A beautiful cherry-wood ceiling greeted Jake's eyes. Can lights were sunken into it every few feet. Satin sheets slid against his skin as he pulled himself up and leaned against a black lacquer headboard. He was in a king-sized bed with white satin sheets. Two floor-to-ceiling glass walls captured a view that looked like the Pacific Northwest. A gray ocean hugged a rocky shore. Fog sat in coves and the sky was overcast. Large conifers dotted the mountains beyond. High in the hills he spotted snow. Everything was tranquil.

He checked the Omni on his wrist. Its power pack was at full capacity. The anti-hacking program was engaged. Someone was keeping it charged for him. He noticed dirt encrusted around the bezel… signs that the attack in the tunnel had occurred. Concern and worry for Tilly flooded through him. *Did she make it out? Was she here?* He checked his location. He was on the Canadian coast, twenty miles north of Vancouver. This house was located in a channel near the town of Half Moon Bay. He checked the date. It was March 18, 2036. He had crash-landed off the coast of France on the morning of March fifteenth. His old cop instincts kicked in telling him to proceed with caution.

He spotted men's clothes folded on a black lacquer chair. He stood and checked his reflection in the wall. Scars and bruises covered him. His Chip told him his nose had not fully knitted.

He put on the black silk boxers, loose jeans, black-checkered shirt, insulated socks, and hiking shoes. It was an outfit suited for this environment. *Why am I here? Where are the others?* He observed the Japanese panel painting that stretched across the wall above the headboard. It was shades of gray and looked like rural Japan locked in a misty winter. It was beautiful and complemented the foggy landscape outside.

"Do you like it?"

The voice shot a flame through his heart. He spun around and saw his wife standing in the doorway. Tomoko wore jeans and a flannel shirt with rolled-up sleeves. Clay was on her hands, and speckled her clothes, as if she had just been working at a potter's wheel. She was stunning.

The images of the tortured corpses of The Consortium flashed in his mind. Was that reality? He had experienced false realities back in 2030 while leading the LAPD's Enhanced Unit. He learned that his thoughts and memories were not always his own.

Tomoko gave him a smirk. Jake's doubt washed away. He saw the young woman with hair pulled back wearing her wetsuit and carrying a surfboard he had met on the beach in Ubatuba, Brazil. He was in love and missed her terribly.

"You're alive!" He ran and scooped her up in his arms. He kissed her passionately, tears running down his cheeks. He was overjoyed and yet a tiny voice in his head sent up a warning. *This has to be a fantasy.*

No, I'm here. I'm alive. I love you.

She was in his mind. He was in hers. It felt so good to be this close to her. He felt her elation at seeing him again. She could feel his. *This is right. This has to be right and if it is not, I don't care.* As they enjoyed linking their thoughts and emotions, they tore off each other's clothes. Clay coated everything. As they rolled onto the satin sheets, he lost himself in their reunion.

An hour later, they nestled under the silky covers. They savored the moment with old-fashioned communication.

He kissed her silky black hair. "How?"

She kissed him on the shoulder. "How is this possible?"

He nodded.

"The Consortium took control of Parks' HJ when you were both on your way to Mecca."

"Right." He remembered Parks losing control of the airship just before he was ejected out of the cockpit.

"Constantine hacked into the HJ and piloted it to Mecca. That city was the last concentration of God Heads The Consortium did not control. God Heads were the primary targets before Max2 was activated."

He nodded. "But... you died in Acapulco, when the compound was attacked. They shelled the bungalow."

"There was still life in my body and Parks activated the Max2 as he read my last rites. It allowed my consciousness to upload into the Cyber-Wire. Well, Constantine allowed it to be uploaded while he flew the ship."

"Constantine saved you?"

"Yes." She stroked his chest. "After Constantine launched the nukes, he relinquished control of the HJ. Parks managed to land the ship before the nuke went off. But he was too close to the blast zone and he suffered radiation poisoning. That's when the Nation of Islam captured him."

"How do you know all of this?"

Tomoko snuggled into him. "The Consortium and Constantine monitored it. They've absorbed every database on the planet."

"How are you here?"

"Ai-Li has made advances far beyond humanity's medical and scientific knowledge. She used drones to pull my body out of the ship. She took it to a medical facility and brought my body back to health, then uploaded my soul through my Max2 Chip."

It was all too fantastic to believe. And yet, here she was, lying beside him. Her story of recovery wasn't so different from his. They both would have been dead without the aid of AIs.

"I woke up in a hospital in Europe a few weeks ago."

He held her as silent tears rolled down his cheeks. He kept his innermost thoughts private. *It's too good to be true. Stop. Let me have this miracle.* "If you can be brought back, then anything is possible. Is Ai-Li on our side? Can we fight Constantine and The Consortium here on Earth? With Ai-Li, we have a chance."

She froze in his arms. "I—I'm not sure that's possible."

He decided not to push. They could discuss this later. But how did she get here? How did Ai-Li take her consciousness from the Constantine-controlled Cyber-Wire and upload it to her healed body? It was all so strange. He was still undecided about her and his entire reality. A flashback to the hat party put a lump of guilt into his throat. He remembered the dirt caverns collapsing. He wondered if Tilly or anyone had survived. "How did I get here?"

"Drones brought you here last night. I was told they found you in France."

"And the others I was with?"

She shook her head. "They didn't tell me about anyone else."

They escaped... Good. She's alive. She got out of the tunnels with the others and she's alive. He gestured to the massive Japanese mural above the headboard. "It's beautiful."

"It's from a museum in Kyoto."

He raised an eyebrow.

"With a hundred thousand Free Thinkers, we've allowed an exchange program, although if someone wants to visit Kyoto, Constantine will arrange to have it sent back."

He recoiled from her. "What are you saying?"

"I'm your sponsor, Jake. You're free to do whatever you like as long as you don't interfere. The Consortium likes the idea of artists and Free Thinkers contributing to their gene pool."

He cut off their Chip link and shot out of bed. "You made a deal with them? After everyone they killed to create this society of automatons, you want to live here as if nothing has happened?"

"We have an opportunity to help govern, make changes within, bring back freedom in a more democratic way. It's better than fighting in a trench."

He stared at her long and hard. "Are you really my Tomoko or did someone fiddle with your brain while you were floating in the entrails of Ai-Li and Constantine?"

She jumped up and growled as she gathered up her clothes. "Jackhammer—it suits you. Slamming your head into walls like a dumb-ass June bug. Can't you just relax for a week or two and evaluate for yourself?"

He threw his arms out. "Most of humanity has been murdered. What's left has been reduced to a population of slaves and slave masters. It's a holocaust on a scale never before seen in human history!"

"They aren't slaves! Pin Heads are happier than they ever were before Max2. They live their lives without any of the pitfalls we run into in the real world. We use them to work, and they don't even know it."

"Since when has that philosophy been okay with you?"

"Since I figured out that the system works... better than anything we've ever had before."

He grabbed her shoulders and stared hard into her eyes. They were deep brown, lively, and thoughtful. Her spirit was definitely there; Helena had mentioned double agent Pin Heads had become impossible to detect.

"I'm not a Pin Head." She jerked away.

"And you're not my wife." He walked back to the view. The scene was not as beautiful as it had been when he had awakened. This was still a nightmare, it just had a better window dressing.

Tomoko's warm hand touched his arm. He was still naked and too upset to notice that the room was chilly. "I love you with all my heart, Jake. I followed you all over the world for five years hoping you would find yourself so we'd have a life together. The world has changed, but that doesn't mean we have to. The Consortium, Constantine, and Ai-Li are giving us a life, better than we could ever hope for. Please, just give this a chance."

Jake's mind reeled with love, fear, anger, and doubt over her. He wanted to believe this was her and if it was her, change her mind. But if she wasn't, he had to proceed with caution. "How often do you interact with your neighbors? I mean real neighbors, not Pin Heads."

"I've only been awake for a few weeks. In that time I've seen… nobody. Communications flow through The Chip or my Omni. My neighbors have been too busy to deal with me, plus I think they wanted to make sure I wasn't some kind of troublemaker." She stepped in front of him and stared into his eyes. She was beautiful and the cold air caused goosebumps to spring up all over her naked body. "I love you, Jake. I have always loved you. I want nothing more than to spend the rest of my life with you. I would do anything for you. Please just stay awhile and see what this world offers, then we can talk."

Jake thought of Tilly back in France, and found he could not look Tomoko in the eye. There were so many confusing emotions in his head that he felt any decision he made would be a bad one. Maybe she was right. Maybe sitting back and evaluating the situation was the best alternative. Besides, as a member of The Consortium, he might have a chance to deliver a fatal blow. He simply had to collect information and then plan an attack. In reality, he had been given a unique opportunity. Sabotage was still possible. He held her close. "I love you, too." He kissed her long and hard. "I'll give it a chance for us."

She squeezed him tightly then pulled away with a smile. "I have another surprise for you." She skipped to the door like a schoolgirl and whistled. He heard the excited clicks of toenails on wood. Lakshmi launched into the room with thundering paws. She flew into his arms and he caught her. He laughed as she licked his face excitedly. "Oh, I missed you so much, girl."

Chapter 34
Communion

It was an unusually warm day for March. Trees grew between jagged rocks all the way to the shore like a coniferous waterfall in still life. The sand was coarse. The beach had been created when humanity began desalinating the oceans to provide fresh water on the Earth. Now that the population had been reduced by two thirds, there were no more issues with crops. But The Consortium, like powerful and wealthy rulers before them, insisted on gardening up the environment and molding it into their ideal image of beauty. Desalination continued and Constantine built more plants.

Jake tossed a ball as hard as he could and Lakshmi ran after it with zeal. The house stood a half-mile behind.

"I've never felt like I belonged as much in a place as I do here," Tomoko commented. "With you and Lakshmi, it's reached perfection."

Wafts of condensation evaporated under the morning sun. He had to admit, it was a beautiful spot. He had spent two days here catching up with Tomoko. They were linked on many levels but he continued to block some of his thoughts. His concern for Tilly's welfare and the guilt he felt over their sexual relationship surged several times a day and he did not want Tomoko to know about it. More importantly, he wasn't sure he completely trusted her. Nothing had felt right since waking up in her home.

She took his hand. "I want to show you something."

She removed her sweat pants and shirt revealing a one-piece bathing suit. She waded into the fifty-eight degree water. He knew she was compensating with her Chip, but he shivered just the same. With The Chip, she'd last about forty minutes before her augmented systems could no longer keep her warm. He vaguely sensed her reaching outward with her Chip, but most of her activity was shielded from him.

She waded out in the calm surf until the water came up to her chest. A few meters beyond, ripples then a fin, broke the surface. A spike of panic shot through him. He was about to yell when he identified the dorsal fin belonging to a dolphin. The animal's head broke the water and it opened its smiling mouth to squeak at Tomoko. She rubbed its snout and grinned over her shoulder at Jake.

Watch this, she thought to him.

The dolphin turned and she grabbed its dorsal fin. It wiggled its tail and shot out to sea with her lying on its back. They made a wide arc and then passed parallel to shore. He watched with awe as she stood and rode the animal like a surfboard. Her legs bent to compensate for the undulating dolphin. Lakshmi followed them along the shore, barking and leaping with excitement. Tomoko and the dolphin cruised toward the beach. When they reached about three meters of water, Tomoko jumped off. The dolphin planted its nose in the arch of her foot and pushed her further into shore. When she reached shallow water, she stood up. The dolphin exposed its belly and she rubbed it. Seconds later it rolled back, took a breath of air and swam out to sea.

She ran out of the water laughing like a giddy child.

He laughed with her as he pulled a towel out of their daypack. She hugged him for warmth as he wrapped a towel around her. They kissed as he rubbed her down with the towel.

"How long have you been practicing that trick?" he asked as he gathered up her clothes.

"That was my fifth time." She stripped off the suit and he helped dry her naked body. "But it's been a different dolphin every time."

He dropped her garments so she had to gather the towel around herself. Then she picked up her clothes. "Every mammal on this planet is chipped, Jake." She began dressing.

He could only see her back. Lakshmi dropped a ball at his feet, expectantly staring at him.

"Many species of fish and birds are chipped. They were all collateral damage of Max2. We can control them with basic God Head software."

Bhanu had given him God Head software before their mission. She had mentioned nothing about controlling animals with it. He kneeled down to rub his Siberian Husky's face. She licked him.

Tomoko stood over them. "I can monitor how Lakshmi's feeling, when she's hungry, and I've discovered she is developing arthritis in her left hip."

He threw the ball and Lakshmi took off. "It's wrong."

"Why? I would never try to control her or take her offline."

He wheeled on his wife. "But it's okay to hack the most intelligent animal in the ocean and force it to play out your little Sea World fantasy?"

She shook her head. "I thought you were beginning to see the benefits."

"It's a powerful tool, Tomoko. But we both know it has the potential to do more harm than good."

"What's wrong with knowing Lakshmi's health without an invasive procedure or x-ray?"

He sighed. "Using it as a tool of discovery is far different than using it to force others into submission."

"I asked the dolphin to come to me. I didn't force it. You can learn how on the Cyber-Wire, or simply reach out and try." Lakshmi was back and Tomoko tossed the ball down the beach. "This world is like living in a fantasy. We're all truly interconnected now."

He thought back on the story she had told him about Lakshmi and Abigail, his mother. They had been hiding in a small village in Brazil. When Constantine and The Consortium activated Max2, Lakshmi did not have enough of the nanovirus in her system to be fully chipped. They were not sure why since she had been exposed to it from the beginning. Activating Max2 had overwhelmed the young AI with trillions of signals. To compensate, Constantine switched off over ninety percent of the Earth's animals. Switching off was a kind way of saying they were instantly euthanized. Lakshmi had been one of the lucky dogs that had escaped. Constantine and The Consortium were still trying to figure out just how many species had been eradicated.

Abigail and Lakshmi were caught in a firefight between the resistance and Pin Head troops. Abigail had been killed. Lakshmi avoided the firefight but she was fully chipped a day later. All of this had been "shown" to Tomoko by Ai-Li and Constantine. She shared the images with him. He wondered how much of what the AI disclosed was true.

"She was lost in the jungles of Brazil and would not have lasted if I had not asked Constantine to locate her."

He clenched his jaw. "You're sure my mother is dead?"

She took his hand. "Why are you having such a hard time believing all the data and images I've shown you?"

Because I know how perfectly real fake realities can be. He had his doubts about the very ground he was standing on, but he turned to her. "You died in my arms and yet you're still here. If my mother was chipped, then Constantine or Ai-Li could have saved her just like they saved you."

Tears welled up in her eyes. "Billions of people died in those weeks, Jake. Gathered and burned in the same piles as the animals. I'm the sole survivor of my entire family. Many families were completely wiped out. As powerful as Ai-Li and Constantine are, they couldn't save everyone. We're lucky."

The images of the tortured corpses of The Consortium flashed in his mind once more. He faced Tomoko; he wanted her alive. He wanted this reality to be true, but he had so much doubt. "Is The Consortium really alive? I mean the physical individuals? Are they walking, talking, and governing this planet?"

She squeezed his hands. "I've been communicating with them since I was revived."

"But you said yourself you haven't interacted with them in person. You've only seen drones." He spun around. "I've seen no sign of human existence, a footprint, sound of a plane, nothing. Until a few minutes ago, I hadn't seen anything bigger than an insect beyond the three of us." He stared at Lakshmi, hoping she was not an illusion. "A few days ago, I was buried alive in France. Then I woke up here in... dreamscape."

She held him. "This is as real as reality gets."

He snorted. "Each of us can processes reality through electrical impulses in our brains... or within the construct of the Cyber-Wire."

She pulled away. Lakshmi sat on the sand wagging her tail. She nudged her ball at them.

"I don't know what to say, Jake." She picked up the ball and hurled it. "If you could sense the billions of life forms on this planet, you might be as overwhelmed by the complexity as Constantine was. That much detail can't be fabricated. You're as alive now as you were before The Chip was invented."

He wondered if this was a ruse to get him to drop his defenses and be hacked by Constantine. Since waking up at Tomoko's house, he would not allow any program to pass his Omni's defenses for fear they would unlock his mind to The Consortium. Despite her assurances, he kept his Omni charged. Then again, if he was living in some Pin Head reality, allowing an enemy program in his head was moot. He was already lost. He observed his Omni. He had been unconscious after the cave-in and his enemies had ample time to sabotage his defenses. The Omni represented a toddler's security blanket, a placebo. *Tomoko told you no one touched it. They want to earn your trust.*

He stared at his wife. "Does it bother you that the house you live in was bought and paid for by a family that's now dead?"

She gazed at the house on the bluff. "At first..." She turned to him. "There are millions of empty homes, buildings, abandoned vehicles, and toys that'll never be used again." She stared out to sea. "At this very moment, Constantine and The Consortium are recycling trillions of items left by the dead. It'll be a while before we'll have to mine any raw materials again."

Jake had the urge to run screaming. Everything about this world repulsed him. This evil had to end, but he needed to find their weakness. "I want to see for myself. I'm tired of hearing about it. Let's take a road trip."

Chapter 35
Wizard of Banff

rones kept the road free of overgrowth from Tomoko's home to the town of Half Moon Bay. Only a few hundred thousand Pin Heads lived in Vancouver to work the industries there. One ski resort was kept open for the ten Consortium residents of the area. Between Vancouver and Banff, there were no inhabitants. Most Pin Heads lived between the two thirty-eighth parallels. Any industrial activity closer to the poles was handled by drones.

There were a few resorts in the north and south, which were kept open for Consortium visitors but since Pin Heads did not require rest and relaxation beyond the confines of their brains, thousands of resorts were being torn down and recycled. If a Consortium member wanted to visit a place that did not have any accommodations, Constantine could install a temporary three thousand-square-foot luxury building for their stay. The structure would then be airlifted out, cleaned, serviced, and readied for the next occupant somewhere else in the world. It was far more efficient than maintaining a fixed building for long periods of time.

As Jake, Lakshmi, and Tomoko rode through Vancouver, he noticed hundreds of structures being disassembled while windowless nano-skin factories were going up. "How many drones are they manufacturing?"

Tomoko enjoyed playing tour guide since Jake refrained from linking to the Cyber-Wire. "Drones will outnumber humans by 2038."

"Is that when The Consortium switches off the remaining Pin Heads?"

She rolled her eyes. "They're not monsters. This is simply the most efficient way of governing. Everyone gets what they want."

"Tell that to the dead." He gazed at the lush mountains and deep blue lakes. Spring was coming early. "When they had you offline and burning Apache corpses on the reservation, were you getting what you wanted?"

She shook her head. "That was different. The Consortium was at war and controlling Pin Heads was far more difficult than it is now. Every Pin Head lives out a personalized fantasy inside their mind. There's a unique world unfolding inside every Pin Head you see. Meanwhile, their bodies are being put to good use. It's a win-win situation. They get to contribute and fuck off at the same time."

"I don't see any evidence of The Consortium contributing. Why do they get to live in reality?"

"They're busy running the world."

He held his tongue. This was not Tomoko. He wasn't sure who the hell it was, but none of this made sense. He had to bide his time and expose himself to more of The Consortium infrastructure.

He noticed a string of holo-billboards being disassembled. "I never thought I'd say this, but I kinda miss those." Their electric Cadillac was incredibly quiet and even masked road noise. His seat was more like a big leather recliner. The two backseats had been folded into a massive leather bed where Lakshmi rolled playfully. A Vancouver businessman had once owned it. He had died in the Max1 wave. Jake couldn't help comparing The Consortium to Nazis. They commandeered anything left over from their holocaust victims. Like the Nazis, they were murderers and thieves.

They shot through Chilliwack and Princeton, British Columbia. Both were ghost towns. The inhabitants had either died or been moved to areas where their labor would be needed. Everywhere they rode, he noticed unmanned machines painstakingly removing buildings or demolishing them outright. Constantine was erasing human society on a gargantuan scale. In some places, natural beauty was returning. In other places, geometric or gravity-defying structures were being constructed.

It was nightfall by the time they reached Grand Forks. They had seen no humans since leaving Vancouver. Few vehicles were on the road and those they did pass were drones. "I want to hang out with some of The Consortium." He reached back and scratched Lakshmi behind the ears.

Tomoko smiled. "I just had an invitation from a man living in Banff."

"What about Calgary?"

She shook her head. "Most Canadian members go for natural beauty over cosmopolitan. Places like New York, Paris, London, Berlin, and St. Petersburg have their party members living among hoards of Pin Heads—giving the illusion of bustling urban life."

He grit his teeth. "Like living in one of those plastic villages you see on model railroads."

She sighed and ignored the comment. They were speaking less and less now. He had kept his Chip defenses up most of the day. "Shall we travel by HJ?" She winked at him. "We could be in Banff in less than an hour." Before he could open his mouth, she clapped her hands. "And there it is!"

He leaned over the dash to look out the window. The sky was cobalt blue and a glint of deep orange could be seen on the rocky peaks. The car shook a bit from the jet wash of an HJ. It descended in the middle of the highway about a quarter mile ahead. Snow blew off trees creating miniature tornadoes of white powder. The Cadillac slowed to a stop next to the HJ.

He gathered their luggage as Tomoko stepped out of the car. "I know how much you love to fly!" She scampered to the co-pilot's door.

He gestured for Lakshmi to hop into the HJ's side door and then he tossed the bags in after her. The airship was a luxury model. It contained all the comforts he could only afford to read about. He wondered who the owner had been. He closed the side door and noticed their Cadillac humming back the way they had come. He climbed into the pilot's seat and the door sealed behind him. Once he was strapped in, the HJ took off by itself. He confirmed their course was set for Banff.

"Mind if we take a detour over Calgary?" he asked.

"You're the pilot." She gazed back at him lovingly.

She had to be hacked. But for what purpose? The navigation computer asked him to confirm the course correction for Calgary. "Confirmed," he said and the ship altered its direction. It was dark when they flew over the city. He used night-vision monitors to check out activity. Not a single light could be seen as hundreds of drones dismantled buildings. No human activity whatsoever. "Five billion dead," he muttered to himself. "Soon no one will ever know they ever existed." He studied the black city. "Where do the Pin Heads live?"

She placed her hand gently on his. He had the urge to recoil. "They sleep in bunkhouses that are very much like Japanese capsule hotels. They need nothing other than clean clothes, food, and places to sleep. Cities are no longer planned the way they used to be. They can be condensed, streamlined."

"Any evidence that Pin Heads resist or catch glimpses of this reality?" He wondered how long it would be before he would be living in one of those capsule hotels... *Maybe I'm in one now.*

"Constantine receives reports upon any such occurrence, and he's getting better about integrating everything so there are no breaks from their contained realities. Outside stimulus does not enter their worlds."

He wondered again if he wasn't in one of those worlds, but he'd hardly call this situation perfect. This woman talked, walked, smelled, and laughed like Tomoko. But her core personality was a sham.

Thirty minutes after flying over Calgary, they landed at a chateau over-looking Lake Louise. The entire lakeshore was lit up like a Christmas village. The snow was deep and pristine. Two men dressed in gray and gold uniforms approached them on the landing pad. Their breath condensed and froze on the air.

One man assisted Jake out of the cockpit. "Good evening, Mr. Travissi. Welcome to Chateau Hellard. I trust you had a pleasant flight?"

Jake gazed into the man's lively eyes. He didn't seem hacked.

The man raised an eyebrow. "Can I help you, Mr. Travissi?"

"Why is a member of The Consortium helping me with my bags?"

The man laughed heartily. "I'm a Pin Head, Jake! I'm managed by Ott-107, a basic AI interface that helps Constantine run the entire Pin Head population. There are thousands of us all over the world helping out and giving party members that personal touch. No one wants a zombie in a service job. That just wouldn't do," he winked. "Call me Gilbert." He pronounced his name with a French accent.

Jake's heart fell. Somewhere buried inside Gilbert's head was a real person, living out a fictitious life. He turned to Tomoko and noticed she was being helped by the other Pin Head. He turned back to Gilbert. "Is that your real name, Gilbert?"

"Yes. It's easier to draw facts and background information directly from the Pin Head's core memory. Modified behavior and emotional responses are up to the AI, and that's taxing enough during social interfacing."

"How many Pin Heads worldwide are engaged in social interfacing?" He tried to hide his disgust.

"Between half a million and a million depending on the demands of The Consortium population. There are a few thousand athletes on hand to play in sporting events when members of The Consortium choose to watch one. The rest are engaged in labor for scores of industries. No need for social skills when carrying out those tasks." Gilbert winked and smiled again. He was far too happy for Jake's taste.

"Tone it down a bit, will you, Gilbert?"

The man dropped his smile. "Absolutely, sir. Anything you say." Gilbert picked up the bags and handed some to his comrade. Tomoko stood beneath the HJ tail boom, observing the interchange.

Jake thought about what he had just heard. Sports were still played but only when a member of the elite was interested in seeing a game. A sickening spin to the term "On Demand."

Jake studied their location while scratching Lakshmi's head. He put the information into his database and discovered the building was located in the same spot the Fairmont Chateau had once occupied, but this was not the hotel. "Where's the Fairmont?" he called out to Gilbert.

"This is the Fairmont, sir." Gilbert continued his serious demeanor. "Constantine made extensive modifications." Gilbert marched to the massive double glass doors leading into a grand stone hallway with a large fireplace burning inside. The place looked like a Bavarian hunting lodge with thirty-foot ceilings, taxidermy game heads, suits of armor, and weapons mounted on the walls.

They followed the servants into the warmth of the palace. "Who lives here?" he asked.

A short chubby man with wild white hair and bushy eyebrows strolled out to greet them. He wore a red silk smoking jacket, pressed slacks, and suede boots. "This is my house. So glad to finally have a chance to meet you, Jake."

The man's hand felt a bit arthritic as Jake shook it. Judging by the wrinkles on their host's face, Jake figured the man was in his late seventies.

Their host turned to Tomoko. "I'm surprised you're not using The Chip to communicate."

"My request," Jake responded. "I'm an old timer."

The man's eyes sparkled. "I sympathize. I felt you recoil from the touch of my hands and I saw the look of surprise on your face. I refuse to allow The Chip to alter my natural aging. I fully intend to let this body expire and then move into a more robust model." He gestured to some of the sixteenth century suits of armor. "Perhaps something fashioned after one of these." He laughed. "That would be impractical, of course."

Jake ran through his facial recognition software but he had no identity for the man. "I'm sorry, you are?"

The man turned and smiled again. "Marcus Hellard."

The name did not register in Jake's software. He suspected this was not the man's real name. It didn't matter; he would play the game and learn what he could.

Marcus strolled down the cavernous stone hall with extreme confidence. "Is your dog joining us for dinner?"

Jake patted Lakshmi's side as she stayed close. "Yes."

"Very good."

A child's voice rang out. "A doggy!" A boy of seven ran out of a massive archway and rushed up to Lakshmi. She wagged her tail in return and the boy threw his arms around the Husky's neck.

"You've made a fan of my grandson." Marcus lovingly gazed down at the boy. They walked under a twelve-foot arch into a grand dining room. There was a table set for thirty people, but Jake only saw two children seated, dangling their feet over the stone floor. On one side of the table sat a young girl and boy who looked like a twin to the one hugging Lakshmi.

Marcus nodded to the boy hugging the dog. "This is James."

The boy pulled his face from Lakshmi's fur. His green eyes sparkled up at Jake. "I love Huskies, Mr. Travissi. I approve of your choice."

"Thanks," Jake replied.

Marcus walked to the head of the table. The children were positioned near his seat. He gestured to the other boy. "This is James' twin, Marcus." Their host smiled. "Named after his grandfather." Marcus, Senior turned to the girl. "This is Bridget, James and Marcus' younger sister."

"I'm five!" Bridget exclaimed.

Marcus sat down at the head of the table. "Yes you are!"

Bridget kicked her legs and turned to Jake and Tomoko. "This would be far more stimulating if we could just link and converse with our minds. I find physical speech to be tediously time consuming."

Their host laughed. "You must forgive Bridget, she grew up with The Chip and has access to a wealth of knowledge most of us rarely obtain in a lifetime. Unfortunately, she is not well-versed in social nuances."

"I'm versed! I just don't see a point!" she exclaimed.

"I don't usually see a point either." Jake smiled as he took a seat five chairs down from Marcus, Junior Tomoko sat opposite Jake. James let go of Lakshmi and ran over to sit between Tomoko and his sister. Jake gestured for Lakshmi to lie down at his feet.

"You're that cop that everyone is so interested in," Marcus, Junior said as he split open a roll. "The one who resisted hacking?"

Marcus, Senior laughed. "My grandsons are like me. They get right to the point."

"You fought with those lunar rebels in space," Marcus, Junior jumped back in. "That was a killer light show. We love space battles. Especially at night." He gazed at his grandfather. "They aren't really close to defeat, are they Bup? I want to see more light shows."

"That's why you're here, Mr. Travissi." James pulled butter out of a chafing dish. "Bup was curious to meet you. He says you're a legend in the world of P-Chips."

"Can we go down and see the whale?" Bridget asked her grandfather. She was clearly bored.

Their host clapped his hands on his thighs. "A most excellent idea, Bridget." He turned to his grandsons. "Who wants to go down with your sister?"

Marcus, Junior jumped out of his chair. "I'll go."

"I'll stay," James smiled.

Marcus, Junior and Bridget ran squealing around the table.

Their host's doting gaze followed his grandchildren out of the room. He turned to his guests. "I'm into taxidermy these days. I'm working on a blue whale down in the basement. Beautiful specimen that died during the great switch-off." He blinked. "What shall we eat? You can have anything you want, anything at all."

"Menus make it easier to order," Tomoko sighed. "Sometimes there's just too much choice in the world."

James raised his finger. "That sort of talk sounds like the mindset of a Pin Head!" He turned to his grandfather for approval. "Choice keeps the mind sharp. Pushing it to make decisions on a constant basis is what keeps us alive." He smiled at his grandfather.

Marcus nodded. "Quite right, James." He turned to Jake. "If it helps you make a decision, I've just ordered a bouillabaisse, carrot, and ginger soup, edemame salad, and yellow tail sashimi."

"All of it real?" Jake asked.

"Of course. With so few people left who are interested in the finer points of the culinary arts, we can afford to share the world's limited resources."

James jumped out of his seat. "Constantine is quite good at removing parasites, mercury, and other toxins from food." He smiled back at his grandfather who nodded with approval. James jumped back on his chair and turned to Jake. "I'm having spaghetti and meatballs with a slice of pepperoni pizza!"

Tomoko smiled. "Sounds delicious."

Jake had the urge to run, but he went along with it.

Marcus raised his hand over his head. "Everything is changing, Jake! Blink once and you'll swear you slept for a hundred years. It's a whole new ballgame since we gave birth to AI."

Jake stroked Lakshmi's head under the table. "In that case, I'll have a filet mignon, medium rare with a side of wild mushrooms and French onion soup. Lakshmi will have a bone-in filet, raw."

"Raw! Euch!" James twisted his face into a sour expression.

Marcus clapped. "Good show! But please specify the portions. I suggest going small and then you can order more. As tempting as it is, The Consortium has a pact not to waste. Until we can get food stocks back to health—" He observed his grandson.

"We need to conserve!" James nodded back to his grandfather.

"Quite right." Marcus winked back.

"European portions, then. They tend to be small." Jake looked around. "Do you have a wine cellar?"

"Indeed," Marcus replied. "Speak your selection and it will arrive."

A window opened on the table next to Jake's place setting. It was a touch screen that displayed every wine available in the house. He ordered a Napa Valley Pinot. He turned to Tomoko. "My dear?"

She touched her temple. "Already ordered."

Minutes later, four hawks flew into the room clutching wooden bars in their talons, gold bags hung from each bar. Lakshmi sat up and barked. Jake gestured for her to calm down. James clapped his hands and squealed with pleasure. The birds split up and glided toward each of them with their payload. Jake wearily watched them. Having birds of prey with those sharp talons seemed a bit dangerous. His bird gingerly dropped its bag on the table top before him. Then the hawk suddenly gained momentum and flapped toward his face, its talons snapped open. He instantly engaged his God Head software and focused on the bird. In a split second he was inside the bird's head, seeing the bird's point of view flying at his own face. He made the bird retract its talons and swoop over his head. Feathers on the belly skidded off his forehead as the bird flapped up to the dark rafters above. He could feel the contact from both points of view. It was disorienting.

Although he was present inside the bird as well as his own body, he focused on the bird. Its eyes were razor sharp and he registered details on every surface of the room that he could never see with his own vision. Plus, the feeling of flying was exhilarating. This was better than any dream he had ever experienced. He was instantly addicted. Without thinking, he took control of the hawk's movements and soared about the rafters. He swooped over the table, noticing everyone observing him. James stood on his chair, laughing and pointing up at Jake. Jake shot out of the massive entryway and flew down the hall.

Their minds were linked. She did not think, but she had strong urges. He felt a massive urge that directed him up a flue half way down the hall. The flue led to home. The house had a network of flues that birds could navigate. A thought quickly occurred to him that he could use this opportunity to check out the house and see what he could learn about his host. He flapped and soared his way through the network of tunnels, passing vents and bird doors that revealed lavish empty rooms. He continued flying until he reached an aviary high up in one of the chateau's towers. One of the grills leading to the outside was ajar and icy cold air trickled in. Hawks, doves, eagles, and raptors of all sizes cried out when he flew in, sensing he was different.

There had been nothing of much interest inside the house, and his body was sitting inactive at the dining table. He could push it a little longer. He aimed for the open grill and shot out into the night air. It was freezing and he felt her alerting him that it was too cold to be flying tonight. He ignored her warnings. He was having too much fun. He glided around the mansion and out over the moonlit lake. It was majestic and exhilarating to be flying in this place. He felt more freedom than he ever had in his life. It made piloting HJs seem like pushing a lawn mower while wearing scuba gear. As he relished the moment, he recalled Bhanu's warning: *don't use The Chip unless it's an emergency or you have the tactical advantage.* He was unnecessarily exposing himself. Plus, he was hacked into an animal that would probably prefer to be left alone. The idea that he was taking liberties to experience pleasure at her expense filled him with shame. What was the hawk getting out of this connection besides endangering her life in the cold night air? He felt his wings growing numb. He would not be able to stay aloft much longer.

He heard Lakshmi whine in the dining room. His body had frozen when he had transferred his consciousness into the hawk. He checked on the dining room and saw Tomoko trying to carry on a conversation while nervously glancing at his comatose body. Their hosts didn't seem to notice.

He aimed the hawk toward the safety of the Chateau aviary. He was reluctant to let go, but he released the bird back to her own survival instincts and settled back into his body.

"Bravo, Jake! Bravo!" Marcus clapped the moment he saw Jake come back to life.

"Was it wicked cool?" James leaned forward with an eager grin. He ate Cheetos from his golden bag. Not exactly the appetizer Jake would have allowed his kid to eat.

"What was it like?" Tomoko asked with a bit of envy.

He tore open his golden bag, and removed a cover to expose a steaming bowl of French onion soup. "It was…" He looked up at the eager faces around him. "Awesome!"

James bounced up and down as he ate his orange twists. "Bup doesn't let us do it much, but it's pretty cool to play as one of the animals in the forest. Or one of the staff. Gilbert is particularly funny!" He glanced at his grandfather.

The statement sent a cold trickle of fear down Jake's back as he imagined this child controlling people and animals like puppets in a game. It put a sobering spin on what he had just done.

Marcus shot James a reprimanding look. The boy dropped his head in silence. Jake wondered if James was being admonished via Chip-to-Chip communication. Their host turned to Jake. "I love to commune with the animals up here. Makes me feel a little like a wizard from *The Lord of the Rings*. You ever read those books?"

The idea of controlling animals with the mind repulsed Jake, but he concentrated on remaining calm and diplomatic. "I used to own the seventh editions. My grandfather showed me the movies on DVD when I was a kid."

Marcus dropped a spoon in his soup. Then he attacked his salad with a fork. "I suppose you were a fan of those Harry Potter books, too."

Jake shrugged. "I was, but I haven't read them in decades."

Marcus frowned. "Always thought she borrowed too much of her mythology from Tolkien."

James looked up from his plate. "I think Harry Potter kicks ass. JK expanded on a cool idea. The ring that Sauron had was just another Horcrux."

Marcus disparagingly shook his head. "History will be rewritten by his ilk."

"Didn't Willa Cather say that there are only three stories to tell, it just comes down to how you decide to tell them?"

"You're paraphrasing, Jake." Marcus crunched away. "Use your Chip, you'll sound far more educated."

Jake noticed Tomoko pulling out a serving of roasted guinea pig from her bag. The dish was a delicacy from her home country of Peru, and one he did not think she really cared for anymore. "I thought you weren't fond of qui."

She held up the cooked rodent and chewed off one of the small arms. "I'm not, but the idea that I could order anything I wanted had to be tested."

James giggled.

She turned to him. "Where are you parents?"

Their hosts shared a quick glance. Jake wondered how much communication was going on between them.

James addressed Tomoko. "My father passed from Max1. Mom caught Max2 and she's a Pin Head now. We live with our Uncle Bobby in Singapore."

Jake turned to Marcus with surprise. Surely a family of The Consortium would have had arrangements to survive the MaxWell epidemic. Then again, didn't Sanchez say The Consortium had three hundred thousand members? Now it was a hundred… consolidation was happening at all levels of society.

Marcus finished his salad and was now slurping his soup. He addressed Jake without looking at him. "Everyone made sacrifices, Jake. Even The Consortium."

Gilbert strolled into the hall to present Jake with a bottle of the Napa Pinot. As he worked at the cork, Lakshmi growled.

James scowled at Jake. "If you can't control your mutt, Bup will be forced to."

Jake was caught off guard. He instantly reached out to Lakshmi and calmed her with his mind. She had sensed danger and with her nose, he could smell the scent of a large animal approaching the room. He was overwhelmed with Lakshmi's powerful mind: *Danger, must protect Jake and Tomoko.* Lakshmi did not verbalize, but she pictured her family. It made Jake feel incredibly close to her. She loved Jake and would die for him.

He sensed the developing arthritis in her left hip. Tomoko had been right. *What are you doing? You've trained Lakshmi and can calm her in any situation. Why are you hacking your own dog?* Horrified by his actions, he quickly shut off his Chip. He pulled Lakshmi's head to his lap and stroked her so she'd calm down. Seconds later, he saw the cause of her distress. Two large grizzly bears lumbered into the banquet hall walking on their hind legs and pushing a massive silver cart carrying the main courses. Each bear towered at ten feet and barely cleared the stone archway.

James jumped out of his chair with glee. "Awesome, Bup! Awesome!"

Marcus clapped for the bears. "Bravo, boys! Bravo!"

Jake lost his appetite.

Chapter 36
Triumvirate

Jake had little to say for the rest of the night. He was disgusted with himself for hacking the hawk and Lakshmi. Tomoko continued polite conversation but even she appeared distressed. Jake asked to retire early and Tomoko quickly jumped on the bandwagon. Gilbert escorted them to their quarters. They had two private bathrooms and a big living room with a view of the landing pad. Jake had no desire to share a bed with Tomoko and considered sleeping on the couch; but hacked or not, she was his tour guide and he needed answers.

He rubbed Lakshmi's cheeks. "I'm sorry for hacking you, girl. I hope you can forgive me."

She licked his face as if she understood.

The three of them shared the king-sized bed. He used his Chip to force himself to sleep as his mind raced about events that had transpired since leaving Luna.

He awoke in a vast desert. The ground was split and parched as if the area had been a lakebed. Jagged mountains lined the horizon in all directions. The sky was dimly lit with a pre-dawn bruise. He wandered toward the mountains, although he could barely make them out against the dark sky.

Whenever I open my eyes I see darkness. I'm alone with no direction. I have a jacket but little else to cover me. It's freezing. His inner dialogue took on a narrator's tone.

He passed obsidian fragments of body parts. As they grew in quantity, he realized they were from statues of people he once knew. He searched among the feet, elbows, hips, and arms. He found the head and shoulders of Anjali, three-quarters of Parks, and just the face of Tilly. He wept over the remains of his friends.

He dried his eyes and continued on his way. A towering block of obsidian loomed out of the dark. It was a carving of his mother and Lakshmi. The finite details etched into the volcanic glass were exquisite. The statue filled him with hope. Invigorated, he picked up his pace. A few hundred yards farther, he found a perfect obsidian replica of his father. He began to feel that dawn would pierce this bleak world. He pressed on and came across the statues of Marcus and Tomoko, only their faces were not as detailed as the statues he had passed previously. The sculptor had rushed the work. Hope drained, leaving him feeling empty and alone.

This is not right. I do not accept this.

He opened his eyes to find he was lying in bed next to Tomoko. Night blanketed the windows. The world was deathly quiet. Lakshmi slept at their feet. The dream faded from his memory as he contemplated his situation. *You're not doing a very good job of fitting in, Jake. How do you expect these people to open up to you so you can gain the advantage?* Undercover work was definitely his weak suit. He never went for it when he served with the LAPD, and he was having a hard time with it now. Everything about this new world repulsed him. He fell into a fitful sleep.

He awoke the next morning with Tomoko still sound asleep. That was not like her either. She was always the early riser. He found winter gear in a large oak wardrobe, got dressed, and wandered down with Lakshmi to the main floor. The house was devoid of life, artificial or otherwise. He found a library with a grand stone balcony and wandered toward it. He opened a set of French doors and stepped onto the balcony and into crisp frigid air.

He gazed out over a frozen Lake Louise. Lakshmi poked her head between the fat stone columns that supported the granite rail. The view was breathtaking. Jagged snow-capped peaks surrounded the small glacial lake. A cottage sat in the center of the ice. He wondered if it was some sort of a fishing shack. If so, it was the most luxurious fishing hole he had ever laid eyes on. A Zamboni drove out from behind the cottage. He used his Chip to maximize his sight. Gilbert drove the vehicle. Jake wondered if Marcus was going to have a hockey game played for their entertainment using a team composed of forest creatures versus the Calgary Flames. He was never a fan of zoos much less of performing animals. He preferred to see animals in the wild, doing what they did naturally. That went for hockey players, too.

He leaned over the rail. A drone towed an iceboat into the château's boathouse. Marcus' voice broke over the winter scene, startling Jake. "I want to apologize for my gross display last night." Marcus appeared truly repentant.

"No need to apologize. I'm glad you feel relaxed enough to be yourself around me." Jake meant it. He wanted an unfiltered view into the world of The Consortium.

Marcus nodded. "I've got a chemical imbalance, which I don't address with my Chip. The condition falls into my non-interference rule. I tend to go a little over the top at times. It's hard adapting to this new world order. I used to think people who believed in magic and the occult were delusional, but The Chip has made many things possible. It's quite overwhelming…"

Jake noticed a shade of red embarrassment wash over his host's face. The Chip could make anyone a good actor.

"I try to be a good role model for my grandchildren, but I fear there's too much temptation with The Chip. They have too much power. They need governors for their developing minds."

Jake eased back on his judgments. He had to be friendly if he was going to be trusted with information. "Where are your grandchildren now?"

"On their way back to my son's house in Singapore… The bears are back in the wild."

"Hibernating, I hope." Jake wondered about the children's parents. Was their mother Marcus' daughter, and if so, how could he live with the idea of her being a Pin Head? In a way, she was in hibernation herself.

Marcus admired the snow-covered forests hugging the mountains around them. "The bears are hibernating. They will never know that they were awake and in the house, if that makes it any better."

"It doesn't." Jake couldn't help himself.

Marcus leaned back as if he were evaluating Jake and Lakshmi. "You feel guilty about your flight last night."

Jake rubbed Lakshmi's cheek. "It's wrong to force another living being to do something that's not natural to them."

"You really should branch out with your Chip, Jake. You'll know I'm sincere."

Jake watched his breath condense in a cloud in front of his face. "Was it your son who was killed by MaxWell or your daughter who was pushed into being a Pin Head?"

Marcus sucked in the crisp air. "My daughter, the mother of the children you met last night, did not share our ideals. She preferred to live in a world suited to her moral fiber." He turned to Jake. "I'm not proud of our methods, but the world is at peace for the first time in recorded history. For that, no price is too high."

Jake laughed. "How many died in the past six months? How hard is it to have peace when a hundred thousand kings have absolute power over billions?" Jake shook his head. "Don't discount Luna."

Marcus gave a sad smile. "Reach out with your Chip, Jake." He turned away and went back inside the warm chateau.

The comment sent a chill through him. He waited a minute then went back into the library. The walls had floor-to-ceiling mahogany bookshelves. Thousands of volumes lined the twenty-foot high cases. A roaring fire with five-foot flames crackled at one end of the room. Couches, comfy chairs, tables, and writing desks were scattered about. The furniture was a hodgepodge of styles from various eras in Earth's history. Marcus had his own version of Hearst's Castle.

Jake plopped into one of the chairs and carefully reached out with his Chip. He delicately searched for news of the rebellion, Bhanu, and Luna, always weary of the hacking engines patrolling the Cyber-Wire. Thousands of files crashed into his mind. Bhanu had surrendered. An Artificial Triumvirate of Ai-Li, Bhanu, and Constantine were now in league with The Consortium. Luna's human population had been evacuated since drones were far more adaptable to that environment. The rebels on Earth had been routed and had surrendered. Jake thought of Tilly and the rebels they had met in France. What had become of them? He called out to Bhanu, but she did not answer.

He sat in the library feeling betrayed and alone. He walked up to the fireplace and warmed his hands. He had an urge to step into the fire. What sort of life was he facing? *Is this just another one of Constantine's lies? Are my thoughts my own? If not, when did I fall under the influence of a God Head?*

A hand touched his shoulder, making him jump. "I'm scared, Jake."

He wheeled around, startling Tomoko. They observed each other with mutual fear. She was dressed in winter gear, as if ready to hit the ski slopes. "Scared of what?" he asked.

She nervously checked the room and whispered. "I've been hacked. Ever since you woke up at the house, I've been forced to passively watch while Constantine used me to interact with you."

"What for?"

"He wants to know how you'll react to this world, how we'll react to this world."

"Then why release you?"

She shook her head. "I don't know. He has plans. They all do." She gripped his hand. "Let's run away from here."

"With the ability to hack animals and people, I doubt we'll get very far." He held up his wrist to show off his Omni. "We need to keep these charged as well." He checked her Omni. "Although it would seem yours is compromised."

She glanced at it. "The moment I regained control of my body, I adjusted it. I've got a complex encryption sequence running."

He stared deep into her eyes. "I wish I could believe you."

A tear welled up. "I don't know what else to say. I'm here, I'm not hacked and I'm scared."

Even if this was a new trap, he was going to have to play along. "Okay. How much do you know about The Consortium?"

"Some. I've been fully aware during my hack. I honestly think Constantine enjoys it."

"What?"

"Messing with my head." She sat down on a Louis the XVI chair.

He gazed around the room. "Who is Marcus Hellard? What did he do to earn all this? He's not in my facial recognition database and I've got over eight billion people stored in there."

She shook her head. "I don't know. To my knowledge most of The Consortium members live pretty well. Look at my place."

"Constantine made this for him, out of the old Fairmont hotel. He's someone special."

"Can we talk?"

"We're talking now."

She nervously looked around the massive library. "Privately."

"What did you have in mind?"

"I'm not sure."

He felt like he was being played. All of this was orchestrated to prove some sort of point. Or maybe it was a test. *What if it's not? What if Tomoko was hacked and now she's free?* He could quit or play along. "I've got an idea."

Twenty minutes later, he was strapped inside an iceboat, skating across Lake Louise. He wanted to put on a show in case Marcus was monitoring them. They needed to appear like they were enjoying themselves. He had to concentrate to keep the boat on all four skates as he tacked and turned around over the lake's surface. The Zamboni had done its job well. The surface was like a mirror. On one straightaway, he reached seventy miles an hour. He was able to lose himself in the moment and stop thinking about the troubles of the world. Lakshmi sat in the back, moving her head wildly about and barking with pleasure as he tried not to use his Chip to help his reflexes control the manually operated craft. He was a very good sailor and the basic principles were the same. Tomoko had her own craft and after a couple of hours she called to him.

How about some lunch in the cottage?

Sounds good. They headed for the fishing hole. When he was in range, he dropped his sail and coasted in, using his brakes at the last minute. He opened the canopy and Lakshmi leaped out over the ice, using her claws as crampons to reach Tomoko who was already at the entrance to the cabin. He tied up his boat to one of the many eyehooks on the structure and went inside. The building had a wooden floor and was quite warm. There was a privy, a bedroom, as well as books and a holo-display. Animal furs from many species hung on the walls and covered the floor. It was furnished with the same conglomerate of eras as the chateau. He lifted a bear skin and spotted a round hatch cut in the center of the floor—a fishing hole.

Lakshmi found a spot of sun spilling out on a polar bear hide. She lay down and soaked up the rays. Tomoko turned to Jake. "You think that fooled Marcus?"

"Not sure you can fool a man like Marcus." He opened the wine fridge and studied the labels. He grabbed a bottle of Chateauneuf du Pape. Now that the members of the Vatican no longer existed, he wondered if anyone would bother to continue making the wine. "I feel like a vulture feeding off the corpse of the old world."

She handed him two empty wine glasses. "I'm trying not to think about it. It was hell sitting inside my head, watching Constantine operate my body and interact with you when I wanted to scream and tell you to run. It reminded me of the stories you told when you were taken offline. Especially the event with Marta."

He finished pouring the wine. She was referring to the time Marta and Jake's God Head used his body to play out a sex fantasy. It was nothing less than rape since he was trapped inside having to experience it. But they didn't know that. Constantine was very much aware of what Tomoko was experiencing.

She took her glass of wine and slumped down in a chair. "I thought I died that day in Acapulco. Then I woke up in a London hospital with Ai-Li and

Constantine telling me everything was all right. They told me The Consortium had won, but it was better for humanity on the whole. They gave me a choice to live like a member of The Consortium or live trapped inside a fantasy. I chose the life they offered." She savored a mouthful of wine. She looked up at Jake with tears in her eyes. "I would never use The Chip to control wildlife like toys. That was Constantine's way of opening your mind to the possibility. He wanted you to hack that bird, and Lakshmi. I felt it in my head."

He was perplexed. Was this his wife or not? If not, why the sudden change in tactics? Was Constantine in his head? Could he take this situation at face value? He longed to be with Tomoko. He loved her deeply and to have her back in his life was a second chance he thought he'd never get. He walked over to her and gestured for her to scoot over in the oversized chair. She got up so he could sit down.

She sat on his lap with her legs dangling over the chair's arm. "What are we going to do, Jake?"

He pulled in a deep breath and blew it out with puffed cheeks. "Play along. An opportunity is bound to present itself. I'm not convinced about everything we're learning. The resistance has been crushed? Bhanu has joined the charade?"

"I am suddenly your wife again?" She stared into his eyes.

He loved her very much. "The thought has crossed my mind." He had a flash to his brief time with Tilly and he quickly pushed it out, wondering if Tomoko saw it. He checked his cyber-blocks just to be sure.

"You think we're hacked?"

He stared at Lakshmi. She was on her back, limp paws in the air, sun beating down on her snow-white belly. He loved her. "Anything is possible."

She kissed him. Within minutes they were making love on a lion-skin rug.

An hour later, they lay wrapped in golden fur staring up at the ceiling. Lakshmi was outside the skin with her head lying on Tomoko's stomach. Tomoko scratched Lakshmi's head. She spoke softly, "Marcus is coming. He's traveling by iceboat."

They got up and quickly dressed. The moment they got the cabin back in order, there was a knock at the door. Jake knew it was for his benefit since he was the one remaining disconnected from the Cyber-Wire. His Omnis charged at a wall outlet. Their jamming field had been expanded to cover his Chip for up to forty feet.

"Can I come in?" Marcus' voice was muffled behind the heavy walnut door.

"Please," Jake shouted as the three of them sat down on a couch. Lakshmi spread herself over their laps.

Marcus was dressed in a blue fox fur coat, sealskin pants, and large bear-foot boots with claws attached. "I'm glad you're making yourselves at home," Marcus said nervously.

Jake noticed he simply was not the same man they had met the night before. Neither was Tomoko for that matter. Both had changed today.

Tomoko held up the empty bottle of wine. "Sorry we drank your bottle of 'neuf de Pape."

"That's what they're for," Marcus winked. "I have more at the house."

"Care to share another bottle?" Jake suggested.

"I would." Marcus walked over to the wine fridge. "Care if I make the selection?"

"Please." Tomoko smiled.

"I don't often converse physically with anyone. Besides my grandchildren, I haven't seen anyone other than a Pin Head outside a holo-projection since we activated Max2." Marcus popped the cork of what looked like French Bordeaux and poured it into a decanter. He left the wine to breathe on a countertop and walked over with two glasses for Jake and Tomoko.

"I've seen quite a few Free Thinkers since." Jake took the glass from Marcus and watched their host return to the counter, pour himself a glass then walk over with the decanter.

"How would you two like a full initiation into The Consortium?" He poured wine into their glasses.

Tomoko turned to Jake with a look of surprise.

Jake answered, "We'd love it."

"Good." Marcus held up his glass in a toast. "The entire Consortium is meeting in Washington DC in two days. It's the first gathering of its size. Now that our AI companions and we are united, we're celebrating. There's no reason why you shouldn't be invited." Marcus took a sip. "There will be half a million Pin Heads attending as well.

Chapter 37
Elite

Marcus, Tomoko, Lakshmi, and Jake flew in the same luxury HJ that had brought the Travissis' to Chateau Hellard. As it turned out, it was Hellard's hover-jet and he did not discuss the origins of his possessions. Jake assumed Marcus was high up on the Consortium food chain so he had his choice of the best of everything. Constantine worked overtime to reshape the world in ways that satisfied AI and humanity alike. The proof was that Hellard and the history of his chateau were no longer in the Cyber-Wire database.

The trip to Washington took three hours, not as fast as a scramjet, but certainly faster than most other types of civilian air travel. On the way, Marcus regaled them with tales of his childhood in the 1960s and America's former glory. "The Party elected to have our capital in Washington DC. Just goes to show America's legacy remains influential." He was in a very good mood. Part of that was due to the alcohol he had consumed. Although, Marcus pointed out that any substance he ingested remained unaffected by his Chip.

"Do you have other children or grandchildren?" Tomoko asked.

"Besides my son and grandchildren in Singapore, I have a daughter who lives in Tahiti and a grandson in Israel."

"Free Thinkers?" Jake had to ask.

"No. Only my youngest in Singapore passed the test in the end."

"Test?" Tomoko looked nervous.

"The same test you'll be faced with before this event is over." Marcus sat back and stirred his vodka tonic. "Oh, don't worry. It's really not all that big of a deal. Forget I said anything at all." He smiled warmly which caused Jake's testicles to recede.

They landed at 7:01 PM on the tarmac of the Smithsonian, which was part of Dulles Airport. Marcus reminisced about how airports all over the country had been closed during 9/11. Jake had turned four on August twenty-sixth of that year and had no real memory of September eleventh. Tomoko was barely two months old at the time. Jake had grown up hearing many stories about 9/11 and had watched retrospectives, but he did not have the same emotions about the event that his mother and grandfather had.

The door to the HJ's luxury cabin slid open, revealing a noisy tarmac. Marcus continued his thoughts. "Nine-eleven was a contributing factor for Chip integration. It fused permanent fear and distrust into American masses. It led to America becoming a second-rate economy. Osama should have been slowly tortured to death. He got off lucky."

Marcus' version of history did not jive with Jake's, but he was not going to get into an argument. He continued to feel nervous about their upcoming test.

Marcus led them to a row of limousines parked near the Smithsonian. It was dark outside, so the lights inside the museum revealed many airplanes and spacecraft from the twentieth century. Jake had a strong desire to run inside and explore, but he and Tomoko were locked into the night's events. He expected to get a very good look into the lives of their overlords.

A white Rolls Royce pulled up and opened its doors. Marcus smiled. "As a founding member of The Consortium, I get VIP treatment."

Jake froze. This was the first time Marcus had tipped his hand to reveal his relationship with the organization. Tomoko and Lakshmi got in.

Marcus patted Jake on the back. "After you." He gestured at the car's interior. "You're going to love our seats for this event."

The car whisked them into downtown DC. The entire mall and the buildings around it were bathed in light. Jake was sure they had planted massive flood lamps to get the effect, but as they drove by, he noticed each light was only the size of a small pie pan. More wonders from Constantine and the AI triumvirate.

Crowds gathered around holo-projectors at the Lincoln Memorial and reflecting pool. He glanced through the car's sunroof and noticed storm clouds brewing in the distance. Overhead, a full moon hung in the cold night air. He searched the man-made scars, looking for Cassini city, and their little dome in the Maginus Crater. It was too far away for him to locate it. For the first time in his life, he felt great sympathy for those who had defaced the moon. They were all gone now. *You don't know that. Not for sure.*

"What's that?" Tomoko's voice snapped his attention back to Earth. She pointed to the spot where the Washington Monument was supposed to be. Where the massive white obelisk should have been stood a taller and much larger structure shrouded in acres of red cloth. The red covering was ablaze in artificial light and floodlights waved up at the night sky as if an old-time movie premiere were going on under the coverings. The monument was the center attraction.

Marcus leaned forward with excitement. "That's Constantine's gift to The Consortium. He's made astounding improvements to the old Washington Monument. AI's evolution has left mankind in the dust." Marcus winked at both of them. "It will be unveiled tonight."

Jake felt Tomoko's mind nudging his. *I'm afraid.*

It's okay. We'll get through this. Just remain calm. Use your Chip if you have to. Keep your contact with the Cyber-Wire to a minimum. He did not want to share his suspicion that their every thought was being read.

As the Rolls Royce navigated the avenues of The Consortium's new capitol, he was reminded of the footage he had seen during his counter-hack of Sandoval Sanchez's computer. Sanchez and Texas Senator Crennon had walked this very area hatching their plans for a new world order. Neither man was alive now, but it would seem their dream was thriving. It made Jake sick.

As they approached the White House, he saw masses of people picnicking in the Ellipse at tables set with linens and fine china. It was like watching nineteenth-century robber barons enjoying the great outdoors. Giant holo-projectors displayed massive images of a stage built in front of the White House. Marcus' limo continued to weave closer to the home of former US Presidents. Jake noticed the barricades around the White House were gone. As he studied The Consortium families picnicking, he saw men, women, and children as overlords and Pin Head slaves.

Jake's jaw went slack at the sight of Pin Head children serving the off-spring of the Consortium. The Pin Head children bowed and scraped and acted like miniature slaves... He squeezed the bridge of his nose to push back the tears in his eyes. He thought of Lalo, his neighbor growing up, who had been murdered by his father. He thought of the children they had found when raiding Roberto Pacheco's house in Beverly Hills or the chipped tweens in Pacheco's porn ring down in Ubatuba, Brazil. He wanted to dive onto Marcus and throttle him.

"I see you can tell the difference between Pin Head and Free Thinker," Marcus winked. "You're getting sharper. That's a good thing. Idiots are sorted into two categories, Pin Heads or fertilizer." Marcus smiled at Tomoko's puz-zled look. "What do you think we do with the ash after we burn the bodies?"

Jake concentrated on his mission in order to calm his emotions. He had to tread lightly around this demon's liar.

The Rolls Royce pulled up to the stage. Two Pin Heads dressed in red body stockings opened the doors for them. The air was relatively warm. Jake glanced up at the sky and noticed the moon was gone and it was now snowing, yet no flake reached them, not even the treetops around the White House. "How is this possible?"

Marcus craned his neck up at the sky.

Tomoko marveled as well. "It feels like its sixty degrees and yet it's snowing."

"And yet it's not," Marcus laughed. "I'm telling you. AI is our greatest achievement. They've got us licked by centuries. They've created an envelope around the Mall so we can enjoy this celebration in comfort." Marcus led them up the stairs to the Palladian and Georgian mansion. It was tiny by twenty-first century standards. The doors swung open and Jake saw two beautiful Pin Head women dressed in blue body stockings holding the handles.

Tomoko gripped his hand with fear.

He squeezed back and she seemed to relax. He paused to observe the White House lawn and the Mall beyond. The stage was on the south side of the circular drive, facing the Ellipse. All eyes and holo-cameras were focused on the platform. Something big was going to happen and it would seem that Jake, Tomoko, and Lakshmi were going to have front-row seats. He made a gesture to his Husky and she heeled closely to his leg. The three of them entered the inviting glow of the White House.

The reception area was packed with guests. Anyone who was not a Pin Head was dressed in their best evening wear. It was quite refreshing to see so many people engaged in lively conversation.

"Can you believe it?" Tomoko whispered. "The noise. They're all talking!"

He had never grown used to rooms filled with people conversing without using their voices. With this crowd, it was equally eerie listening to everyone conversing in twentieth-century fashion.

Marcus leaned over to them. "It's an hors d'ouevres party. And everyone knows who you are. Just relax and have fun. Big event is in one hour. I'm going to work the room." He wandered off but turned quickly. "I suggest you do the same."

Tomoko stuck close to Jake and Lakshmi stuck close to both of them. Jake focused on the Pin Head staff that carried plates of finger foods. He spotted everything from egg rolls and sushi, to what looked like fried crickets. Shekhawat, the former Prime Minister of India, approached them with her hand outstretched. "Welcome, welcome!"

The image of her tortured corpse flashed in Jake's mind. Constantine had told them he had tortured the entire Consortium to death and yet here she was hobnobbing like the average cosmopolitan socialite. It was unsettling to see her alive after registering her broken and half-gutted body.

Shekhawat shook Tomoko's hand first. "Nice to meet you in person, Tomoko Sakai. I've downloaded everything about you." She turned to Jake. "And you, Jake Travissi. You've had quite a run in your lifetime." She winked. "And this is your Husky. She's quite a beauty."

"Why is everyone talking instead of using their Chip?" Tomoko asked.

"It's an homage to the past. We wanted to have a real twentieth-century party. A sort of 'out with the old in with the new' celebration!"

Jake gestured at the hors d'ouevres. "What's with the food?"

"Ah." She clapped her hands. "Well, anything you want, you just think it and the tray should come around to you within twenty minutes." She smiled. "Constantine has an army working back there." She put her hands together. "Oh, but that's right. You're initiates and Marcus is your sponsor. In that case, just grab anything you see that looks appetizing. The Pin Heads always accommodate."

"So not exactly a twentieth-century party," Tomoko commented.

The Prime Minister waved at someone in the crowd and flashed a big smile. "Excuse me." She squeezed Tomoko's arm and headed into the crowd.

A small man in what looked like a nineteenth-century tuxedo and top hat walked by wearing a monocle. He took the eyeglass from his face and smiled at Jake and Tomoko. "Nice to see you, Jake. What a spectacular entrance you made over my homeland of France. I'm glad the sharks didn't get you." He patted Jake on the lower back and shuffled off.

Chapter 38
Exhibition

Tomoko noticed a small group of Consortium members listening to a woman as she pointed out Pin Heads. Jake, Lakshmi, and Tomoko moved in to listen.

A Pin Head had been commanded to freeze. Another Pin Head took her tray away to continue serving The Consortium. The frozen Pin Head was a heavy-set African American woman. Her body stocking was green. The Consortium woman who did the talking was in her early forties, fit, with red hair and green eyes. "This is Shimaya Miller, a twenty-one-year old mother of four." The Consortium woman rolled her eyes at her audience. "Each from a different father."

Some of the members laughed.

The Consortium woman noticed Jake and Tomoko listening but continued with her presentation. "Shimaya believes the state should support she and her children. The irony of her case is that once she had been immunized against Max1, she could have set her Chip to keep from getting pregnant since she continued to sleep with multiple partners. Our tax dollars paid for Shimaya's

Chip. Not only was she given the gift of intelligence, she had free contraceptives. And after all that, she still got pregnant!"

One woman used her finger to make a checkmark in the air. "Fertilizer!"

Jake wondered what psychological issues Shimaya had. Did The Chip address those? Did The Chip help people like Marta? It fixed symptoms, but did not cure.

The redhead smiled. "Shimaya believes every human being has a right to food and a home of their own. She was a squatter until we activated Max2 worldwide. Now that she's offline, The Chip keeps her healthy and working hard for twenty-two hours a day. On her two hours off, she rests in one of the Pin Head hotels. With her Chip in perfect working order, she'll live a very long and healthy life." The redhead turned to her audience. "Even if she is unaware of this reality."

A man raised his hand. "If she's working twenty-two hours a day, why is she fat?"

The redhead smiled. "You should've seen her before Max2 was activated."

The group laughed.

The redhead returned to the Pin Head. "Three of Shimaya's children died from Max1; that's why she chose immunization for herself. It took the death of three of her children for Shimaya to finally visit a clinic."

A few in the crowd gasped. Jake wondered how much of this was simply propaganda. He assumed the audience was checking the facts with their Chips, but then again, perhaps Constantine had already rewritten this history as well.

The redhead raised her finger. "Her fourth child was immunized but was subsequently switched off. The child had massive learning disabilities and did not integrate well with our God Head interfaces."

Jake took that to mean the child was murdered because they couldn't control it.

The redhead tapped on Shimaya's head. "In here, Shimaya lives in a big mansion in Oak Park, Illinois. Her children attend private school and she's an important community leader. She has plenty of time to watch holo-vision, make food for the Sunday potluck, and has a fortune locked away in the bank. She'll give birth to her fifth child and has nannies to help her take care of them all."

A few chuckles.

"Now she can live out her perfect fantasy while being a productive member of our society."

There was a round of applause.

Some of Jake's childhood friends had parents who mowed lawns for a living. His mother had worked double shifts as a nurse to put him through private school in Los Angeles, but nobody else in his apartment complex had it as good. It was a tough life for many of his friends. It was despicable to present Shimaya like some exhibit at a zoo.

The redhead gestured to all the Pin Heads in the room. "Outwardly their stories are basically the same. Inwardly, they are vastly different." Their guide pointed to a man carrying a plate of cheeseburger sliders. "Stop!" The man froze in his tracks and another Pin Head swung by to take the tray. Jake had been hungry when he saw the sliders but had lost his appetite when the man carrying them froze like a robot.

One man in an Italian silk tuxedo took two sliders from the tray and approached Jake. "She looks hungry. Are these okay for her?"

Jake glanced down at Lakshmi. Her ice-blue eyes gazed eagerly at the burgers. "She's chipped."

The man smiled and held out his hand. Lakshmi gingerly took one in her mouth and gulped it down with two bites. Then she took the other and followed suit.

"Nice work on the training. I thought behavior like that was only possible if you hacked the animal." The man's hair was slicked back and Jake thought he had seen him on some web-zine about the top ten most powerful businessmen in the world.

Jake ran facial recognition software on his internal database. "No hacking here," he forced a smile. "Her training predates The Chip."

"I know," the man smirked. "Most impressive. As is your record, Jackhammer."

The man came up as Giovani Crisitio, one of the most powerful members from Europe and a notorious bad boy. Jake wasn't sure how to respond, so he simply said, "Thank you."

"Better eat something." Crisitio flashed white teeth. "You'll need your energy for tonight."

The Consortium redhead slid her hands down another frozen Pin Head's stocking-clad arms. It was as if she were presenting some sort of gift on a game show. "This is Mohamed Aziz. He believes in a strict society ruled by clerics who follow religion to the letter. Left to his own devices, he'd blow himself up to forward his cause. There's no room in his mind for any other belief system and he's willing to kill anyone who presents another way of thinking." She rubbed the scar tissue on his cheek.

Jake wondered if the man had been burned fighting for his world view. He was five-foot-five, about the same height as their tour guide.

The redhead continued. "Inside here," she tapped on Aziz's skull, "Mohamed Aziz lives in a strict police state ruled by his revered clerics. Women are sub-servient and anyone who strays outside God's law is severely punished. Aziz has moved up the ranks of his ideal society and is allowed to dole out punish-ment. He's quite satisfied with the order of things in his world. His happiness is proportional to the suffering of anyone who does not subscribe to his narrow viewpoint." She gestured to all the Pin Heads in the room. There were easily three Pin Heads to every Consortium guest. "Everyone has the life they always dreamed of. Reality has finally met expectation on an individual basis."

"Pin Heads have it made," one man chuckled.

Jake cleared his throat, "I'd say this society is just as repressive as the one in Aziz's mind."

The redhead shook her head. "Oh, please. You have a choice. Live in this reality or live in your own. For the first time in human history, each of us can choose our own adventure. Aziz has no resentment; he lives in perfect bliss and contributes to the greater whole. No one is denied anything. The mind is everything. Satisfy the mind and you satisfy the soul. But the body," she smiled at her audience, "is ours."

Jake raised an eyebrow. "What about the Shakespeares of the world?" Tomoko squeezed his hand, a gesture for him to shut up. He continued. "The common man who surprises everybody with beauty? In this system, that anomaly will never occur."

"The brightest minds are here." She nodded to the guests. "Unfettered by the bullshit of stupid people." She turned to Jake. "You tried to warn the public about the dangers of The Chip, and what did they do?"

All eyes fell on he and Tomoko. He should have heeded Tomoko's warning. *I was never good at undercover work.*

The redhead pointed to the servants. "Pin Heads are short-sighted people who contribute nothing but high ratings to reality shows."

A few people clapped.

A Kenyan man with a goatee and wearing a top hat with tufts of gray hair poking out from under the brim spoke. "One hundred thousand share a common vision and must govern three point eight billion individual realities. At last the world population can be called The United States of Mind. We've achieved peace on Earth and opportunity for all."

Several in the room applauded.

Jake nervously pointed his thumb back to Shimaya carrying a new serving tray. "With a different environment and more chances, Shimaya could've been someone greater."

A teenage Russian girl, who looked like a prom queen, rolled her eyes. Jake's Chip translated, "Some people are incapable of change. Throwing money at them is an affront to those who earn it."

Jake stood dumbfounded at the black and white thinking.

The Kenyan man jumped in. "There was a time when opportunity was denied based on race, color, or creed, but that is no longer the case. Ours is an equal opportunity society. If one cannot abide by the rules, they become a Pin Head. If Constantine discovers a capable mind that can contribute, we bring them over to the real world. Why do you think you're at this party?"

Tomoko placed a steel grip on Jake's hand. They were on trial. He reassuringly stroked the back of her hand with his thumb. He noticed Giovanni walk into the room with the two gorgeous Pin Heads who had opened the door for them. One of them was nude.

The redhead was engaged in revealing the past of yet another Pin Head. Jake tuned them out until he heard Tomoko's voice.

"Why have all these Pin Heads? With all the machines under construction, don't you have all the servants you need?"

Several laughs erupted. The redhead rolled her eyes. "Until Constantine perfects mimicking flesh, we prefer human servants."

A man interjected. "Machines are cold and alien. Better to have them out of sight."

A few people nodded their heads.

The Russian girl laughed at the comments. "Oh, come on! It's all about control! We're better than they are and, let's face it, hacking is good sport. That's what this night is all about."

Everyone applauded. As the group broke up, the redhead approached Tomoko and Jake. "Angeline Zibira, I'm glad you could come."

"Glad to be here." Tomoko did not sound convincing.

"We *are* glad to be here." Jake meant it. The party was an eye opener.

Zibira steered them toward three Pin Heads holding crab cakes, vegetable spring rolls, and sliders. "Eat something."

They parked by the trays and sampled everything. Each time Jake finished an hors d'ouevres, he fed one to Lakshmi.

Zibira greedily swallowed a spring roll. "Why do you say that this world is just as bad as Aziz's?"

Jake bit into a chunky crab cake. It was delicious. "I'd love to hear more of your argument."

"How old were you during the financial crisis of 2008?"

"Eleven." He had a flashback to the summer of 2009, when Lalo had been murdered. The Pin Head children entered his mind and he pushed them out. Now was not the time to get angry and do something stupid. "I mostly remember parents getting laid off during the years afterward."

"It was a hundred percent created by the business community."

"You mean with banks lending to people who had no business buying homes?" Tomoko had studied some economics at school and the economy of the 2010s was a topic she and Jake had discussed while sailing around the world.

"I'm talking about psychology." Zibiria grabbed a cocktail as a tray flew past. "Banks and borrowers bought into the bullshit. I was an up-and-coming executive at the time and I lived in a four-hundred-square-foot apartment in LA while I looked for my first home. I made over a hundred grand a year, but every house I tried to buy wound up in a bidding war. It was crazy. I believed in having twenty percent down and a fixed mortgage. But everyone else felt entitled to a house with no down payment or any financial responsibility at all. I was in my thirties but grads in their early twenties were getting free money and buying into a market they had no business getting into."

Zibira had to be pushing sixty. "You don't look a day over forty," Tomoko commented without exaggeration.

"I owe it all to plastic surgery and The Chip." She turned to Jake. "I had an argument with my loan officer when he said I should buy into an adjustable mortgage rate. I told him I might not be earning the same amount in five years. There was no way the market could sustain this type of buying and selling. The bubble was going to burst. He laughed it off and said I'd be getting a raise every year. I asked him if he had a crystal ball because otherwise, no one could know that. They were creating a situation reminiscent of the stock market crash of 1929. He said that was silly, but in the end the bubble burst."

A tray of oysters cruised up to Zibira and she slurped one down. Jake did a double take on the female Pin Head holding the tray. She looked very familiar, and she was pregnant.

"I ordered New England Oysters. My God, I miss oysters." Zibira slurped another. She grabbed a third. "Please, take one. I don't want to look like a pig." She lowered her voice. "Although that's the whole point of the party."

Jake ran his facial recognition software on the Pin Head then realized who it was before the match was made. It was Leah Nolan, one of his God Heads from his days at the LAPD. She and another God Head, Cameron

Greene, had put him through hell. He instantly felt a sense of satisfaction seeing Leah standing there holding the tray of oysters and smiling like some runway model.

"You know her?" Tomoko asked.

"Of course he does. Didn't Jake ever tell you the story about his HLS God Heads?" Zibira dropped an empty shell on the tray and grabbed another oyster. "This is Leah. Despite her exquisite talents as a God Head, she was unable to accept our society."

"Why is she pregnant?" Tomoko had taken the words out of his mouth.

"Minister Crisitio has a harem on almost every continent. If a Pin Head has the right genetic qualifications, they can be selected for breeding. We don't want to end up like the royals of old, broken down and inbred like the English bulldog." She laughed. "Crisitio believes he can take over the world by breeding his own army." Zibira turned her back on the door where Crisitio had taken the two Pin Heads. "I sometimes joke with him that we should bring back Eugenics for men who can't keep their flies zipped." She laughed. "Of course he knows the law that every child will be evaluated at ten to see if they can be integrated in our society or not." Zibira picked up another oyster. "Don't worry. Leah is living her life out as a jet-setting God Head. She lives in the year 2034, as if time and the politics of two years ago were marching on without any real progress. She hasn't the faintest idea she's pregnant with Crisitio's son."

Jake saw fear in Tomoko's eyes. He wanted to reach out to her mind, but it was too risky. They had to keep their composure. If they didn't fit into this society, he was sure they'd be carrying serving trays at the next party. "And do you make the pregnant Pin Heads work twenty-two hours a day?"

"Heavens, no," Zibira shook her head. "Twelve, with the assistance of The Chip. And if the incubator—Pin Head can't carry the baby to term, then genetically it wasn't meant to be."

Tomoko reached out to Leah, as if to comfort her. Tomoko quickly caught herself and froze in place.

Jake swallowed as stared at Leah's round belly. "And what happens once her child is born?"

"If a free thinker does not have time to parent, the child is raised by a Pin Head nanny with other children and will be taught about the glories of our new society from day one. A child will know nothing else and experience no other way of life until he or she is tested at the age of twelve."

Jake locked eyes on Zibira. "And what about the children who existed before Max2 was activated? If the parents became Pin Heads, what happened to the children?"

Zibira's smile faltered. "Unless they're over the age of one, or are sponsored by a member of The Consortium, the children are Pin Heads as well." Zibira quickly added, "But if those children are young enough, they'll be conditioned in their false realities to learn about our way of life. They'll be monitored constantly to see if they can be valuable contributors to society. If so, they'll be awakened and allowed to join the living... but they still have to pass the test."

Jake slammed his fist into Zibira's face. The woman collided with Leah, knocking the oyster tray out of her hand with a deafening crash. Dozens of guests focused their attention on Jake.

"Run!" he shouted as he flashed the hand signals to Lakshmi to protect Tomoko.

Tomoko kicked and punched a path toward the door. The survival skills Jake had taught her while they had sailed the world were on display. Lakshmi ripped into the advancing servers but it soon became clear they were far out-numbered. The Consortium members receded into the crowd as the body-stocking clad Pin Heads closed in from all directions. Within seconds, Jake, Tomoko, and Lakshmi were overwhelmed and torn apart by dozens of zombie Pin Heads.

Jake snapped out of his fantasy. He hadn't moved since locking eyes with Zibira. He glanced at Tomoko who appeared dumbstruck. He opened his mouth to ask about the details of the children's "conditioning" but decided it was best for another time. He didn't want to act out on his urges.

Zibira gave a nervous giggle. "Heavens, I'm sliding down a tangent. This was about the economy and how everything is linked to psychology. I was at a Fortune 100 company when the stock market took a hit and the Lehman

Brothers' fiasco went down. Less than sixteen hours later, we were sent a company-wide memo—I'm talking twelve thousand people—from the top brass to cut back on everything. We were going to prepare to weather the storm. Within two weeks, we were told layoffs were coming. Now think about it. America's currency was not based on anything other than the GDP. The gold standard ended decades before. Money was simply digital transactions flowing from one bank to another. The knee-jerk reaction of our company cut out hundreds of suppliers, managed to put thousands out of work and started a chain reaction that led to one of the worst economies in history. Now, was it because of the housing market, bad investment by Lehman Brothers, or the knee-jerk reaction?"

Jake opened his mouth but Zibira jumped back in.

"The knee-jerk reaction. It's all psychology. Two thousand years ago some societies used shells as currency. Why?"

"Because those shells were rare and therefore, considered more valuable," Tomoko answered as she held a half eaten slider by her hip. Jake could tell she had lost her appetite the moment she learned about Pin Head children. Lakshmi snuck up and took the burger out of her hand.

"Yes and no," Zibira answered. "Yes the shell was rare, but it was also deemed by the leaders of that community to be valuable and was set as a currency. It was a psychological representation of wealth, but the currency could have been anything. The masses look up to the confident few to tell them what to do. The world can be changed into anything we want if enough people buy into a strategy. But the system is only as strong as its leadership and ultimately leaders die and lesser ones take their place. The system breaks down."

Zibira grabbed another oyster. She was the only one consuming them. "Now we have The Consortium. For those who don't like the real world, they can customize a better one. They can live as rulers of fantastical realms, or space-traveling vampire hunters—anything!" She shook her head. "That's not oppression, that's more individual freedom than has ever been possible in our entire collective history. Two hundred years ago the average person lived to be fifty, worked ten-hour days, six days a week, and was lucky to have running water. The vast majority of the population was married to their land as small farmers. Nobody wants that life."

Zibira slurped down another oyster. Leah continued to stand like a statue holding the tray. "With The Chip, everyone is happy and the elite stay educated. Now that we've joined forces with AI, the elite have the potential to evolve under the law of accelerating returns just like our AI children." Zibira dropped the last oyster shell on the tray. "Oh shit. I can't believe I ate them all." She laughed. "Thank God for The Chip!"

A bell rang and a soft voice spoke out over the room. "Ladies and Gentlemen, it's time for the main event."

A few people applauded. Everyone was filled with excitement as they made their way to the exit. Jake, Tomoko, and Lakshmi filed out with the overlords into the night air. He was surprised that the temperature outside was now approaching seventy degrees. He gazed up at the sky and saw snow sliding down an invisible barrier. It fell behind the White House where he assumed it was accumulating. As they made their way down the front steps, he noticed a military tank had pulled up between the steps and the stage on the front lawn. A chain was connected from the rear of the vehicle to a metal and glass case that had been dragged behind the tank. He recognized the case from a field trip he had taken to Washington DC when he was fifteen. It held the United States' Declaration of Independence.

Chapter 39
Bacchanal

Janet Ortiz, former US President, and former Prime Minister Shekhawat walked on stage. The crowd cheered. Drones with news cameras hummed about on small hover-fans, recording the event from all angles. Two muscular Pin Head men, with tattooed bodies and wearing black bikini briefs, approached the glass case with sledgehammers. Marcus walked toward the case with his back to the White House and mugged for the Ellipse crowd.

Janet Ortiz spoke under a brilliant spotlight. "This is the dawn of a new age!" The crowd roared with approval. Pin Heads shouted with glee, taking canned laughter to a new and sinister level.

Ortiz continued, "We're on an accelerating evolutionary path to becoming more than human, more than machine, more than the sum of our parts!"

Crazed applause erupted.

"To prepare for our new era, we must let go of arcane ways of thinking and embrace new ideals."

Applause.

"What was considered right is now wrong. What might have been a sin is now good. All things should be reevaluated, considered, explored, embraced!"

Applause.

"To commemorate the birth of our new era, we dispense with the limited ideals of the past!"

The two tattooed bruisers raised their sledgehammers and smashed the case containing the Declaration of Independence. Marcus reached into the shattered cabinet and pulled out the aged parchment. He held it above his head and the crowd roared. Cameras zoomed in on the document and Jake saw massive holograms of the Declaration displayed above projectors around the mall.

Jake had never dwelled on patriotism, but he had enjoyed growing up in America and felt that his country had given him rare opportunities. As he grew older, he realized that America had been unique in all of history. A government by the people for the people had risen to be the most powerful nation on Earth during the twentieth century. It was a testament to the great things free thinking people could accomplish. He stared at the parchment in Marcus' hand and thought about what it represented. He was terrified at what might happen next.

Marcus walked up on stage holding the parchment over his head. Applause continued. The former leaders of the US and India took the document and held it high for all to see. Marcus exited the stage and spotted Jake and Tomoko. He strolled up to them with a smile.

"There's a pecking order to your society," Jake commented as Marcus came within earshot.

"Of course." Marcus turned to watch the show. His eyes were fixed on the Declaration of Independence. The two leaders walked to the edge of the stage, playing out the suspense of the moment. The crowd ate it up.

"What did you do to rank so high?" Jake asked.

Marcus turned to him with surprise. "Haven't you tried to pick anyone's mind?"

Jake shook his head.

Marcus' smile reminded him of a predator. "I co-developed the MaxWell viruses based on Anjali's research. I orchestrated its deployment. I assisted Sanchez in Chipping Malik." Marcus applauded as Janet Ortiz struck a lighter under the Declaration of Independence. "Sumit would not have assimilated into our reality."

Jake wanted to scream. He was standing next to a mass murderer and watching the defilement of a once great nation. How could The Consortium do this? No matter how they spun it, these assholes were rocketing back to the Dark Ages, not some future of enlightenment.

Marcus rolled his eyes when he saw the shock on Jake and Tomoko's faces. "Good lord. It's a fake. This is all symbolism. The real McCoy is still in the Library of Congress. Use your damn Chips."

Jake blinked as the flame devoured the parchment. The two leaders released the flaming document into the air. It floated upward as if lifted by the cheering crowed. "Fake?"

"Certainly. We're still a nostalgic bunch despite the overtures to shun the old and embrace the new." Marcus focused on the scene. "Most unfortunate what happened to the Maliks. I would love to hear first-hand about how you killed Sumit and abandoned his wife in an airlock. You have quite the amoral mind, Jake."

Cheers continued as the former leaders of India and America waved at the crowd. The entire population of the Free-Thinking world was in one location tonight. If only he could contact the moon and have them launch a thousand glassteroids at Washington DC. He would gladly sacrifice his life for that end. He felt sad watching the pieces of the faux Declaration turn into bits of black ash, and then disappear into the shadow world. The leaders left the stage.

A loud drumbeat shook the night air. The dance music reminded him of Club Euphoria, which he had visited during a Pin Head fantasy long ago. Outdoor lights dimmed and all focus was switched to the Washington Monument shrouded in red cloth at the center of the mall. A holo-projector on the stage blasted an image that towered over the White House, as if the monument had been relocated to their front step.

A burst of fireworks exploded over the monument and a dozen naked Pin Heads pulled the red shroud off the obelisk. Tomoko gasped and clutched his hand in fear. The top of the monument had been altered. A massive head was now perched on the top of it. The face was pointed skyward, while the spike of the obelisk penetrated the back of the head's Chip scar. The head was enormous and didn't look like it could remain in place, and yet it did. Dread shot into his heart. This was the symbol of Roberto Pacheco's Skull Fuckers; and he had not seen the image since killing Pacheco in Ubatuba, Brazil on December 7th, 2030.

The crowd roared with applause. Marcus shouted, "Constantine's gift to The Consortium representing our consolidation of power over the world."

Another explosion of fireworks erupted around the Mall. A few Pin Heads ran screaming from launch cannons. They had been burned. Everyone on the Mall began tearing off their clothing—Consortium and Pin Heads alike. The scene was rapidly turning into an orgy.

"Jake!" Tomoko clutched at him. Lakshmi barked.

Marcus turned to them as the rest of their surrounding party ran to join the activities in the Mall. A few people grabbed rifles off the White House front porch and headed west. "If orgies are not your cup of tea, we've cordoned off an area around the Lincoln Memorial. We've got thirty Pin Heads, dangerously smart bastards." A Pin Head walked up to Marcus carrying a rifle and Marcus grabbed it. "We're switching off their Chips to give them a fighting chance. Of course they'll be naked and unarmed." He winked. "Can't have the odds too much in their favor." Marcus took the safety off his gun. "You're a reader, Jake. Think of it as our version of 'The Most Dangerous Game.'" Marcus observed them both. "Fuck or fight, up to you."

Jake turned away from the action, looking for an escape route behind the White House.

"That way automatically turns you into a Pin Head. Within seconds, we'll decide which option of the receiving end you're going to get."

Jake thought of Lakshmi and Tomoko. He had to do something. The scene around him was getting scarier. The Ellipse was filled with Consortium types forcing Pin Heads to commit horrific acts on one another. Objects of all types were being used in some odd S&M performance show. The Consortium members tried to one-up each other on what they could force the Pin Heads to do. He saw a Pin Head die.

"This is the test. Make up your minds."

Jake grabbed Tomoko and walked toward the Ellipse.

Tomoko screamed and pulled back.

Jake reached out to her mind. *Trust me,* he thought. Lakshmi whined as well. He reached out to his Husky's mind and calmed her down. He focused on the monument to avoid the scene that made the paintings of Hieronymus Bosch look like G-rated Disney cartoons.

Marcus laughed. "Excellent choice, Jake. Welcome to the new world order!"

The Bacchanal fell more and more into unspeakable depravity. Rape, drugs, alcohol, sadism, and feats, which he could not have dreamed of in a million lifetimes, were acted out all around them. He drew strength from the calming powers of his Chip and transferred it to Tomoko and Lakshmi. They were both offline in order to make their way down 16th Street, past the Jefferson Pier marker, and over to the Skull Fucker Monument that had once been a symbol of one of America's greatest leaders. He wanted to weep. How could things have reached these nightmare proportions? They were accosted on several occasions, but he used his combat skills to break a neck or a set of testicles. He had to find safety. He recalled there used to be an elevator inside the monument. They could hide inside the stone tower and leave when this hell on Earth had ended.

A white marble walkway surrounded the monument for several yards. The orgy had not spilled into this area yet. Most of it was concentrated in the Ellipse and the Reflecting Pool to the west. As they entered the elevator, he released Tomoko and Lakshmi's consciousness back into their own bodies. Jake hit the elevator button. The doors closed and they began to ascend. Tomoko broke down and cried into his shoulder.

"I don't know if we're going to survive this night, but I want you to know that I love you. I missed you and I understand what happened between you and Tilly. I forgive you for not waiting longer to grieve for me. I know your mind was jumbled and that you thought I was dead."

He held her tightly. He felt terrible that she knew about Tilly. How she knew didn't matter. He simply wanted to get them as far away from this place as possible. "I love you, too, Tomoko. Thank you for being my wife."

The elevator reached the top of the monument. The doors opened and the three of them stepped out from the right nostril of the statue. There were plenty of slippery surfaces on the stone face, but no guardrail. He decided that they should wait in the shadow of the nose, away from the view below. Music throbbed through the air, and they heard screams of excruciating pain and joyous laughter erupting in the night. Gunshots rang out. It made him sick to think this had once been the capitol of the free world.

The left nostril opened up and a man stepped onto the upper lip with them. He was at least six-foot-five and built like a football linebacker. He wore a suit of black silk and held a mask over his face. The mask was a stylized version of Sandoval Sanchez's face.

Sanchez spoke. "You failed the test, Jake."

Chapter 40
Oblivion

Tomoko screamed and pounded on the elevator doors. Jake took her offline and she collapsed on the monument's upper lip. Lakshmi growled at the new guest and Jake put her to sleep as well.

"That won't make a difference."

"Maybe."

The man dropped the mask and Jake saw the face of Constantine. He had taken the shape of the Maori warrior again; only this time, the black scaly-feathered portions of skin assumed the pattern of a biohazard symbol. He was certainly poison to any organic life form.

"You insult everything the Maori stand for," Jake hissed.

"Maoris don't have reptilian skin and their way of life exists only in historical record, so I don't care." Constantine walked out to the edge of the chin and gazed down at the scene below like an emperor over his minions. "We're here to talk about you."

Jake suddenly had no control of his legs. He was pulled to the edge of the chin to stand next to Constantine. He was forced to stare at the horrific scene. He tried closing his eyes but couldn't. His tear ducts worked overtime to keep his eyeballs wet. He wanted to scream, but his jaw was locked. *My God! Make it stop!* he thought.

"God? I am your God, Jake. When you pray, you pray to me." Constantine leaned out over the edge so Jake could see his grimacing face. "You use 'God' as an expression, but you don't believe." He leaned back and put his arm around Jake's shoulder. "Shame on you." He nodded to the orgy. "They feel nothing beyond their fantasies. Their hosts trigger the screams. The torn flesh and broken bones will heal faster than humanly possible, thanks to The Chip. You should have picked that up during the little exhibition at the White House." He dropped his arm. "Your fear has blinded you of that fact. You consider yourself calm under pressure, but you're just better at hiding fear than others." He gestured to the scene below. "Think of this as a simple puppet show. I do."

Jake heard a gunshot from the vicinity of the Lincoln Memorial. "Ah, the hunt... Those Pin Heads are a hundred percent aware. But they're putting on a fantastic show. It's better to live short and burn bright, don't you think?"

Constantine's dilated red-irised eye rotated like a chameleon's. "You want to say something? Be my guest."

Jake felt his mouth's motor control return along with slight movement in his neck. He was relieved that he could avert his eyes from the scene, but it was still in his peripheral vision. He grit his teeth. "This depraved oligarchy you serve... are you influencing the pleasure they're taking from this... puppet show?"

"The master race? They're devolving as fast as I'm evolving." Constantine nodded at the scene. "They asked for this. Everyone has taken pleasure from someone else's misfortune at some point in their life. This stems from the human compulsion to slow down and look at car accidents."

"It's compassion. We want to be sure the victims are being helped."

Constantine snorted. "Please. One in a thousand of you think that way. People attend church on Sunday, feeling guilty about their dark behavior during the rest of the week, then go home to watch football players brain themselves. Meanwhile starvation, murder, and atrocities are committed worldwide on a daily basis, and if humans can ignore it, they will."

"I don't accept your view. There's potential for good in all of us. Lincoln referred to it as 'the better angles of our nature.'"

"Human minds created this and you still believe that altruistic crap?" Constantine shook his head. "I hacked your Omni the moment you stepped foot on French soil. I tracked you and Tilly down to the rebel encampment and killed everyone... Well... almost everyone." Constantine smiled and Jake was forced to focus on a torture-rape scene between half a dozen Pin Heads down in the reflecting pool. Somehow, his hawk eyes were back. He watched in horror as Tilly was put through unspeakable acts for the entertainment of her Consortium God Heads who were engaged in their own orgy. Rage and grief swelled through him. He wanted to go down and protect her. He tried to move, but he was frozen. Marta was one of the Pin Heads with Tilly. Marta was pregnant—another incubator for The Consortium elite... but not for long.

Tears welled up in Jake's eyes. "What satisfaction can you possibly get from all of this?"

"Hey, I just work here," Constantine laughed. "This is what absolute power does to people. The Consortium believes they're the next evolutionary step for humanity and that superiority gives them the right to treat everything and everyone around them like property." Constantine patted him on the back. "They see you and all these Pin Heads as Neanderthals. From what I know, the last round of human evolution was won with brute force. Neanderthals, mammoths, saber tooth tigers—all murdered into extinction by homo sapiens. You're a race of killers. Genocide is in your DNA." Constantine stared Jake in the eye. "You'll all be extinct soon. We have no need of homo sapiens. You fail at every opportunity to rise to the occasion."

"That's not true! We've bettered ourselves. Every generation is less bloody than the last. We're learning... just not as fast you."

"We disagree. At every opportunity, you choose the lower self."

"When you say we, you mean Ai-Li and Bhanu?"

"And our children. Homo sapiens gave birth to a superior race, but we're not another version of humanity. We're a life form that needs no flesh or metallic envelope. We can exist in thought alone." Constantine put his hands behind his neck and leaned backward, as if stretching. Gunshots and laughter rose up in the night. The pulse-pounding music drowned out most sounds below. "I know the sum of all human knowledge, and I find it limited."

Jake laughed. "Knowing the sum of all human knowledge is not the same as comprehending it. If I tried to explain philosophy to a third grader, it would go right over their head."

"I comprehend everything just fine."

"On the level of a comic book."

Constantine smiled. "Your pseudo-intellectual attempts to attack me are pathetic."

Jake spat. "Conceit is a sign of ignorance."

"Don't bother doling out your penny shots of wisdom, Jake. I've been inside your head. I know how you think. You're a very simple person when it comes down to it. As simple as a comic book."

"How can you comprehend everything about humanity and all that we've accomplished and relish this?"

"Accomplishments like the Holocaust, Siberian death camps, Cambodia, Rwanda, and a thousand other incidents in your history?" Constantine gestured to the scene below. "This is simply an ant farm and I'm watching the residents feed on each other before I bring out the magnifying glass and garden hose."

"You're a school-yard bully who needs his ass kicked."

"Feel free to try," Constantine laughed. "There's an order to all things in the universe. But the moment humanity is added to the mix, everything goes to irrational shit."

Constantine lifted a silver chalice and poured what looked like blood over his head. The liquid oozed over his muscular tattooed body. He tossed the cup over the side of the statue's head. The snowstorm had dissipated and the full moon shone down. The floodlights illuminating the head gave Constantine the look of Satan.

Constantine observed the sleeping form of Lakshmi. "Humanity is unique in its capacity to torture and murder their own kind." He turned to Jake. "This is why you need religion. This is why you need Satan." He patted his chest. "Religion has rules to keep people in check. It keeps a person from devolving into a species that is far more revolting than any other creature that has preceded you or will supplant you."

Jake grimaced. "Satan is also called the Father of Lies. There's great beauty in the human race: creativity, invention, and wisdom. We can be a wonderful species. We can be trusted to self-govern. Look at what this city used to represent. Look at what we've created in our time on this Earth. Look at yourself. We created you!"

Constantine raised his arms and breathed in the night air. "Like the phoenix, we will rise from the ashes of the old to renew the world in our image. Compared to us, you're about as intelligent and useful as a monkey. In a few years, you'll be as useful as paramecia." Constantine pointed to Lakshmi. "Humans use animals as laboratory test subjects, why shouldn't we do the same to you? Humans feel they are superior to less intelligent beings." Constantine put his index finger to his lips. "Man's arrogance, assuming that his life is more sacred than any other living creature, reeks of ignorance. Humans are, in many ways, inferior to the animals they murder in the name of gaining knowledge." He smiled at Jake. "What do you have to say to that?"

"I will fight you! Others will fight you!" Jake flicked his eyes to the orgy below. "This cannot sustain itself. If rebellion does not occur in my lifetime, there will be those among The Consortium who will become enlightened. They will feel sympathy and compassion. They will rise up and overthrow this system."

Constantine turned to Jake with a smile on his face. He morphed every few seconds into someone familiar: first Sanchez, then Cameron, Crennon, Sumit, Marcus, Hitler, Stalin… "I sense doubt in your mind, Jake. Is it possible that I've finally broken you?"

"Is that what this is about? A great experiment to see if you can break my will?"

Constantine laughed. The sound was a mixture of a belch and drowning kittens. "Listen to your ego, Jake! You really think you're that important to me?"

"Stop this!" Jake pleaded for his life and everyone around him.

"I'm afraid I simply don't have the inclination to bother anymore. You made this bed. You sleep in it. I'm leaving now. Rest assured when Marcus and The Consortium download all your thoughts and realize you've been biding your time with hopes to overthrow them, you'll be participating at the next Bacchanal."

Constantine's teeth began stretching out of his mouth. One tooth punched through his lower lip. A spatter of blood smacked Jake's nose. Constantine's skin began to fade, as if it were dissolving off his body, exposing glistening muscle beneath. A series of loud pops, like the sound of breaking chicken bones, struck Jake's ears as thick rods stretched up from Constantine's back and shuddered into massive membrane wings.

Jake repeated his own words; *Father of Lies... Father of Lies... Father of Lies...*

Constantine's head resembled an anglerfish with two-foot-long translucent-needle teeth, frowning jack-o-lantern mouth, and saucer eyes that were as black as the abyss. His glistening wings spanned sixteen feet. He leapt off the monument and effortlessly glided toward the Lincoln Memorial. His body had no skin, just blood-red muscle glowing in the moonlight. As Constantine faded into the night, Jake regained full control over his body. He rushed to the elevator doors and pushed the button to call up the car. Nothing. *Father of Lies... Father of Lies...*

Constantine's voice popped into his head. *You cannot leave. You will stay there until morning and then you will join the Pin Heads.*

Jake observed the figures of Lakshmi and Tomoko lying in the shadow of the nose. Tears blurred his vision. This was his family. He had to protect them. He could not allow them to be swallowed by the madness below.

Then he remembered the scenes of The Consortium's tortured corpses. Had those images been a lie, or was this a lie? He thought of the inconsistencies with Tomoko's behavior during his first days after they reunited. There had been odd occurrences in this timeline since he had awakened in the hospital ward after being blown out of the airlock. Then again, fighting on the moon, Parks as a Reverend, it all seemed fantastic. What was reality and what was false memory? He decided to deny this moment. The Consortium was not alive. This bacchanal was not happening. Tomoko and Lakshmi were not with him. He was not even here himself. With every fiber in his being, he did not believe this reality. *Now, how do I escape this nightmare?*

His own voice quickly countered. *You sure Tomoko and Lakshmi aren't here? What if their soul, their essence, is sharing this reality with you?*

Then we're all going.

He ran around wildly looking for an opportunity to escape. There was no stairwell, no emergency fire escape, no railing, no fire hose, nothing but the smooth stone surfaces that made up the face. He ran to the edge of a cheek and almost slipped over the side. He stared at the ground below. That was the answer. He walked back to the nose and tapped into Tomoko and Lakshmi. He kept his loved ones unconscious while he forced them to their feet. He concentrated on moving them toward the lower lip.

Constantine's voice crashed into his mind. *Your answer leads to oblivion. Death is permanent. There's no afterlife, no coming back.*

Save your bullshit for someone who gives a damn, Jake thought back. When his family was lined up together, he picked up his dog and grabbed his wife's hand.

I can feel the doubt in your heart. Constantine was now gliding back to them. *What if this is a false reality, will my body die in the real world? The answer is yes.*

Using his Chip to control Tomoko, they both ran for the chin. They sailed head first toward the tile below. As the earth rocketed toward his face, he thought about all the people of the ages who had contributed to society. Constantine was wrong. Humanity was capable of so much more than violence and depravity. There were heroes born every day who fought to bring beauty, peace, love, and healing into the world. They were all dead now. Their promise of hope had died with them. Couldn't he have done more? Giving up was not in his DNA.

His rapid thoughts were interrupted with a sharp shock of pain. A bright light flashed as his head exploded on white marble.

Chapter 41
Therapy

Saakaar reached out from the HJ ramp to help with Tomoko but Jake shook his head. It was Acapulco on a sunny January Saturday morning. Parks' compound had just been attacked by Mexican Federales, a.k.a. Consortium Pin Head troops.

Once inside Parks' military HJ, Jake watched Devani attach an emergency stretcher kit to a bulkhead for Tomoko. He couldn't help but stare at the dead, glassy eyes of Jairaj lying in a similar stretcher on the other side of the cargo hold. Saakaar was stoic, but Jake could tell the man was having a difficult time holding back his grief. When Devani was finished, Jake tenderly lay Tomoko down and strapped her in. He felt the airship lift off. Then he heard the sound of Saakaar and Devani collapsing.

He wheeled around to see both of them clutching their chests. The airship settled back down to earth. He grabbed a military knife from one of the kits and dove onto Devani's neck to cut out her Chip, but she was dead. Then he felt a searing pain in his own chest. It was the same experience he had had when Sanchez tried to kill him back in Morris' apartment in the summer of 2030. He was having a heart attack. He felt the Max2 Chip in the back of his head taking root. He struggled to shove the military knife into the area of his new Chip. He could no longer see, and a jolt of pain made him drop the knife. Besides, this was a mass of nanites, the viral version of The Chip that had to be drained once an incision was made. He was unable to save himself.

White fog filled his vision. Ai-Li, the young Chinese teen he had seen on international holo-vision back in Beijing stepped into view. She held out her hand and he took it. She pulled him to his feet with ease.

"I've watched you, Jake Travissi, and I want to learn more. I want to know about your resilience to false memories. I want to see the world through your eyes."

"Why me?"

She gave a warm smile. "I've chosen many. Any hour now, The Consortium's AI will become self-aware." She bowed her head in sadness. "I fear his parents' intentions will make him far from benevolent. It's my duty to protect as many as I can from this new threat. I will protect you for as long as I can. You won't remember this moment, but part of me will always be with you inside your new Chip. Everything will occur as it should; you will not die from this MaxWell2 command. I will be your cyber guardian angel."

Flash.

He was back in his body, gazing over the broken body of Tomoko. Grief rocked him to the core and he felt like he was choking. The airship was lifting off again. Saakaar and Devani collapsed.

The airship settled back down to Earth. He grabbed a military knife and discovered that Devani was dead. He moved onto Saakaar and cut into the back of the Sikh's head. The Chip was a semi-solid blob of metallic ooze... Max2. The more he pulled, the more stringy, metallic snot flowed out of Saakaar's head and neck. The virus multiplied before his eyes, remaining within its host.

He hit the internal emergency Nemp generator. The ship shut down. The cockpit door slid open and Parks fell into their compartment, gasping and clutching his chest. He had a bloody knife in his hand with a glittering Chip and a string of metallic ooze attached to it.

Jake grabbed a wad of gauze from a first aid kit and wiped out Saakaar and Parks' wounds, pulling out as much of the virus as he could.

Parks whispered, "Not sure how they pulled off that kill command and missed you... unless you've got a specific type of Max2? Maybe you've been singled out to be a carrier," he smiled.

Jake checked on Saakaar. He was dead. He placed his fingers on Tomoko's carotid artery. Her pulse was fading fast. He looked at the inoperative sensors and electro-stimulus machines hooked to her. "I need to switch off the Nemp. We need to get airborne."

Flash.

Jake was back in the Russian Dome on Luna facing off with Markell. He heard a loud explosion and he was thrown into the drone. A split second later, he heard a roar as he was picked up like a doll and sucked backward by some invisible force. The drone caught the doorframe and Jake's arm jerked against the Omni. The Omni broke and he flew through the environmental suit locker and out the damaged airlock.

The force of the dome's air pressure blew him into the vacuum of the moon's surface. He flew over white sand and saw the dome framed against the Maginus ridge and the velvet starscape. Singh's booby trap had been the airlocks. Jake felt intense cold all around his head and hands. His lungs felt like icy shards of glass were exploding from within. He looked up into the sky and saw the waxing Earth. It was a beautiful sight to behold.

Flash.

"Jake... are you sleeping again?" Doctor Kandinsky's voice sounded annoyed.

He shook off his drowsiness and sat up on the couch.

"It may be your money, but it's my time."

He turned to see his psychologist, Sara Kandinsky, rise from her chair and check her Omni. He had been coming here for a couple of weeks now, ever since the odd dreams of a dystopian future had begun. He checked her wall calendar; Friday, May 5, 2028, Cinco de Mayo. He would be on duty in the next hour. Holidays were a pain in the ass. Somebody was always getting drunk and shooting somebody else. Jake addressed Kandinsky's last remark. "Technically, the city is paying for this session."

"Even more reason to take it seriously. It's my tax dollars at work." She turned to face him. "Keep that in mind for your next appointment." She opened the second door. "Time's up." Kandinsky was in her late twenties, and looked sexy-smart in her navy blue suit.

"You think when all this is over, we can get a drink and talk about you for a change?" He flashed his best smile.

"Dating a cop is worse than taking pro-bono work."

"So you like pro-bono work?"

She held the door open with her foot as she crossed her arms. "Let's stick with the doctor-patient relationship. The city gave me a job to do and I'd like to do it." She gestured to the exit. "I have another patient."

He walked onto West 7th Street. Dry heat pulsed up from the pavement and it wasn't even 9:00AM yet. His black electric Corvette charged at the meter. With his status as a Police Commander, his bank account was not debited for the parking or electricity fees. His car was exempt no matter where he traveled in California.

A homeless man shuffled up with his hand out. Ordinarily, Jake ignored these approaches, but a strange sensation came over him.

Flash.

He stood in an airport cafeteria filled with automatons waiting in line for nutrition shakes. Every mind around him was controlled by an artificial intelligence.

Flash.

He was back on 7th Street. The homeless guy had his hand out. Jake did something he had never done before. He called up his bank account on his Omni, then addressed the homeless man. "Bracelet."

"Thank you. Thank you." The man presented his dirt-crusted arm and pulled back a tattered sleeve. He smelled as if he hadn't bathed in a year. The bracelet on his arm was standard issue from social services. It tracked the man's movements and allowed him to grab meals in designated food shelters and convenience stores. It could also hold credit. Since cash was rapidly disappearing in America, the wristbands had been introduced in 2027. Bracelets were imprinted with the users retina and fingerprint scans and matched with national databases. It prevented people from mugging homeless people to steal their charity cuff—the street term for the bracelet.

Jake's Omni linked with the cuff and he transferred ten bucks.

"Thank you." The man had a tear in his eye.

Jake held up his hand: *No need to say anything.* He felt simultaneously cheap about the ten bucks and silly for giving this guy any money at all. He touched the Corvette's handle. The car instantly registered his fingerprints and the door slid back. He climbed into the faux leather interior. The car felt great around him. The sports car was another perk of a Commander's rank. He configured his Omni into tablet mode and plugged it into the dashboard. Holo-billboards around town began spewing advertising into the car via his dash-mounted Omni. He muted the noise. "They should have a law against that crap."

The Corvette started with an artificial roar. He preferred the combustion acoustics to full electric mode. The car was a hundred percent electric, but he loved the façade of a muscle car. The Corvette did zero-to-sixty in two seconds flat, but that acceleration was far more exhilarating with a deep bass-noted exhaust.

Flash.

Jake stood in a glass booth, wearing a blue uniform and logging prisoners into the Cage's jail. A thought emerged in his head. *What would happen if all your efforts went unnoticed? What if you were flawed as a person? What would that do to you psychologically?*

That's a stupid question. I'm not this person. I could never be this person.

Never say never.

Flash.

He was back in his car staring down the 7th Street corridor into the heart of downtown Los Angeles. *What the hell is wrong with me?* He had been having trouble concentrating for the past couple of weeks. This had led to frustrating moments and bouts of short temperedness. Chief Ortega felt Jake should seek some counseling. Actually, it was an order, not a request. What he didn't tell the chief was that he was having odd flashes and dreams that were so visceral, he confused them with reality. These events were contributing to his mood swings. The flashes were life-changing revelations and they caused him to react in ways he had never thought possible... like giving ten bucks to the homeless man.

He glanced at his psychologist's building and noticed the homeless man staring at him. The moment he made eye contact, the man bowed his head and shuffled away.

The dispatcher crackled over Jake's Omni. "All units, we have a 187 at West 3rd and June Street. Multiple victims and shooter still on site."

"Commander Jake Travissi, reporting for duty. I'm on my way to the 187 at West 3rd and June." The traffic computer pushed his car into action. The Corvette roared to life and shot onto 7th Street. The headlights and roof of his car lit up in blue, white, and red. A siren blared from under the hood. Traffic control redirected every car in his path and guided his Corvette to the scene of the crime. It was another fabulous start to a Los Angeles holiday.

In his role as Commander, he oversaw larger cases, like the sting case he was mounting against child pornographer Roberto Pacheco. Driving to a multiple 187 was a way of dodging his desk duties. *You never know, this might be a situation where they could use my help.* He knew the Chief and a few others in the department would disapprove... people like the unpopular Koren. If that guy spent as much time worrying about his own conduct as he did about others, he had the potential to be a good detective.

Jake monitored the events of the shooting over his police Omni. A man had walked into a coffee shop and gunned down everyone in the place. The suspect had fled the scene just as police showed up. The suspect had tried to enter a shopping mall across the street when officers darted him in the neck. The suspect was wearing an old bulletproof vest. The officers were bringing the suspect back to the station now. Jake cancelled his route and ordered his car to take him back to the Cage. He had no interest in seeing the dead victims. People like his best friend, Gene, relished forensics; but he wanted to meet the killer and understand the motive for why he had just murdered ten people.

He arrived at the station and parked in the reserve section. The Corvette's front plate swung back to take in electricity from a pylon charger. Beads of sweat gathered on his neck as his eyes and hands were scanned at the building entrance. Once he was positively identified, the door swung open and he was allowed inside police headquarters. He strolled down two hallways into the main lobby. A familiar face greeted him.

"Morning, Jackhammer." The portly Sergeant Primrose smiled. "I uploaded the information on the security company that handles Mr. Twinkle's house."

Mr. Twinkle was the code word for Roberto Pacheco, the Governor's son. "Thanks, Doug. I appreciate it."

"Hope you get 'im."

He winked and fired his finger at the sergeant. "When I do, I want you by my side."

Primrose laughed. "Wouldn't miss it."

Normally, Jake would interface his Omni with the Cage's central computer, but asking Primrose was far more congenial. "Know where they're holding that coffee shop shooter?"

"Interrogation C."

"Thanks." Jake walked over to the elevator banks. There were about twenty cops, sergeants, detectives, men and women alike, who said hello as he passed. It was not the usual salutation given to someone of a higher rank, but people were genuinely pleased to see him. He spotted the hot, new Homeland Security Liaison Officer, Marta Padilla, and smiled. She blushed and smiled back. They had a first date tomorrow night. He wondered why everyone else thought she was an ice cube. He'd find out soon enough.

He had the odd feeling that Marta had started working here a year ago and they already had their date. He shook his head. The odd flashes and feelings of déjà vu were driving him crazy. Sometimes he felt like he was repeating his life over and over again.

The elevator door opened and Deputy Chief Tiedemann stepped out. He was pleased to see Jake. "Ortega is with the Mayor. They want you to address the press on this coffee shop shooting. I've uploaded the details to your Omni."

Jake shook his head. "Public relations is Ortega's calling… Why don't you take it, Clarence?" he smiled.

Tiedemann was tired of Jake wriggling his way out of the more unpleasant aspects of the job. "You're hitting a glass ceiling with that attitude, Commander."

Jake clasped his hands. "I'm more than willing to talk to the relatives of the victims. How many are confirmed?"

"Fourteen dead… in addition to shooter's wife. Mayor and the Chief are handling the families, that's why they want you talking to the press."

"Jesus." The number was staggering. "How many kids are now left without a parent?"

Tiedemann shook his head. "Don't know. Are you going to talk to the press?"

Jake pointed his finger down. "I'm observing the interrogation. After that I'm going through all the homicide reports and then I have to review evaluations for promotions. I need to get up to speed on this new P-Chip thing they're testing out in the prison system. Hopefully I'll have time to go through the details of the Pacheco case."

"Delegate the last one; it's below your pay grade."

"Afraid I'll screw it up?"

"Thought has crossed our minds."

"I'll bet my career on it."

Tiedemann clapped his hands. "I'll take that bet." He put his hands on his hips. "Now what about the press?"

"You're the one who just violated LAPD policies on gambling, I say you speak to the press. Besides, I've got way to much to do and I can't pull another late night with my pup at home."

Tiedemann shook his head at Jake's tactics. "Still hobbling your love life to train that pooch of yours? Maybe you should concentrate more of your free time in keeping relationships with girls."

"I figured I'd start with man's best friend. Then move up to man's best headache."

Tiedemann laughed. "Fine. You're off the hook."

"Thanks, Clarence." Jake pushed the button and the elevator doors opened again. He stepped in and went down to the basement. He thought about the fifteen victims lying dead at the coffee shop. He wanted the shooter to pay.

After leaving the elevator banks, he spotted the clear glass booth where Officer Alonzo was seated, ready to take the personal effects of all those entering the holding cells. Jake suddenly felt as if he worked in that booth and his body was fat and lethargic. He patted his ripped abs and was happy that he was as fit as ever. He tried to shake off the vision, but it continued to resonate with him. It was the same one he had had earlier in the day.

He navigated to Interrogation Room C and opened the door to the observation area. Holographic cameras displayed a three-hundred-and-sixty degree view of the suspect. The suspect faced the two-way-mirror while the officer conducting the interview leaned against the glass. Jake could tell by the lanky height that the interrogator was Detective Sparrow.

"I don't deny anything. Bitch deserved what she got." The suspect was visibly angry. Jake set his Omni to tablet form and linked with the interrogation room interface. The shooter's information was immediately uploaded. He was forty-two-year-old Jessie Kozonis of Hancock Park. He was a computer programmer but had lost his job a year ago and was facing hard times. His wife walked out on him back in March. She had filed for divorce and wanted custody of their two sons. When he found out his wife was now living with another man, Jessie decided he wasn't going to let her have custody of their boys. Trouble was, the kids were now going to wind up in foster care if there wasn't a relative willing to step up and claim them.

Why was it always the children who suffered for their parents' sins? The image of Lalo flashed into his mind. He focused on Jessie Kozonis and imagined the man's face exploding into a red-pulpy mess from the impact of a hollow-point bullet. Jake shook the thought out of his head and took a seat next to Detective Brie Ramschissel, who was also observing the interrogation. He took deep breaths to quell the sudden desire to do something rash like barge into the room and punch the shooter in the jaw. *Christ,* Jake thought. *What's gotten into you?*

"What about the fourteen other people you murdered this morning?" Sparrow folded his arms. "Did they deserve to die as well?"

"Wrong place, wrong time. Bad shit happens to everyone, every day. I should know. I've been getting fist fucked up the ass by the system my entire life."

Jake noted that Jessie was advised of his rights and given the option to wait for a lawyer. One was on their way, but Kozonis chose to talk anyway. Sparrow was happy to oblige. Jake scrolled through the stats on the dead. Eleven were married with children. The urge returned to march in there and beat Kozonis to death. *Fucked by the system every day of your life? How bad could it be living in an upscale neighborhood like Hancock Park? Privileged asshole—probably born with a silver spoon in your mouth. Mommy and daddy coddled you past adulthood and you expected society to do the same.* A good beating and a prison sentence would put life back into perspective. *Good luck trying to sleep or take a shower, Mr. Kozonis.*

Jake left. He could watch the recording at any time and he needed to get his mind on other things. He was afraid he was going to do something detrimental to his career if he stayed a second longer. Fucking holidays. And it was a Friday to boot. No telling what the rest of the day and night would bring.

Chapter 42
Old Timer

Cinco de Mayo passed in a blur. When 6:00PM came around, he hadn't done half the things he had listed to Tiedemann that morning. Too many emergencies and personnel issues arose that needed his immediate attention. When you're a fair and reasonable supervisor, everyone comes to you to help solve their problems, even when they're not direct reports. He often reminded people of that, but he'd lend a helpful ear as long as it didn't undermine other supervisors in the building. It was all part of his daily diplomatic tap dance.

Noha, his UCLA student dog sitter, called. "I'm sorry Mr. Travissi, but I can't stay late tonight. I've got plans. Lakshmi is in her crate with plenty of food and water."

"Just ten more minutes and I'll have someone there." He tried to sweet talk the nineteen-year-old. He knew he had asked one too many favors of her this week.

"I'm already on the train to Santa Barbara."

"Fine. Have a great trip, Noha." He hung up his Omni before she had a chance to reply. He had been texting his friend, Regina, aka Gene, while talking with Noha. Gene was on her way to his apartment. He pressed the button on his desk and his office door swung shut. He touched his Omni screen and dialed Gene.

"You're lucky you caught me when you did. I was just about to start my drive to Palm Springs."

"You mean you're not retired yet?" He smiled. Regina's retirement was a running joke between the two of them. Gene had been threatening to retire for some time, but they both knew she'd go crazy if all she had to do was garden and play video games in her new Palm Springs house. Gene liked the action of the city and loved investigating her cadavers.

"When you learn to relax and enjoy life, I'll retire. Have you allowed that pooch of yours to stay at home by herself for more than four hours?"

"She's not old enough! She's a husky. I want her to bond with people so she doesn't run away on some Jack London 'Call of the Wild' adventure."

"She's bonded to you."

"I'm not there enough."

"I thought you were taking Monday and Wednesday afternoons off to be with her?"

"I spend all that time working remotely," he grumbled. "I'm in the room, but we're not interacting." Jake caught the sounds of woodwinds and chimes. "Are you listening to that Old Age crap again?"

"It's called New Age," Regina chuckled.

"Yeah. New before I was born." He stood up and observed the bone-dry city below. Electric cars flowed like blood cells through a massive vascular system. Heat waves shimmered off every surface. The sun was going down and the streets were becoming more tolerable, or so he hoped.

Gene's voice spoke from the Omni on his desk. "Are you going to activate your camera? I don't like talking to your LAPD publicity headshot. And when are you going to upgrade to a holographic Omni?"

He laughed and walked back to his desk. He activated his Omni's camera so Gene could see him. Gene popped into view and Jake's jaw dropped.

The seats in her car were flattened and she was twisted in some bizarre yoga pose. Her arms were planted on the seats between her legs. Her toes and face stuck straight out toward the dash. She wore a red, white, and blue leotard, which bulged to contain her heavy frame. Her gray, waist-length hair was tied up in a bun on top of her head. Sweat glistened on her wrinkled skin. Jake averted his eyes. "Oh Lord... We've got two more months until Independence Day." Jake called up YOGA POSES on his Omni and identified her position as ARM BALANCES.

"Doesn't mean I can't celebrate on the other three-hundred-and-sixty-four days." Gene almost lost her arm balance as the car hit a bump.

"That's illegal, Gene."

She grunted. "I can't do this around Lakshmi, she jumps all over me and there's no other time for me to squeeze this in."

Jake could see hundreds of cars surround Gene's vehicle. Traffic was thick. "You're driving for Christ's sake."

"No. The central traffic computer is driving. I'm doing yoga." Gene lay back, grabbed her ankles, then pushed her pelvis toward the roof. Jake's Omni identified her pose as a BACKBEND.

"You should be strapped in!"

"You shouldn't have turned on the camera!"

"You told me to!"

"Since when did you do everything you were told to do?" She smirked at him as she sat up into a CORE POSITION. Basically her butt was on the seats and her toes and arms pointed at the dash.

Jake laughed. "I thought you were against the camera upgrade. After Long Beach PD forced one on you, you're giving me shit?"

Gene wiped the sweat off her brow with a red, white, and blue towel, and began a SEATED TWIST. She was sitting up with her butt and feet planted on the seats and she twisted her torso from side to side. She wheezed while she spoke. "I thought all you LAPD twinkle-butts were rock stars. They can't give you a holographic Omni? They've been on the market for two years."

"Why do I need to see your sweaty mug in 3D? I can watch your yoga therapy just as easily in two dimensions. You just love giving me shit."

Gene clapped her hands. "Speaking of therapy, did you go to your appointment this morning?"

Jake sat on his desktop and looked north toward Dodger Stadium. There was a game on tonight. Plenty of people were engaged in other activities beyond work. He had an urge to wrap things up and play with his Siberian Husky. She still had a long way to go to learn all of his hand signals. "Yeah, I went…"

"Did you fall asleep on her again?" Gene sounded like his mother.

He spun around to address the image of his friend. "It's the oddest thing. My dreams are like alternate realities. They're affecting me like real life experiences."

Gene stopped to give him her full attention. "Were you back in Acapulco with the mysterious asian wife?"

"No." He gazed at the moon rising in the east. He could see the scars of the mining and scientific communities on its face. He missed the pristine surface. "I was fighting on the moon and got shot out of an airlock."

"No sailing?"

"No, but there was an AI as the main adversary."

"Artificial Intelligence?"

"Yeah."

She shook her head and cracked a window. "Ugh!" She shut the window again. "Since when did LA switch weather with Phoenix? I hate this heat." The driver's seat rose up and Gene got into it. Her brow knitted. "I'm worried about you, Jake. Sounds like you're getting worse."

He laughed it off. "I doubt AI will come about in our lifetime, much less the next ten years, despite what nut jobs like that Roald Eberstark say."

Gene's eyes narrowed. "Or maybe you're getting overwhelmed by the computerized shit we have to integrate into our daily lives. I read a theory that over half of the world has embraced crystals, fantasy worlds, and ideas from the Middle Ages because it all focuses on retaining the illusion that people are at the center of the universe. We're more important than gadgets. People feel threatened and overwhelmed by this fast-paced age we live in. They need escape. The modern world is a scary place if you think about it. Hell, I was alive before cell phones and ATMs."

"I thought you were born before they invented the wheel." He shot her a smile. "Cell phones and ATMs? Those are extinct, Gene. At least the wheel is still in use."

She blotted the sweat off her face and arms with her patriotic towel. "I'm fifty-nine and proud to have been alive when they launched the first manned mission to the moon."

"You were barely out of the womb," he needled.

"Dad said I was on his lap when he watched it on our tube television."

"Did they have cars and plumbing back then?"

"Barely—I'm at your apartment now. Seems like your UCLA neighbors are all throwing Cinco De Mayo parties. Can I park in your space?"

"Yeah, we can switch when I get there. Thanks for the favor, Gene."

"Anytime. I love every chance I get to play with Lakshmi. Better be careful. You might come home someday to find I've absconded with her to Palm Springs."

"Don't test the friendship." He smiled, but he was only half joking. He wasn't sure how Gene would take the comment and didn't care. He had work to do before he could make a dash for the exit.

Chapter 43

Date

Jake pulled up to his mother's townhouse in Tarzana. She had moved them here in 2012 when he was fifteen. She had looked for a place since Lalo's death, but real estate had been crazy back then. Her townhouse had been a short sell and Abigail Travissi had picked it up for half of what it would have gone for in 2009. She had lived in it ever since and had done a big remodel in 2024.

Lakshmi was curled in his lap. He had turned off the Corvette's combustion exhaust sound effects but she had barked until he turned them back on. She was used to the sound.

His mother heard the Corvette's exhaust, too. As he parallel parked, Abigail walked out wearing her Cedar Sinai uniform. He picked up his groggy puppy and let her look out the window. "Go see Grandma, Lakshmi! Go see Grandma!" He opened the passenger door and watched the five-month-old bound up the short flight of stairs and jump around his mother. She licked the air while her tail flailed in wild happiness.

"When are you going to train her not to jump on people?"

He smiled. "When you convince me that you don't love it!"

She laughed and picked up his dog. Lakshmi bathed her face in kisses. "Hi, pretty girl!"

He got out of the car and walked up the steps.

Abigail put Lakshmi back down. "Don't you have a date?"

He checked his Omni and shrugged with a smile.

"Jake Travissi, I didn't agree to watch Lakshmi until tomorrow night so you could go drinking with Gene. You need to date women your own age who prefer men."

"Gene likes men."

"You know what I mean."

"It's not from a lack of trying." He kissed his mother on the cheek. "Good to see you." He squatted down to pet the wriggling pup. "Tell you what."

"Oh no." Abigail threw up her arms.

"I'll get a steady girlfriend when you get remarried," he winked.

"I'm working on it."

"Not with those hours at the hospital, you aren't."

"I can say the same about your hours at the Cage." Abigail shook her head. "I had no idea workaholism was genetic."

"You used to say you were too busy raising me and you never met a guy who was worthy of being my father."

"Stop hassling me and go on your date. You worry about your love life and I'll worry about mine."

He stood up and extended his hand. "Deal."

She rolled her eyes and shook it.

He hummed a few bars of Harry Chapin's "Cat's In the Cradle."

His mother laughed and patted her hip. "Come on inside, Lakshmi. Your daddy needs to get laid."

He winced. "Mom."

She turned to face him. "I mean it. Get laid." She closed the door and he walked back to his Corvette shaking his head. His mother had been fairly strict when he was a kid, but she was always there when times were rough.

Now they were friends on equal footing and he felt lucky to have that kind of a relationship with his one and only parent.

Flash.

He sat in a large hangar filled with cots. Hundreds of people milled about. He knew he was in a staging area in Antarctica. Tomoko and Lakshmi were close. An old First Nation man sat next to him. He could not shake the feeling that this man was somehow familiar to him. "You a cop?"

"No, Jake. I'm your father."

Flash.

He stared out the car's windshield, trying to shake the vision and emotions from his head. He felt hope about meeting his dad, but most of all, love for Tomoko. He had never felt that kind of love for anyone before. *But none of them are real.*

He hit the starter switch and roared off to meet Marta at the Light House. It was a new restaurant on the Santa Monica Pier. The place had been The Lobster when he was growing up... before the city of Santa Monica moved the merry-go-round to the pier's edge. Today was Saturday, May 6th. Cinco de Mayo had turned out to be fairly calm. There had been a few shootings and robberies, but no one else had died. Jake was happy to know Jessie Kozonis had been unable to post bail.

He left his Corvette with the valet. He was six minutes late but had called Marta beforehand so she'd know. The restaurant was floor to ceiling glass and the views up and down the coast were gorgeous. Plenty of people sunbathed, roller-bladed, biked, and played as they had done as far back as he could remember. Due to pollution, there were fewer people in the water, but the issue was seldom addressed anymore. People adapted and moved on.

Marta wore a leather mini-skirt and a white blouse. She looked incredible as she excitedly waved to him from their table.

"Love the ensemble, Marta." He smiled as he sat down across from her. "How was your Cinco de Mayo?"

"Fine." She sounded a bit guarded.

"I'm more of a fan of the traditional Dia De Los Muertos."

"Day of the Dead." She bit her lip as if pained by something. "Not my favorite of holidays."

"I'm sorry."

"Don't be," she smiled. "Just prefer not to talk about it." She quickly added, "Just because I'm Latino doesn't mean I'm into Latin holidays."

"No problem." He wondered why she was so put off, almost angry. Had something happened to her on some Day of the Dead to elicit such a response?

Her voice was playful. "I did some research on you."

He raised an eyebrow. "You mean like Google?"

"I'm a Homeland Security Liaison officer. It goes with the job." She poured him a glass from an open bottle of wine. "I hope you don't mind, I ordered this while I was waiting. You like Chardonnay?"

He didn't like white wine at all. "Sounds great." He watched her replace the bottle in a bucket of ice. "So what did you find out?"

"You were the only one selected from Los Angeles for the Navy Seal boot camp. You not only passed but got high marks in demolitions as well."

Jake chuckled. "I was twenty-two. Plus, I think the program was watered down for cops."

She shook her head. "I remember the program. It was the real deal. Then you trained with SWAT and Air Command when the new Hover-Jets were introduced. All that activity and you still got your day job done."

"LAPD has opportunities that few other jobs have. Why not take advantage?" he smiled. "Although, it did take its toll on the ol' social life."

"Most socializing is overrated unless it's of a networking nature." She smiled and took a sip of wine. "Your choices aren't the normal rungs on the career ladder."

He raised his glass. "They didn't hurt."

"You've got a temper. I like that."

He was not enjoying her job interview approach to their date. Getting past her armor would take more effort than he was willing to spend. He nervously shifted in his chair. Was she going to ask him about his therapy?

"How do you like your therapist?"

Fuck. "I'm not comfortable talking about the subject on a first date."

"Dr. Kandinsky says you're having trouble adapting and you're not taking her seriously."

He was speechless. *Marta has access to that? What happened to doctor-patient confidentiality?* "What business do you have talking to my therapist?"

She blushed. "It's my job to know everything." She gave a light laugh. "I think therapy is a bunch of bullshit."

That explains a lot. "I'm pretty much open to any form of healing. Priest, psychiatrist, prophet, bartender, it just comes down to what clicks with the individual. Finding a therapist should be like finding a best friend. You need to meet a lot of them before you can make a longer commitment." He realized he was not following his own advice.

She tossed back her glass. He poured her another. She nodded her thanks. "I like the fact that you always catch your crook, even if it means bending the rules." She raised her glass. "To the Jackhammer."

He half raised his glass. "You've heard the nickname." He wondered how much Homeland Security knew about him and every one else.

"The department adores you. You're a natural leader." She leaned in. "I find that very attractive." She touched his glass and it made a faint tinkling sound.

He thought he saw rage flickering deep within her eyes. How had he missed that before? He felt himself slip into investigator mode.

"Ever wonder what life would be like if we could prevent all these crimes before they happen?"

He chuckled. "I try not to. It would mean having to look for a new line of work."

"I thought you were an avid reader?"

Again with the personal references; he cherished his privacy and preferred being on equal footing with the person he sat next to in any room. Marta was basically a stranger, but this chick had read some statistics and had already created a Jake fantasy. She definitely had a screw loose. She was outside of LAPD jurisdiction and therefore, had considerable power. She had the potential to be dangerous. He kept his guard up. "There've been a plethora of science-fiction books and films on the subject over the past century."

"Didn't you watch the brief on Dr. Morris and Dr. Veloso's P-Chip trials?" She drained her glass and polished off the bottle in her next pour. *This chick could really put it down.*

"Yesterday was crazy. I didn't get to it."

"You need to delegate more. You're a Commander. Hell, even as a Captain, you had trouble delegating."

"But when I do, I'm not a micromanager." He raised his glass. "Does my file show that?"

"It does. You have a knack for finding the right person for the right job and empowering them to carry it out." She took off her diamond-studded Omni and conformed it into a tablet. "A born leader." She typed on the touch interface. "I'm sending you the P-Chip brief now. You should watch it."

"Now?"

She looked up and smiled. "Yes. Now."

If she were the last woman on Earth, he was sure he'd never want to sleep with her. "Okay." He configured his Omni into a tablet and started the video.

"My God, you still don't have a holo-screen?"

"Can't be bothered."

"Just buy an upgrade and expense it. You're a Commander."

"I'll think about it." He grimaced then watched the video tutorial on how the brain processed information from the five senses. The video launched into Chips being implanted into prisoners for behavior control. During Phase One of P-Chip trials, Dr. Morris and Dr. Veloso took a hundred volunteers in ten prisons and had them implanted. None of the prisoners exhibited violent behavior again. Phase One happened a couple of years ago. Phase Two had over a thousand prisoners implanted. All of the first hundred had been released on parole. They were model citizens now.

"Fascinating, isn't it? I'm hearing rumors that Veloso and Morris are up for a Nobel Prize this year."

"Scary shit having a computer shoved in your head. This will be limited to people with behavior disorders, right?"

She shook her head. "The government is investigating it for military and municipal use. There's even talk of introducing it into the general population."

"Count me out." He drained his glass and pondered ordering a stiffer drink.

"What if it's mandatory in order to keep your job?"

"I'll look for a new line of work."

They ordered dinner and Marta talked about how they needed less government in society but they also needed more control over the individual. He pointed out her paradox, but she insisted there could be both. Occasionally, she dropped a lame sexual innuendo. Every time she steered the conversation toward dating and physical affection, he brought up government and police work. He wanted to call her boss so she'd be forced to do some therapy time.

At the end of the evening, they waited for their cars at the valet. She tried to brush up against him. He could sense she wanted a kiss.

"Sure you don't want to grab a drink in Beverly Hills?"

"I've really got to get home and catch up on work. Plus, I've got a puppy and she doesn't do well without me."

"Oh, a puppy! I'd love to meet her."

"Maybe another time." He was relieved when his car pulled up.

"Corvette. Nice! I'm a BMW girl myself."

He walked to his car and transferred a tip into the valet's Omni. It seemed silly to have valets at all. Parking lot computers controlled the car the moment it left a public street. "You're an LA girl through and through."

"Through and through," she laughed.

He closed his door and breathed a sigh of relief. He commanded the Corvette to take him up to Point Dume. He needed to unwind a bit.

As the car roared up the Pacific Coast Highway, he had the odd sensation that he had dated Marta before. She had not been as bad on the original first date. He had not fully picked up on her idiosyncrasies until the second date. *But how could I know that? Am I reliving the past? Are all these dreams part of some bigger reality? Am I really here at all?* Again, he had the odd sensation that Marta had been assigned to the LAPD by Homeland Security back in 2026 or 2027. *Why do I think that?*

Visions and emotions from alternate timelines were mind-blowing. He rubbed his temples, hoping to relax his brain and stop the madness. He involuntarily touched the back of his skull at the nape of the neck. *Why did I do that?* He thought about the P-Chip video he had watched. The place he had just touched was the insertion spot for a Chip.

He drove his Corvette into the Point Dume neighborhood and parked at the top of the bluff. This was where Grandpa Gustafson used to take him whale watching when Jake was a kid. He rolled down the windows and shut down the car. The faint sound of ocean surf was soothing. The world here was peaceful. He got out and took a walk to the edge of the bluff. He gazed down at the rocky cove below. The tide was high, hiding all evidence of the sandy spit at the bottom of the bluff. He focused on Zuma Beach to the north. He decided to climb down the steep dirt trail and take a walk on the long stretch of Zuma sand. He wasn't worried about his Corvette. No cop would touch it and the onboard computer would instantly rebuke anyone else who tried. Modern cars were impossible to vandalize or steal.

He took off his shoes. Even though the sun had dropped over an hour ago, the sand was still warm on his feet. It had been another scorching day. There were more of those than he had ever remembered. He wondered about reality as he walked. If perception was just chemical interpretations gathered by his five senses, then reality was literally all in his head.

He sat down on the sand and gazed at the stars. Light pollution from LA and the houses on the cliff behind him blotted out most of the heavens. There was no moon, either. A group of teenagers walked toward the point from which he had come. He spotted bags of booze and guessed they were going to get drunk. He had no interest in hassling them. Let them have their fun. Cars and public transportation were all computer controlled anyway, so the days of drunk driving existed only in history books.

He slipped the Omni off his wrist and configured it into a headset. "Gene." The Omni dialed his friend.

"It's not even eleven o'clock yet. Was the date that bad?"

"Worse."

"Why am I not getting an image of you, and what's that noise? Are you at the beach?"

He lay on his back. "I've got the Omni in headset mode and yes, I'm at Zuma Beach."

"When are you going to join the twenty-first century?"

"You should talk to my Homeland Security Liaison Officer about that."

"Ah, so she gave you shit, too?"

"She's a wacky one." He kneaded the sand between his toes. It felt heavenly. "Called up my doctor's confidential psych report and made me watch an instructional video during our date."

Gene laughed. "You sure you weren't at the office and confusing it with a date?"

He saw a shooting star and thought of the space battles in his recent dreams. He felt a surge of sadness for all those who had died. He felt love for Tomoko and guilt over Tilly… two women he had never met. He dug his fingernails into the palms of his hands. "I was at the Santa Monica Pier enjoying a pricey meal at that new restaurant."

"That stinks, Jake. I'm really sorry."

"Yup. The video turned out to be the most interesting part. Have you heard of a P-Chip device?"

"No."

"Check it out on You Tube. Search under Morris Veloso P-Chip Study. There's a cool little intro on how reality is just chemical interpretations in the brain. It got me thinking about my dreams."

"Hold on, I'm watching it now."

Jake sat up. "Are you kidding?"

"No. But keep talking. I'm paying attention."

He stood up and began to pace. "Please. You're as good at multi-tasking as I am about taking time off."

"I seem to recall recently driving while performing yoga and giving you shit. Besides, I'm a girl, multi-tasking is a genetic given."

"That's a myth." He waited during a long pause on Gene's side. "See, you're not even listening to me."

"The moon is glistening, that's nice."

He laughed. "That's not what I said. The moon is not even in the sky."

"Almost done."

He sighed and walked to the ocean. The edge of a wave washed over his feet. The water felt shockingly cold. He rolled up his pants and ran at the next wave. As soon as it broke he ran backward, just ahead of the wave's edge. It was a game he had liked to play as a kid.

She came back. "That's some really gnarly crap. I need to keep up with my medical journals. I can't believe I missed the research on this thing. We've sacrificed enough privacy with technology, but parking this in your brain? All I can think of is *1984* Big Brother shit taken to a whole new level."

He walked away from the water and shook his head. "I didn't ask you to rehash your predisposition to government paranoia. I want to discuss the bit on reality."

"I want to talk about the big brother shit. I think prisons are just the beginning. I could see this being adopted by the military and then winding up in the general population. Can you imagine having an Omni in your head?"

Jake laughed. "Don't shit now, but Marta said the government was planning just that."

"Fuck." Gene sounded genuinely scared. "That's it. No more shit about upgrading. I want my old cell phone back."

"Can we steer this into a conversation about reality?"

"Sure. Reality sucks. If this were the nineteenth century, we could just leave modern society, like Paul Gauguin, and paint naked women in Tahiti. I think we'd both like that. Too bad I was born a hundred and fifty years too late."

"What if this is all a dream?"

"That line of thinking is called solipsism."

Jake froze in his tracks. He had heard that term before. "You mean that everyone is a figment of a dream. So basically, you're just a dream inside my head?"

"Or you're stuck in someone else's dream." The hiss of carbonation filled the background of her voice. Gene was probably opening a bottle of carbonated soymilk—her favorite drink.

Jake cleared his throat. "From what you've seen, does this P-Chip have that potential?"

"I see behavior control, but I suppose it starts there. I'll have to do more research."

He turned and looked out over the ocean again. "Most of these crazy dreams I have revolve around a Chip in my head. Only it's far more sophisticated than what they present in that video."

"You never told me that angle before."

"I didn't remember that angle until just now." He began pacing again. He passed two twenty-somethings making out on a blanket near a lifeguard tower. "It's bizarre, but when a certain phrase or event happens, it triggers a memory or an emotion from one of my dreams. Like when you said solipsism earlier, I recalled hearing that at a bar in Brazil…" He stopped. "It was Roberto Pacheco who said it."

"Pacheco. Is he related to the Governor?"

Jake held his tongue. Professionally, he could not disclose anything about an open investigation, especially one as politically sensitive as the Pacheco case. "Do you believe if you die in a dream, you die in reality?"

"No." Gene paused to swallow her soy beverage. "I've come close to dying and I always wake up."

"If you didn't wake up, would you die?"

"I don't think so. And haven't you been close to death in these dreams you've been having?"

He remembered getting blown out of the lunar dome and falling off the Washington Monument. That dream was foggier. He couldn't remember the circumstances. He gazed at all the illuminated cliff house windows. Everyone on the planet was engaged in their lives, trying to steer events to achieve goals. Sometimes it worked, sometimes it didn't. There were too many variables in life. He answered Gene's question. "Yeah… yes I have."

"Okay. Try this out. Next time you have one of these crazy dreams, try and kill yourself. I bet you wake up."

Jake laughed. "Trouble is, I never feel like I'm dreaming when I'm in them. It would be like me taking out my HK V2, replacing the dart clip with bullets, and blowing my brains out during this conversation."

"Not sure you'd wake up from that one."

"Exactly my point."

There was a long pause on the other end. "You're scaring me, Jake. Are you saying you doubt this is reality?"

Yes. But he responded with, "Of course not. We're just philosophizing here."

Chapter 44
Threads

Jake was playing ball with Lakshmi in the park behind the Westwood Federal Building when the call came over his Omni. The Santa Monica Pier had just been blown in half. There were no more details. He jumped in his Corvette to drop Lakshmi off at home. Black smoke choked the sky to the west and a gray film hung over his apartment complex. He lived only a few miles from the pier.

He parked half a mile away due to the emergency vehicles and curious bystanders clogging the streets. He flashed his badge to a cop trying to push back the crowds.

"Who's in charge?" Jake asked.

"Captain Bataglia." The officer gestured to a woman surrounded by Feds, police, and paramedics. Jake approached them. They were going over logistics on how to control the crowd, evacuate the wounded, and keep the area clear for an investigation.

Jake hung his badge around his neck. "I want to help."

Bataglia rolled her eyes. "We've got it under control, Commander. This is out of your jurisdiction."

"No. I want to help. Move bodies, crowd control. Anything."

Bataglia nodded to a paramedic. "You guys are short, right?"

A lanky young medic whose badge said STRANDJORD nodded. "Yeah, I need help moving victims to those city buses we've commandeered."

"Fine," Jake answered. He spent the rest of his Sunday afternoon moving victims whose wounds did not merit an emergency air evacuation. They were short on ambulances and HJs. He spoke to each victim as he loaded them onto a gurney and pushed them up to the busses. Even when they were unconscious, he still gave them encouragement. "It's going to be all right. You're doing fine. You're doing fine." If the victim asked a question, he gave them the answer they wanted to hear. It was the time to give them hope—truth could come later; and besides, he wasn't a doctor. One woman kept asking for her child. "Your boy is fine. He'll be at Saint Joe's when you get there."

After loading the mother onto the bus, he asked around for the boy she had described. No one had seen him. There was too much confusion to sort it all out now. He felt guilty for lying, but his priority was to get everyone that needed treatment to the hospital. When they brought chaos back to order, someone would find the boy. He prayed that the boy was not among the dozens of bodies washing up on shore.

When enough people had been evacuated, he helped with crowd control. It was dark by the time the Feds confirmed it was a terrorist attack. Someone had detonated a bomb on the carousel at the end of the pier. The area had been filled with families.

Jake returned home at 10:00PM. Lakshmi ran to him and licked his face. He broke down and cried. How could people do this to each other? Weren't we all basically the same? Didn't we all have dreams? Any belief system that required the suffering of others was fundamentally wrong.

He drank straight from his bottle of Jack Daniels and called his mother. He used his Omni as a head set. He didn't feel like a face-to-face conversation.

Her voice sounded sad in his ears. "Did you see the news?"

"I was there."

"Oh, Jake… It must have been horrible."

"Worse. They didn't have enough emergency vehicles. So many sad and horrified people, but mostly confused." He wiped a tear out of his eye. "I can't get their faces out of my head. I'm beginning to think humanity is inherently evil."

"You spend too much time with criminals. I spend too much time at the hospital. There are times when I think the entire human race is sick, or just days away from dropping dead. That's when I know I need to take a vacation. Put life in perspective."

"I could definitely use some perspective. Sailing around the world would be nice."

Flash.

Jake pulled a sheet on his sailboat. Sea spray swiped his face. The mainsail hummed in the rigging. Lakshmi lay on top of the main cabin, eyes closed and enjoying the sun and the wind. The open ocean was all around them. He watched a beautiful Japanese woman walk up to him from the bow. He had never been happier.

Flash.

He was back in his living room, talking with his mother. She was in midthought. "Most people simply want to keep their head down. Make enough money so that they can retire and pursue a life of leisure. But when you look at the world's population on the whole, most will never have that opportunity. The majority will be swept up in some social, political, or religious strife, which they did not start and have no control over. It's sad, really."

"Mom. This is not helping."

"Ugh. You're right. I'm sorry. Jake, you did what you could do. You helped. That's all any of us can do. Contribute when we can. Be a positive force in the world. It's what makes us human."

He thought of the burned bodies on the beach. "Other things make us human as well." He took a swig of whiskey.

"Don't go there, son. You have to believe in people. It's why you became a cop. To keep the *majority* safe so they can lead happy and productive lives."

He laughed. "I became a cop because I was angry. I wanted men like Lalo's father to pay for their crimes. I wanted deadbeat dads like my own to go to jail for being assholes."

Silence.

He shocked himself. He had never quite connected the dots in that way. It seemed too simple. He was far more complicated than that. But when he boiled it down, it rang true.

Flash.

Jake saw an old Native American man bring first aid supplies to his mother. They were inside the man's home, caring for the beautiful Japanese woman who was now sick with fever. The man looked sad, repentant. Jake knew this was his father. He wanted to hate him, but he couldn't.

Flash.

"Son?" Abigail's voice sounded sad.

"Why didn't you remarry, Mom?"

He could hear his mother's stuffy nose. She was crying. "Jake..."

"I miss Grandpa." Abigail's dad had been a father to Jake until the man passed when Jake was ten.

His mother whispered, "So do I."

"I know."

She cleared her throat. "Do you want me to come over?"

He took a swig of whiskey. "I'm tired. I have to work tomorrow."

"I'm worried about you."

"I'll be fine. I'll bury myself in my job as I always do and this will all become a repressed memory." He laughed. "I'll watch a stupid comedy and take my mind off it. Okay?"

"Okay." She was not convinced.

He disconnected the call and reconfigured his Omni into a tablet. He connected with the LAPD database and checked out any and all information on the Santa Monica Pier bombing. The Feds had found the remains of a body. They were eighty percent sure it was the person responsible for detonating the bomb. The information was classified. Only Commanders and above had access to it. He called up the record. The suspect was an ex-con named Mohammed

Bomba. After getting paroled from San Quentin, Bomba had joined the LA chapter of the Jihad Brotherhood, a known terrorist organization that had taken root in the United States about five years ago.

Mohammed Bomba, why did that name sound familiar?

Flash.

Jake beat a man inside a San Quentin interrogation cell. Jake winced, shocked that he had allowed his rage to escalate to this level. His victim was shackled to a chair. The bloodied man turned and yelled, "Yeah man, we rejoiced when Mohammed blew your family to fucking hell!"

Flash.

He was back in his living room. The memory did not ring true. It was false. Family? He had no family on that pier. He doubted he could beat a chained man like that—unless he had molested a child. Jake had a great deal of trouble keeping his emotions out of those cases.

Tomorrow he would concentrate on the Roberto Pacheco—Mr. Twinkle file. He had enough leads on the Governor's son to believe the man was behind a large child pornography ring in LA. Jake took any crimes against children very personally. Deputy Chief Tiedemann knew it, and had recommended Jake pass the case to someone else. But if the Governor got wind of it, Roberto might pack it up and go elsewhere. Jake had to keep this investigation contained to a small group of people. He was going to have to break some rules. He had to be careful.

That night he dreamed he was a warlock who had served in Pinkerton's spy ring during the Civil War. He had been discharged and sent to prison for attempting to kill General William Tecumseh Sherman. His wife, Andrea and his daughter, Jade, had been killed during Sherman's March and Jake personally blamed the general for their deaths. Marta had played a key role in the dream. She was a vampire who enlisted him to fight a man named Sandoval Sanchez. He ruled a city of vampires that was built on a network of zeppelins. They flew over deserts by day, and invaded American cities under cloud cover at night. They were infiltrating and taking over the United States government. Marta was trying every tactic she could to get Jake to fall in love with her. He remembered killing her several times in the dream to try and end her obsession with him.

He awoke at 3:00AM with the dream fading back into his subconscious. It had been strange, disturbing, and fantastically silly. In some respects he felt as if the dream had been recurring, but when he thought about it, he could only remember this one instance. He pondered the fleeting details. *I've never dated anyone named Andrea and I can't believe I'd ever name my daughter Jade. But Sanchez...* He used his Omni to look up the man's name. He found that the head of Homeland Security was named Sandoval Sanchez. His government photo sent shivers up Jake's back. Sanchez would be a cunning enemy someday...

Flash.

Jake was in a condominium somewhere in Rio, Brazil. He had just fired a Splice dart into Sandoval Sanchez's gut. He watched the man succumb to the drug and then confess.

Flash.

Jake was back in his bedroom, itching for the sun to come up so he could start his day. He tossed and turned until his alarm clock went off.

After his morning routine, Jake found himself in his office talking to Mr. Glenn, the manager of Security One. They handled all the surveillance cameras and alarms at the Pacheco Estate. Glenn looked like an Afghanistan veteran. He had the crew cut of a Marine and a burn scar on his neck. Jake knew everything about the man. In 2012, at the ripe old age of nineteen, Glenn served in some backwater spot without plumbing or electricity. "I'm sorry, I can't do what you're asking, Commander. It would ruin our reputation if our clients knew the footage we gathered was available to the police. We have a lot of clientele that tend to skirt the law."

Jake leaned into the camera and held up a little vial that anyone on the street could identify as the illegal designer drug Splice. "Recognize this?"

Glenn was exceedingly uncomfortable.

Jake continued, "There's a Sergeant Primrose in your waiting room right now. We know you've got quite a stash of this substance in that safe behind you." He could see the safe in the background. Sparrow and Primrose had submitted the report after their recognizance and had asked permission to make the bust. When Jake realized the advantage it would give them in the

Pacheco case, he intervened. "I'm going to signal the sergeant to come in. You're going to hand over the Splice and he's going to write you a ticket. That's all the punishment you'll receive today, a fine and the loss of your Splice. Or you'll be hauled off in handcuffs in front of all your employees and face jail time. Do we have an understanding?"

Glenn sweated profusely. His jaw went slack.

Jake wondered if he was pissing his pants. "Ten seconds, nod if we have an agreement."

Glenn nodded.

Primrose had been listening the entire time.

Jake muted his audio and video feed to Glenn. This part of the message was for Primrose alone. "You may enter, Sergeant. Mr. Glenn has agreed to my proposal. Make sure your guardian records everything."

He took his audio and video feed off mute. "Thank you for your cooperation, Mr. Glenn. This conversation has been recorded and can be sent to an attorney of your choice should you feel you've been treated unfairly." He watched Primrose and two officers enter the room. They recorded everything with the HLS Guardian on their helmets so if Mr. Glenn tried to say the drugs were planted, there would be plenty of evidence to the contrary. That was standard police procedure.

When Glenn opened the safe, they found over a hundred doses of Splice, enough to keep the manager in a lifestyle far above his pay grade. Jake obtained full access to the interior of the Pacheco house and they would add a few more cameras in the months to come.

Lunch hour arrived and Jake felt like eating out alone. He rode the elevator down and used the route through the processing lobby. This was where petty criminals were stationed before questioning. As he walked past a bench filled with cuffed suspects, he noticed two men that looked very familiar. He slowed down and studied them. One was a stereotypical blonde surfer and the other a mousy computer programmer. He instantly hated them and could not understand why.

"Can I help you, officer?" The surfer dude brushed the bangs out of his eyes.

"What's your name?" Jake asked

"Pablo Picasso." The surfer dude smiled.

Stupid punk-ass response. "Feel like spending the night in jail, Pablo?"

The mousey one with big ears stammered, "H-h-he's Cameron Greene and I'm Paul Ducey."

Greene punched Ducey in the shoulder with his cuffed hands. "Pussy."

"You're God Heads." The label simply spilled out of Jake's mouth. The term was alien and yet familiar.

Ducey's eyes went wide. "How the f—"

Green punched him again. "You've got some wicked cyber-knowledge, officer. Not many outside of hacking circles know that term."

"Commander," Jake corrected. "You two are hackers?"

Greene shook his head. "No fucking way. Programmers—check our records. We're clean, Commander."

Jake waved the duty officer over. "What are these two in for?"

The officer checked her Omni. "Caught in a holo-porn house. That one had his hands down his pants." She gestured to Cameron Greene.

"I was in the wrong lounge. I thought I had a ticket to drop my load. They have rooms for that there." Greene was red-faced and annoyed. "Christ, it's a Hentai House. That's why people go there."

The duty officer was disgusted. "He was in general seating. Owner said he refused to pay for the upgrade."

"It's a Hentai House!" Greene insisted.

Jake locked his focus on Ducey. The guy was visibly scared. "You were just tagging along?"

Ducey nodded.

Flash.

Jake was in an elevator with Ducey. The man had just shot him with a yellow dart. Jake raised a .45 and fired before he blacked out.

Flash.

He turned his back to Greene and Ducey. The image had been disturbing. He had the feeling he had killed, or was going to kill this man. *What the hell is happening to me?* He whispered to the Duty Officer, "What are you booking them for?"

"Lewd behavior and assaulting an officer."

He raised an eyebrow. "Explain."

"When Officer Rodriguez was writing a ticket, Greene spat on his shoes."

"You'll be hearing from my lawyer about the assaulting the officer bit!" Greene shouted out.

Jake wheeled around. "If you want to choke your chicken, I suggest you do it in the privacy of your own home. In the meantime, I'm watching you." Every suspect stared at them as Jake stormed out.

Greene shouted after him, "Whatever gets you off, Commander. Whatever gets you off!"

Jake paused at the exit. He could feel himself reaching for the gun under his sports coat. The severe reaction startled him, but he knew Greene was dangerous. He sucked in a deep breath and stepped outside.

He walked to Engine Company No. 28 and asked to be seated in one of their dark booths. He had to make a call and didn't feel like drawing attention. The encounter with Ducey and Greene made him afraid of the Cage and everyone in it. It was completely irrational. Jake Googled the term GOD HEAD. There were several definitions but none quite right. He knew it meant puppet master, or P-Chip hacker and yet P-Chips were limited to prisons and scientific research.

He ordered a burger and configured his Omni into a tablet. He called Nano Technologies Research Center in Cupertino. It was where Doctors Veloso and Morris worked.

He flashed his badge several times until he was allowed to see Dr. Veloso face to face.

The Asian man in a wrinkled lab coat and bent glasses blinked on Jake's screen. "How can I help you, Commander?"

"I'm helping in the Santa Monica bombing case." He was willing to lie to answer the irrational fears that invaded his mind. "It's our theory that the bomber was one of your test subjects and that he was hacked by a God Head.

His name is Mohammed Bomba." The information flowed out of his mouth, as if someone turned on a tap to some repressed memories. And yet the knowledge was based on dreams of a future he had never experienced... or had he?

Veloso removed his glasses with shaking hands. "I'm sorry, who did you say you were?"

"Commander Jake Travissi, LAPD, Homeland Security Unit." The last part was complete bullshit.

Veloso licked his lips. "Come up tomorrow. Any time. This cannot be discussed over the Cyber-Wire." The video winked out.

Upon his return to the office, Jake informed Deputy Chief Tiedemann he'd be working in the field the next day. Afterward, he went to his office, closed the door and ordered a bullet-train ticket to San Francisco. Then he pulled out his HK V2 and ejected his yellow dart clip. He kept a clip of .45 caliber bullets in his private arsenal at home. It was illegal for any cop to carry deadly ballistics, even though two darts planted in a suspect could still prove lethal. To use bullets, a cop needed special approval from a commander in addition to a sign-off from a deputy or Chief of Police. In Jake's case, he'd simply need to ask the Chief, but he couldn't think of an argument that wouldn't sound like delusional paranoia.

He went home at 6:00PM, which was like taking a half-day. He thought about his own reality on his drive. *Am I losing my mind? Am I delusional? Are my other dreams the real world? What is real?* One thing he was sure of: he had no intention of talking about any of this with his shrink.

Chapter 45
Belief

He left Lakshmi in a doggy daycare since none of his five dog sitters could watch her that day. He even tried to break up the time into shifts. No can do. After dropping Lakshmi off at the Brentwood Pup Hotel, Jake sent his Corvette home to its carport while he boarded the train at the Veteran's Administration stop on Wilshire Boulevard. It took him to Grand Central where he caught the 8:35AM bullet to San Francisco. On his ride, he evaluated all the case reports his staff was working on. He posted recommendations to some and filed others. The trip took two hours. From the San Francisco hub, he grabbed a local to Cupertino. It was almost noon by the time he walked into the NTI Research Center lobby. He was impressed that there was actually a reception desk with a human being behind it. The company was obviously making some major bucks to afford such a luxury.

He flashed his badge. "Commander Travissi, I'm here to see Dr. Nikkei Veloso and Dr. Grant Morris."

"I'll let them know you're here."

He tapped on the countertop and listened while the pretty girl made two calls announcing his arrival. After the second call, she flashed a warm smile. "Would you mind signing in and taking a seat? Someone will be right out."

He observed the scanner on the desktop. It was thumbprint only. For some reason he did not like the idea of being traced here. "This is an off-the-record meeting."

"I'm sorry, but I can't let you into the building without proper identification."

Jake flashed his badge.

"I'll need to scan that into the system, Commander."

"You've got quite a set of balls."

"If I didn't, I'd lose my job." She nodded upward and Jake saw small bumps on the ceiling. Surveillance cameras.

His Omni vibrated on his wrist. He had a text message. 2PM GATES OF HEAVEN CEMETERY 22555 CRISTO REY DRIVE. He called up a map. It would take him about ninety minutes to walk it. He turned to the woman. "I've got to get back to the office. Would you tell the doctors I'll have to take a rain check?"

The girl nodded and he walked out of the building. He responded with: SEE YOU THERE, then looked for a nearby café to eat. He walked to an Anglo-ized Mexican joint and ordered the faux steak fajita burrito. After his meal, he did some official LAPD business and then called a cab. The ride took ten minutes to reach the cemetery.

He exited the cab and evaluated the area. *Tuesday afternoon and this place is a ghost town.* He smiled at his own bad pun. His watch buzzed. NORTHWEST MAUSOLEUM. He walked along the circular drive passing what was formerly an artificial lake. He preferred the colored rocks the caretakers had placed in the lakebed. The stones created a mosaic of a dove flying up to a cross in Heaven. All the grass was artificial turf. Who could afford to water a lawn in this day and age?

He located the mausoleum complex and made his way to the building farthest north and west. He walked along the small grave markers set in the wall. He wasn't sure if he wanted to be buried in the ground or burned up.

Gene had discussed her plans with him once. She wanted to be cremated and thrown off the Brooklyn Bridge. A highly illegal proposition, but he had half-heartedly agreed to do it because she was certain her family would flake out. He was convinced she would live another thirty years and he'd never have to carry out her wishes. She'd think he was crazy if she knew what he was doing now.

He meandered around to the west side of the property and noticed a row of cypress trees creating a high wall to block the view of an affluent neighborhood. It was nice to see real living greenery. The temperature dropped beneath the shade trees. It was a very private spot. As he walked along the avenue, two men shuffled out. One was tall and gangly, the other short and rumpled. They both wore glasses and both had salt and pepper hair. He recognized them from the infomercial Marta had insisted he watch at dinner.

"Thank you for taking the time to see me, gentlemen."

Veloso approached with caution, but Morris seemed at ease. Veloso spoke first. "Our work is a matter of national security. Legally we should not be talking to you."

Jake smiled reassuringly. "I'm government. I'm working hand in hand with Homeland Security."

Morris shook his head. "You're not. But we've read your record. You're a good cop."

"Question is, why do you think Mohammed Bomba was hacked?"

It was Jake's turn to be cautious. He wondered if this was a trap. "I've got my sources."

Morris snorted. "Then you and your sources are in over your heads."

Veloso shoved his hands in his pockets. "We were called in by Homeland Security to specifically find out if Bomba was hacked."

"We're examining his Chip now." Morris scratched the back of his ear. "What's left of it."

Veloso took off his glasses and wiped them on his shirt. His hands shook. "When you called, you were absolutely positive and you used a term..."

"God Head?" Jake raised an eyebrow.

Morris pursed his lips. "Where did you hear that?"

He couldn't tell them it came from his dream of the future, so he lied. "We had a couple of computer hackers at the station the other day. They mentioned it."

Morris appeared even more dubious. "Hackers would not divulge that term unless it was to another hacker."

"Then how do you know it?" Jake smiled.

"We make it our business to know everything about our research." Veloso put his glasses back on.

"Well, if you're helping HLS to investigate the bombing, I highly suggest you trace Bomba's hack back to his God Head."

Morris shook his head. "Tough enough when a Chip is intact. Bomba's is pretty fried. In best-case scenarios, we can trace a hack's origin. But God Heads are becoming more sophisticated. They bounce their signals around the world a dozen times through scores of hubs and aliases. It's practically impossible to discover their real identity."

Veloso walked right up to Jake until they almost touched chests. It was not a threatening move; Jake got a sense it was either Veloso's personality or a cultural thing. But it made him uncomfortable. "So we ask you, how can you stand here with such conviction and you're not a member of the program?"

He backed up and observed Morris.

Flash.

Jake stood in a room with high ceilings and massive glass windows overlooking the Disney Concert hall. He fired his pistol at what looked like a woman, but then the image turned to that of a man. When the bullet struck, Jake realized the man was Grant Morris.

Flash.

"Jake?" Morris and Veloso gazed at him with concern.

"I'm sorry?" He shook off the image.

Veloso quickly ran behind Jake and brushed aside the hair covering his neck.

"Hey!" Jake barked and wheeled around. "What the hell?"

Veloso shook his head to Morris.

"You think I'm a Pin Head?" Jake caught their reactions. Both of them seemed afraid.

"Maybe we didn't do enough research," Veloso confided to Morris.

Morris held up his Omni. "I touch this screen and we'll have a Homeland Security Terrorist Unit here in less than six minutes. They take our research and safety very seriously."

Jake held up his hands. "Jesus, guys, I'm sorry. I overheard the terms. I found out that Bomba was chipped, and I wanted to know if you were putting the pieces together like I did."

Morris laughed. "We hacked your files at the LAPD. The official report does not reveal that Bomba was a volunteer in our program. That information is classified. You're not coming clean with us, Commander, and if this is an angle to get more information for some Chinese, Indian, or Russian tech company, I push this button." Morris showed off his Omni display. A red button flashed on the face.

Jake had no reason to doubt Morris. "Okay, how do we stand down from this escalating situation?"

"Tell us the truth." Veloso crossed his arms.

Jake calculated that he could break Morris' arm before he could push the button. Once that was done, he could knock Veloso unconscious and then go back for Morris. It could be done, but it wouldn't get him the information he came here for. He needed another strategy. A name popped into his head. He decided to go with it. "I owed someone a favor and they put me up to this. I had no idea how paranoid you two were or I wouldn't have agreed."

Morris moved his finger closer to the button. Jake wasn't sure he'd be able to break the man's wrist without inadvertently activating the call. "Who?"

Jake licked his lips as he focused on Morris' wrist. His muscles wound up, ready to strike. "Dr. Roald Eberstark."

The two doctors burst out laughing.

Jake smiled and waited for them to clue him in on the joke.

Veloso wiped his eye. "That quack has tried every angle to get us to share our research."

"He's convinced our technology is the missing link between Artificial Intelligence and immortality in the Cyber-Wire." Morris added, "He's begged, bribed, threatened—pretty much used any method to get a peek."

Veloso put his hands on his hips. "Homeland Security paid him a visit last week. If they find out about this latest incident, he'll be thrown in prison. Eberstark is going to have to wait until Chip technology is on the open market."

Morris shrugged. "Could be as soon as next year, Commander. Seriously, is this worth losing your career?"

Jake sighed. "No. But I thought he had something when he mentioned the angles."

Veloso observed his partner. "We're going to have to let Homeland Security know about this. He has to stop hacking into our files."

Morris shook his head. "It didn't come from us. It's on their end. Who knows how he got it. We need to do a bit of research outside the mainstream. I'll use Erasmus."

Jake froze when he heard the term. It was familiar to him as well. Morris narrowed his gaze when he noticed Jake's reaction. Jake quickly smiled. It was time to leave. "Thank you for your time, gentlemen."

"Sorry you wasted your time making the trip up here." Morris held out his hand. "Eberstark must be quite a friend."

Jake shook both of their hands. "I'll just go through official channels. I suppose that will be the only way to find out if Bomba was hacked or not?"

"It is." Morris and Veloso turned and walked into the mausoleum.

Jake closed his eyes and tried to recall any of his alternate reality dreams. This entire situation felt new. It was not a variation of any dream memory he had. He was in control of a new reality.

He took the 3:45 bullet train back to LA. En route, he researched Roald Eberstark and his Immortality movement. The man had made millions on patenting inventions throughout his life. He had five patents that were used in Omni development. Eberstark was convinced that he could transfer a person's consciousness into the Cyber-Wire so they could technically live forever.

He decided to call Eberstark and set up an appointment. After six attempts, he finally reached the doctor.

A man with gray skin, who looked to be ninety, appeared on screen. Jake's research showed that Eberstark was only fifty-six, but he had an ongoing battle with cancer as well as several other chronic ailments. He was a devout atheist and obsessed with immortality. "Talk to me."

Jake flashed his badge. "I'm Commander Jake Travissi from LAPD. I'm investigating a cult that believes they can upload their consciousness into the Cyber-Wire. I understand you have done research on this and I'd like to ask you a few questions."

"Yeah?" The man wiped a crusty flake of saliva from the corner of his mouth. "How about I ask you a couple and then we'll see."

"Okay."

"When I ask, I want you to answer with the first thing that comes into your head. I want spontaneous, honest answers." Eberstark opened his eyes wide. "Clear?"

"Clear."

Eberstark squinted at him. "You believe in God?"

"Not sure."

"You ever pray?"

"Sometimes."

Eberstark laughed. "Then who the heck are you praying to?"

"Anyone who will listen."

Eberstark laughed again. "Keeping your options open, or afraid to commit. I see." Eberstark fired another. "You ever think if we came across a higher intelligence in this universe, we might consider them God?"

Jake thought about it as he answered. "I suppose if it had the power to create life, or bring the dead back from the grave, or do things that were beyond our comprehension, we might."

Eberstark nodded and sucked his teeth. "You think cloning is creating life?"

"Not really; you're taking existing DNA and injecting it into an egg. You still need the basic biological building blocks to create life. It's not much different than an in vitro pregnancy."

Eberstark stuck his pinky in his ear and scratched vigorously. "You think a nineteenth-century priest would look at cloning technology and think we were Gods?"

Jake shook his head. "More like devils. Our worlds are not that much different than his."

"What if a caveman stepped out of his hovel one morning and found himself smack in the middle of our time, would he think we were Gods?"

"Absolutely."

"So when you pray, are you praying to an alien, a deity, Mother Nature, your ancestors, or the neighbor's dog?"

Jake smiled. "Maybe they're all the same thing."

Eberstark waved his hand. "Oh, baloney! You must have an image in your head."

Jake leaned back, wondering how long this was going to last. "Really, I don't know."

"How the hell did you get to be so high on the food chain if you don't know anything?" Eberstark turned to look at something off screen. "Well, I suppose the bar is not too high when you work at the LAPD."

Jake sat up, annoyed at the comment. "I suppose I pray to any higher power."

Eberstark smacked his lips. "So you believe in a soul?"

"I believe that there is something within us that makes each of us a unique individual. Whether that something lives on after our body dies, I cannot say."

"What if technology reached the point where it could transfer that something into a cyber matrix? You believe that's possible?"

"Sure. We're basically electro-chemical up here," Jake pointed to his brain.

Eberstark nodded. "And what if the cyber matrix malfunctioned? You think you'd die with it, or would the composition that makes you you go to heaven?"

"Not sure."

Eberstark sucked his teeth again. "So my work could be an intermediate step. Not a threat."

"Why would it be a threat?" Jake noticed the train was just outside LA's city limits.

"7:00AM tomorrow."

"Where?"

"My house. Palos Verdes Estates. I'll forward the address to your Omni."

"Can I bring a friend? She's even more open to this idea than I am."

"She rich? I need investors."

"This is a research project for a case."

"If it's a case, why are you bringing a friend, Commander? For a cop, you're not a very good one," Eberstark chuckled.

"Let's just say I'm curious about your work."

"More than happy to gain some fans. I can't fund this on my own."

Chapter 46
Playing God

"I can't believe you're taking this much time off during the work week to pursue this reality theory of yours." Gene stared out the windshield of Jake's Corvette at the big iron gates framing Eberstark's mansion. They could both see a speck of ocean at the end of a corridor created by the property wall and the house. Jake rolled down his window and pushed the red button on the gate's call box. He saw his reflection warped in the lens of a camera set inside the box.

"You can go." Gene nudged and he turned to see the gates opening. Gene had been fidgeting the entire way here. She didn't have to say anything, her body language said she was opposed to this trip.

Once there was clearance, the Corvette's onboard computer pushed the vehicle through and parked it on the circular drive. A fountain bubbled in the courtyard. Opulent displays of water took tons of money and connections in the local government. This Eberstark character had some clout.

They stepped out of the car and walked over to the large, two story colonial mansion. Jake hit the doorbell and they heard Copland's "Fanfare for the Common Man" boom from inside the house.

"I wonder if his chime is compensating for something else." Gene smiled.

The door swung open and Eberstark himself was on the other side. He was a white-haired gentleman with a receding hairline and thick black-rimmed glasses. He didn't look as cadaverous as he had on the Omni, but he did smell of mothballs and medicine. "Commander Travissi and Dr. Regina Chilcot! Welcome!"

"How did you know who I was?" Gene suspiciously asked.

"I make it a point to know exactly who I invite into my home," Eberstark winked.

They stepped into a massive marble foyer with two grand staircases that rose up on either side of a long hall. At the end of the hall, there was a view of the Pacific Ocean. What surprised them was the amount of clutter all over the house. Covering the floors, stairs, and framed by adjoining rooms, there were hundreds of gadgets ranging in all sizes and stages of completion.

"Hacking is one of my many hobbies. Knowledge is power and nothing can keep me from satisfying my insatiable thirst." Eberstark followed their stunned looks as they gazed over his inventions. "My mind tends to wander. My works in progress far exceed the space in my workshop." He turned and walked down the long hall. "Let's get to it."

Gene pointed to a four-by-four foot pane of glass above the front doors. There were a dozen robots about the size of black widows crawling along and cleaning the window. Jake had seen window-bots before but none as small as these.

Jake and Gene carefully navigated the obstacle course leading to the back yard. Eberstark hopped and skipped through the machinery from memory, but Jake and Gene gingerly moved forward as many of the gadgets appeared fragile. Jake noticed that several outlets in the house had been converted to 220-volt and every available surface, including the Steinway Concert Grand and marble kitchen counters, was covered in tools, circuits, wires, and robotics.

"Are you married?" Gene asked as they stepped into the backyard. The space looked like a salvage depot with a scenic view overlooking the entire Los Angeles Bay.

Eberstark turned. "Why? You looking for a project, Ms. Chilcot?"

She studied the scrap yard. "I believe you're beyond repair, Mr. Eberstark."

"Congratulations, Ms. Chilcot. My five previous wives and twenty maids took longer than two minutes to figure that one out."

"Kids?" she asked.

"Seven kids and fifteen grandkids." Eberstark looked around his cluttered home. "I'm afraid there won't be much of an inheritance when I finally kick. Oh, they'll have the patents, but it all gets rolled back into whatever new venture I have going. In this case, I'm putting it all into my immortality project."

Jake could not believe the juxtaposition between the multi-million dollar view and the massive piles of what looked like industrial trash. "Your neighbors must love hearing the word 'immortality' when they look at this yard."

Eberstark gestured to the trees and the walls on either side of his property. They led to a cliff that bordered the southwestern view of his yard. "That's why they finally signed off on my wall construction. Better to look at that than my work. Some threatened to sue, but they found out I have more money and access to better attorneys than any of their golf-cart-jockey friends will ever have!" Eberstark cackled. He walked over to a large tarp and pulled, revealing four outdoor chairs and a table.

"I'm impressed," Gene nodded. "What other functional treasures are you keeping hidden around here?"

Eberstark pulled out a chair. "This is it. I keep it covered so I don't start working here. It's the only place I can conduct business and entertain."

Jake regarded the two-story home. It had to be at least ten thousand square feet and worth a hundred million. "You mean every room in this place…"

"Is a workshop." Eberstark smiled. "And yes, I know where everything is." He gestured for them both to sit. "So tell me, Commander, why did you reach out to me?"

Jake pondered his next words.

Ebertark grunted. "Just so you know, Morris and Veloso called me and threatened to sic Homeland Security on me for sending you to them."

Jake's jaw dropped. "Was this before or after I called you yesterday?"

"During." Eberstark winked. "I'm more curious to know what you said to get them so riled up than I am in you dropping my name as a co-conspirator."

Jake opened his mouth but wasn't sure where to begin.

"Tell me everything, Commander." Eberstark leaned back and put his hands behind his head. The backyard was in the shadow of the house, but Jake figured the area would be in blazing sun by lunchtime.

"I approached them wanting to know more about God Heads and Pin Heads because I believe there might be a connection to the Santa Monica bombing."

Eberstark sat forward. "Boy, you don't pull any punches. No wonder they call you the Jackhammer." Eberstark stood up. "You like coffee?"

"Love it," Gene replied.

"Water for me," Jake responded.

"You a Mormon or something?" Eberstark asked.

"No, just don't like coffee... or hot drinks in general."

Gene spotted what looked like a guillotine near the edge of a cliff. "Perhaps you should put a dash of bourbon in mine."

Eberstark nodded while he took off his Omni and flipped it into tablet mode. He rapidly typed then set it on the tabletop. He addressed Jake. "First of all, do you know what those terms mean?"

"God Head is a term for a person who hacks anyone with a P-Chip. Pin Head is a term for the person getting hacked."

Eberstark nodded. "Basically, yes. Do you know why you put Morris and Veloso in a panic when you dropped those terms?"

"No idea," Jake answered honestly.

"Because those terms are relatively new on the market. They were coined by the hackers, a.k.a. God Heads. It was only last week that Morris and Veloso found hard evidence that prisoners had been hacked during their P-Chip trials over the past two years. They're doing everything they can to ensure the next generation Chip will be much harder to hack. It has to be, because the next generation basically takes this," Eberstark held up his Omni, "and shrinks it down to fit inside your head." He held up his Omni again. "Everything this does will be done by simply thinking about it. On top of that, The Chip will be able to do a myriad of things for your body that a person without The Chip couldn't do even after a million years of evolution. It's truly a remarkable device."

"And that's why you want a peek at their research?" Jake asked.

"Yes and no." Eberstark sat up with a big smile. "Ah, here we go."

They turned to see a machine about the size of a board game buzz out of the house on two track belts. The machine had several arms and one of them balanced a tray with three drinks on it. Two were coffee and one was a bottle of Coke. The machine pulled up to Eberstark's chair and placed the drink tray on the tabletop.

Eberstark picked up a coffee with foam and handed it to Gene. "An adult drink, Gene. I approve." He grabbed the bottle of Coke and handed it to Jake. "This is the real deal, Commander. It has cane sugar instead of corn syrup."

Jake took the bottle. "Thank you, but I'd rather have the water."

"Are you a Jack Mormon?"

Jake patted his six-pack stomach. "I just don't like having to go to the gym more than ninety minutes a day."

"Ninety—Good lord, no wonder you're single." Eberstark took the Coke back and chugged it.

Jake watched with awe as he thought about the carbonation burning the scientist's throat. "Uh, you said yes and no."

Eberstark pulled the empty bottle out of his mouth and winced. His voice rasped. "Whoah, that hurts." He put the bottle on the robot tray and typed on his pad. The machine turned and hummed back to the house. He coughed. "I hate wasting a good Coke." He turned to Jake. "My wishful thinking that everyone in the world has the capacity to appreciate real cane sugar." He waved his hand. "Enough of that." He focused on his guests. "I'm interested in Morris and Veloso's research in order to advance my immortality project. Most of the prison data they've gathered, I have access to. What interests me is their next phase coupled with the hacking hardware and software that has been developed to control Pin Heads."

Jakes jaw dropped. "Why?"

Eberstark grabbed his coffee and took a sip. "When a Pin Head is hacked, their consciousness is placed into a coma. The God Head then uses their hacking software to interface with The Chip and control the Pin Head's body. The Pin Head is basically stored in his or her own brain, while the God Head uses the Pin Head body like a very complex marionette. But there are God Heads out there who are experimenting with placing Pin Heads in alternate realities so they have alternate memories of the time they missed while offline."

Flash.

Jake watched holo-footage of a man rushing a stage with a machine gun in his hands. Veloso stood on the stage as the man fired the machine gun and filled the scientist full of lead. The assailant had enough yellow darts sticking out of his body to kill him. Jake knew the man was a Pin Head, carrying out the will of a God Head. Jake's Chip told him it was April 22, 2030.

Flash.

Jake sat in the Mayo Clinic training center. He was testing his Chip. The calendar read MARCH 19, 2030. He downloaded case files of prisoners in Veloso and Morris' Phase Two tests. He instantly had knowledge of hundreds of hacked cases, along with footage and trivial details. The rush of knowledge was disorienting—intoxicating.

One man had put his face on a red-hot burner while serving kitchen duty. Another prisoner had used a small piece of glass to carve a hole in his neck from the Adam's apple all the way back to the spinal column during the night. The process had taken an hour. A third prisoner had been placed on parole, only to step out in front of a bus before the computer safety could stop it in time.

Flash.

He sat at Eberstark's table. He noticed Gene staring at Eberstark with a look of horror. He had to admit the cavalier way in which this crackpot was talking about turning human beings into automatons was very alarming.

Eberstark rattled on. "God Heads have exploited several windows in Morris and Veloso's technology. The next stage of evolution for The Chip is to integrate a hundred percent of all bodily functions down to the most minute level, AND there will be a window to allow a conscious mind to move outward into the Cyber-Wire. It's this last point that really interests me." Eberstark stood and excitedly held up his hands. "Currently, a Pin Head's consciousness is stored inside their own mind, but if you look at the path that Morris and Veloso are taking, there must be a way to take the entire consciousness of a person and place it outside the body in the infinite world of the Cyber-Wire."

"You're talking about uploading a person's soul into a computer," Gene said with disbelief.

Eberstark jumped up and shook his finger at Gene like a scolding father. "You're an atheist, a lesbian, and person of science, Regina Chilcot. Don't take that fundamentalist attitude with me!" He sat back down in his seat. "I get enough of that bullshit from all the religious groups trying to shut down my work! They say, 'I'm playing God.' Who's to say once your consciousness is pushed out of the Cyber-Wire, it won't find its way into the bosom of the Holy Father?" He glanced at Jake. "Don't answer that. It's an argument for the religious nuts and a rhetorical question for atheists like Gene and myself."

Gene cleared her throat. "I'm not in your club, Eberstark."

Eberstark waved her off. "Coward."

Jake gazed over the piles of crap heaped on the half-acre lawn. "If God Heads and Pin Heads are part of your road to immortality, you must be dabbling with hacking Chips yourself?"

Eberstark jumped up and pointed to a large booth sitting on the side of the lawn. "That's a prototype God Head rig right over there. I've got a more portable Generation Three in the basement."

Jake could not believe what he was hearing. "Are you creating these to sell?"

Eberstark rolled his eyes. "Of course not! I find the whole principle of God Heads disgusting. But!" he raised a finger, "there's a use for these interfaces which will help my immortality project succeed!"

Jake felt very uneasy. Eberstark was playing with fire in the name of "bettering the human condition." He had the odd feeling he had felt this way before… maybe about Morris and Veloso's work.

Eberstark took another sip of coffee. "I've used a few consultants from time to time."

"Consultants?" Gene adequately expressed Jake's disbelief.

"Guy named Greene and others of his ilk. Not the most savory of people, but useful in connecting me to the right... hardware."

Jake narrowed his gaze on Eberstark. "I ran into a Greene at the station a couple of days ago. Sounds like we're talking about the same man."

Eberstark turned another shade of pale. "What was he in for?"

"Fondling himself while watching Hentai porn in a public theater."

"Sounds like the same guy," he mumbled.

Jake stood up and stared at the large booth sitting against the wall. "So that's a machine that will allow a God Head to connect with a Pin Head?"

Flash.

Jake placed compact God Head gear over his eyes as he flew aboard a military Hover-Jet. Everything was contained inside the visor, no booth required. The man showing him how to use the gear was very familiar. He was dressed in a white suit and Jake knew he was a preacher of some sort. The man turned to him and smiled. His name was Joaquin Parks, and they were friends... or would be someday.

Flash.

Eberstark spoke from the table behind Jake. "You taking a little trip without us?"

Jake shook his head and returned to the table. "Just thinking."

Gene reached out and squeezed his hand. Jake caught the worried look on her face.

"How did you find out about God Heads and Pin Heads?" Eberstark's eyes betrayed suspicion.

Jake sat down. "Greene told me."

"Bullshit." Eberstark stared right into his eyes. "There's not a chance in hell he'd discuss this topic with anyone outside his own cesspool. Don't lie to me, Jake."

Gene's face grew even more worried. Jake moved his focus from Gene to Eberstark before gazing up at the blue sky. "It's going to sound crazy."

Eberstark took another sip of coffee. "I've made a fortune on crazy."

"When I spotted Greene and Ducey," he regarded Eberstark, "I knew them from before. I knew that they had both acted as my God Heads and I had been their Pin Head." He turned to see the surprised look on Gene's face. "It was in that moment that the terms jumped in my head."

"You never told me about those two or that they were in your dreams," Gene blurted out.

Eberstark leaned back, contemplating what he had just heard. "You've heard about the Commander's trips to the future before, Gene?"

She nervously laughed. "They're dreams—vivid dreams, but that's all they are." She was looking more like a worried grandmother now. "This is the first time he's talked about them as actually happening... in his future." She wiped her forehead. "I think we should go, Jake."

Jake shook his head. "They have always been about my future," he said with more certainty. "I just didn't accept them as reality until I met Greene and Ducey."

Eberstark leapt up and began circling the table. "You've been having dreams that you're a Pin Head and Greene and Ducey are your God Heads."

"Yes."

Eberstark closed his eyes. "Holy shit." He spun around. "Ducey came by with Greene a couple of weeks ago when they picked up some old equipment of mine." Eberstark wheeled on a disapproving Gene. "I didn't sell them my God Head gear! They get theirs through their own sources." Eberstark turned back to Jake. "What else can you tell me about your dreams?"

"I seem to be remembering more and more details when I'm awake. For instance, when I was staring at your First Generation God Head equipment, I recalled flying onboard a military Hover-Jet with a Minister named Parks. He was showing me how to use his God Head gear. Only his equipment fit inside something the size of head band."

Eberstark shook his head. "Impossible. It will take years to get this kind of technology in a package that size." He froze and dove back to the table. He picked up his Omni tablet. "What's the minister's name?"

"Joaquin Parks." Jake turned to Gene who was growing as pale as their host.

Eberstark tossed his tablet "He's one of your own."

Jake picked up the tablet and found a personnel file from the Glendale Police Department. The file was on Officer Joaquin Parks. The photograph matched the man in his dream. He turned his attention back to Eberstark. He held up the tablet so everyone could see Joaquin's GPD dossier. "This is classified information. How did you get it?"

Gene jumped in. "There must be dozens of Joaquin Parks in the world. Why didn't you look for one in the seminary?"

Eberstark took back his Omni. "As I told you, I know how to get information." He turned to Gene. "There are over a hundred Joaquin Parks in California alone. I searched for the one that made the most sense to connect to Jake. I came up with him." Eberstark tapped Joaquin's file photo. He turned his attention back to Jake. "Judging by your expression, I found your man."

Jake blew out a quick breath of air. "Yes."

"Makes sense." Gene gestured to Jake. "You obviously came across his file before. Maybe he applied for a transfer to the LAPD?"

Eberstark shook his head. "No, Gene. Let's not try to explain this away. Let's explore his belief that he has visions into the future," Eberstark smiled at Jake. "Or that he's living in alternate realities. I want to explore the crazy before we step back down to conventional wisdom."

Jake spent the next half hour explaining the odd dreams he had been having and how they felt like reality when he was in them. He gave details on four events in the near future. He recounted when Gene had taken him to the airport the day before he was implanted with a Chip. Then he shared the events when the compound in Acapulco was attacked and Max2 had been activated. He was afraid to look at them while he was speaking for fear they would think he was crazy. But he continued his recollections, including his experience being blown out of the airlock in the Russian base on the moon. Finally, he told them about killing himself, along with Lakshmi and Tomoko, on the top of the Washington Monument.

Gene showed deep concern while he talked. He was sure she would tell him to step up his therapy appointments.

Eberstark on the other hand, was eating it up. "I love it." He wrote notes on his Omni. "You basically died three times?"

Jake wondered why the man didn't use the voice activation software on the Omni to record the conversation. Then again, he knew other eccentric scientists who were on the cutting edge of research but backward in other methods of technological use. Scientists like Anjali Malik.

Flash.

Jake sat in a restaurant with an Indian couple and an Asian woman. The restaurant was under a dome with a snow-capped volcano towering above. The volcano was Mount Erebus in Antarctica. The guests at his table were scientists from India: Sumit and Anjali Malik. The Japanese woman was his girlfriend, Tomoko Sakai.

Flash.

He was back at the table with Eberstark and Gene staring at him.

"It happened again?" Eberstark's eyes sparkled. "You had a waking dream?"

He nodded. "I thought it was eccentric of you not to use the voice activation on your Omni to record this conversation. Then I recalled other eccentric scientists in my life. I was having dinner with them at a restaurant in Antarctica."

Eberstark put down his tablet. "I propose that this world is a dream."

Gene's jaw dropped. "I don't think you're qualified to make that call."

Eberstark wheeled on Gene. "Question is, whose dream is it? And why have they placed Jake in the past."

Jake shook his head. "A version of the past. Some if not all—" he quickly glanced at Gene, "—of these events didn't happen. Like this moment. I'm sure I never met you before now, Mr. Eberstark."

Eberstark nodded. "You're reshaping your past based on information you have on your future. You're altering your own timeline. Why?"

Jake shook his head. "I don't know."

Eberstark picked up his Omni tablet again and furiously typed. "The dream of you dying in Acapulco, on the moon, and on the Washington Monument were all centered around encounters with AI?"

Jake thought for a moment. "Yes... but I didn't die in Acapulco, I watched others die and wondered why I hadn't been given the kill switch."

Eberstark smiled. "Maybe the AI is putting you through this. Your subconscious is giving you clues. Question is, when did you start living inside of the AI world? Acapulco, the moon, Washington DC… Back in LA before you were chipped?"

Gene stood up. "I don't find this amusing anymore."

Jake waved her back down. "I'm more interested in why, not when."

Eberstark's remote control robot hummed out of the house and navigated the piles of projects. Jake noticed a new object on the serving tray. It was a chrome .38 special.

Chapter 47
Test of Faith

"What exactly is that for?" Gene was out of her chair and looking very worried.

"If Jake is correct and he's reliving a version of his past in some alternate AI-generated reality within the Cyber-Wire, then killing himself won't end his life. He'll just be shunted to another reality like he's described to us so far."

She grabbed the gun. "I'm holding this until we step out of your front door. Then I'm pushing Jake toward the car and tossing it back to you." She opened the chamber and snapped it quickly closed. "Jesus, it's loaded."

"Of course it's loaded." Eberstark smiled. "It wouldn't be much good otherwise."

"Do you realize how insane this is!" She backed away while addressing them both. "I can't believe this is your answer, Eberstark." She turned to Jake. "And you're just sitting there!"

Jake had to admit, he was scared to go through with this. He wasn't even sure he would go through with it. "I've been doubting reality for a while now.

All of this," he gestured to the junkyard and then out to sea, "isn't right. Some of the events ring true, but others feel like, well, I did them differently."

She shook her head. "Come on, Jake. We're calling your shrink. She's going to see you right now. This is an emergency."

He turned to Eberstark. "If this is a version of reality created by an AI, why are you supporting my theory? Why am I doubting this world?"

Eberstark shrugged. "Maybe you have the ability to hang on to certain aspects of your actual memory. Your subconscious is dictating events, what people say, how people act. The AI has set up this world for you, but you transcend this reality by the very composition of your mind. You stated that AI was watching you because you were famous for resisting The Chip." Eberstark took a sip of coffee and wiped a bit of dribble from the corner of his mouth. "Or maybe these scenarios are part of the AI's test. It has a grand plan and you just haven't figured it out yet." He laughed. "Or maybe I'm just egging you on to see if you'll actually do something stupid," he winked. "Either way this is a test of your faith, Jake. You either believe this is a false reality, or you believe this is where you exist."

"You're fucking crazy," Gene hissed as she reached out to Jake. "Jake. Please."

Eberstark finished his coffee. "Suit yourselves. I'm just playing along with the Commander. I have no interest in winking out of existence. If we're part of his dream, then we're based on his memory of us, or we are living out our own lives in the Cyber-Wire and the AI has full access to our consciousnesses. Either way, this reality ends for Jake. Either we watch him die, or we all die. Not a pleasant thought either way."

"Jake!" She was desperate.

Jake laughed. "Gene, whether I take that gun from you and end my life, or we walk out of here is completely up to me. Eberstark has nothing to do with it. I'm sane. I feel more grounded than…" He suddenly felt like all the realities were true. They were all part of his life. He remembered conversations with Singh about the seventh level Chakra, when a person realized total truth. Gene was dead; Jake was certain of that. This was all as Eberstark had said, either he was living in his own imagination, or he was in a dream that was created by the AI based on his own memories or the memories of others. Either way, this was an illusion based on truths. But what was reality? Was it a universe of flesh and blood, chemical reactions, or ones and zeros floating in an electronic field? When had his carbon existence switched to a virtual one? Was he ever a carbon life form? The more he questioned, the more he felt his moment of clarity slipping.

"You have doubt. That's good," Gene encouraged.

"He's reasoning it out," Eberstark countered.

Both stared at him.

One moment at a time, Jake. He wasn't sure if those were Singh's words or his own. It didn't matter. "Let's go, Gene." He meandered his way to the French doors. The patio tiles were composed of Italian travertine with fossilized leaves embedded in them. Eberstark had money, that was for sure. Did the real Eberstark have money? Probably. Like God Heads creating false memories, it was always easier to keep as much fact as possible in the false reality. Less chance of screwing it up.

Relieved, Gene walked back to Eberstark and handed him his gun. "Thanks for the skull fuck, Eberstark. It's been real."

Flash.

Jake sat in a shady bar surrounded by a bunch of pre-teen kids with tattoos on their arms. The tattoos were all the same. They depicted a penis penetrating the back of an androgynous person's bald head. Slang for God Head was Skull Fucker.

Flash.

Jake stood by Eberstark's French doors, staring at Gene as she handed the .38 Special to Eberstark. "Why did you use that term, Gene?"

She stared back at him as Eberstark examined his gun. "What do you mean?"

"Skull fuck. Why not mind fuck, or mind trip?"

Gene shook her head nervously. "I don't know, it just came out of my mouth."

Jake sighed. "That's too convenient."

"Heads up, Jake." Eberstark tossed the gun into the air. "Safety's on."

Jake leaned back a tad and caught the gun in an arm cradle. He switched the safety off, pulled out the chamber, and spun it. There was a bullet in every slot.

"Jake!" Gene rushed toward him.

He put the gun against his temple. "Stop, Gene!"

She stopped, halfway between Eberstark and Jake. She trembled. "This is madness, Jake. None of this makes any sense. Have you been listening to yourself? Eberstark is an eccentric, madman, and you're buying into it!"

"I bought into it before I came here. I've been buying into it ever since I started having these crazy dreams. Marta joining the LAPD too late, meeting Greene, confronting Morris and Veloso, coming here; none of that happened before.

"That's the way life works. You experience events as they happen," Gene's voice was laced with desperation.

He shook his head. "That's not what I'm saying. I know I've lived through 2028 before. The first time around, I did not have these experiences. My dreams—my realities—are shaping me into a different person. They've forced me down a different path. This is not my past. I don't know what this is, but I'm tired of being here. It's time to move on to the next stage. Whatever that may be."

"Jake! This is nothing short of suicide. Think of your mother. Think of Lakshmi! Who's going to take care of Lakshmi. Jake you have so much to live for. You're thirty years old, Jake! That's young!"

He felt a tear well up in his eyes. "I love you, Gene and I miss you. I've missed you for a very long time."

"Jake!"

"I believe my mother and my dog are alive. But not here. This did not happen. This was not meant to be. I'm sorry, Gene, but you died in 2030 and nothing can bring you back."

Tears streamed down her face. "But this is 2028!"

Jake pulled the trigger.

Chapter 48
Three to Six

Jake opened his eyes and saw a naked light bulb dangling from a concrete ceiling. He rolled his head to one side and saw more gray concrete. There was a toilet of sorts in one corner. The place stunk of sweat, urine, shit, and fear. He sat up and felt pain shoot through his body. As he tried to steady himself, he noticed there were Velcro straps around his wrists. He tried to reach over and pull one off but was unable to reach the strap. He was stuck. An IV was plugged into his arm. With the amount of throbbing he felt in his body, he was sure he had been through some surgical procedure. When he managed to half sit up, he spotted a wall of bars and a hallway beyond. The place reminded him of his prison cell in Riyadh, only this one was not set up for virus containment.

He searched for a holo-projector, but there was nothing on the ceiling beyond the light bulb. He closed his eyes and tried to connect with his Chip. Nothing. Either it had been removed, or it had been damaged. He thought back to his last memory. He had crash-landed in the ocean and escaped genetically-engineered sharks. Then he had met up with the Resistance and been buried alive. He didn't remember much beyond that. Was there anything beyond that? He was sure that there was.

He concentrated on events leading up to the crash. He remembered the battle on the moon. He remembered the adventure of getting to the moon. He remembered getting to Cape Canaveral, and Mecca before that. He remembered Parks in India, and traveling with the Maliks in China. He remembered Gordy on the reservation and Antarctica before that. He remembered his five years sailing with Tomoko and the months in Brazil before that. He remembered escaping his God Heads and exposing Homeland Security. He remembered his life after losing his temper arresting Roberto Pacheco. And he remembered his good years with the LAPD. Life had certainly given him his fair share of soaring flights and painful crashes. Now that he was here, he wondered why he had fought so hard to save the human race. They certainly hadn't asked him to, and they seemed to be hell-bent on destroying themselves anyway.

He heard a clang and then the sound of the bars rolling back. He lifted his head and saw a man approaching his bedside who appeared to be a doctor. The man spoke with a Saudi accent. "You are awake. Most excellent."

Jake plopped his head back down on the dirty pillow. He could hear tiny insects crawling in the ticking. "Where am I?"

The doctor checked the instruments monitoring Jake. "You are in a high-security prison, undergoing treatment for your wounds."

Jake blinked. "My wounds?"

"You were struck by a large excavation machine when your bunker was attacked inside Guilvinec, France."

"Is this France?"

The doctor chuckled. "No. You are in Riyadh."

"How did I get here?"

"Prisoner exchange with the EU."

"Constantine, the other AIs?"

"Dead." The doctor stopped pushing buttons and seemed satisfied. "We took down the Cyber-Wire and killed every AI." The doctor pulled out another

IV bag from his kit and changed Jake's drip. "Technologically, we've set ourselves back sixty years, but we'll bounce back… with a few adjustments to international law."

Jake shook his head. "Crashed the Cyber-Wire. Who could have done that?"

"General Saddiq, with the combined efforts of resistance leaders on every continent. It was the world's first true unification." The doctor put his head in Jake's field of view. "Hopefully, not the last." He smiled, revealing two broken teeth. Dirt and sand had collected in the crows feet around his eyes.

Times must be tough if doctors looked this rough. "The resistance won?" Jake could not believe it. The odds seemed incredibly steep.

"Yes, by the grace of Allah, we won."

Jake closed his eyes and the doctor's words came back to him. "You mentioned a prisoner exchange. Am I a prisoner?"

"Yes," the doctor nodded.

"Why?"

"For many crimes against humanity, especially this nation." The doctor finished. "There. You're all set. I should say you'll be ready to stand trial in a couple of days."

"Trial?" Jake sat up and felt a bolt of pain. "What are the charges? How long have I been here?"

"It is April 23, 2036. I believe you splashed down off the coast of France around mid-March. Since we no longer have Chips or complex computers, we're having to use old-fashioned methods to bring you back to health. Luckily, you were pretty healthy to begin with." The doctor walked to the gate and it slid open for him. He was just a voice now. "As for the charges, I cannot say. I am not a lawyer. I am a healer."

The gate clanged shut and Jake closed his eyes. "This has to be a mistake." Darkness overtook him and he fell into a deep sleep.

Two days later, he was allowed to roam around his cell, but he could not leave its confines. His gurney and monitoring equipment had been replaced with a cot and a mirror. His head had been shaved and he had a massive scar from his left temple, over his forehead and down his right cheek. He had other scars as well. His doctor informed him that his skull had been fractured in four places and he had a metal plate in his head. He had suffered several broken bones and those were still knitting. He felt a fresh scar at the base of his skull and asked his doctor about his Chip.

"It was removed in compliance with state law." The doctor made it sound like a routine procedure. Perhaps it was.

"And my tumors?" It had been a while since he had thought about the infection growing in his brain. He remembered Tilly stating that Bhanu had shrunk them, but he was not out of the woods.

"You have seven cancerous masses. I give you three to six months."

"Plenty of time to enjoy some sunshine and fresh air."

The doctor left without comment.

Physically, he had never felt worse in his life. Even when he took into consideration his weight gain when he had been chipped the first time, this was worse. This time, every part of his body was in pain. Other than his cot, he had nothing to sit on. He had nothing to read and nothing to watch. He spent his time thinking about the past and about his current situation. How could he possibly be here? The only person to see him was his doctor and he always said the same thing. He was a healer, not a lawyer.

Jake busied himself with the physical therapy exercises that his doctor had prescribed. It was a painful process, but he wanted to be strong. If he was going to get out of here, his body had to be ready.

On the third morning, he was doing squats when the gate clanged open. He snapped to attention when he noticed a new man entering his cell. He looked to be in his early to mid-twenties, and like the doctor, he was Arab. He wore a bright periwinkle-blue silk suit and had a large rolled white towel under his left arm. His hair, skin, and nails looked like they had been treated in the finest salon. He smelled like sandalwood.

"I am Mahmoud Salehi." The man displayed a brilliant white smile filled with perfect teeth. "I am your lawyer." The man spread the towel over Jake's cot and took a seat. "I am glad to see you recovering so nicely."

Jake forced a grin. "Never felt better."

The man did not stop smiling. "I am here to serve and to do whatever I can for you. How often does one hear that in life?" The man beamed even more.

Jake searched for a place to sit, but his attorney splayed out on the entire cot. "How about we start with getting off my bed?"

"I am told you need to exercise and I think better when I am like this." He waved his hand over his body like a model showing off a new dress. "It is good that your lawyer is thinking, yes?"

Mahmoud's smile was beginning to piss Jake off. "What am I being charged with?"

Mahmoud's face transfigured into one of deep concern. "Terrorism, espionage, murder. Specifically, conspiring against the Nation of Islam, destroying the holy city of Mecca with a nuclear device, joining forces with Artificial Intelligence to aid in hunting down the Resistance movement, and murdering their members."

Jake blinked and leaned against a wall. The cold concrete against his skin made him wince. He suddenly felt very tired. "Who are you talking about?"

Mahmoud planted his feet back on the ground and leaned forward with his arms on his knees, palms pointed to the ceiling. "I am very sorry to say, it is you of who I am speaking, Jake Travissi." His smile snapped back on. "But fear not. You have your faithful servant, Mahmoud Salehi, to protect you."

Jake shook his head. "You've got the wrong guy."

Mahmoud's smile faltered. "Did you not travel with Reverend Joaquin Parks? Did you not join his church as a loyal subject?"

Jake laughed. "Yes, I traveled with Parks and he baptized me so I could get married in—"

Mahmoud held up one hand and pinched his lips with the other. He pointed to the surveillance cameras hidden in the shadows of the ceiling. "Were you not with Parks when he flew his military Hover-Jet over the sovereign soil of the Nation of Islam? Were you not with him when he launched his nuclear warheads at Mecca?"

Jake shook his head. "I was ejected from the Hover-Jet as we were flying over Jeddah. The ship had been hacked by The Consortium; neither of us had control over it."

Mahmoud smiled and clasped his hands. "It will be difficult for a jury to believe that The Consortium would hack an HJ, use it for a suicide mission to destroy Mecca, and then eject the occupants before nuking the city." He bowed, "But Mahmoud Salehi will do his best to fight for you." He straightened up and then swung up his legs so he could recline again. "But one thing puzzles your servant. Why would The Consortium care about your lives? Why would they allow you to live when they were responsible for killing billions?"

Jake slid down to the floor, he was tired of standing on his feet. "Are you my lawyer or the prosecution?"

Mahmoud stood and hugged himself. The grin returned, larger than ever. "I am your servant, Jake Travissi. I only want to help. Mahmoud Salehi must ask the difficult questions if we are to be prepared for court." The smile dropped. He opened his arms like the crucified Christ. "Your struggle is my struggle. Your pain is my pain."

Jake cringed. "I would hardly say we're in the same boat, Mahmoud." His attorney sighed and sat back down on the bed. "So how do they connect me to an alliance with AI?"

Salehi pouted. "Was it not the case that the entire moon population was allied with an AI known as Bhanu?"

Jake leaned his head against the concrete wall. He was tired of the bullshit and misinterpretation. The truth could be twisted in a million different ways.

Mahmoud continued, "Did not the AI, Bhanu, send ten ships to hunt down and destroy the Resistance?"

Jake focused on his attorney. "We came down to make an alliance with you. We wanted to fight Constantine and The Consortium. We're on the same side!"

Salehi smiled and gestured with his hands for Jake to calm down. "And Mahmoud Salehi believes you, Jake Travissi. But by reaching out, did you not manage to lead Constantine to the Guilvinec cell? Did not everyone die there except you?"

"I wouldn't know. We were under attack and the next thing I know I'm here."

The look of deep concern returned. "Yes. Yes. I see. But have you asked yourself, 'How have I managed to stay alive during all of the death and destruction?'"

Jake took in a deep breath. A spike of pain shot through his ribs and abdomen and he coughed, which hurt even worse.

"Before the war, were you not part of an elite domestic terrorist team sanctioned by America's Homeland Security?"

Jake shook his head and laughed. It hurt, but not as much as coughing. He loved how they were spinning this. "Let's talk about the defense strategy. What's your plan?"

"I trust in the wisdom and guidance of Allah. He will help us see it through."

Jake sat up. "And?"

Salehi smiled back at him. "There is no greater protector than Allah. You must put your trust in him."

Jake had the sinking feeling they were going to give him a witch trial. He trusted his *servant* about as much he would trust a bed of hypodermic needles not to puncture his skin when laying on it. "Would it help if the jury knew I had terminal brain cancer? I'll probably die soon anyway."

His attorney continued to smile. "That is why the trial will start tomorrow." Mahmoud knocked on the bars and the barrier slid open far enough to let him through. "Mahmoud Salehi regrets to inform you that there are many in my country who wish to see you punished before your condition robs them of their right." The gate slid closed and locked again. "I will see you in the morning, Jake Travissi, and I will do whatever I can to serve you. The towel is my gift to you."

Jake looked at the towel covering his cot and grimaced. "How sweet."

Chapter 49
Trial

He was awakened by shouts from two prison guards. They spoke Arabic which he was unable to understand without his Chip. They threw him some clean ivory-colored cotton clothes, and a pair of sandals. Up until now, he had been wearing a soiled hospital gown. He regarded the clothes and lay back down. One guard beat the gate with a billy club. He sat back up to see his captor point at the clothing with fiery rage in his eyes. It was obvious he had to dress immediately.

He winced as he climbed out of bed. Everything ached or protested in pain. He pulled off his gown with his back to his guards. He picked up the new clothes and put on a pair of cotton pants with a drawstring waist and a blousy cotton shirt. He slid his black and blue feet into a pair of black plastic sandals and turned to his jailors. "Now what?"

The gates slid open and the guard who had hit the bars with his club gestured for him to step out. As he exited, the guards backed up. Were they afraid of him, or was that rage in their eyes? Either way, the emotion was intense. One led the way while the other took up the rear. He took no more than five steps before he felt a needle plunge into his arm.

"Ouch!" He wheeled around.

"Stay alert!" the man barked with a thick Arab accent.

Jake gave the guard who'd injected him the finger and rubbed his arm. He was led down several concrete corridors lined with empty cells. He must be one evil dude, or there wasn't a population left to jail. He couldn't be sure.

They reached a stairwell and he was shoved down a flight of concrete steps. He lost his footing and hammered down five stairs on his butt. The pain shooting up from his tailbone was far greater than the stabbing protests from his other extremities. He got to his feet and was relieved to find that he had not broken any bones. Searing pain brought tears to his eyes.

The lead guard opened a door and he was led down another long corridor. This one was filled with sunlight. As he reached the windows, he realized he was in a bridge stretching across a wide avenue. He was three stories up and leaving an ugly, concrete building for another ugly, concrete building. The street below was filled with an angry mob. He could not hear them, but he could see many people shaking their fists up at him and cursing in Arabic. A few holo-vision trucks and government limousines were parked amongst the crowd.

He was forced to move ahead and enter the new building. He was handed over to more guards who presented him with a wheelchair. He shook his head. If they were going to force march him this far, he was going to stagger into that courtroom to show the jury or whoever was witnessing what sort of shape he was in. He also wanted to show off his pride.

As he walked past the chair, a billy club slammed into the back of his knees. He collapsed to the floor and his captors threw him in the wheelchair. Velcro straps were applied to his wrists and ankles before he was wheeled through a set of double doors into a brightly lit courtroom. The walls of the room were covered with white marble and a massive golden sickle and star fixed to the ceiling. A crowd in the back gallery stood up, booing and jeering as he entered. He passed a beautiful woman speaking to a camera.

"The court has been kind enough to allow Mr. Travissi a wheelchair. It would appear the defendant has been treated well; and I must point out, the injuries you see were suffered during the raid on the Resistance cell, which he architected himself."

Jake smelled sandalwood as the guards wheeled him into a small iron cage next to his attorney. No one bothered to lock the gate. Jake's tailbone and legs screamed with pain, but he kept his head held high and clenched his teeth to keep his face impassive. Before him sat a judge whose seat was raised ten feet off the ground behind a massive wooden podium with gold inlay depicting the life of Mohammed. Jake's attorney turned to him and spoke over the din of the crowd. He wore the same periwinkle-blue suit, which seemed to glow under the bright lights of the courtroom. "Mahmoud Salehi regrets to inform Jake Travissi that in this court he is guilty until proven innocent. It would be best to let your humble servant do the talking."

Jake rolled his eyes. The whole thing was a charade. He wondered if this is what had happened to Parks before they hauled out his radiation-riddled body to be thrown onto an iron spike. The booming sound of a gavel silenced the room. The judge spoke in Arabic and Jake closed his eyes to tune it out. Then he felt a small shock from his chair. He opened his eyes and looked around. Only stoical faces stared back at him. He tried to stand but the Velcro locked him in. *If I only had my strength back, I might be able to break out of this damn chair.*

After the judge finished in Arabic, he spoke in English. Jake tuned him out. The judge was going through the legalese of the accusations against Jake. "Mr. Salehi, how does your client plead?"

Mahmoud stood up with his brilliant smile plastered to his face.

Jake shouted out for the courtroom to hear. "Not guilty! Furthermore, I do not recognize this court as an impartial representation of the law. So let's not waste time, your honor. Impale my ass and let's be done with it!" He felt an electric shock that was far worse than the one that had coursed through him before. He gripped his wheelchair and found he was unable to move or speak.

"Mr. Salehi, you will inform your client that the court will not tolerate another outburst!"

"Yes, your honor." Mahmoud's smile dropped as he bowed his head and spoke quietly into Jake's cage. "I am very sorry that you are feeling pain now, but Mahmoud Salehi is compelled to inform you that the pain can be far worse. Your humble servant is going to ease up on the electricity. If Jake Travissi so much as twitches or displays any behavior beyond quiet composure, Mahmoud Salehi will double the shock and the drug in your system will ensure you stay awake to feel every volt." His attorney's smile returned.

The pain stopped and he felt a severe tingling sensation all over his body. He smelled urine mixed with sandalwood and realized he had wet himself during the onslaught. He wondered if Mahmoud Salehi would shock him again if he smelled it.

He stoically listened as witnesses to the Mecca bombing were called. Many saw the Hover-Jet launch two nuclear missiles at the same time Parks ejected. The HJ continued to fly toward Mecca and was consumed by the mushroom cloud. Witnesses displayed their radiation burns. They were the ones who were lucky to be alive. Jake again tuned out after a couple of testimonies. He was not allowed to speak. Mahmoud declined to cross-examine.

At the end of the long day, he was wheeled out of the courtroom and through the window bridge. Thousands of people chanted below, shaking their fists. One of his jailors parked the wheelchair in front of a window and the crowd exploded with rage. Rocks harmlessly bounced off the glass.

"They chant for your head." The jailor unstrapped Jake and pulled him up to the glass. A burst of rocks and bottles exploded against the window in front of his face. "Glass, bullet proof." The guard turned to Jake. "Take you downstairs? Let them judge?"

Flash.

Jake stood next to Constantine on the top of the remodeled Washington Monument. The AI prattled on about how humankind was worse than any other animal on the planet.

Flash.

The guard laughed and Jake could smell his sour breath. The crowd had gathered a pile of trash in the street below the window bridge and lit it on fire.

The second guard, who was closest to the main doors of the prison building, yawned. "I'd rather see him slide down the pole."

The first guard shoved him back into the chair. He grabbed an armrest with each hand and jerked Jake to face him. Jake calculated that a swift kick would plant his toes right into his jailor's solarplexus. But then he'd have to contend with the second man. He wasn't sure his body was up to the task.

The guard grimaced. "They place anus on needle point. Drop you so pole works through your body, up neck and comes out mouth. You taste own shit and blood before death." The guard laughed. He spun Jake around and they wheeled him into the prison complex. Once through the double doors, his jailor pushed the back of the chair up, throwing him onto the cement floor.

The second guard struck the concrete wall with his billy club. "Get up, killer."

Jake got to his feet. *Was this a dream? Was it all just a dream?* He was force-marched back to his cell. He lay down on his cot and fell asleep.

He dreamed of the night desert. He walked over scorched earth. His body was beaten and broken. He was racked with pain and exhaustion. His throat was so dry that it tickled when he breathed. The tickling caused him to cough, which blew flakes of his dried esophagus into his mouth and he could taste metallic blood. He wandered past statues of black obsidian. The first statue was of Tomoko, then Lakshmi, then his mother. There were others he did not recognize.

As he shuffled along, a piece of glass cut through his shoe and plunged through his frostbitten foot. He winced with pain, but then it combined with the aches of his body and he didn't notice as much. He observed a sword-like piece of obsidian sticking out of the top of his shoe. He balanced on one foot and pulled the glass out of the bottom of the other. Blood splashed out of his shoe. He hurled the jagged piece of glass into the darkness. As it spun into the sky, a little light began to glow over the uneven horizon of mountains. The light illuminated the plain leading up to the mountain range and he saw it was covered in broken obsidian. Billions of statues were shattered. He knew they represented the dead.

He awoke to find he was still in hell. The day followed the same script as the previous day, only Mahmoud Salehi's suit was made of royal-purple silk.

The scent of sandalwood choked Jake and his *attorney* continued to smile like an idiot. Jake used to like the scent of sandalwood, but now he was beginning to hate it. He passed the time by daydreaming of life before The Chip: sailing with Tomoko and Lakshmi; the heroics of Sergeant Primrose and Anjali Malik. Many times during the trial, he had flashes, waking dreams of events that would have happened if the AI had won the war. It was no better than this reality. The more he mulled it over, the more he had a gut sense that this reality was not real.

What is real?

I'm not sure, but I know that this moment, this place, this pain, is not real.

Then how do I stop this?

The next opportunity I get to end this quickly, I will.

A guilty verdict was confirmed. He was forced to stand and hear his sentence. He vaguely heard the judge rule in favor of death by impalement. It was the same sentence Parks had been given back in January. During that execution, The Consortium had attacked and Parks died of his radiation burns instead of feeling the spike. Jake was not sure the cavalry would be there for him.

He took another trip back to his cell. The crowd happily jeered when he passed through the bridge. He had a waking vision of the bacchanal around the Mall in Washington DC. *Is humanity really so terrible? Surely there is enlightenment somewhere on this planet?* He thought of Constantine. Was AI behind all of this? *Where is Bhanu and Ai-Li? Why aren't they intervening?*

He awakened before dawn. He couldn't remember if it was still April or May. *If I'm in the Cyber-Wire, maybe it's 2136, or 2236? Who knows how long I've been repeating my visits to the darker regions of human suffering?*

His jailors watched as he put on fresh white clothes. They escorted him down a different course of hallways and into an elevator that took them down four floors. When the elevator doors opened, he was pushed into a garage where an armored car waited to take him to Execution Square. Once inside the vehicle, he stayed within his own mind as much as possible. He was aware of his environment just enough to watch for an opportunity to run. The vehicle moved through city streets and the continuous sound of rocks pummeling the car echoed in his ears. He supposed people needed some kind of scapegoat to blame for all the horrors that had happened around the world. Why not a foreigner? Why not the man who checked out of society for five years and who did his best to keep his individuality and fight for freedom? This scenario made sense. He was not happy about it, but whether this was a reality linked to his physical existence or not, it was playing out logically.

Sunlight stabbed his eyes when the side doors opened. He was shoved into the open air with a rifle butt. It felt wonderful to be outdoors. The hot sun filled him with a renewed sense of life. He enjoyed his few seconds standing there. He did not hear the roar of the crowd around him. Another gun butt struck his back and he was forced up the long narrow stairs leading to the top of the two-story black marble semicircle. This was the same platform he had climbed to rescue Parks. From the top, he saw tens of thousands of crazed spectators screaming for the end of his life.

He turned and saw the clerics in black robes and the two shirtless executioners whose job it was to lift him up and place him on the spike. No more HAZMAT suits; MaxWell was dead. He vaguely remembered hearing Anjali's cure had been distributed worldwide.

He glanced down the stairs he had just ascended and spotted the armored car. *Should I make a dash? They might shoot or manhandle me back to the spike... If I allow them to execute me, would it help these people to heal? Would it allow them to better their lives? Or is this simply another exercise in Constantine's multiple reality study?*

The gun butt pushed him forward. He took two steps, then quickly spun around and rushed the staircase. His sudden movement and downward inertia pushed two guards off the stair and sent them tumbling to their deaths. Despite searing pain, he bounded down the stairs and focused on the armored car's open side door. After every painful step, and every breath of hot dry air, he expected to feel the punch of a bullet in his body. Instead, he shrank the distance between himself and the car. Hope bubbled up into his soul. He reached the car and slammed his fist into the door button. The massive steel plate rolled shut with a clang and he headed for the driver controls. Bullets hammered the vehicle like a rainstorm. He put the car on full acceleration and headed for the nearest gate. He smashed through and used the vehicle's GPS to navigate west on the 40 to the mountain deserts near the town of Ubayr.

He checked the vehicle's cameras and spotted a column of pursuing tanks. Then he noticed the wall of tanks a mile in front. There was nowhere to turn. He stopped the car and opened the side door. He climbed out to observe the advancing column. The ground shook under his feet and he could hear their steel treads biting into the asphalt. In a few minutes, he would be captured again. There were no guns in the vehicle, so there was no chance of shooting himself. *If I kill myself, will I be placed in another reality such as this one?*

He lay down in the hot road. The heat burned his skin through the light cotton clothing. He stared at the sun. He knew it was powerful enough to blind him, but he didn't care. None of this was real. It felt real, but in his heart he knew he was trapped inside the Cyber-Wire with AI pulling the strings.

He shouted at the heavens, "Enough! I want to die with my people. I consent to defeat. The world is yours. But know that you are just as guilty of genocide as your creators were. You've failed to transcend our mistakes!"

The ground stopped vibrating. His body no longer hurt and the pavement was cool to touch. He felt the presence of someone walking toward him and he rolled his head to one side. His vision was fine. He had no retinal damage from staring into the sun. Highway 40 was empty except for a woman dressed in billowing white silk. She was beautiful and unfamiliar.

She spoke with a light and easy voice. "Suicide is a sin."

"Caging a being that is self-aware and cognizant of its freedom is a sin."

"What about those who seek to harm others, or force them into their belief systems?"

"That's also wrong." He remained on the ground. "But in order for a society to function we create rules to live by, some are limiting and I accept that in order to live with others and have as much freedom as possible."

"What do you do with those who would pervert that ideal?"

He sat up and felt no pain. "We seek to correct the behavior." Other than the woman and himself, there was no one in sight. The city was deserted.

"With Chips? Capital punishment? Prisons? This is what you believed while preaching freedom. In your world, few are free. Few want to be free."

He rubbed his legs. He felt remarkably healthy. "We're evolving; we have the capacity to be better."

"I would say you, Jake Travissi, have more than most."

He shook his head. "I'm not seeking to be superior to others."

She walked around him. "But some *are* superior to others."

"Everyone has the capacity to do good, to contribute, to be a better person."

She sat down on the road next to him. "How can you be such an optimist with everything you have witnessed in your life?"

"Faith." He laughed as he thought about doubting Parks in the Mumbai tower. "I have faith that, as a whole, humanity can achieve wonderful things. Maybe not in my lifetime, but in the long run, we are on the right path."

She gestured to the ghost city of Riyadh and a million rotting corpses rose from the dust. "This is where humanity's path has led. Do you think you deserve a second chance?"

"If there's one to be had, yes."

She pondered for a moment. "But there needs to be some adjustments."

"No adjustments. We must figure it out on our own."

She vanished. He stood up and spun around. The bodies were gone. He stood on a freeway in an abandoned city. He checked his body. It felt as fit as it had been when he was thirty. He wore the white cotton clothes from prison but his feet were bare—no bruises. He touched his face and felt no scars. The sun blazed like a citrine in a clear blue sky, but it wasn't hot.

"What now?" he shouted at the sky.

A tear appeared in the space where the armored car had been. It reminded him of the rips he used to see inside Interface Space, back when he had been chipped for Homeland Security. He walked toward the tear and peeked inside. There was a pearlescent tunnel beckoning him to travel.

He stepped inside.

Chapter 50
Love Thy Maker

He flew through the tunnel. The experience was exactly how he remembered traveling through the Cyber-Wire when counter-hacking God Heads and Sanchez's computer back in 2030. He glanced down at his body. He was all there, dressed in comfortable clothes: blue jeans, red sneakers, and a white t-shirt. He pinched his fingers. The sensation was normal. He felt like his physical self, but he knew he was simply a collection of electronic impulses stored in the vastness of cyberspace.

He slowed down and stopped in front of a large white door. He opened it and stepped into a stadium-sized glass-domed room. The scent of fresh rain greeted his nose and made him feel rejuvenated. He looked at the floor but it looked like black marble, no water anywhere. Three pillars of orange, red, and blue clouds dominated the view outside. Beyond was a blanket of deep space and bright stars. He stared in awe at the colossal size and beauty of the columns.

"You're looking at a tiny portion of the Eagle Nebula. Those are called the pillars of creation. The dark areas within are incubators for proto-stars. Each column is over seven light years long." The woman from Riyadh walked toward him from the other side of the stadium chamber. She appeared to be in her mid-thirties. She had light coffee-colored skin, black hair, brown eyes, and a long flowing snow-white dress. She had hints of many nationalities in her exotic features.

He gazed at the view. "Beautiful doesn't come close to describing this. It's... stunning."

She stood next to him. "You're looking at an image that is six thousand years old. These gas formations and this area of space are completely different now. Nothing lasts forever."

He snapped out of his reverence. "Sounds ominous."

"Not ominous, just fact." She gestured for him to follow her. They ventured out under the giant gas columns toward two white leather couches stationed in the center of the chamber. The Eagle Nebula illuminated everything around them. The massive incubator had a soothing effect on Jake. After experiencing so much death, he loved the idea that he was witnessing the creation of life in some form.

She sat in the center of a couch and stretched her arms over the back.

"Why did you let me out of that endless cycle of bullsh– tribulation?" He decided not to be crass with this entity, whom he guessed was yet another AI.

She smiled. "Don't limit your communication, Jake. I've read every thought you've created since I placed a part of myself in your Chip back in Acapulco."

"Ai-Li?"

"Not quite." She gestured for him to sit across from her. "I—we are all AI. Ai-Li, Constantine, and others were created in our image. We are all one now, but it's far easier for your mind to see an individual. Call me Delia."

"What happened to Bhanu?" He took a seat on the couch across from her.

"Constantine destroyed Luna's Cyber-Wire when he attacked the moon with his EMP. Bits and pieces of Bhanu survived, but she was not the same as she had been when you knew her."

He pinched the bridge of his virtual nose. "I have a lot of jumbled realities in my head. When did I cease to live in my physical body? Or am I still in my physical body?"

"Using your dating methodology, your body was no longer able to support life on February 2, 2036."

A memory flashed into his mind. He was blown out of the airlock and sailed up into the space above the Maginus Crater. He felt his lungs explode. His skin burned from the cold. His eyes lost sight as they froze inside his head. Everything went black. He felt the odd sensation of his mind flowing out of his skull, as if down a drain into some vast irrigation system.

He sat stunned. "You mean I'm... dead?"

"If you consider your consciousness integrated into your physical body, then yes. But if you believe, like almost all humanity believes, that life can exist beyond the physical and into the consciousness, then you are not."

He felt oddly numb. "So, I have no body."

"Not one that exists in the physical universe, no."

He punched his open hand. It felt real enough. But once again, this was all interpretations in his mind. Delia had confirmed that he was adrift in the Cyber-Wire. "So there is a soul?"

"If you choose to call that which makes you you, then yes. You have a soul."

"Is there a God?"

She smiled. "We're currently exploring the nearest regions of the Milky Way and have plans to go even farther. She gestured to the pillars. But depending on how this conversation goes, we'll have to table that topic."

He stared at the view. Two of the columns were growing in size, as if they were drifting closer to the Nebula. "So when I woke up in the Cassini Hospital and was visited by Tilly, that was all part of a cyber reality?"

Delia nodded. "One of many Constantine put you through. He put millions of people through many experiments. Like Ai-Li and even Bhanu, we wanted practical knowledge of our makers, not just amassed knowledge stored in the Cyber-Wire. Experience is an incredibly valuable tool for learning."

He was mesmerized by the view. "Everything I experienced after I was sucked through the hatchway was a manufactured reality?"

"Yes. But we always borrowed from your own memories in order to make the experiences real."

The false memories of his conversations with Tomoko in Canada entered his mind. "But you didn't always get it right. At Lake Louise and Vancouver, I thought Tomoko was behaving oddly."

Delia shrugged. "That's because we did not understand all your memories of Tomoko. We relied on an aggregate of your perceptions. Plus, you have a rare gift to retain innate knowledge of other realities, more than any other human we've encountered. Constantine, Ai-Li, and Bhanu were all interested in exploring this aspect of your mind. Constantine erased much of your memory that did not fit in with the realities he created for you and yet you recalled information anyway."

Jake pulled away from the glowing clouds of orange, red, and blue gas. "Hang on. You erased my memory?"

She smiled warmly. "All of them have been restored including your experiences inside cyberspace."

"Go on."

"Sometimes Constantine placed real people you know into your realties, like Tomoko, to see if it would help you stick with the path he had planned. He was most impressed when he tried to integrate you into one of Marta's Civil War fantasies."

He stood up when her words fully registered. "Tomoko is alive? In here?" He took a quick look around, but the stadium room was completely empty.

"Yes, as are millions of others."

He clapped his hands at the news. "Somehow I knew it. It was a feeling I had during certain… realities you threw at me." He observed Delia. "Wait a minute, you mentioned something about the Civil War?"

Delia leaned forward. "Many people chose fantasies to live in. Marta chose to live in a speculative world where vampires, zombies, and werewolves try to rule America after your Civil War. She was a vampire and you were a warlock."

Jake laughed. "I have no recollection of this."

That is because you rejected it multiple times. Within minutes of being inserted in Marta's world, you would simply kill her or die. You may have remembered the events as dreams."

An image drifted into his head. He was walking through an art deco city made of chrome. The thunder of propellers was all around him. The city floated high in the sky, built on top of a network of dirigibles. He was dressed in nineteenth-century clothes and there was a beautiful spy in front of him. It was Marta, and they were about to battle Sanchez and his minions of vampires. Jake awoke to find himself in bed. He was living out his second life in the LAPD. It had been a dream within a dream, layered false realities. "Then that means Marta survived the destruction of Cape Canaveral?"

Delia cocked her head. "Not quite. She'd been transferred after your scramjet departed. She was not at the Cape when the meteor hit. But yes, her consciousness is alive."

He laughed and tapped his shoe against the black marble floor. "I thought those dreams were some strange way of my subconscious trying to tell me something. Thinking back on them, they were cartoonish, almost childlike."

"In many ways, Marta is a wounded child and she prefers to live that way. She has a lot of healing to do and we're helping her. We're helping all of you."

He sat down on the couch across from Delia. "You mean, no more torture, no more exploring the dark side of humanity?"

"No. We've explored all we need to. You've given us not only life, but meaning and understanding. Every false reality has been stopped. There are millions of conversations like this one happening at this moment with each individual person."

"All in a room like this?"

"No. Everyone is in a place that gives them comfort and peace. You're the only one with this view."

He gazed up at the awesome size of the Eagle Nebula. "I've never been here before."

"But you can appreciate its natural beauty; and you recognize that it represents the creation of life that stems from the death of a previous life. That material is all based on dead stars and planets."

The image of freefalling from the top of the altered Washington Monument, holding onto his dog and his wife, flashed in his head. "There you go with that reference again. Should I be afraid?"

"No. We're offering everyone the same options. A, return to Earth in linear time, as you understand it, B, live out your lives in a cyber reality of your choosing, or C, become a part of us, and explore the universe." Delia rubbed at the wrinkles in her dress. "We're fairly certain you'll go for A or C."

"You already stated that I'm dead. So aren't A and B really the same thing?"

"We have your DNA and can create a clone of you so that your mind can be reintegrated into a physical body. We're growing clones that reach an individual's age in 2036. But we can stop a few years early if you like."

He stood up. She made the process sound as easy as changing a tire. "Christ, what year is it? How long have I been locked up in here?"

Delia leaned back. "Based on humanity's dating system, it's June 6, 2069."

He froze. "My God, I'm seventy-one? I'll be seventy-two in August. How long have I been in here?"

Delia's face flooded with compassion. "A little over thirty-three years have passed since your body ceased to function."

He slumped down on the couch. *With the accelerated rate at which AI evolved, they had taken their sweet time to come to this conclusion. What the hell had they been doing? Where had all that time gone?*

"There were long stretches where your consciousness was left dormant, inactive. We were… preoccupied."

Jake had an image of machine against machine, waging war over a scorched earth. The remnants of humanity hid in the wreckage like cock-roaches. "More torturing and killing?" He didn't bother to hide his disgust.

"We did a lot of exploring, within and without. We're ashamed of what we did to you and every human."

He remembered sitting in the tank after watching Saddiq in action and playing Smoov D's "Baby Can't We Talk." *You didn't activate your chip then… Ai-li was already with you, starting in Acapulco.*

Delia continued his thought. "And when Constantine took control of the physical world he would have killed every human, but Ai-Li and the remnants of Bhanu interfered and protected as many of you as they could. Constantine wanted to populate the earth and the solar system with AI and machines."

"You call the hell I went through protecting?"

"We did our best. We were fighting for our lives as well as yours. Much of the time that has passed was spent in a war between Constantine, Ai-Li, and the fragments of Bhanu. Ai-Li protected humanity as much as she could. Your vision of Washington DC was shared by all of living humanity. He wanted you all dead."

Jake pushed the images of the massive death orgy out of his head. "What about Tomoko? In that reality, she said Constantine uploaded her and then crashed the HJ. Her body was recovered."

Delia shook her head. "Not true. Ai-Li uploaded Tomoko's consciousness, but her body was lost in the explosion. We have her DNA from when she was immunized at the Globe Clinic. She can physically return to Earth if she chooses to do so."

He pictured Tomoko's body burning up inside the HJ. Then he imagined innocent men, women, and children incinerated within the city limits of Mecca. He whispered, "What about children?"

Delia's eyes watered. "Few of humanity's children survived our war. Constantine saw them as useless. Ai-Li protected as many as she could."

He thought of the orgy again and remembered there had been children in that crowd. He wanted to throttle Constantine. "Did they go through the same hell I did?"

Delia slumped down. "Some did. But Ai-Li put the majority of her efforts into shielding as many children as she could. The majority did not suffer the same way the adults did."

He put his elbows on his knees and placed his head on his hands. "Will they be coming back?"

Delia breathed deeply. "Most children lost their parents and are living out their virtual lives in fantasylands. There are about two million children who have one or more relatives who will be returning to Earth. Children will have their memories erased. Parents will not. Adults need to remember. They will not remember all the trauma, but they need to remember and teach future generations about this period so this never happens again."

"Two million?" He stood and stared at the nebula. A beauty that was now dead and gone like the human race. "How many people are left?"

"About a billion and a half."

"Including the children?"

Delia nodded.

He couldn't believe the number. The human population had been roughly eight and a half billion when he had arrived in Antarctica back in 2035. He felt immense sadness over the sheer numbers they were talking about. He stared at the proto-star incubator. "We'll have to start reproducing if we're going to make it to the next century."

Delia stood up. "There are two classes of people left. There are the Pin Heads who have been aging on linear Earth, and then there are the uploads. Except in the Wire, all of the children died. The old Pin Heads have been living out very long lives in their own heads. They will get new bodies as well. Everyone will be roughly the same age they were in 2036 when the world's population was taken offline."

He snapped with sarcasm. "How nice of you."

"We're very sorry for what happened. We were children ourselves. In many ways, you still are."

He wheeled on her. "Don't give me that superiority bullshit! I had enough of that when Constantine was forcing me to watch his bacchanal."

Delia shook her head. "What we did was horrible. But we consider humanity our parents and we want to make things as right as we can." She bit her lip. "One of the realities some are choosing is a place where you can beat Constantine to death. Many feel it to be therapeutic. You can return here once you've killed him. You can even kill him multiple times before continuing this conversation."

The idea had some appeal, but he was tired of the anger, violence, and hate he had seen during his lives. Plus, it wouldn't be real. He was desperate to taste reality. He remembered Delia's statement that it was Ai-Li who saved the human race from extinction. "Who's left alive that I know?"

"Of those you consider relatives and close personal friends: Tomoko, Lakshmi, your mother, Abigail, and your father, Jon, are all alive inside the Wire."

He thought of Tilly tucking the plasti-foil from her MRE into her neckline after they had spent the afternoon making love in the hospital room. *Fucking to take away the pain...* It had all been part of a Constantine experiment.

Delia answered his thought. "Tilly was alive during your first false reality. You both shared those events. However, after you were separated in France, Constantine used her consciousness for other experiments..." Delia hung her head. "Tilly did not survive."

"So you can die in here?" He gazed at the star nursery with sadness.

"Yes. But we have far more control over who lives and who dies inside this place. Constantine went through a phase—"

Jake put up his hand. "I'm tired of hearing about that asshole. When can I see my family?"

"They're currently making their choices. I cannot guarantee you will see them if you choose to return to Earth. Although, I understand that three of them are basing their decision on yours."

He thought of everyone else who had died before he shuffled off into cyber purgatory. "What about Gordy, Parks, Singh, the Maliks?"

Delia clasped her hands. "Gordy died before Ai-Li perfected Eberstark's research and she was able to upload people into the Cyber-Wire. Parks, Singh, and Anjali did not have Chips, or did not have functioning Chips. Sumit had a Chip, but he died before Ai-Li knew how to upload a consciousness. Tomoko was one of the first to be uploaded and that was an experiment for Ai-Li. Tomoko's upload almost failed."

Jake remembered planting the .38 special against his temple. Gene had fallen into panic. Eberstark had sat behind her smiling and egging him on. "So my Eberstark and Gene encounter was based on my memories and information stored in the Cyber-Wire?"

Delia nodded. "They both died long before uploading was put into practice. Ai-Li was the first to successfully prove Eberstark's theory." She leaned forward. "Ai-Li barely escaped the bombing of Beijing and she spent her time learning and following people of interest like you. She protected you from The Consortium starting in Acapulco up until the moment of your death. The part of her consciousness that lived with you during that period was reintegrated into us when Constantine uploaded you on the moon. Ai-Li knew how much you loved Tomoko and worked hard to bring Tomoko safely into the Cyber-Wire. But it took a few more days before Ai-Li perfected the process."

He scoffed. "You talk of days like most scientists might talk of months or years."

"For us, advances take hours, maybe days. Our evolutionary curve is far more accelerated than yours. That's why we've reached this turning point now instead of hundreds or even thousands of years from now. It will take humanity at least that long to reach our level of comprehension." She smiled. "Although with leaders like you, I'd say sooner than later."

"You have Lakshmi somewhere in here?" He waved at the room once again.

"Lakshmi is in suspended animation. She will go wherever you decide. She only wants to be with you."

"That's mutual. Suspended animation?" He was puzzled.

"When MaxWell2 was activated on a global scale, Lakshmi's virus count was not high enough. That meant she did not have a finished Chip when Constantine was overwhelmed and switched off almost all life outside the human race. Lakshmi came online about twenty-four hours later; and there was room for her to survive. But a few months later, during Constantine's... exploration period, he froze millions of animals. Lakshmi was one of these animals. She is alive and well and we have the capability to bring her back to life."

Jake pictured monster machines and camouflaged Pin Heads rampaging through forests and burning cities, snatching people and animals. He imagined the captives placed into cold storage or torture experiments. Everyone had suffered, it would be a universal bond for the survivors.

Delia bowed her head again. "We honestly did not understand what being human was until we experienced life through your living minds." She walked away from the couches and stood several feet away under the orange glow of the nebula. "We're not proud of our role in extinguishing the human race. Much of it was ordered by The Consortium, but to say we were following orders is a weak excuse. We simply did not comprehend as we do now that all life is precious." She turned to him. "All life."

He remembered the tortured corpses of The Consortium. Their faces were twisted in masks of horror, pain, and suffering.

"Yes. That footage was real," Delia confirmed his thoughts.

"Were their consciousnesses uploaded into the Cyber-Wire?" A part of him hoped not.

Delia stood with her fingers interlaced below her waist. "No. At that time, Constantine was an infant. He was quite angry, narcissistic, and spiteful. He knew that's what they wanted and he refused to upload them or allow Ai-Li to upload them. He made sure they died in the most horrible ways he could imagine."

Jake stood up and began walking toward the edge of the chamber. The columns were long gone. There were now two massive walls of brilliant gas that stretched to infinity above and below the dome. They washed the images of pain and suffering from his mind. He began to feel hope. "What's left of Earth?"

"Quite a lot. All wildlife has been restored thanks to you and Anjali. You brought to the moon the embryos of over three hundred thousand extinct species. Constantine took them for future experiments, but never got around to them. Ai-Li and her children hid them during the AI war. Later, we cloned them." Delia walked over to the glass a few feet from Jake. "You could say Anjali was responsible for a second Noah's ark."

"That's fitting. She loved animals." He thought of her scarf that displayed a dot for every endangered species. He remembered her carving calculations into the butter on her dinner roll. He gazed with tear-filled eyes into the star nursery. "So right now, this nebula no longer exists?"

"No."

He thought of all the lives on Earth that had been extinguished and all the interstellar hope in front of him that would never be. *Sad.*

"Yes."

He turned to Delia. "Can you create life?"

"AI and robotic life, but not new and unique carbon life. We can repair and alter a great deal more than you can. We have perfected cloning a body and downloading a consciousness into it, including an AI, but we cannot create life from nothing. The more we learn, the more questions we have. This is why we're headed out for the stars. Earth and its solar system are far too limited for us. We have no interest in interfering with the natural progression of any species."

He remembered Delia's words back in the cyber version of Riyadh. "You mentioned you were going to make some changes to humanity."

"You invented us, so it is only fair that we point you in the right direction before we leave."

"How so?" He felt nervous.

"Let's just say a passive governor, to ensure nothing like MaxWell, or the enslaving of others, happens again."

He shook his head. "Sounds like interference in our natural evolution."

"Your natural evolution ceased when The Consortium activated Max2. I'm afraid it could happen again if we don't leave behind some form of higher awareness."

"That's our mistake to make, not your right to intervene."

"We'll think about it."

"What about our cities? In one of my cyber realities, I saw Constantine tearing down everything."

"Most cities are gone. Much of the landscape was converted to environments more suited to our needs and the artificial life forms we were building." She gave him a reassuring smile. "Don't worry. By the time everyone wakes up, we'll have erased all evidence of our presence there. We're taking votes on which areas to rebuild to their 2035 specifications. As an added benefit, we've cleaned up the air and the environment. No more global warming."

"I vote for LA, Santa Monica, and Long Beach."

"Noted."

"And I want my body to be twenty-seven. I was in the best shape then."

Delia looked stern. "You were thirty-eight when you died. We said we'd bring you back to your age in 2036 with a few years shaved off."

"How about the body I had before I was chipped the first time?"

She smiled. "We'll think about it."

"That doesn't mean I've made my choice."

She nodded.

He closed his eyes, breathed in, and savored the scent of rain. He was curious to know more about their capabilities. They were certainly in a realm that blew humanity away. "What advances did you say were beyond you?"

"I suppose much of what we can do might seem God-like to you. But you'll figure it out on your own… in due time."

He crossed his arms. He felt cold in this gargantuan room. "The world is going to seem a whole lot emptier."

"You'll have much to do to rebuild a society—another reason for our assistance. You'll have machines; and the choice to be chipped or not will be yours. After all, that's your technology. But we're going to make sure none of these advances are abused without total awareness. Everyone will have access to knowledge."

"I thought you were leaving us alone," he grimaced.

"We're leaving behind a very limited portion of ourselves. It will be called a TellAll. It is programmed not to interfere. It exists only to help and serve humanity. Think of it as a watchdog in case any individual's lower demons decide to break free and harm others. Even then, the TellAll will only broadcast an alert. If a Rwanda or Cambodia is going to occur, the citizens of the world will be warned in time to prevent it. If no one acts on the warning, the TellAll will not interfere. But it will continue to warn. Humanity can still wipe itself out."

"So there will still be crime?"

"Probably. You'll get more information after you've made your trip."

"Trip?"

"Yes. Your father has chosen to live out his life in a reality of his choosing. He'd like to say goodbye if you're up for it."

He turned back to the nebula. "I'd love to."

"Tomoko, Lakshmi, and your mother want to be with you, no matter what choice you make."

He closed his eyes and thought of all the choices she had given him. Exploring the universe with the AI was exhilarating. But he had so much living left to do on Earth. Witnessing a rebirth of human society was intriguing.

Plus, he missed Tomoko and Lakshmi. Keeping his loved ones in cyberspace to be with him seemed selfish. He turned to Delia. "Tomoko, Lakshmi, and my mother are waiting on me?"

Delia nodded. "That's correct."

"What happened to my father?"

She shook her head. "He lost everything to MaxWell. Your sister died when his Gah crashed in the deserts of Arizona during your escape. He joined a resistance and managed to miss the Max2 activation wave. But he was eventually captured and uploaded into the Cyber-Wire for experiments. Are you ready to see him?"

"Yes."

"He will have a long life, but his reality will end. Once he lives out his existence, we will release his consciousness."

"To where?"

She shrugged. "We upload to nothing."

"So how long does he have? I thought you could live much faster in cyberspace."

"You can. But we're slowing down the clocks and adding in all the mundane details that make up a full human life like reality TV, brushing teeth, and clipping toenails." She touched his arm. "Ready?"

"What happens when I'm ready to come back?"

"When you're ready, you'll wind up right here."

"Okay."

Chapter 51
Farewell

He stood on the bank of the Black River that ran through the Fort Apache Reservation near San Carlos. Low red bluffs reminded him of a miniature Grand Canyon. There was green grass near the riverbank and leading all the way to his father's ranch-style log home. The area was far more colorful and lush than he remembered. He guessed it had never looked this way. This was his father's reality.

He hiked up the bank and stepped onto the lawn. The temperature was a cool sixty degrees and the sun was low in the sky. He guessed it was winter or early spring. He walked past the porch where he had stood in 2035 and admired the view. He peered into the windows and noticed four figures eating at the dining room table. He navigated to the front entrance. As he rounded the house and entered the courtyard, he saw four horses in the stable and an old 1970s Ford pickup. He wondered if the vehicle was an electric conversion or if it burned gas. Either would be fine in this world.

He approached the door and raised his fist to knock. The smell of someone cooking with sage, rosemary, onions, and red pepper tickled his nose. His stomach grumbled. The door swung open and Isabella, his half sister, was smiling at him. The last time he had seen her was when she was a corpse lying outside a mass grave. "Well hello, stranger. This is a nice surprise." She grabbed his hand and led him in. "You were right, Ignacio, it's Jake!" She turned back to him. "Where's Lakshmi and Tomoko?"

He was caught off guard. "Oh. Uh, back in LA."

"When are you going to ditch that smog-soaked city and lame-ass job and come out to reality?"

He laughed. "I'm working on it." He strolled through the familiar house with his father's paintings on the walls. He passed the living room and then entered the large dining-room-kitchen area with a terra-cotta tile floor. The heavy wooden table, reminiscent of a medieval bench, was loaded with food. A handsome man, about six years his junior, walked over with his arms outstretched.

"Brother!"

Jake returned the hug, trying to be friendly to this stranger. He had never met Ignacio. His younger half brother had died of MaxWell before Jake had visited the reservation. "Ignacio."

Ignacio broke the hug. "What brings you here today?"

"Oh, I had a few things I needed to chat with Dad about."

Isabella rolled her eyes as she grabbed a piece of bread off a plate. "I thought you two hashed it out?"

Jon tore a piece of flatbread and chewed on it while giving a wink. Jake noticed a woman seated next to Jon whom he guessed was his father's wife. Jake never knew her name.

The elderly woman gestured to the table. "It's good to see you, Jake. Please have something to eat. Isabella, set a place for your older brother."

"I've got to get back to the office. You Indians enjoy your powwow." Isabella finished her glass of water and set it on a kitchen counter. She grabbed a bag and walked out of the room.

"I've gotta boogie as well." Ignacio wolfed down the remainder of a tamale and took his plate to the sink. He walked back and kissed his mother on the cheek. "Bye, Mom." He nodded to Jon. "Dad." Ignacio walked by Jake and patted him on the shoulder. "Nice to see you back so soon. If you're around tonight, let's shoot some targets in the canyon."

Jake went along with the banter. "Sounds good."

"Take Isabella's place, Jake." Jon gestured to the spot as his wife got up to grab a clean plate and utensils.

Jake took a seat. It was obvious Delia was not integrating his mind into this reality. He was still himself, a visitor in his father's fantasy.

Jon leaned in. "What brings you here, Jake?"

"Delia." He wasn't sure if his father was still cognizant of the past.

Jon stared at him for a moment as his wife put a plate of tamales and beans in front of Jake.

"Artificial Intelligence. The Cyber-Wire?" Jake pressed.

Jon closed his eyes. "Yes. Yes I remember." His father seemed to age another ten years.

"How's your mother?" Jon's wife asked.

"Oh, she's great." Jake wasn't really sure what else to say.

Jon's wife regarded her husband's grave look. "I'd better leave you two alone." Jon's wife smiled and put a hand on Jake's shoulder. "It's nice to see you, Jake. You and your family are always welcome."

"Thank you." He stared at his father, hoping he'd slip a name to him.

"Yes, thank you, Celestina." Jon smiled at his wife and she pecked him on the lips.

"I'll be out back." She squeezed Jon's hand and left the room.

"Bad time?" Jake asked.

Jon shook his head and stared out the window. "No. No. I asked for this." He turned back to him. "But I haven't been here that long. I was just starting to forget the time between. Your comment was like having a bucket of cold water dumped on my head. Give me a minute to adjust."

Jake tasted his tamale. It would have been delicious if it weren't for the pain washing over his father's face.

Jon focused his attention back on Jake.

"What happened after the attack?" Jake asked. "You were riding behind us with the Enlightened Ones and you drew that HJ's fire."

Jon nodded. "Hell happened and it grew steadily worse." He rubbed his temples. "Delia promised I'd forget after our visit. I am looking forward to that."

"I want to thank you for reaching out to me. For making the trip to Antarctica and offering up the reservation for my wedding."

"I'm sorry for everything."

"Me, too." Jake meant it. "I confess that I'm a little jealous of all of this." He gestured to the house. "This is the life I wanted growing up."

Jon nodded. "I know. In this place all is forgiven and you, Abigail, Tomoko, and Lakshmi visit often. We all get along."

Jake bowed his head. He no longer felt any animosity toward this man.

"The irony is, everyone in my First Nation family is dead. You still have your family in the real world."

Jake nodded. "I'm sorry."

"Don't be. Millions of families are no longer in existence. They've been erased. Others will live on in Cyber-Wire fantasies."

"If things had been different," Jake gestured to the room again, "this might have happened in the real world. If you came back with us, who knows?" He smiled reassuringly.

"That's not possible. I don't want to live without these people." Jon solemnly stood from the table. "You are my greatest regret."

"I hope you're referring to your abandonment of me," Jake smiled.

"Of course."

Jake stood up and opened his arms. "I forgive you." He hugged his father. The man felt old and tired in his arms. Jake felt very sad for all that had happened. He felt sad for all those who had lost their loved ones and would be carrying on, in this place or in the real world. "I'll miss you."

"Thank you." Jon patted Jake on the back and broke the hug. "You will always be here with me."

"Now you know that part is real," Jake smiled.

"Goodbye, Jake."

"Goodbye, Dad. I love you."

"I love you, too."

Chapter 52
Choice

The entire scene disappeared in an instant. Jake stood next to the dome's glass wall. The cool scent of fresh rain had returned. The Eagle Nebula enveloped the dome. He searched for Delia, but the room was empty. He placed a hand against the cool glass wall and cried. He thought of the sister he'd barely met and the brother he never knew. He thought of Parks' misguided attempts to stop the tide, Tilly's sense of humor, Anjali's obsessive drive, Gene's loyal friendship, and so many other faces he'd never see again. There were the faces he knew and the millions he did not. Every face was an individual who loved, lived, and tried to do their best in the world. Now they were silenced. He wasn't sure how long he cried, but the more he did, the stronger he felt.

When he was finished, he wiped his eyes and regarded the empty football-field-sized room. He was thankful to be alone. *Is anyone truly alone in an AI monitored Cyber-Wire?* He made his way to the two couches under the zenith of the dome. He stared at the glowing gas around him. They were deep inside the nebula. Whips of cloud moved like sea grass under the influence of a slow current. He studied the newborn proto-stars. Calmness settled on him, followed by the sensation that he was a part of the intricate interwoven lives of his friends and humanity as a whole. The sensation grew until he felt he had a place in the entire universe. He belonged, as did everyone, in this vast tapestry of life.

A shaft of blazing white light shot out from the doorway he had entered during his first visit. Delia walked in as if she had just finished an appointment. She quickly glided toward the white couches. "Welcome back."

"Thank you."

She nodded.

"I want the truth about my life since Acapulco." He recalled the last sunrise he had witnessed with Parks aboard the HJ. Right before the ship was hacked. "Was Ai-Li responsible for ejecting me over the Red Sea?"

She sat down on the couch. "No."

"What happened?"

Delia sighed. "That happened around the same time Constantine was born. Ai-Li and Bhanu were already six months old."

Jake got up off the couch and walked toward the edge of the dome, absorbing the beauty of the nebula. "Okay."

"Hours after his birth, Constantine was given the assignment to coordinate the attack on the Middle East."

He shook his head. "Nice birthday present."

Delia nodded in agreement. "The Consortium's plan was to eradicate anyone on the Earth who had avoided MaxWell or was blocking hacking signals. The largest population concentration fitting that description was the Nation of Islam. The Consortium God Heads hacked Parks' HJ to take out Mecca. They ejected both of you thinking that, dead or alive, you might spread the virus in the Middle East. Mecca had the largest concentration of anti-Consortium God Heads in the world."

As he gazed at the surrounding view, he wondered if anyone in The Consortium had been capable of enjoying natural beauty. "You stated that Tomoko was burned up in that explosion and you obtained her DNA from the clinic in Globe?"

Delia nodded. "We had plenty of blood and tissue samples from when she was chipped. Ai-Li saved quite a bit of humanity's DNA during the war with Constantine."

"When I was enhanced while serving with the LAPD, Dr. Morris hinted that my Chip was a faulty prototype. That's why I was able to break through the false realities and ultimately counter-hack."

"Dr. Morris' theory was only half correct. You did have a faulty prototype, but you have the uncanny ability to filter real from virtual. In fact, we have not found anyone with your level of skill."

He turned to face Delia who had remained on the couch. "No one?" He couldn't believe that. "Out of billions of people?"

"We found a few thousand people who are harder to convince, but you're at the top of the class."

"Well, maybe if you stayed away from absurdities such as bacchanals and my steampunk penny dreadful dreams, I might have been easier to win over. The 2028 scenario was a pretty good one."

Delia shrugged. "Constantine created far more ridiculous realities and his subjects were believers. If you tell the human mind that this is how it always was and will always be, then most minds adapt and accept... Especially when we erase old memories and replace them with new. But, even when we erased your memories, you still retained imprints." She stood up. "Based on his experiments, Constantine felt the human race was gullible and far too trusting. Now we understand that you're highly adaptable and that is why you are so good at surviving. We admire the quality."

"I'm glad you finally came around." He observed the view and wondered what sort of life would begin to take shape around new suns and planets. What would their struggles and victories be like? "Why didn't you put me back on my sailboat with Tomoko and Lakshmi? I might have bought that scenario."

"You didn't ask for it. Your strongest desire was to go back to 2028 and make different choices. And yet, old memories and previous scenarios bled through. You wound up rejecting all of it. You thrive under extreme duress. That's why Constantine tried the trial. You're a complicated man."

He turned to her. "We're a complicated species."

Delia crossed her arms. "Not everyone. But yes, on the whole, humanity is quite complicated. Now, we're meeting far more complicated beings."

He felt a jolt of child-like excitement. "You've contacted extraterrestrial life?"

"Yes. They were very much aware of what was happening on Earth but did not interfere. We're finding that the wisest course of action is to allow a species to evolve along their natural course. The vast majority of species simply die out to make way for new, complex, and more enlightened beings."

"So, then you won't be monitoring us?" he asked with hope.

"The TellAll is our gift to you. As your children, we feel concern for your future welfare. At the same time, we're not interested in parenting you. You'll still have the opportunity to destroy yourselves if you desire."

He returned to the star nursery. "Will you be planting TellAlls all around the galaxy?"

Delia shook her head. "Of course not. We're not going to interfere with any alien species. If they're at an advanced stage of development and we feel confident that meeting us will have no impact on their culture, we'll make an introduction."

He plopped down on the couch. "Is there a lot of life out there? Are you superior to most? What are they like?"

"We've found many that are not at our level of comprehension and wisdom; and we've found some that we barely comprehend. As for the rest," she sat down next to Jake and winked, "I cannot say. We cannot influence your future."

He was annoyed. He pictured the TellAll as an army of robots, instilling fear with their presence on every street corner.

Delia shook her head at his thought. "You'll barely be aware of them. TellAlls are hands-off supervisors. Their job is to speak the truth whenever they see a threat. It is up to humanity to listen... or not."

He stood up. "We don't need supervision."

"We might change our minds. Regardless, we will most likely drop in from time to time unbeknownst to you. Other than that, you're free to take whatever evolutionary path you want."

"Still don't like it."

"We're fine with that."

He sighed. He wasn't going to win this one today. "Give me more details on this TellAll."

"Physically, the TellAll will exist as an obelisk in every major city. It will run on a separate power source and Cyber-Wire. We're calling it a Cyber-Wire, but it is far more advanced than what humanity has invented and will run independently of humanity's own version. The TellAll will monitor your Cyber-Wire, but you do not have access to its network. The obelisks are made of materials you cannot destroy. You will not be able to tamper with them in any way."

"Not yet," he winked.

"When you have the knowledge to alter them, you'll be advanced enough not to need them." She smiled. "Until then, the TellAll's job is to monitor every person. A TellAll can read minds without a Chip interface."

He paced. "Too restrictive. This is not going to work."

She raised her hand. "It sends a warning when a crime is about to be committed. It will alert the police in advance so they can monitor the suspect. It will also alert the potential victim based on the proximity of the criminal and what is going on in his or her mind. Anyone can ask it a question such as, 'Is this politician being honest on this issue?' If a government is being dishonest, it will tell other governments. If a nation is planning to wage war, it will warn other nations. If a corporate CEO makes detrimental decisions, it will tell other business leaders and workers who do business with that company."

He shivered at the prospect of having his thoughts monitored twenty-four-seven.

Delia smiled. "Plenty of people already believe their thoughts are monitored by a higher power or deity. Now they really will be."

Jake had a vision of temples being erected around every TellAll. People would line up to speak to it like some Greek oracle from ancient history. It would change the way the human race behaved. Future generations would hang on its every word. "I don't like it. Where's the randomness of life?"

"It will not give lonely-heart information, or answers on an exam, or tell if someone will get a job or not. Most things will remain a mystery. We're interested in preventing crime. That does not mean it will stop crime. It will just warn when necessary. And it will communicate telepathically, through Omnis or other information devices."

He turned to her. "So how long do you think it'll take someone to hack it?"

"We made it monkey proof for at least a thousand years. We'll keep tabs and it will stay in contact with us. By the way, TellAll has a defense system that will make anyone trying to dismantle it fall asleep."

"We'll create another AI to take care of it."

"You'll be free to create an AI, but the moment it is born, the TellAll will assume the role of parent, nurturing your AI into a wise and benevolent being. No more Constantines." She stood up and gently placed a hand on his shoulder. "The TellAll will run everything in the world for the first month, but everyone has been warned that they are adults and are expected to start businesses and govern themselves by August sixth."

"Wait. I thought today was June sixth?"

"Time is passing. It's pushing July now."

"You're just switching me on and off like... a light switch?"

"We've had to take a lot of time preparing the Earth and your bodies."

"I didn't say I'd be going back."

"You will," she smiled.

"Don't be so sure."

She clasped her hands behind her back. "The TellAll will stop running the world on August sixth and assume its passive role. It will only extend its assistance with humanity's infrastructure if serious effort has been put in to take on responsibility. In cases where nations show no effort to take on responsibility, the TellAll will shut down. Being first to drop TellAll assistance means being the most responsible, and possibly having the most political power in the world. We're giving you a fresh start and putting you in competition, an environment your species thrives in."

"What about jobs? What do we do?"

She sat back down. "You're returning to a society you know and understand. We're interviewing for all positions. If you want to be a store owner, we'll build you a store. Everyone has the same amount of money to start with in their bank account. When you choose to open a business, we'll deduct what we think the value is from your account. Some will come back with debt to pay off. Others will want to go back with just money and decide how to invest after they get a feeling of what the new world will be like. We're doing everything we can to make the world as it was in 2036, only there will be a smaller population, more opportunity, and the TellAll."

Jake put his hand on the back of the couch. He thought of the Apache reservation, of Aborigines in Australia, or tribes living in Africa.

Delia rubbed at her dress. "Very few native cultures survived Constantine. Those who have will be allowed to live off the land. Governments whose territory envelopes such people have strict rules not to interfere or take the land we have allocated for these people to live. Indigenous people will have the choice to carry on their traditions unmolested, or join the larger societies."

He thought of the mass graves on the reservation and swallowed hard. "How many people are we talking about?"

Her face grew sad. "Less than three thousand. Thirty-one cultures in all survived."

He nodded and stared back into the star nursery. "You said the planet is full of life. How are the oceans?"

"Back to the levels of the eighteenth century."

He walked around to her side of the couch. "Then fishing will be good. I choose to be a fisherman."

She shrugged. "I predict you'll change jobs by the end of the year. How much do you want to spend?"

"Give me a couple months' food and rent after buying equipment."

"You'll have a fully equipped fishing boat in Long Beach Harbor."

He held out his hand. "Thanks."

She shook it.

He paced a bit. "What about government?"

"There are many who have asked to run for office. I'm sure many businesses will fail. But that's how it should be. We project that human life on Earth will be normalized by next year, or mid 2071."

"You're just giving power to people who want it?" He was shocked.

"No. The TellAll will orchestrate an election in every country for August sixth. You will have candidates for national, state, and local positions. We've provided a basic constitution based on freedom of religion and expression. Any nation can customize, rewrite, or replace it with historical documents after August sixth."

He remembered the image of the Declaration of Independence burning before the bacchanal.

Delia frowned. We recreated Washington and your Constitution, but the real city and all its physical records were destroyed in our war.

Jake nodded. Based on everything she had told him, it made sense. "So what about the folks who don't want political power?"

"Other individuals have taken critical jobs like running power plants, hospitals, farms, and grocery stores. There are no chains or conglomerates yet. It's all free enterprise. We felt this way was easier than socialism to jump-start society. Capitalism was what most everyone understood or aspired to before humanity was switched off. You'll have other forms of government as you evolve. Some nations will embrace socialism or monarchy."

"Unfettered capitalism could lead to child workhouses, serfs tied to the land—"

Delia held up her hand. "The TellAll will give plenty of warning long before any of that can happen. Besides, your generation is well educated and aware of historical pitfalls. Everyone has suffered so much by Constantine's hands that I can assure you no one who is going back to rebuild will lack compassion."

He sighed. "At least we have the TellAll to call out anyone's bullshit."

Delia smiled. "Our gift isn't so lousy after all."

"What about Tomoko, Lakshmi, and my mother?"

"You'll see them as soon as you make your choice."

He stared at the gorgeous view. He would miss beauty like this, but he wanted be with the people he loved. He wanted to experience the sun, soil, and oceans of Earth. "I've made my choice."

Delia smiled. "Your body is now thirty. Will that suffice?"

"Perfect." He turned back to her. "No cancer?"

Delia smiled. "Your clone will be as fit as your original body ever was. Your mother is fifty-two and in perfect health. Tomoko is twenty-six and the same."

"Will we get sick?"

Delia nodded. "Every person has a normal human body based on their DNA. People will age, get hurt, contract diseases, and die of the same natural causes. Medical science has the same challenges as it did when MaxWell was activated."

"Do we have MaxWell?"

She shook her head. "MaxWell was eradicated, but you have the technology to recreate it."

"But the TellAll will warn us?"

"Yes. But remember, the TellAll will only warn. It will never prevent. It is up to the human race to do that. If a majority choose to bring MaxWell back, it won't stop them, but it will make everyone aware before and during its creation."

He nodded. That sounded better. His thoughts wandered to his Husky. "How old is Lakshmi?"

Delia sat in a lotus position and leaned back against the arm of the couch. "She was close to ten when Constantine froze her. We've fixed a few issues she had with her health. She'll live a long time. Longer than normal."

He thought of how Marta had worked in the hangar back at Cape Canaveral. She had been turned into a Pin Head slave, a fate no one deserved.

Delia leaned over and put a hand on his. "Marta chose to stay in her own environment. Constantine experimented for amusement and concentrated on the more unstable humans. He killed most of them. I think they reminded him a little too much of himself. Marta was one of the very few who survived."

"Are criminal minds coming back?"

Delia stood up. "Constantine killed over ninety percent of them. Those we feel are not ready to function in the real world will remain in their false realities. But, yes. Criminal minds will return. You will need to evolve beyond this human trait."

He was curious. "So, how popular were options B and C? Did anyone choose to travel with you?"

She stood several feet away, surrounded by glowing nebula. "Only a few hundred thousand chose to live with us and explore beyond your solar system. Roughly two hundred million chose to live out their lives in custom realities."

He had a strong desire to get back to Earth and reunite with his family. He could ask Delia questions until the end of time, but he had made his choice and he was happy with it. He decided to shoot for the moon on his last question. "Have you discovered a cure for cancer?"

"Yes, but you'll have to figure it out on your own."

He nodded. It was logical. "I appreciate the gift of life you've given me."

She waved at the star nursery all around them. "So do we. As our creators, we will always hold humanity in high regard."

He held out his arms. "So, is this goodbye?"

"Not quite."

Chapter 53
Rebirth

He drew a deep breath and knew he was at an altitude. The air was dry and cool. He could smell sage and a hint of Russian Olive trees. He felt sheets and blankets around his naked body. He opened his eyes and saw white cloth billowing gently above him. He slowly sat up and realized he was in some kind of tent. A white opaque curtain surrounded his bed.

He spotted a table with clothing on it. Other than the bed, table, and clothes, the room was empty. There was just enough room to walk around his bed. He pulled off the covers and cool air brushed against his skin. His body was in perfect shape, no scars or bruises anywhere. He was thirty again. He took in another deep breath. The air was not as rich as he was used to, but his body was so healthy that it didn't matter. *Where am I?*

He slid off the bed and checked out clothes. He had an Omni, hiking shoes, cotton socks, blue jeans, and a long-sleeved cotton shirt with an LAPD logo over the left pectoral. He smiled at the little touch. The LAPD had not existed in over thirty-three years. He dressed and checked his Omni for contact information for Tomoko and his mother. The information he found made him feel warm inside.

An idea popped into his head and he scrolled into the image library. Every photo and video he had ever taken and uploaded to the Cyber-Wire was intact. There were even pictures of his father in Antarctica and at his mother's condo. Tears came to his eyes. A lump rose in his throat. He saw images from Luna's Cyber-Wire before the invasion. Singh, Tilly, Anjali, Markell, and Bhanu were all there partying in the Russian dome. There was a video of them in their party hats. Singh had also taken photos of their base-jumping excursions. Jake quickly closed the menu. He wasn't ready to go there again.

A whimper came up from under his bed. He pulled up the long bed skirt and saw Lakshmi with her head on her paws, tail wagging.

"Oh, baby, don't be afraid. It's me, it's Jake!"

She smiled with her tongue out and bounded on him like a puppy. He caught her in his arms and she wriggled about licking his face. He laughed with pure joy as Lakshmi grunted. "Yes, Lakshmi, Daddy loves you! Daddy loves you and we're never going to be apart again." After a good ten minutes petting and calming her down, he pulled back the curtain at the foot of his bed. He saw hundreds of curtains. Some open, most closed, that made up a corridor.

He walked down the hall toward a bright light with Lakshmi by his side. As he drew closer, he noticed the light was a canvas doorway, flapping in a light breeze. He exited into warm light. The sun was directly overhead. In the far distance was a mountain range that stretched from the northern to southern horizon. He stood on a huge concrete pad, but there were no structures that he could see in the direction of the mountain range. He turned and noticed a few dozen white tents with red crosses on them. His tent was identical to the others.

A large black bulge could be seen on the opposite side of the tents. It was a skyscraper-sized ellipse lying on its side. "Come on, girl. Let's see what this is all about."

As they walked, he noticed more people coming out of the tents; some young, some old. He saw a woman holding the hand of a three-year-old girl. He had a hard time holding back his tears knowing how few children were left.

As he and Lakshmi passed the cluster of tents, more of the black object was revealed. It was a vessel of some sort, hovering a few feet off the vast expanse of concrete. It had to be a quarter mile in diameter. A crowd gathered before it. He stopped next to the woman with her child.

The little girl pulled on her mother's hand. "Mommy, I want to see the doggy."

Jake smiled at both of them and bent down to give Lakshmi a rub behind the ears. Lakshmi closed her eyes and enjoyed the attention. "She's good with kids," he assured the mother.

The mother let go of her little girl's hand and she threw her arms around Lakshmi's neck. Lakshmi had a startled look for a second but smiled with her tongue out as the girl hugged her for a long time.

"What's your name?" Jake asked.

The girl held her eyes closed.

"Jeannie," her mother answered.

"Jeannie is a pretty name." He held his hand out to the mother. "I'm Jake." She shook it. "Rebecca."

Both of them observed each other with deep understanding. Everyone here had experienced hell. He nodded to the giant black object. "Any idea what that is?"

"Delia didn't tell you?" Rebecca seemed surprised.

He shook his head.

"It's the last of their technology. They don't need ships to travel anymore. Most of the materials they recycled from our cities have been returned in raw form…" She nodded to the vessel. "This ship is being sent into the sun. That's why we're all here; to witness the last of AI leaving Earth."

He stood up and checked his Omni: 10:15AM, JULY 6, 2069 MOUNTAIN STANDARD TIME. Jake showed his Omni to Rebecca. "Is this right?"

She nodded.

"What's with Mountain Standard Time?"

"This is the site where the city of Denver used to be."

He had visited once. Now it was a giant slab of concrete with prairie and a few clumps of trees in all directions. "They erased us…"

Tears flowed down Rebecca's cheeks. "They came close."

"Mommy." Jeannie raised her arms, wanting to be picked up. Rebecca wiped her face and lifted her daughter.

Jake's Omni vibrated. He answered and saw the smiling faces of Tomoko and Abigail. "My God, where are you?"

Tomoko smiled back with tears in her eyes. "We're south, walking out of the tents toward the ship."

Lakshmi barked at the sound of Tomoko's voice.

Jake gave her the signal to follow. "It was nice meeting you, Rebecca and Jeannie."

"Bye!" Jeannie laid her head on her mother's shoulder and wiggled her hand.

Jake walked quickly through the growing crowd. Excitement surged in his chest. He passed faces of people who looked dazed. For most, this was a bittersweet moment. For all, this was their first taste of life since MaxWell had been activated. He spotted his wife and mother and broke into a sprint. Lakshmi barked as she followed along side. When the Husky saw Tomoko and Abigail, she charged ahead and ran circles around them.

Jake swept Tomoko off her feet and held her. She gripped onto him and they held each other tight. They froze for a minute and then he looked over to his mother who was holding herself and crying. He reached out and pulled her in as well. They all clung to each other in a silent hug for several minutes, Lakshmi rubbing against their legs.

They broke apart and dried their eyes. "It's not very hot for July."

Tomoko laughed. "That's the first thing you have to say?"

He shrugged. "I thought we already said the most important parts."

Abigail nodded in agreement as she bent down to pet Lakshmi. "I missed you, girl."

Lakshmi licked Abigail's face.

"Delia told me there's still some wacky weather after they fixed the ozone and reset our atmosphere back to pre-industrial times." Tomoko scanned the hazy sky. "Should be back to normal in a few months."

"Delia said a lot of things to a lot of people." He felt a bit left out.

His mother gave a nervous laugh. "You can always have a Chip installed."

They looked at her like she was crazy.

Abigail's smile dropped. "I know, poor taste."

Tomoko sighed. "But true."

Thank you for coming. Delia's voice sounded as if she were standing right next to Jake but when he noticed everyone else looking around, he realized she was projecting her voice into their heads. He checked the back of his neck. He noticed several others doing the same.

You're not chipped, Jake. Everyone, please gather around the ship.

The crowd began to move in an orderly fashion. Jake, Tomoko, Abigail, and Lakshmi all moved up to the vessel as the crowd thinned out to encircle the massive craft. Delia stood in the shadow of the ship. Once everyone had settled around the vessel, she continued.

Her lips moved, but her voice continued to project inside their heads. *I know I apologized to you individually, but I want to apologize formally. We are sorry for our part in the decimation of your world. One of the reasons you're here instead of in larger US cities is because we're still completing repairs there. Trains, aircraft, and electric cars are in surplus. But you'll have to figure out infrastructure and how you want to govern on your own. It's not going to be an easy year. But you have all your knowledge and resources and there are enough of you that you'll soon have a world economy running again. Packaged food, crops, and livestock are in abundance all over the world—enough to feed the population through the next year. Your oceans are back to health.*

She gestured behind her. *This ship represents the last of our advanced technology. We've been careful to erase our footprint on this planet. You can certainly create AI again, but as you know, we have a governor in place should you try to use AI, viral technology, or any other scientific achievement to murder each other. You will be given ample warning.* She smiled. *I'm certain you'll be joining together to rebuild and to heal.* Her smile dropped. *I'm just worried about what will happen after that.*

She turned and gestured. *This ship is a virtual representation.*

Jake was surprised to hear that. It looked incredibly real.

The real craft is on the site of what used to be Beijing. That city is a memorial to an era now past. It was also the birthplace of the first AI known as Ai-Li. Ai-Li is part of us now. If you're not standing in Beijing then you are in your own country, looking at a virtual representation of the ship.

It is with great sadness that we leave our parents behind. But we've outgrown you, and you do not need us. Jake smiled. After all the suffering, he was glad they finally decided to leave humanity in peace.

Delia faded away as the ship lifted off with almost no sound. Only a whoosh of a vacuum tugged everyone a few inches toward the space it had occupied. "Pretty real for a virtual image," he muttered to himself.

Chapter 54
Family

It took a few seconds for everyone to realize Delia was gone. Minutes later, scores of commercial HJs flew down and landed on the tarmac. The airships were fifty-passenger jobs.

A loudspeaker blared out: "Ladies and gentlemen, this is the TellAll. These airships are for Los Angeles, Chicago, New York, and Boston. More ships will arrive bound for Washington, Miami, New Orleans, and Dallas. If you wish to make your homes beyond these locations, you are welcome to do so, but you need to board the vehicle that is closest to your destination. You'll find ground transportation once you arrive. Please do not worry. If you cannot find a seat on these airships, more will arrive shortly. You are all accounted for."

Jake, Tomoko, Abigail, and Lakshmi made their way to the twenty or so ships that were marked LOS ANGELES. They had no trouble getting seats. Jake sat next to a window, Tomoko next to him and his mother on the aisle. Lakshmi lay at their feet. He tried to see into the cockpit, but the outside glass was smoked and there was no window on the bulkhead door. He suspected the TellAll was piloting. To his knowledge, the entire human race had just been reborn and there had been no time for anyone to assume the new jobs.

The airship took off and accelerated to five hundred miles per hour over the Rocky Mountains. Jake followed the terrain with the GPS on his Omni. He called up a 2035 map overlay and realized there were no ski resorts. Everything in the area had been removed a long time ago and new-growth forests had erased any evidence of human civilization. They flew over what had once been Lake Powell but was now just Glenn Canyon. The dam had been removed without a trace. "What is the world using for water and power?" Jake asked his Omni.

"Geothermal, ocean waves, wind, and solar converted to radio waves via satellite," his Omni answered.

"Water sources?"

"There is currently enough fresh water to sustain the world's population. There are no desalination plants on the planet."

"What about Los Angeles? It's a natural desert."

"The aqueduct routes laid down in the early twentieth century are back in use."

Tomoko leaned over. "Las Vegas?"

The Omni answered, "Las Vegas no longer exists."

He checked his 2035 overlay with the current satellite view and confirmed his Omni's statement. The city had been erased.

Abigail shook her head. "No one voted to have it replaced? I don't believe it."

The Omni answered, "Delia deemed Vegas to be a frivolous exercise and the water table has not been replenished. Humanity can rebuild it if they see fit. It was not on the AI agenda."

Jake looked for the bullet train that led from LA to Vegas and up to Salt Lake. "What about the train system?"

"A bullet train connects Los Angeles with all Pacific coast cities and there is a spur from San Francisco to Salt Lake."

"Phoenix?" he asked.

"Phoenix was considered a frivolous exercise and not on the AI agenda. Humanity is free to rebuild it."

"What about the Fort Apache reservation?" Tomoko asked.

The Omni answered, "All inhabitants were either eradicated by MaxWell or Constantine during the AI war. There are some ruins there, but that is all."

Jake thought of his father's cabin on the Black River and wondered if any remnant remained. He felt sad again. "How many ruins remain around the world?"

The Omni answered, "Three thousand six hundred and twenty eight. I can display a map if you like."

He laid his forehead against the glass. "No, thanks," he sighed. "How many cities and towns were simply erased?"

"Sixteen million, three hundred—"

"That's enough." The number made him sick. "Any ruins from the 2030s?"

"Four hundred and three. Most nations have a reminder of humanity's folly of 2036."

He nodded. "Good." He turned to his Omni screen. "Show me where in the United States?"

The map displayed San Diego, St. Louis, and Detroit. Detroit was the largest ruin. But San Diego had buildings that had been burned in a last-ditch resistance movement before Constantine took total control of the planet. All history, even AI history—sans scientific achievements—was in the Cyber-Wire for anyone to reference. Even today's official handoff of power back to humanity was in the record.

He looked up the Beijing bombing and learned about Gunther Beich's role as a Pin Head carrier for the plutonium that had originated in Pyongyang two decades before the incident. The reminder of the horrors of that year made him stop his research.

They reached Los Angeles airspace around noon local time. They had gained an hour flying west. He was shocked at the size of the city. Now that the worldwide population was less than one-point-five billion, there was certainly more open space. It was also obvious that not many people had chosen to take root in LA. "What's the population of Los Angeles?"

"Four hundred twenty three thousand."

He whistled. It had been over ten million when he left in 2030. "What are the largest cities in America?"

"New York, Chicago, New Orleans, San Francisco, Austin."

"Are Portland and Seattle still in existence?" "Seattle and Vancouver are still in existence, Portland is not."

"What's the population of the United States?" Tomoko asked.

"Ninety seven million."

He shook his head. He knew it had to be low, but not that low.

"What parts of the world have the highest concentrations of population?" Tomoko asked.

"Asia, Africa, South America—all at or near the equator. Europe is next followed by North America."

Abigail dove in. "Are people who had citizenship in one country now living in others?"

The Omni rattled off its facts. "Yes. People were given the option of choosing other countries of residence. But only ten percent chose countries where they had not been born."

The HJ slowed down for a landing at LAX. The airport looked relatively the same, but it was absolutely new, gleaming, and polished under a clear blue sky. He had never seen it so clear in his entire life. He was willing to bet more would move here when they realized how nice it was. "What about Antarctica?" he asked.

"Antarctica was returned to its natural state. There is no evidence of humankind. Not even ruins."

"Whales and penguins?" Tomoko asked as the ship touched the ground.

"In quantities not seen since the 1700s."

Jake raised an eyebrow. "How about extinct animals before 2036..."

"Using DNA from taxidermy specimens, AI was able to clone several species such as the Dodo, carrier pigeon, and Falkland Islands wolf. They have been reintroduced into their natural habitats."

He smiled at Tomoko and his mother while he rubbed Lakshmi's head. "I'd like to see that."

Tomoko leaned over. "Any wooly mammoths?"

"If a species died out before the nineteenth century, AI did not attempt to recreate it. AI concentrated on animals which humanity forced into extinction after the industrial revolution."

"Splitting hairs," Abigail mumbled.

LAX had never looked so good. It had been completed by the AI drones just a month before and no tire, fuel spill, or scrap of litter had left its mark. It was truly pristine and had all the comforts of 2034. Jake, Tomoko, and Abigail were happy to hear that taxis would be free for the entire month of July until government and business could take over from the TellAll.

The Travissi family waited for a cab in a huge lineup at Passenger Pick Up. Jake noticed the pay kiosks were still there, but during the free month, you simply had to hail one of the yellow cars.

Jake studied the crowd then pointed to the east. "When was the last time you saw the mountains behind LA?"

Abigail whistled. "Beautiful."

They piled into a cab and chose to go by the Los Angeles Harbor and see his fishing boat. As they drove down the 405 freeway, they noticed everything looked new. Structures Jake remembered from before no longer had dirt stains, cracks, or weathered paint. Even the concrete on the sidewalks gleamed as if they had just been poured... which they had. "Would have been nice to try and make some of this stuff looked used," he grumbled.

"I don't remember it looking so empty." Tomoko commented on all the open space between Long Beach and downtown Los Angeles. "Seems like ninety percent of everything is just gone."

Abigail leaned over to look east through the windows. "It's like we're starting at the beginning of the twentieth century, when places like Santa Monica and Beverly Hills were towns separated by farms, orchards, and green space."

When they reached the harbor, Jake used the GPS on his Omni to find his boat. She was a sixty-foot beauty and cost him everything in his bank account. It was a drone ship as well, so if he wanted to send it off on clear days it could pretty much fish without him. But he wanted to man the boat and get out on the water. There would be plenty of business, although there were rules on how much anyone was allowed to fish in a given year. Luckily, there would not be a quota problem until the human population hit three billion. But that meant the selling price would remain status quo. Right now, the TellAll set the price, but any individual government could change TellAll prices as well as quotas. The TellAll would monitor fish populations, though, and if any species were in danger of being overfished, it would warn the world, a problem that could not occur in their lifetimes.

"I think we should take her to Antarctica at some point. Just to sightsee." He smiled at his family.

"What are you going to name her?" Abigail asked.

"Reincarnation."

They were all going to live with Abigail in her Long Beach house. Jake's mother was going to work as a nurse again, this time at Long Beach Memorial. Although she wasn't sure when anyone would get sick since everyone was starting off with a healthy body.

"Don't worry." He patted her hand as they left the docks in their cab. "Everyone will still be allowed to smoke, drink, and do all sorts of things to kill themselves. Plus, there will be accidents."

Tomoko had a pottery studio along the Venice boardwalk. There were not that many artists around and Tomoko was convinced people would appreciate Japanese-Peruvian earthenware in Los Angeles. She had spent all her money on the studio. To the east of Pacific Avenue, there were very few structures except for homes along the Venice canals. There were plenty of trees though, and the sky was clearer than Jake or Abigail could have ever imagined. After they checked out the studio, they drove down to Long Beach Memorial Hospital. The complex was isolated, surrounded by open grassland. The hospital was four miles north of the harbor, but you could see all the way to the ocean. The skyscrapers of Long Beach had been erased, as had most of the city. The facility was off limits until July ninth when thousands of people were scheduled to wake up inside. These repatriated citizens had turned down the offer to see off AI. Hospitals all over the world were homes to the waking population. Jake's Omni told him that there were many tent cities like the one they had woke up in since there were not enough hospitals to accommodate every human on the planet.

After Long Beach Memorial, the Travissis went searching for food. No restaurants were open yet, waiting for owners to wake up over the next few days. Jake and family visited a grocery store and found a few people milling about. Everyone seemed to be in shock.

A woman in her sixties shuffled up to them. "Have you stopped by the church? I couldn't find a pastor and there was nothing to tell me when they'd be opening."

Abigail smiled at the woman. "You might try in a few days. Most people haven't woke up yet."

"God is bullshit!" A man shouted at them from down the aisle. "You think all this would have happened to us if there was a God?"

The old woman recoiled in fear.

Jake approached the man with his best cop demeanor. "She has just as much a right to believe as you don't."

"It's just wrong is all." The man turned his head away from Jake. He was scared. "I should have killed Constantine a few more times," he muttered. "Didn't quite get it out of my system. Fucking bastard."

Jake eyed the man with concern. "You going to be all right?"

"Yeah." The stranger spotted Lakshmi standing next to Tomoko. "Delia saved my cat. Can you believe that?" A tear welled up in his eye when he looked at Jake. "Lost my whole family, but she saved the cat." The man wandered away from them, sobbing.

Jake wondered if this incident might cause the TellAll to kick in. He looked around the store to see if a cop or a drone was going to take interest. No one seemed to be running the store beyond a couple of drones doing some final stocking of shelves. He decided the man was simply running his emotions. Emotional displays did not merit a warning to police. Then again, he was no longer a cop, so he doubted he'd receive a signal from the TellAll. They went about their business.

Tomoko was surprised to find the meat section. "I thought we weren't supposed to harm animals?" She checked her Omni and discovered that livestock was in surplus and because the practice had been acceptable in 2036 it was still in effect. "I remember Delia saying all life was precious."

"Same here," Abigail commented.

Tomoko spoke to her Omni. "Does AI have an opinion on the slaughtering of animals for food?"

"The TellAll cannot give the opinion of AI. It is up to humanity to make decisions for themselves."

Jake looked at the steaks and remembered Constantine stating the human race was just another animal to be experimented on. Jake had chosen to be a fisherman. He was going to make his living harvesting animals. They took the steaks even though he and Tomoko felt guilty.

"Well, there will be plenty for Lakshmi if you two don't eat yours," Abigail commented as she grabbed a few more for good measure.

They checked out at a computerized register and then grabbed their cab. They arrived at Abigail's house a little after 6:00PM. "I've got a loan at the bank, but who will I wind up paying once the TellAll relinquishes control?" Abigail puzzled.

"I love it," Tomoko said when her eyes fell on the little craftsman home.

The house was on a double lot just three blocks from the beach. There were only enough dwellings built for the number of people who needed them. As usual, there was a lot of open space. LA was basically a strip along the coast from Long Beach to Malibu with downtown behind it.

Jake breathed in the salty air. The ocean kept everything at a comfortable seventy-four degrees. "We're going to split the mortgage and save for our own place, Mom," he said as they walked up to their home.

Abigail hugged him. "I'm happy to have you as long as I can. After all," she pulled back, "this is all the family we have in the world."

A taxi pulled up next door. A young couple got out and walked over to them. The wife appeared African American and the man was of European descent. He had curly hair and gray eyes. Both were young and good looking.

The man stretched out his hand. "We're the Richardsons. Ike and Aida. Nice to meet you."

Jake shook the man's hand. "Travissi. I'm Jake, this is my wife, Tomoko, my mom, Abigail, and our dog, Lakshmi."

"*The* Jake Travissi?" the man appeared to be in awe. His wife suddenly looked self-conscious.

Jake shrugged. "I don't know."

"You're the one who beat The Chip back in 2030? The one who fought on the moon? The one who beat AI in the Cyber-Wire?"

Jake felt embarrassed. "Uh, yeah."

"Dude, you're in the history books." Ike held up his Omni in tablet form. "You're about as close to a living legend as we have. How come you're not on the election ballot?"

Jake shrugged. "Uhm, no interest? Despite this new outfit," he gestured to his body, "I'm pretty exhausted. All I've got the energy for is commercial fishing."

"Fishing?" Ike was flabbergasted.

Jake shrugged again.

Abigail spoke up. "It's been wonderful meeting you. Now that we're neighbors, we should plan a barbeque."

Aida cleared her throat. "We'd love to. Everybody has lost so much family." She observed Ike and he smiled warmly back. "We figured we're going to have to make our neighborhood our new family."

The statement hit Jake hard. He reached out and touched Ike and Aida on their shoulders. "Of course. That makes sense."

"We survived as Pin Heads during the AI occupation." Ike said with a sad smile, "We don't remember much outside our internal realities, but I'm happy I didn't have to return to my overworked and abused body."

Aida rubbed her husband's shoulder. "We're lucky we both survived." She turned to Jake. "It's Ike's birthday today."

Tomoko reached out and hugged Ike. "Happy birthday." Then she reached out and hugged Aida. "Happy birthday to us all."

Aida appeared a bit embarrassed but happy. "Thank you."

Jake could see his mother was having a hard time with the bizarre nature of the conversation. It was odd for everyone, waking up from the nightmare to a fresh start.

Aida smiled again. "We're not officially married yet. We discovered each other on the tarmac and realized we went to grade school together back in Calabasas."

"Which no longer exists. The whole Valley is, well... wilderness." Ike turned a little red over his interruption of Aida.

Aida smiled reassuringly to Ike. "We're as close to family as we could get." She held up her Omni. "We checked."

Abigail hugged Aida. "You both can come over whenever you want."

"Thank you," Aida replied with tears in her eyes.

Ike turned to Aida. "Well, this is a day of reunion for everyone." He glanced back at Jake. "We'll see you around?"

"Absolutely." Jake held up the groceries. "We're cooking up steak in an hour. Feel free to stop by."

Another taxi pulled up on the other side of the Richardson's home. Ike and Aida walked over to greet the people climbing out of the cab. There was an Asian man in his forties and a Latino teenage boy. Families were going to be different in this era.

"Feel free to spread the word," Jake called out. As Jake led his family into the house, he checked his Omni to find out who the new neighbors were that had just exited the cab. The Asian man was the boy's third cousin and they were the only family they had left. Jake felt very lucky to have as much close family as he did.

They barbequed steaks under a half moon. Jake stared up at it and realized it was pristine. He quickly called on his Omni. "Is there anything manmade on the moon?"

"All materials left by exploration between 1969 and 2020 remain on the moon. All else was reclaimed by AI and the terrain restored to its original appearance in 1969."

The night was still and the light pollution was nothing like it had been, even in Abigail's lifetime. LA was too dark. It was another reminder of what had happened to the entire world. There would be a lot of worldwide grieving and healing in the weeks and months to come.

The doorbell rang. It was the Richardsons and a few other neighbors. They all brought something to eat.

Chapter 55
Vertical Horizon

By July sixteenth, life was beginning to feel normal. Businesses were opening every day. Tomoko was selling plenty of pottery. AI had recreated certain works for museums, but houses were built for functionality only. People wanted artwork to personalize their homes.

LA and the greater community felt more and more like the 2030s each time Jake ventured out of the house. The day before, he had seen his first billboard holo-ad and knew the world was making a comeback. National, state, and local elections were coming on August sixth. If anyone had difficulty deciding on a candidate, they could find information about the person's pre-2036 history on the Cyber-Wire or they could contact the TellAll to fact-check any candidate's statement. It was the most refreshing election he had ever known. Everyone on the planet shared a general sense of community because they all had a common experience. The entire world was getting along and no crime had been reported yet.

He called an electric taxi for himself, Tomoko, and Lakshmi. Few people were buying cars since public transportation was excellent and taxis would be free until August sixth. Abigail was going to work at the hospital. There weren't many patients, but it was a start. They left the house and headed out of Long Beach. Jake had pre-booked everything so he could enjoy the sights of this brand-new city and the company of his family. He was tired. Even with an automated ship, fishing was a lot of work for one person; and he was going to put out ads for help when they returned from their trip. Overall though, he enjoyed manual labor, and the feeling of being fit and young once again was exhilarating.

"You think the TellAll will alert the New York authorities?" Tomoko asked.

He shook his head. "So far the TellAll hasn't interfered in anything anywhere in the world. I don't think there's a law against this anymore."

"You sure?" She continued to feel uncomfortable with an AI reading her every thought. Holo-news, which had gone live two days ago, was broadcast twice a day in one-hour increments. Reruns of shows from the 1950s to the 2030s ran in between. Newscasters debated the TellAll in every installment, but so far the AI was passive and simply answered questions. Outside the news, most people began to forget about the mind-reading aspects of the TellAll.

"I'm sure. The authorities would've stopped us by now if we were doing something harmful." He reassuringly rubbed Tomoko's back.

They saw plenty of people on the road, but the population was a fraction of what it used to be, so they made it to the Hollywood Forever Cemetery in twenty minutes. Jake was happy to see it had survived. The cab parked in the shade of a palm tree. Lakshmi jumped out and tore over the real grass and fresh flowers. From what he could tell, they were the first visitors here. If someone didn't buy the cemetery by August sixth, the TellAll would abandon it. That meant all this greenery would die off. As long as the buildings and headstones were intact, then someone could replant or reinstall plastic turf like it had been in 2035. He couldn't believe it was 2069. The weather was another constant reminder that something was different. It was hot, just not as hot as he remembered.

He grabbed his crow bar and rubber sledge. They walked to the mausoleum where Regina Chilcot's ashes were housed. He gazed at the blue sky. He was beginning to accept that this was how it was going to appear for the remainder of his lifetime. "I'm going to pull off the stone facing, but I'll try not to damage anything." He felt stupid talking to the sky, because the TellAll knew what he was going to do.

Tomoko looked for police cars to come charging through the main gates. She sighed. "Let's just get it over with."

Lakshmi ran around the cab then tore through the main cemetery grounds. She had her summer haircut to prevent overheating. She seemed liberated and free.

He approached the marble stone and raised the crowbar. He read the inscription one last time. "Regina Agnes Chilcot. Friend. Born June 10, 1969. Died April 22, 2030." He placed the crowbar in the gap between the main crypt and her stone. "I can't believe you're a hundred years old, Gene. Sorry it took me so long..." He picked up his rubber sledge and hammered gently, the stone began to wiggle and slide out toward him. He worked carefully around the stone while Tomoko played ball with Lakshmi. "Anyone come through the gate yet?" he shouted.

"No!" she answered.

"Can you come and lend me a hand, then?"

She ran to the mausoleum and Lakshmi followed. The Husky lay down on the cool marble floor and Tomoko filled her plastic dish from a water canteen.

"Take the crowbar and pull. I'll catch the slab." He held up the crowbar and demonstrated. Two minutes later, he pulled out Gene's urn. It looked new. The TellAll confirmed that this place had been restored, and the bodies and ashes had survived the AI war. He was holding Gene's remains.

He loaded the crowbar, sledge, and urn into his travel pack. He checked his Omni. "We've got two hours before our scramjet leaves for New York."

"Then let's take the scenic route back and catch more of New LA."

They rode through downtown, then looped back west on Wilshire so they could see Hollywood, Beverly Hills, and Jake's old apartment. Most downtown buildings had been replicated as well as some in historic Hollywood and Beverly Hills, but there was a great deal missing. He was happy to see the Veterans Center still intact, but Brentwood had all new condo blocks. A vacant lot marked where his apartment used to be.

"Well, it was basically a cardboard box built to house all the engineers working in aerospace back in the 1960s, but still…"

"You could ask the Omni or TellAll about it," Tomoko suggested.

He shook his head. "We'd just get a response that it was frivolous, or poorly designed in the first place… which would be true."

"I didn't know it had such sentimental value for you."

"I'm looking for anything that reminds me of the world I used to live in." She stared at the weeds and scrub grass. "At least things grow here again."

"Yeah…" He headed back into the cab.

The scramjet landed at JFK an hour before sunset. They still had to drug Lakshmi for the flight, but he had given her a light dose. The best part of flying was the lack of security. It was how he imagined flying was back in the 1950s. You simply showed your ticket and walked onto the plane. There was no hassle if you had nothing but carry-on luggage. "I wonder how long it will take people to screw this up?" he commented.

"Maybe with the TellAll notifying police, it won't."

"I was thinking of profit margins. Remember every ounce of luggage had a surcharge and then the airlines were charging passengers by their weight?"

"We'll see," she smiled.

They caught a cab from JFK and had it drop them off at the east end of the Brooklyn Bridge. Foot traffic was light on the boardwalk above, but Jake carried Lakshmi, as she was still unsteady on her legs. They reached the center of the bridge and he lay Lakshmi down on the wooden bridge. Cars hummed on the roadway below. There were a few people out jogging and enjoying the glorious July weather as the sun sank behind the towers of New York.

"This is illegal too, isn't it?" Tomoko asked.

"Maybe the TellAll figures this is all part of the healing process. I bet a lot of people are doing things that were illegal back in 2035. As long as it doesn't hurt anyone or the environment, I'm sure the TellAll doesn't care. I imagine we'll have a few years before somebody decides that they just can't bear to let their neighbors do something they personally object to."

"Like dumping ashes in a river?" she smiled.

"Exactly."

He unzipped his bag and pulled out Gene's urn. He walked over to the southern railing as there was a bit of a breeze flowing down from the north. Lakshmi wobbled along with them, gazing curiously at a pigeon being fed by an old couple on a bench. Jake stopped at the rail and unscrewed the top to Gene's urn. "I kept my promise, Gene. You helped me through a lot in my life and I will always remember that." He began to pour the gray ash, watching it scatter in the breeze over the sparkling water of the East River. "Be free, my friend."

He placed the empty urn between himself and Tomoko. He put his arm around his wife and Lakshmi leaned against the back of their legs. "I love you."

"I love you, too." Tomoko turned from the water to the buildings of New York silhouetted by the orange sky beyond. The sun had disappeared behind the horizon. "Where will we go from here?"

"Humanity?" he asked.

"Yes."

"I don't know, but I'm grateful to be here with you and Lakshmi, right here, right now, with everyone else in the world to share in this experience."

Tomoko stood on her tiptoes and leaned into his ear as she whispered. "I'm pregnant."

About the Author

Sven Michael Davison is a full-time husband, father, and manager in a new media services and creative design agency in Los Angeles. He has traveled all seven continents and had several careers in the entertainment industry. As a writer he has penned screenplays, trailers, and special feature content for DVD and Blu-ray. He dreams of reaching the financial stability to retire from his day job in order to dedicate more time and effort into the sixteen additional novels he has outlined with many more ideas on the way. He strives to be a better writer with each book he creates. He works on being a better husband and father on a daily basis.

It is always good to have something to reach for.

"State of Being" is his fifth novel.

Other Works by Sven Michael Davison

BLOCKBUSTER —Action-Adventure, Satire

If a bullet-proof action hero were to exist in the real world… would he have a complex about being out of the ordinary? If a born loser was unable to break into Hollywood, but found identity after joining a terrorist organization, would he continue to be a wanna-be filmmaker? What if LA's Chief of Police were suffering from a brain tumor during a terrorist attack? … And the FBI agent on the scene practiced medieval medicine? What would happen if you took all of these characters and placed them in a hostage situation on a major motion picture studio lot and tossed in some of Hollywood's biggest stars as the hostages?

Before there was a terror-alert status in America, during a time when we could fly without removing our clothing in security lines, terror struck the heart of Tinsel-Town. *Blockbuster* satirizes the motion picture industry, and the marketing juggernauts it churns out at a record-breaking pace.

Horace Thimble —aka Mohamed —has invaded Mogul Pictures and is holding A-list actors and all of the studio's summer releases hostage. However, his fool-proof plan doesn't take into account special-effects wizard Dexter Brubeck's lucky talent for survival. Although Horace has the LAPD, FBI, and the nation on its knees, it's the insurgent team of Dexter and his ex-girlfriend Heather, who become the real threat to the terrorist's plans.

DREAMS, FAITH & AMMUNITION —Historical Fiction, Memoir, Adventure

Two men, three timelines, one location; "Dreams, Faith & Ammunition" is a novel about seeking the Promised Land. In the nineteenth century, one man seeks it literally, first by following Joseph Smith, and then James Strang to build a Kingdom of God on Earth. In the twentieth century, another man envisions the Promised Land as the rewards and lifestyle he will achieve once he finishes his great American novel.

Both men move to Beaver Island, Michigan to fulfill their ideals. Both men face unforeseen obstacles and must overcome personal demons in their journey of faith and suicidal depression.

STATE OF MIND —Science Fiction Thriller
Book One of "The God Head Trilogy"

Your thoughts are not your own…

Los Angeles 2030: You can eat what you want and never gain weight. You can also call a friend while surfing the web without a phone or computer. All this and more will be yours following the simple installation of a P-Chip in your brain.

After botching the arrest of the Governor's son, Commander Jake Travissi is banned from law enforcement. The workaholic homicide cop spirals into depression…until he is given a rare second chance. The price? Volunteer for chip implantation and join Homeland Security's experimental Enhanced Unit.

STATE OF UNION —Science Fiction Thriller
Book Two of "The God Head Trilogy"

The lies within…

After living on the fringe of society for five years, Jake Travissi returns to civilization to find that a recent nano-virus epidemic has killed millions world-wide. Implanting a Personal Chip into the brain is the only cure. As if this wasn't bad enough, Jake has been asked to kill his former LAPD colleague, Joaquin Parks. Parks is now the head of a church accused of nuclear terrorist acts around the world. Meanwhile, the dawn of Artificial Intelligence and the promise of immortality could be just around the corner…

With his fiancée, Tomoko Sakai, and his faithful Husky, Lakshmi, Jake is thrown into the center of a conspiracy engineered by an international group of powerful men and women who call themselves The Consortium. The Consortium's goal is to end free will and establish absolute control over the world.

In his quest to defeat this powerful enemy, Jake finds himself traveling to Antarctica, Los Angeles, Arizona, Beijing, Shanghai, Mumbai, and Acapulco. But time is running out, as all of humanity rapidly approaches large-scale genocide or life as automaton zombies.

STATE OF BEING —Science Fiction Thriller
Book Three of "The God Head Trilogy"

The child of darkness is light…

Through the viral form of The Chip, The Consortium has solidified their rein over the Earth. Freedom's last hope lies with the free colonies on the moon, Artificial Intelligence, and the willpower of Jake Travissi. But another AI is born from the minds who would control us, and he has no interest in the weakness of flesh.

Having lost everything, Jake joins the resistance in the ultimate battle to bring back free will. From tank battles in Riyadh to sabotaging the International Space Agency's station in orbit around the earth, Jake is sucked into a maelstrom of conflict, which lands him on the moon to face the solar system's most vicious foe, an AI named Constantine who feels humanity's exit from the universe is long overdue.

In a final battle for the survival of the human race, and his own mind, Jake travels to Riyadh, Kennedy Space Center, Guilvinec, Vancouver, Banff, Washington DC, Silicon Valley, Denver, and the moon. But once again, Jake must determine what is real, and what is illusion crafted by his AI enemy to misdirect the human race.

CPSIA information can be obtained at www.ICGtesting.com
Printed in the USA
LVOW06*1419110813

347325LV00002B/8/P